Star

Kirsten opened one end of the large brown envelope and gingerly eased out her complimentary copy of *Time*. What she noticed first was the name Beaton curving in bold black capital letters around her left shoulder with all the possessiveness of a lover's hand. To her chagrin, a tremor of excitement rippled through her. The Kirsten that Andrew Beaton had portrayed was a far different Kirsten from the one photographed by either Anthony Armstrong-Jones or Richard Avedon. His Kirsten was a twenty-six-year-old enigma—vulnerable yet aloof, innocent yet sensual too. A bewitching blend of the come-hither and stay-away in her luminous violent eyes, an ambiguous promise in the upward tilt of her parted lips. The totality of it, however, came as a devastating shock to her. Andrew Beaton had seen the same face she herself saw each time she looked in the mirror after she and Michael had made love.

Everyone had an opinion about the cover, everyone had an opinion about the article. And Kirsten was in demand everywhere. It was as though the entire world had suddenly discovered her, and the American press immediately capitalized on it by turning Kirsten into something the classical world had never had before—its first true media personality.

So Many Promises

Nomi Berger

BANTAM BOOKS

TORONTO • NEW YORK • LONDON • SYDNEY • AUCKLAND

SO MANY PROMISES

A Bantam Book / September 1988

Published simultaneously in Canada by Seal Books.

ISBN 0-553-27206-3

Bantam Books are published by Bantam Books, a division of Bantam Doubleday Dell Publishing Group, Inc. Its trademark, consisting of the words "Bantam Books" and the portrayal of a rooster, is Registered in U.S. Patent and Trademark Office and in other countries. Marca Registrada. Bantam Books, 666 Fifth Avenue, New York, New York 10103.

PRINTED IN THE UNITED STATES OF AMERICA

KR   0 9 8 7 6 5 4 3 2 1

With loving thanks from the author to:
Howard for his unwavering support;
Carolyn for her devoted perseverance;
Bernard for walking me onto the stage
of Carnegie Hall;
And Carmen for providing the inspiration.

Prelude

1983

She stood in their way, a magnificent obstacle, and the city stepped graciously around her.

She was a woman who commanded attention. Perhaps it was the startling blackness of her suit, or the black veil obscuring her features, or the worn paper shopping bag clutched in one of her small, gloved hands. Perhaps it was the way she defied the crowds in order to remain where she was, or her obvious fascination with the yellow brick and terra cotta building at the corner of Fifty-seventh Street and Seventh Avenue. Whatever it was, not even the most jaded New Yorker could pass by without giving her a second glance.

Unaware of the curiosity she was arousing, the woman continued her loving sweep of the building, following every Roman arch, each fluted column, cornice and cupid. In the pale March sun, the building's façade gleamed like gold. Yet even without the sun, it still would have seemed golden to her. The building was her shrine, and she a silent worshiper, someone who had once laid a dream at the foot of its majestic altar.

But then, this was Carnegie Hall. And Carnegie Hall had been created especially for dreams. Inside its grand auditorium, some of those dreams lived, most died, a few even grew to greatness. It was a gathering place for greatness. All the greats had conducted here: Toscanini, Stokowski, Eastbourne, Ormandy, Bernstein, von Karajan. The best soloists had performed here: Stern, Perlman, Rubinstein, Horowitz, Rostropovich, Cliburn. And tonight was his turn.

Her gaze descended slowly, coming to rest on the poster inside the marquee box in front of the main entrance. Even from this distance she was able to see his face on the poster and the wonderful dreaminess in his eyes. It was the same dreaminess her own eyes once had. Armstrong-Jones had discovered it, Beaton had captured it, and Avedon had immortalized it. Turning her head to the right, she glanced up

Fifty-seventh Street toward Ninth Avenue, to where her dream had originally begun. It was only a matter of two blocks, yet it could just as easily have been two miles. It had taken her an entire lifetime to realize that distances can be distorted when blurred by the brilliance of a dream.

The shopping bag was getting heavy. She shifted it from her left hand to her right and slowly rotated her aching wrist. The gold charms on the bracelet she was wearing began to jangle. It was a happy sound and it made her smile. She wondered if he would even remember the bracelet. Her smile dissolved, to be replaced by a frown of deep concern. Tonight after she told him the truth, she knew she might never see him again. She swallowed hard and looked back up at the poster. It was a risk she would have to take; she had no other choice. She had run out of time. With her eyes still focused on his face, she stepped off the curb, unaware of the approaching car.

The glancing blow of the car's left fender sent her sprawling onto the pavement. In an instinctual move to protect her hands, she had flung out her arms, causing the charm bracelet to snap apart and the shopping bag to slip from her fingers. Caught by the breeze, pieces of sheet music, like errant white gulls, began soaring and dipping high above her head. While several passersby dashed about trying to retrieve the music, a young man knelt by her side and peeled off one of her gloves to feel for a pulse.

With her hat askew and its veil partially raised, the shimmer of her silvered hair framed a face of haunting beauty and indeterminate age. Awed by the perfection of her features, the young man dropped her hand and simply stared at her. A moment later he was brushed aside by another man rushing to take his place. Picking up the broken charm bracelet, he dropped it into the pocket of his jacket, then with both hands cushioning the woman's head, he bent close to her ear and started whispering her name.

But she couldn't hear the man's whispers or the wail of the siren as the ambulance whisked her toward Bellevue. She couldn't hear anything but the music playing softly inside her head. It was her favorite of all Claude Debussy's works, his impressionistic masterpiece, "Reflets dans l'Eau." As they slid her from the stretcher onto one of the examining tables in the emergency room of the giant hospital, her eyes flicked open. The glare of the lights caught her full in the face. But she was seeing other lights now. She sighed and closed her eyes again. The music became fainter. Soon all she could hear was the applause.

Andante

1946–1952

1

"Brava! Brava!"

"Encore!"

"Brava!"

She rose from the piano and swept regally to the center of the stage, where the lights formed an iridescent halo around her. Pressing both hands over her heart, she sank gracefully to one knee and bowed her head. The applause continued to soar, swirling around her like a warm, dense wave, gathering strength, lifting her higher and higher.

"Brava!"

"Brava, Kirsten, brava!"

Her wide eyes were brimming, the tears transforming their violet irises into rainbow-colored prisms which the lights reflected back at the audience. Overwhelmed and humbled by their outpouring of affection, she kissed the tips of her fingers and threw her arms wide to embrace the entire hall. The audience responded to her expansive gesture by rising as a single body and giving her a standing ovation.

"Kirsten?"

She was shaken from her reverie by a bony hand on her shoulder. Standing over her desk was her eighth-grade history teacher, his protuberant brown eyes magnified into giant, unblinking orbs of disapproval by the thick glasses he was wearing.

"Was there any particular reason for your staying behind today, Kirsten?" Harmon Widemann asked the slightly dazed-looking thirteen-year-old.

Kirsten glanced around the empty classroom and grimaced. "I guess I was somewhere else," she said.

"Yes, I guess you were." Being somewhere else wasn't unusual for Kirsten Harald. "Who was my competition this time, may I ask, Chopin or Brahms?"

"Neither of them," she admitted somewhat sheepishly.

"Oh, who then?"

"Not who, Mr. Widemann, what. It was the applause."

"Applause!" The word virtually shot out of the man's mouth. "If you spent a bit more time *studying* history instead of daydreaming about *making* history, my dear young Kirsten, you wouldn't be doing as poorly in this subject as you are. Applause indeed."

Kirsten squirmed in her seat and concentrated on the dented metal cap of her inkwell.

"Well, what are you waiting for? Go on, go on." Widemann made rapid fanning motions with his hands as though trying to sweep her away. "I've got to lock up in here."

"Yes, sir." Kirsten immediately gathered up her books and slid out of her seat, nearly tripping over one of the man's size-twelve shoes in the process. She bolted from the classroom, then fairly spun down the two flights of stairs leading to the ground floor. It wasn't until she had pushed her way through one of the heavy wooden doors opening onto the school yard that she finally stopped to catch her breath.

The unexpected brilliance of the late afternoon sun was like a flashbulb exploding in her face. New York was writhing in the grip of an unusual heat wave, and although it was the second week in October, it felt more like mid-August, with the air a choking mixture of gasoline fumes, rotting garbage, and human sweat. Momentarily disoriented by the sun's stinging glare, Kirsten juggled her heavy armload of books and tried to get her bearings.

"Well, well, well, if it isn't little miss perfect."

Wheeling around, Kirsten found herself looking up at a tall, gangly girl with long red braids.

"Too good for us mere mortals," added her friend, a short, pretty girl with flyaway brown curls. "You'd better run home to your piano before the bogeyman catches you."

As if on cue, both girls broke into a chorus of laughter and ran to join five others who were waiting for them by the school yard gate. Soon all seven girls were snickering at Kirsten and staring across the yard at her. She was mortified, her cheeks burning, her body flinching and twitching as though she were being publicly flogged. All seven mocking stares seemed to be intent on melting her down. Refusing to allow the girls the satisfaction of seeing her cry, she squared her shoulders and raised her head proudly. She didn't blink once as she forced herself to walk stiff-backed past the girls and out of the school yard. Only she would ever know how close her bottom lip had come to quivering and how painfully knotted her stomach had been.

Through all her early years of schooling, Kirsten's most enduring lesson was one she had learned *outside* the classroom: children don't like anyone who is different. And because of her awesome musical abilities, she *was* different. Different and special. Her specialness prevented her from fitting in with her classmates, and for that she had been permanently ostracized, her peers' way of punishing her for prefering the piano to them. The result was a loneliness so penetrating she always felt chilled, as though she were sitting in a constant draft.

Frightened by these feelings of alienation, she occasionally found herself regretting her choice and regarding her natural talent as more of a curse than a blessing. How many times had she longed to abandon her rigidly disciplined routine and do nothing but play for a while? How many times had she ached to be like most thirteen-year-olds, who thought only about new ways to wear their hair, experimented with lipstick and nail polish, and giggled about boys? How many times had she watched a secret being passed from one best friend to another, and yearned for a special friend with whom she could share a thousand such secrets?

But she had no time for friends, no time for experimenting, no time even for play. To protect her hands from possible injury, she never took gym and never participated in sports. Her nails had to be clipped so short that the only polish she wore was clear and primarily for strengthening purposes. Because she took piano lessons twice a week, practiced for three hours on school days and for six hours daily on weekends, she was never available for the proverbial after-school soda, Saturday night slumber party, or Sunday afternoon movie.

She lived a life of splendid isolation, in solitary confinement, her sights narrowed into what was appropriately termed "tunnel vision." But in spite of her momentary pangs of regret, she was a most willing and committed prisoner, dedicated to the pursuit of one goal and one goal only: musical greatness. The seductive and alluring gleam of brilliance at the end of that long, dark tunnel. The shimmering promise of immortality that made all the sacrifices in its name more than worth it.

But even she knew sacrifices weren't enough to guarantee

success; only a few ever made it. The rest were doomed to lives of frustrated ordinariness, with perhaps a scrapbook half filled with lukewarm reviews and a faded rose or two to remind them of their thwarted assault on the mountain. Most of them turned to teaching, some joined orchestras or chamber music ensembles, others became accompanists. All together these failed potential soloists formed the broad base of a pyramid whose lofty pinnacle was jealously guarded and ruled by a sacred few. Despite whatever obstacles lay ahead for her, Kirsten had no intention of widening that already overcrowded base; she was fully determined to scale it and join those chosen few at the summit.

"Hey, kid, whatsa matter wit' you, you tryin' to get yourself killed or somethin'?"

Cursing loudly, the irate man took his hand off the horn and stuck his head back inside his DeSoto. Kirsten peered first at the car, then at the traffic light, and gasped. She had stopped right in the middle of Fifty-fifth Street without even realizing it, and while she was standing there, the light had turned red. She sprinted to the curb with her heart beating like a tom-tom and ran the final block home, nearly colliding with her father directly in front of their apartment building.

"Oop la!" Emil Harald caught hold of his daughter to keep her from losing her balance.

Kirsten responded with a whoop of sheer joy and automatically raised her face for a kiss.

Looking down at his beautiful daughter, Emil reacted to her heartbreaking vulnerability the way he always did—with a deep sigh and the overwhelming urge to wrap his arms around her and protect her. But after he had planted a warm kiss on her smooth, high forehead, he settled for simply draping an arm around her shoulders and leading her up the chipped stone steps of the building. Tugging open the outside glass door, whose surface was nothing but a spiderweb of thin cracks held together with strips of graying tape, he ushered Kirsten into the dingy white-tiled lobby and rang for the elevator.

The dank, humid box reeked of fried food, unwashed pets and drying urine, and the moment the rusty metal door clanged shut behind them, Kirsten leaned up against her father with a sigh. To her, this tall, gaunt man with the wavy blond hair, the face carved out of some friendly northern oak, and the voice like a soothing whisper of wind represented home. He was safety and security, comfort and caring, a wellspring of solace, support, and strength for her to draw from whenever the task of behaving like an adult in an adult's world became too much for the thirteen-year-old girl she still was. She had commended her heart to him at birth and he had been holding it in his large, capable hands like a sacred trust ever since.

The elevator lurched to a stop on the sixth floor and the door inched open with a reluctant screech. A row of naked light bulbs, some lit, others burned out, hung from the peeling gray ceiling and pointed the way down the hall with all the certainty of a drunk trying to walk a straight line home.

"Are you excited about tonight, Kirsty?" Emil asked as they headed down the dismal hallway toward the last door on the left.

"Excited?" For a moment she seemed confused. But then, in a sudden warm rush, she remembered. "Oh, yes, Pappy, yes," she said, giving him a smile that deepened the dimple in her right cheek and lent a disarming impishness to her tender beauty. Tonight she was being taken to hear her first concert at Carnegie Hall. She had no words to describe her excitement—she always expressed herself far more eloquently at the keyboard—and had she been near her piano, she knew she would have been dashing off a lively Chopin scherzo.

"Kirsty?"

Emil was nodding at the faded brown door to their apartment. This was her cue. Standing as straight as she could, she threw back her shoulders, thrust out her gently pointed chin, and slipped her performer's mask firmly into place. Doorways were made for grand entrances, she had been taught, even this one, as dilapidated as it was. When Emil saw she was ready, he flung the door open with a flourish and watched in wry amusement as Kirsten made another of her dazzling entrances into the dreary half light of their shabby home.

"You're late, *cara mia!*" Gianna Rudini Harald, an older but no less beautiful version of her daughter, burst out of the kitchen, only to stop short when she found her husband standing there. "And you!" she exclaimed with a wide smile. "You're wonderfully early."

Emil stooped to kiss his wife on the mouth. "Day shifts this week, remember?"

Gianna returned the embrace of the man she adored with

an ardor that made Kirsten blush. She was always embarrassed by their easy demonstrativeness, feeling like an intruder witnessing something too intimate to be shared. She started to back out of the living room, narrowly missing the sharp corner of her aunt Sophia's baby grand, then continued on tiptoe into her own room. In size it was only slightly larger than her aunt's piano, and three of its four cracking walls were papered with the covers from the hundreds of Carnegie Hall programs her mother had been collecting for her over the years.

She tossed her books onto her scarred maple dresser and threw open her window to catch whatever she could of the tepid afternoon breeze. Holding her heavy black hair away from her neck, she gazed out at the soot-stained configuration of roofs and chimneys and twisting metal fire escapes that zigged and zagged across her field of vision. Everything she saw was stained and crumbling, splattered with pigeon droppings and coated with grime. The alleys were littered with stacks of empty cardboard cartons and piles of bound newspapers, and clogged with rusting and battered metal trash cans overflowing with garbage. Overhead, clotheslines crisscrossed and soot-flecked clothes swung limply in a vain attempt to dry. Such were the boundaries of her squalid world and its seediness only served to reinforce her determination to eventually rid herself of its cloying, clinging stench.

"Someday," she said aloud to a pair of roosting pigeons on the roof of the building across the street. Someday her music would take her out of the slums and set her on top of the concert world. Someday she would pay her parents back for their faith and love and support by cushioning them in luxury soft enough to erase from their memories the stark meanness of the lives they were leading now. "Someday," she vowed again. "I swear it."

"Here's your dress for tonight, *carissima*," Gianna called softly from the doorway where she was standing, both arms lost in the fullness of the dress's filmy double skirt. "I've just finished pressing it so I think we'd better lay it across your bed to keep it from creasing."

Kirsten's throat tightened as she gazed at the tangible proof of her mother's love for her. Gianna had used all of her precious free time over the last two weeks to make her this dress, and the result was a beautiful copy of a pale blue organdy party dress Kirsten had seen in the window of Bonwit

Teller. Hers was made of rayon instead of organdy, but otherwise the two dresses were identical, with the same short capped sleeves, wide, flaring skirt, and royal blue velvet sash that tied in a bow at the waist.

"*Grazie, Mama,*" Kirsten whispered, giving her mother a long, hard squeeze.

Gianna returned her daughter's hug, then steered her back into the living room. "If you really want to thank me," she said, laughing, "you can play me my favorite song."

Kirsten was only too happy to oblige. Seating herself at the secondhand piano which she polished daily with loving care, she flipped open the lid and flexed her fingers several times to relax them. Then she closed her eyes and summoned up a mental image of the first page of Beethoven's "Moonlight Sonata." Bending low over the keyboard, she struck the opening notes of the piece with a pureness and clarity that came not so much from years of practice as from rare and inspired genius.

As her fingers swept over the keys, she could feel the music beginning to ripple through her in sweet, soothing waves. The sensation spread slowly. It soaked through her skin, seeped into her bones, and surged through her bloodstream to saturate her very soul. She grew impervious to her deep loneliness and blind to the shabbiness of her surroundings. She was transported, lost in a blissful state where she and her music were one.

She was convinced that the music was already inside her when she was born. It kept her gloriously alive, and she was, in turn, a prelude and a sonata, an étude and a full concerto, a gavotte and a waltz, a mazurka and a polonaise. Every note she played, each scale, arpeggio, trill, and chord was a cause for celebration. Her favorite composers were the Romantics, whom she knew intimately and who matched her many moods: Mahler and Strauss for dreamy interludes; Rachmaninoff, Tchaikovsky, and Schumann for times of emotion and drama; Brahms, Chopin, and Liszt for moments filled with romantic longings. For a girl with no friends, they were her friends.

The ability to fuse herself so successfully with her music remained as much a source of wonderment to Kirsten as the powers her hands possessed. Her talent had been discovered by sheer accident when, at the age of five, she had sat down at the piano in her aunt Sophia's parlor, and played the entire "Moonlight Sonata" just the way she had heard it played countless times by Vladimir Horowitz on one of her mother's scratchy seventy-eight recordings. She immediately assumed she had done something terribly wrong when she heard a word she didn't understand being passed around the parlor from one nodding relative to the other. The word was prodigy.

When she asked her mother what the word meant, the vague explanation she received was accompanied by a waterfall of tears, kisses, and frantic little hugs, all of which only frightened her more. But the day Aunt Sophia made her a present of the secondhand baby grand, all her fears vanished. Being a prodigy had to be a good thing, she decided, especially if it meant being able to play the piano whenever she wanted. But it took another three years and a series of pitifully inadequate teachers before the redoubtable Russian concert pianist, Natalya Federenko finally taught Kirsten the true meaning of the word prodigy, with all its implications. To be a concert pianist like her teacher was soon Kirsten's own ambition; to be the greatest classical pianist in the world became her ultimate goal. When she confided this to Natalya, she took that first step toward realizing her dream. Dedicating herself to it was the next step.

This she did on the way to Aunt Sophia's for dinner one cold but clear Sunday afternoon in late January. She asked her parents to stop at Carnegie Hall first, and while they waited for her on the corner, she approached the main entrance to the hall alone. Tucking her coat carefully around her knees, she knelt down on the icy bottom step and bowed her head. With her eyes closed and both hands clasped below her chin, she solemnly committed herself to her dream. She swore to forsake everything in the name of her music, to resist all temptation and remain faithful to her goal no matter what. Then she kissed the shiny new penny she had found on the sidewalk outside their apartment building the day before and placed it on the topmost step to seal her pledge.

She had remained faithful to that pledge ever since.

At seven-thirty Gianna knocked on Kirsten's door and asked if she was ready. Instead of a reply, she was greeted by a cry for help and a panting, red-faced girl who had been straining unsuccessfully for several minutes to do up the back of her dress.

"The zipper's stuck," Kirsten said as she turned around to show her mother.

"This shouldn't be too difficult," Gianna reassured her.

"Hold still now, that's a good girl. There, what did I tell you, it's all fixed." The zipper slid upward with a smooth silken purr and Kirsten sighed with relief. "Now then," said Gianna, giving her daughter a peck on her slim, fine-boned nose, "let me have a good look at you."

Kirsten promptly obliged by turning a series of slow pirouettes in front of her mirror. Gianna's dark eyes filled with tears as she gazed lovingly at the exquisite, heart-shaped face of her only child.

"You look like a princess, *carissima*," she murmured, "a beautiful little princess."

"Oh, I love you, Mama," Kirsten cried, wrapping her arms around her mother's neck and squeezing her tightly. "I love you and Pappy so much, and I wish you were coming with us tonight, I really do. It just doesn't seem fair somehow."

"Fair has nothing to do with it, *cara mia*." Gianna's voice was gently chiding. "This is the way it was meant to be. I never wanted you to see Carnegie Hall the way I've always seen it. Now, forget this business of fair or not fair, and go have a wonderful time."

"Are you ready, Kirsty?" Emil called out from the living room, cutting short Kirsten's continued protest.

"Coming, Pappy." She was meeting Natalya outside Carnegie Hall, and although it was just two blocks away, her father insisted on walking her over.

"Your escort awaits, Miss Harald." As his daughter came out of her room, Emil greeted her with a deep, formal bow and a mischievous gleam in his crackling blue eyes.

"Thank you, kind sir." Kirsten dropped him a low curtsy in return, then linked her arm through his.

"Now, try to remember everything for me, won't you, *bella*?" Gianna asked as she walked them to the elevator. "How the women were dressed, if there were any celebrities in the audience, whether or not the concert—"

"The elevator, Mama." Kirsten quickly gave her mother one last hug.

"And don't forget to bring home a program," Gianna shouted as the door began to close.

"Three of them, Mama," Kirsten called back, "one for each of us."

Once outside the building, Kirsten grabbed her father's hand to keep from giving in to the mad impulse to race down the street and shout to everyone she passed that she, Kirsten

Harald from Ninth Avenue, was on her way to Carnegie Hall
to hear the great Arthur Rubinstein perform. Carnegie Hall.
How magical those two words were. She repeated them to
herself over and over again. Carnegie Hall. Carnegie Hall.
Home of the New York Philharmonic, host to the greatest
musical talents in the world, repository for her own precious
dream. Even after they had arrived at the concert hall's main
entrance, she still had difficulty convincing herself she was
really and truly there.

"Is anything wrong, Kirsty?" asked her father, who had
been studying her closely all this time.

"Of course not, Pappy. Why?"

"You were just frowning."

"Oh." She gave a slight shrug. "I guess I'm a bit disappointed in tonight's conductor. I was hoping to see someone
like Stokowski or Toscanini conducting Rubinstein, not some
unknown."

"Michael Eastbourne may be an unknown to you, young
lady," cracked a sharp female voice at Kirsten's elbow, "but
he certainly isn't unknown on the continent. Really! You
Americans."

The elderly woman who had made the comment looked as
arrogant as her crisply accented English had sounded, and
her pale gray eyes were as cold as the diamond choker she
wore around her thin, leathery neck. Kirsten stared after the
woman as she was helped up the steps by a man in a chauffeur's uniform, then turned to her father with a stricken
expression on her face.

"The rich sometimes have a way of making a person feel
small," Emil said in that gentle voice of his. "But don't ever
let them intimidate you, Kirsty, because you've been blessed
with a gift that makes you richer than anyone."

In spite of her father's comforting words, Kirsten was shaken
by the woman's contempt. Balling both hands into fists, she
knew the only way to control her emotions was to find something else to concentrate on. Casting about for just such a
diversion, her gaze flitted past the tall wooden marquee box a
few feet from her, then froze, and quickly backtracked. What
began as nothing more than a cursory glance evolved into a
wide-eyed, disbelieving stare. To her astonishment, she actually felt her jaw drop as she continued to peruse the two
photographs on the poster inside the glass-enclosed box. She
immediately recognized Arthur Rubinstein, but not the other

man. How could she have possibly recognized him, she asked herself; she hadn't even heard of Michael Eastbourne until Natalya had invited her to this concert.

"Handsome, isn't he?"

Kirsten jumped, her heart sinking. But this time, to her immense relief, it was only Natalya coming toward them, her tall, imposing presence preceded as usual by her deep percussive voice. Her brisk walk was more of a lope, with her long arms and long legs churning the air like the blades of a human threshing machine. Her russet-tinted hair was looped into an intricate bun at the nape of her neck, and gigantic silver earrings studded with topazes and garnets swung from her ears like metallic icicles, lightly grazing the shoulders of the russet and silver silk caftan she was wearing.

Kirsten reached up and gave her teacher a hug. Yet her gaze remained riveted on the poster the entire time. Her breathing momentarily faltered. After that, every breath she took was strangely rapid and shallow. Natalya was wrong. Michael Eastbourne was more than just handsome. And something in his eyes was making it all but impossible for her to look away.

"He studied with Toscanini, you know," Natalya hastened to inform her. "Think of it, Kirishka, only twenty-seven, and already he's being called the most dynamic and innovative conductor of the decade."

"Is he British?" Kirsten asked, recalling the accent of the woman who had taken such pleasure in berating her earlier.

"Only by choice." Natalya sounded somewhat scornful. "He lives in London now, but he was born in Boston."

While she digested this particular bit of information, she continued to study Michael Eastbourne's remarkable face feature by feature. She was so preoccupied that she didn't even know her father had gone until Natalya began to lead her, the way one leads a blind person, up the very stone steps she had once knelt on and into the vast white and gold hall she had always worshiped from afar.

"Your programs, Kirishka," whispered Natalya, pressing them into the limp hands of the girl, who seemed to have gone into a sort of trance. "All three of them," she added, giving Kirsten a slight nudge. When all she got in return was a glassy-eyed stare, she gave up on subtlety. "Move!" she barked, one elongated index finger pointing imperiously to their seats in Row E.

Kirsten plunged toward her seat and sank into its plush red softness with a dreamy sigh. Then began her first hungry sweep of the legendary hall, devouring everything in sight: the semi-circular tiers of seats and private boxes; the white fluted columns; the rich plaster ornamentation, gold medallions, and twinkling wall sconces; the heads of the hundreds of men and women making up the audience. She had purposely saved the stage for last. Drawing a deep breath, she swung her gaze round full circle, then stopped. She was immediately bewitched. Swathed by white and gold brocade curtains and drenched in light, the stage rose before her, beckoning to her.

Transfixed, she saw herself sweeping across the pale, highly varnished floor of that stage, the folds of her long lavender gown—she had long ago decided to wear only lavender onstage to compliment the color of her eyes—rustling like leaves about her feet. She saw herself bowing to the audience while the applause rose and enveloped her. She saw herself seated at the nine-foot Steinway and heard the first note she struck ring out across the silent hall, proclaiming to all the world that Kirsten Harald had arrived.

Natalya watched the rapt expression on Kirsten's face and smiled. Was she imagining herself up there, she wondered. Kirsten belonged in Carnegie Hall, of that there was no doubt. Never in all her years as a pianist and teacher had Natalya seen a dream burn as brightly as the one burning within the diminutive girl beside her. Never had she known this rare a gift to have been so generously bestowed or so graciously received.

After only one lesson Natalya knew she had discovered genius in the then eight-year-old girl, miraculously spawned after fifteen years of a childless marriage by an Italian mother working as a cleaning woman at Carnegie Hall and a Norwegian father employed as a doorman at the Algonquin Hotel and appropriately, named after Norway's celebrated Wagnerian soprano, Kirsten Flagstad. Natalya had been so eager to work with Kirsten that she had reduced her usual fee by two thirds for these proud, hardworking people, and in the five years since that astounding first lesson, she had been slowly leading her cherished pupil up the same steep path she herself had once climbed.

The lights dimmed and Kirsten stiffened expectantly as Michael Eastbourne came striding onto the stage. His walk was liquid motion, his graceful movements those of a man keeping time to some lilting melody only he could hear. Even his bow possessed that same remarkable fluidity, like the bow of a gracious host welcoming a group of close friends to his home. But when he opened the evening's program with Claude Debussy's dramatic tone poem, "La Mer," that deceptive casualness disappeared, to be replaced instead by an electrifying intensity.

Kirsten leaned forward in her seat, fixating now on the young conductor's hands. They were as lyrical and expressive as his walk had been, commanding and controlling, but tender, too, as they masterfully unfurled Debussy's moving tribute to the sea he had loved so much. Mesmerized by the music, Kirsten once again forgot where she was. Soon the only sound she could hear was the sea rising from its gentle resting state to be whipped into a frothing, thundering frenzy by the howling winds.

It was then that she began to understand the special genius of Michael Eastbourne. What made his interpretation of a piece so brilliant was his ability to translate even the most obscure message into something meaningful and comprehensible, then direct it outward to the audience. He was magnificent, Kirsten decided in a state of near delirium, truly magnificent.

Following a tumultuous round of applause that seemed to last forever, Eastbourne escorted Arthur Rubinstein onto the stage. Kirsten held her breath as the fabled Polish pianist sat down at the gleaming Steinway to play her favorite of all piano concertos: Rachmaninoff's intensely romantic C minor concerto. By the middle of the first movement she had already begun to visualize herself at the keyboard. It was she whom Eastbourne was using as his medium to transmit Rachmaninoff's hauntingly bittersweet music from the page to the audience; she, not Rubinstein. A pulse fluttered in her throat as she pictured herself beginning the achingly beautiful portion of the third and final movement that always made her cry. With the music tugging mercilessly at her heart and tapping all her body's strength, she and the orchestra continued to soar upward, stretching and reaching and straining, until they crescendoed together at last in one splendid, soul-wrenching burst of melodic brilliance.

She collapsed against the back of her seat, her face flushed, her dress plastered to her skin, her arms weak. While the rest of the audience was roaring its approval in a series of deafening volleys, Kirsten remained silent, waiting for her strength to return, and with it, the self she seemed to have misplaced. She longed to spring to her feet with all the others, but she couldn't move. She felt energized and enervated at the same time; completely drained, yet filled to overflowing.

The concert ended at ten-thirty and Kirsten followed Natalya out of the hall feeling numb and strangely bereft, as though she had just been abandoned by someone she loved. She allowed herself to be carried along with the crowds spilling down the steps onto Fifty-seventh Street, but as soon as her own feet touched the pavement, she knew she couldn't leave without one final look at the poster.

"Something tells me you were quite impressed with young Mr. Eastbourne," Natalya remarked as she followed her transported pupil over to the marquee box again.

All Kirsten could manage was a slightly distracted nod while she concentrated on memorizing every feature of the face of the man she now considered her own personal discovery. The poetic gentleness shaping and defining his face combined with the lingering effects of his music suddenly made her want to weep.

"One day this man's going to conduct me, Natalya," she whispered. "I swear to you he will."

She didn't doubt it for a minute. In fact, she could already envision their names linked together, their faces sharing marquee boxes throughout the country and around the world.

"You'll help me, won't you, Natalya?" Conviction had transformed her luminous violet eyes into glittering amethysts as she reached out for her teacher's hand.

"Of course I will, Kirishka." The woman took the small, warm hand in hers and kissed it. "Haven't I always?"

2

"May I help you, young lady?"

Kirsten stiffened at the sound of the man's familiar voice but pretended not to have heard him.

"This is becoming quite a habit, isn't it?" he asked, not unkindly. "What's it been now, six times?"

Kirsten finally stopped playing. "Five," she told him. "Forgive me, five."

She kept her head down and waited, hoping he would go away, but unfortunately the man showed no immediate signs of doing so. Oh well, she thought. Drawing in a deep breath, she released it as a long, dramatic sigh, then slowly and with studied dignity slid out from behind the Steinway. With shoulders squared, she turned to face him and stood as tall as her five feet three inches would permit.

"I *am* a musician, you know," she informed him in a cool, level voice.

"Oh, I can believe that." Folding his arms, he studied her with a bemused half-smile on his face. He was far more serious than his tone implied. In fact, every time he heard her play, moving from one Steinway to another, like a gourmand sampling the food at a buffet, he held himself back, hoping she would finish with her experimenting and leave before he was forced to ask her to.

"I've been studying with Natalya Federenko for eight years now." Kirsten's jewellike eyes dared him to contradict her.

"Wonderful pianist in her time, Federenko."

Frowning, Kirsten hastily tried another tack. "Doesn't Steinway sell pianos anymore?"

Now it was the salesman's turn to frown. "Of course we do."

"And don't you often lend them out to concert pianists for their New York appearances?"

"We do."

"Then how am I supposed to know which piano to choose if I'm not allowed to try any of them first?"

Good point, he was tempted to answer, but didn't. "Don't you think you're a bit young to be worrying about that right now?"

Kirsten bristled. Why did adults always have to resort to the same kind of blackmail when they felt they were losing an argument. "I'm sixteen," she declared. "Mozart was playing the harpsichord at three, and no one ever told him he was too young."

"Touché, madame," the man replied with a grudging smile. Then, as Kirsten continued to stand there and glower at him, he took a quick look around and nodded toward the piano. "I'll probably lose my job for this," he said, "but who am I to thwart another Mozart? One more piece, all right? But only one."

Kirsten was gleeful as she plunked herself down on the bench again.

"Well, now that I've risked my job for you, Miss Mozart," said the salesman, "don't you think I ought to know your name?"

"It's Kirsten. Kirsten Harald, with two a's." The dimple deepened in her cheek. "What's yours?"

"Ralph Bowers. Why?"

"So I can send you a ticket to my first performance at Carnegie Hall." And with that she launched happily into a spirited Chopin polonaise.

Kirsten had recently begun trying out new pianos the way most girls her age tried on new clothes. To her acutely tuned ear, Aunt Sophia's piano was starting to sound thin; its touch had become too familiar, its action boringly predictable. She had pushed the secondhand piano to its limit and it was time she expanded. No two pianos were alike—each had its own particular voice, its own distinctive temperament—and if she hoped to continue her growth as a serious musician, she knew she should be familiarizing herself with as many of those voices and temperaments as possible.

But there was a second equally important reason for her coming to the Steinway Building. She wanted to be discovered.

Over the last three years she had given numerous recitals together with Natalya's other students, and had performed alone several times in various church basements and community halls, but nothing more substantial than that. She had yet to be reviewed, yet to find a single critic who had even heard the name Kirsten Harald. From the day-old newspapers her father brought home from the hotel, she had begun to read about *other* women pianists making names for themselves in a world still overwhelmingly dominated by men. Women like Lili Kraus, Myra Hess, and Roslyn Tureck. And she felt a budding spiritual kinship with them even as she found herself envying them their success.

If she were ever to join their exclusive ranks, she needed to be reviewed—favorably and often. Until that happened, however, she had decided to seek an alternate route by finding herself either a sponsor—someone highly connected to open all the necessary doors for her—or an agent to

represent her or a conductor willing to risk having an unknown soloist perform with his orchestra. And if an actress
like Lana Turner could be discovered in a drugstore, what
more appropriate place for a pianist to be discovered than the
showroom of Steinway & Sons?

When she left the Steinway Building—again without having been discovered—she consoled herself by taking a brisk
walk over to Joseph Patelson, the prestigious music store on
West Fifty-sixth Street. Clutched in her hand was a small
blue plastic change purse bulging with her current month's
savings. Due to the number of recitals she had been giving,
she had been forced to take additional lessons and buy nearly
twice as much sheet music as before. The increased expenses
had severely strained her parents' already tight budget, and
despite their initial protests, Kirsten had insisted on contrib-
uting in some way. The result was that she began baby-sitting
on weekends and working Sunday afternoons at the corner
candy store. Once a month she gathered up her earnings and
went to Patelson's, and this month, to her delight, she had
managed to save enough to buy both Schumann's "Fantasia"
and the entire collection of Chopin preludes Natalya wanted
her to learn.

After picking up the two works, she continued browsing for
a while through Patelson's extensive selection of sheet music,
then wandered toward the rear of the store, where the records were sold, and started idly flipping through them. She
had just reached the letter E when she suddenly remembered that Michael Eastbourne had recently recorded Rachmaninoff's Second Piano Concerto with pianist Rudolph Serkin
and the London Symphony. With a quiver of excitement, she
began to search in earnest through the tightly packed rows of
records for the letter R.

Each time she came across another work of Rachmaninoff's,
her stomach muscles would automatically contract, then just
as quickly relax the moment she read some other conductor's
name on the album cover. Munch. Stokowski. Ormandy.
Another Munch. Beecham. Szell. She sucked in her breath
and held it. With only two recordings left, she had finally
found the one she was looking for.

The cover showed Michael Eastbourne with both arms
raised, the baton clasped lightly in his right hand, his head
turned toward Serkin, who was seated at the keyboard. Kir-

sten stood there entranced for what seemed an eternity before she could even bring herself to take the album out and
examine it more closely. As she began greedily absorbing
every detail of the photograph, she was no longer in Patelson's
but back inside Carnegie Hall, hearing her beloved concerto
being played the way she had heard it played that night three
years before. The piece had been so indelibly imprinted upon
her brain that even the memory of its searing beauty still had
the power to reduce her to tears.

"Excuse me, miss, but we're closing."

Kirsten was so startled by the sound of the soft-spoken
voice behind her that she nearly dropped the record. Recov-
ering just in time to save both the record and her pride, she
turned and thanked the salesgirl with a slightly wobbly smile
and watched her walk away. She was in a bit of a quandary
now, knowing she couldn't afford to buy the sheet music *and*
the album. It took her just five seconds to decide. Back went
the sheet music with only the slightest twinge of guilt. Then
she tucked the record album under her arm and marched
over to the cashier.

"You're lucky, you know," he said as he slid the album into
a bag and taped it shut. "This is the last recording of
Eastbourne's we've got. They seem to disappear almost as
quickly as they come in."

While he was talking, Kirsten had emptied the contents of
her change purse onto the counter and had begun counting
out her money, praying anxiously with each growing mound
of quarters, dimes, and nickels that she would have enough.
She made it with twenty cents to spare. Again she felt a tiny
twinge of guilt; she wouldn't be able to buy the sheet music
she needed for another month. But the guilt dissolved as
soon as the cashier handed her her package. She hugged it to
her chest with an unabashed squeal of delight and hurried
out of the store. She had just bought her very first record.
That it was one of Michael Eastbourne's made the purchase
all the more precious.

Finding this album had been like discovering Michael
Eastbourne all over again. She couldn't wait to get home and
play it. She was nearly halfway there when the thought
suddenly struck her: If she had discovered Michael Eastbourne,
why couldn't Michael Eastbourne discover her? Surely that
wouldn't be too difficult. All she had to do was find some way

of letting him know she existed. And what better place to start than with the Rachmaninoff?

Buoyed by the utter outlandishness of the idea, she listened to his recording with a highly critical ear, studying it until she was convinced she had worn out the threads. She marveled at the subtle variations in Rubinstein's and Serkin's interpretation of the same music, knowing her own interpretation would be entirely different from either. By the time she was finally ready to tackle the Rachmaninoff, she knew just what that interpretation was going to be. She had no sheet music, of course; all she had was her superlative memory, her passionate love for the piece, and her unshakable belief in her own ability. She allowed herself two weeks to perfect it. It took her twelve days. And on the thirteenth, she played the entire concerto through for Natalya for the first time.

"You did this all by ear, Kirishka!" The unflappable Russian was dumbfounded. "Remarkable," she muttered, "simply remarkable. I must find someone to listen to you play. You're more than ready now." She began to pace her living room floor, stopping only long enough to pour herself a cup of tea from the huge brass samovar she always kept filled. "Aha! I've got an idea." She slammed the porcelain cup and saucer down on an antique marble console and clapped her hands twice to get Kirsten's full attention. "Eduard van Beinum of the Amsterdam Concertgebouw will be in town sometime next week to guest-conduct the Philharmonic. Eduard and I are old friends, and he has more international connections than anyone I know. I'll try to arrange for him to hear you. Yes," she said with an emphatic nod of her aristocratic head, "that's precisely what I'll do." But one look at Kirsten's glowing face and she quickly forestalled what she knew was coming. "Don't even think about playing the Rachmaninoff for him," she warned.

"But—"

"No buts. Without an orchestra, your playing, no matter how brilliant, will have only half the impact. No, Kirishka, for van Beinum we'll need something special, something dazzling. And I know just the piece." Rummaging through her sheet music, she finally found what she wanted and waved it high in the air above her head. "First we'll give him a Schumann, a Grieg, and perhaps a Mendelssohn or a Liszt, and then, my darling Kirishka, we'll give him this: Prokofiev's 'Toccata.' "

She thrust the music at Kirsten and stepped back to await her pupil's reaction. She wasn't disappointed. At the sight of such a complicated piece, its pages black with a myriad of thirty-second and sixty-fourth notes, Kirsten blanched.

"Don't be afraid of it, Kirishka, you'll master it in no time, I promise you. Now, go home and do nothing but look at it. Study it until you've absorbed it completely, then start to work on the fingering." She gave Kirsten a kiss on both cheeks and led her over to the door. "Remember, no more work on the concerto. You're to devote yourself solely to Mr. Prokofiev now."

The next morning Natalya called to confirm that she had indeed arranged for van Beinum to hear Kirsten on Wednesday at four o'clock in Carnegie Hall, Room 851. When Kirsten put down the phone she was trembling with excitement. In exactly five days she would be auditioning for the world-renowned Eduard van Beinum. Five days. She gave her head a shake and tried to absorb the shock of it all. She would have hugged herself if panic hadn't suddenly glued both her arms to her sides. Five days. And here she was, caught somewhere between elation and pure, unadulterated terror. She gulped hard several times, then ordered herself to calm down. This was the moment she had dreamed about and worked toward and waited for, and she fully intended to wring every second's worth of glory out of it. Gritting her teeth, she hardened herself in preparation for the task ahead and set off to do battle with Prokofiev.

Whether it was the complexity of the piece or the deadline ticking away like a clock inside her head, the combination made her doubly critical of everything she did—from the intricate fingering she was struggling to master, to the subtle tonal shadings she was striving to perfect, to the relentless pace she needed to maintain while making it all seem effortless. She was certain she was boring holes in the sheet music with her eyes and wearing grooves in the keys with the pads of her fingers as she went over the piece again and again and again, usually hearing nothing but her own mistakes. It was as invigorating an exercise as it was frustrating, but she was grimly determined to master the impossible piece and play it for van Beinum as it had never been played before.

She practiced until midnight for three consecutive nights

without any objection from her parents. But on the fourth night her father startled her by coming into the living room at ten and pleading with her to stop.

"It's enough, Kirsty," he said. "I'm surprised you aren't playing that piece in your sleep by now."

"I *am* playing it in my sleep." Kirsten fought back a yawn and stretched. Her fingers were sore, the muscles in her arms throbbing, her eyes strained from memorizing so many tiny black notes, yet she still wasn't ready to quit for the night.

"Come, Kirsty, please," Emil persisted in spite of her obvious reluctance to do what he asked. "I want you to go to bed now. There's time enough for this tomorrow."

Kirsten wavered for another moment, then finally gave in. Emil helped her up, noting her bloodshot eyes and the purple smudges of fatigue underlining them. She was driving herself mercilessly, and at what a cost. He returned her good-night kiss with a forced smile, but he wasn't smiling as he watched her stumble twice on her way out of the room. He cursed under his breath and waited for her bedroom door to close. Then he lowered the lid over the keyboard and turned out all the lights.

At precisely three forty-five on Wednesday, Kirsten walked down the eighth-floor corridor of Carnegie Hall toward Room 851 with a dry mouth and a wildly pounding heart. Both her mother and Natalya had wanted to come with her, but she had wanted to do this on her own. Now she was beginning to regret her decision; she could have used the moral support. She peered twice at the black numbers painted on the nondescript-looking door, frowned, then promptly checked the numbers again. There had to be some mistake. From behind the closed door came the sound of Mendelssohn's "Rondo Cappricioso," while just outside the door sat three girls of varying ages and two young men who looked to be in their twenties, staring either at their feet or at the ceiling and pretending to be oblivious to everything around them.

Suddenly, Kirsten couldn't swallow and her knees threatened to give way beneath her. She looked up at the face of the clock on the wall, noting the time, and wondered with mounting trepidation if all these people were waiting for van Beinum too.

"Holy Christ!" someone bellowed, and Kirsten whirled

around to see a rangy young man charging toward her. His thin face was nearly as red as his curly hair. "You here for an audition too?" he asked. "What time did they tell you to come?"

Kirsten cleared her throat. "Four o'clock."

"Great, that's just great!" He rolled his eyes and cocked his head in the direction of the other five outside the door. "Join the club. Hold on a minute and I'll get you a chair." Glancing up at the clock, he muttered something Kirsten couldn't quite make out, but she could well imagine what it was.

She sank onto the vinyl seat of the cold metal bridge chair the young man brought her, sighed, and crossed her legs at the ankle. Resting the back of her head against the wall, she dropped her sheet music onto her lap, closed her eyes, and tried to pretend that she was alone. How naive of her to have imagined Natalya was the only teacher in New York who knew van Beinum. How stupid of her to have assumed she would be the only student to play for him while he was in town. There were probably hundreds of aspiring pianists, not to mention violinists, cellists, flutists—the list made her stomach turn over—sitting on similar chairs outside similar studio doors all over the world, just waiting for him to hear them when he happened to be in their particular town.

In desperation she tried imagining she was somewhere else. She pictured herself at the piano, running through the program she had prepared for her audition, playing each piece in turn, and ending in a blaze of triumph with the "Toccata." She could feel herself beginning to smile, knowing she had accomplished what she had set out to do. She had assaulted the treacherous little piece and conquered it, tamed it, and claimed it as her own.

The sudden silence made her open her eyes and look anxiously around her. The door of the studio was ajar, and the girl next to her was the only one still sitting there. Kirsten gazed up at the clock and gasped. It was nearly six. It wasn't possible! She leapt up from her chair, sending her sheet music flying, and slammed right into the young man with the curly red hair.

"I'm sorry," he mumbled, giving her a look meant to include the other girl as well. "Look, what can I say? He just ran out of time. He had a six-fifteen rehearsal."

"But I was told he would hear me at four," Kirsten insisted through lips that were growing numb.

"I know, kid, but you saw the others here. They were told the exact same thing. Happens every time."

"It isn't fair." Kirsten shook her head, forcing back the tears. "I was told to be here at four and I *was* here. I waited for two hours . . . and . . . and nothing . . . they promised me . . . I just don't understand . . ." She knew she was babbling, but she couldn't stop herself. The words kept tumbling out of her mouth like beads breaking loose from a necklace and hitting the floor, then bouncing off in all directions.

"Hey!" He held up his hands and started backing away from her. "I just work here, you know, there's nothing I can do."

"Then why tell us to be here and not even have the decency to apol—"

"Face it, kid!" he snapped. "You're not the only one looking to be discovered." And with that, he stalked off down the hall.

Kirsten stared after him open-mouthed, not moving, barely breathing. It seemed hours had elapsed before she had the strength to turn around and see that her sheet music was still scattered all over the floor and that the other girl had gone. A large hole opened up inside her then, draining away all of her feelings and leaving her mind blank. Before she quite realized what she was doing, she had walked into Room 851 and switched on the light. The Baldwin was still open, the bench pulled out, as though someone had gotten up in a hurry and left. She sat down on the bench and found, to her astonishment, that it was still slightly warm.

You're not the only one looking to be discovered. The harsh words kept echoing over and over again in her ears. Five days ago she had been an unknown pianist with a dream and a promise to believe in. Five days later she was that same unknown pianist with the same dream, only now she was struggling to come to terms with what would undoubtedly be the first of many broken promises. Nothing had changed at all. As far as the music world was concerned, Kirsten Harald still didn't exist.

They had asked her here today to play for them, and that was exactly what she intended to do, even if there was no one around to hear her. Centering herself at the keyboard, she began with Schumann's "Carnaval," the first piece she would have played for van Beinum. By the time she began her

second selection, Grieg's Sonata in E Minor, the warmth had
returned to her hands and a sense of calm had replaced the
icy numbness she had experienced earlier. But behind the
calm there was a newly hardened resolve. She would show
them, all of them. They might break *their* promises, but she
would never break hers. She would become the greatest
concert pianist in the world, with or without their help. And
when she was, she would wait for them to come to her.

3

"Kirishka, you're doing it again!" Natalya clapped for Kirsten
to stop. "You're playing that passage like a lament. I want a
happy sound here, a happy one, do you understand? Good.
Now, try it once more." But it wasn't much better this time
either, and that wasn't like Kirsten at all. "What's wrong,
Kirishka, a touch of spring fever perhaps?"

Kirsten only shrugged.

"Something else then?"

Now she was embarrassed. Leaning forward with her hands
clasped between her knees, Kirsten bowed her head and kept
her eyes trained on middle C. "Have you ever been in love,
Natalya?" she whispered.

"What?"

Kirsten reddened. "Have you—"

"I heard the question," snapped the older woman. "I was
simply wondering what suddenly made you ask it."

The words came spilling out in a nervous rush. "Do you
realize that I turned eighteen yesterday, I'm graduating from
high school next week, and I've never even been out on a
date?"

"That's because you've had more important things to do,"
Natalya retorted, scowling slightly as she studied the back of
Kirsten's head. "Anyone with a talent as great as yours doesn't
risk diluting it, not even with love, in spite of what the
storybooks say. You have no room in your life for a storybook
romance, Kirishka, not if you intend to become a truly great
classical pianist. Are you listening to me?" She cupped Kirsten's chin in her hand and forced the girl to look at her.

"Stay true to your music, Kirishka, and it will stay true to you. It will be your most faithful friend and ally, never deceiving or abandoning you the way a man will. It will serve as the instrument for your desires, the receptacle for your hopes, the vehicle for your frustrations. Love, on the other hand, will only deplete your creative energies, dull your ambition, and divert you from the path you've chosen for yourself. If you allow yourself to be distracted even for a moment, Kirishka, you'll lose everything—yourself, your gift, but above all, your dream."

Kirsten sat quietly while she absorbed Natalya's well-intentioned advice, but instead of being reassured by it, she felt more confused and frightened than ever.

"I don't understand why I can't have both," she ventured almost meekly. "Both love *and* music."

"Because for you, love *is* music."

"Perhaps," she conceded somewhat reluctantly. "But I'd still like to have at least one date before I die, even if it's just to see what I'm not missing."

Or *missing*, nattered the same small insistent voice that had been nattering away at her a good deal lately. She was convinced she was missing out on something, but she didn't quite know what. All she did know was that there were strange new feelings deep in her body which she could neither comprehend nor control. Stirrings, unsettling and disconcerting, a kind of twitchy restlessness for which there seemed to be no remedy. It was as though someone were tickling her insides with a feather, stroking back and forth and up and down, making her feel tingly and warm and strangely shivery all at the same time. There was an urgency to these feelings that made her want to press up against sharp corners or squeeze her legs tightly together at the knees or grind her hips into the sagging mattress on her bed. And that made her feel guilty. Guilty and ashamed and a little bit dirty.

She couldn't even bring herself to mention her feelings to her mother. Asking Natalya about love was the closest she had ever come to admitting to another person that for the first time in her life she had begun to think seriously about something besides music. The very idea of it was tantamount to blasphemy, nothing short of sacrilege, and that further compounded her guilt. Only an act of contrition had the power to purge her body of its treacherous sensations and her mind of its double burden of guilt. And only her music could guarantee her the kind of cleansing absolution she needed. She had put off suffering her penance long enough.

"Natalya," she said, her mind made up, "I want to learn Brahms's Second Piano Concerto." It was his most challenging concerto and therefore the most fitting as her penance.

"The Brahms, impossible! Absolutely impossible!"

Kirsten was completely taken aback. "Impossible, why?"

"Because you would mutilate it," came the uncompromising reply. "You're too young, too inexperienced. You lack the depth and maturity a work as complex as the Brahms demands if it's to live and breathe. You'd be cheating your audiences *and* Brahms if you tried to learn it now."

Kirsten's initial enthusiasm was quickly turning into a bruised kind of bewilderment.

"You're simply not ready yet, Kirishka," the other woman continued in a softer, slightly appeasing tone. "You need to live first, to enrich yourself day by day, experience by experience, and that takes time, a lot of time. Once you've lived, my darling, truly lived, you'll be more than adequately equipped to pay the Brahms the homage it deserves."

"Then find me something else, Natalya," she begged in a desperate voice. "Just find me something, please."

Natalya found a piano competition for her to enter. The Wycliffe Trent Piano Competition was a worldwide solo competition named after the brilliant British pianist who had died tragically in 1940 at the young age of twenty-eight. It was held every April in the auditorium of New York University's downtown campus, and awarded the first-place winner a cash prize of one thousand dollars as well as recital dates in Boston, Cleveland, Philadelphia, and Chicago. Ironically, not a single American had ever won the ten-year-old competition, a dismal precedent which Kirsten was intent on breaking.

She woke up at four on the morning of the competition, bathed in perspiration, her body shaking and her teeth chattering. Twenty minutes later the chills gave way to undulating waves of prickly heat. By six she couldn't remember a single note of Beethoven's "Appassionata," the piece she had selected to play for the first round of the competition. She got out of bed and practiced feverishly until eight, stopping just long enough to bolt down a piece of toast and a glass of milk before returning to the piano to practice some more. At nine she was standing in the living room, wearing a scratchy blue and red wool dress, clutching the purse that matched her new imitation patent leather pumps, and staring balefully at her mother.

"Ready?" Gianna asked, opening the front door.

Kirsten took a single step forward, then stopped. Clapping a hand over her mouth, she raced down the hallway to the bathroom, where she promptly threw up her breakfast.

On the bus down to Greenwich Village, Kirsten sat with her head resting against her mother's shoulder, feeling like a child on her way to the dentist for the first time.

"If I ever decide to enter another competition," she said, groaning, "please talk me out of it."

"And if I tried," Gianna responded with a knowing smile, "do you honestly believe you'd listen?"

Kirsten chuckled. "Probably not."

For the remainder of the ride she managed to forget about her aching stomach by concentrating on the Beethoven and pulling it apart note by note. But the moment they started up the steps of the auditorium, she could feel a fresh wave of nausea beginning to rise threateningly inside her. With nothing left in her stomach, all she succeeded in producing were a few feeble hiccups. She caught her mother regarding her with a strange expression on her face and forced herself to smile as though nothing were wrong. Then the two of them joined hands and started down the long, congested corridor together.

Once again the sight of so many other aspiring pianists was like a slap of cold reality in the face, a painful throwback to that ghastly experience outside Room 851 in Carnegie Hall. When she had entered this competition, it had never occurred to her that she might not win. But as she looked around her now, she was suddenly seized by a shattering and immobilizing spasm of self-doubt. Mumbling a hasty apology to her mother, she left her just outside the doors of the recital hall and ran for the nearest ladies' room. When she emerged some moments later, she found her mother talking with Natalya and hurried over to join them. But no sooner had she greeted her teacher with a hug and the requisite peck on both cheeks than she had to go to the bathroom all over again.

"No, you don't," Natalya decided for her.

"Yes, I do."

"It's only nerves."

"It's my bladder," she countered.

"*And* your sudden doubts about your ability."

With teeth clenched, Kirsten snapped up the bait. "I have no doubts whatsoever about my ability."

"You don't?"

"No, I don't."

"Good." Natalya gave her a resounding slap on the back. "Then relax."

The qualifying round was set to begin at one, and Kirsten wasn't scheduled to play until four. At noon, when Gianna suggested they get some lunch, Kirsten hung back; she was still busily sizing up her fellow competitors, all of whom had so many grim-faced people clustered around them that they looked astonishingly like small, armed enemy camps. Of the thirty-two contestants there, only one girl appeared to be completely alone. Kirsten's first impulse was to feel sorry for her, but when the girl glanced up and found she was being observed, the look she threw Kirsten was so piercingly cold that she actually shivered. It was the same look the elderly woman had given her the night of the Rubinstein concert.

And like that woman, the girl, who was perhaps two or three years older than Kirsten, also carried herself with the instinctual hauteur of the upper class. Although not a conventional beauty, she was striking nonetheless, slender and quite tall, and her pale blond hair had been pulled back from her face and tied at the nape of her neck with a wide black velvet ribbon. She was wearing a simple sleeveless black sheath; her only jewelry was a single strand of large, luminous white pearls; and her low-heeled pumps, with their broad black grosgrain bows, were genuine patent, not imitation like Kirsten's. She seemed so self-contained, so secure in her aloneness that any circle of support around her would have been utterly superfluous. Although admittedly intrigued by the enigmatic blond, Kirsten's pride had been badly wounded, and she stubbornly refused to be the first to look away. She resolutely held her ground until the other girl broke their stare by turning her back on all of them. Quietly satisfied, Kirsten was finally ready to leave the hall.

Lois Eldershaw was used to people staring at her. Whether out of curiosity, admiration, or pity, it had ceased to matter years ago. But to have been so thoroughly scrutinized by such a shabby little urchin was insufferable. The pretensions of the girl, the airs! Lois shuddered. Who did she think she was, this presumptuous nobody with the mismatched pair of human bookends on either side of her?

The moment she had come down the corridor, Lois had recognized her as the last one to have arrived that day for an audition for Eduard van Beinum. She could feel her chest beginning to constrict. She didn't know what galled her more, van Beinum's rude dismissal of her after hearing her play only one piece, or the girl's acting as though she had never seen her before. Lois may have been used to being stared at, but she certainly wasn't used to being forgotten that easily.

At a Chock Full O'Nuts just down the street from the auditorium Gianna and Natalya each ordered cream cheese sandwiches and coffee for themselves, while Kirsten, who was too nervous to eat, asked for only a glass of water. But she couldn't even manage to drink it, not with her throat clamped shut around an image of the haughty blond girl's face. She closed her eyes and all she saw was another pair of eyes, pale-lashed and frosty blue, trying to stare her down. For the second time that day, she couldn't recall a single note of the "Appassionata," and by the time four o'clock rolled around, she was so disoriented that Natalya had to help her up after her name had already been announced twice over the loudspeaker.

She walked with her back straight and knees knocking all the way down the aisle toward the stage. Giving the six judges her most gracious smile, she mounted the steps with cautious dignity. She seated herself at the piano, felt around for the damper pedal with the toe of her right shoe, and immediately got up to adjust the height of the stool. Once she was satisfied, she folded her hands in her lap, closed her eyes, and summoned up the image of the first page of the Beethoven. She raised her hands and allowed them to hover gracefully above the keyboard for one brief, dramatic moment before bringing them down and striking the first eloquent chord of the "Appassionata." As those opening chords filled her ears and floated out over the hushed auditorium, she felt the music enfold her like a warm, protective mantle and spirit her blissfully away.

She was a dreamer lost inside her music, alternately playful and tender, teasing and earnest. And as she played, her body followed the melody's seductively winding path in one continuous, swaying clockwise motion. It was a glorious taste of eternity, one of those rare, cherished moments when she knew how it felt to be immortal. She dreaded her inevitable descent to earth but submitted to it graciously nevertheless; and when she struck that final note, she even paused a moment before allowing her arms to fall slowly to her sides, signaling the end.

Her exit was as properly dignified as her entrance had been, but as she started back up the aisle, her body was quivering. To make matters worse, she couldn't remember where her seat was. An eerie lightheadedness began turning her joints to rubber as she continued her search for her mother and Natalya without being able to locate them. Looking up, she suddenly found herself gazing into the glacial blue eyes of the blond who had just left her own seat on the aisle. Something inside Kirsten snapped. She took several more faltering steps, then slumped to the floor in a dead faint.

She opened her eyes to find her mother and Natalya bending over her as she lay stretched out on a leather couch in one of the university's administrative offices.

"That will teach you to go without food," Natalya scolded as she raised Kirsten's head and held a paper cup to her lips. "I would have much preferred vodka, of course, but I suppose water will have to do for now. Come, Kirishka, drink up."

But Kirsten didn't want any water; she wanted to know if she had been disqualified from the competition. Natalya snorted at the absurdity of the question and shook her head.

"Disqualified, ha! You're a superb showman, Kirishka, with a marvelous sense of timing. You at least had the good sense to faint *after* your performance."

"Was I good?"

"Good? You were sublime."

"Was I, Mama?"

Gianna was beaming. "Wonderful, *carissima*, truly wonderful."

"A word of caution, however," Natalya interjected as Kirsten struggled to sit up. "You have a very strong competitor in a girl by the name of Lois Eldershaw."

Kirsten was instantly on guard. "Who?"

"The young lady who played after you."

"Was she blond, wearing a black dress?"

"You know her?"

"Hardly." Kirsten swung her legs over the side of the couch and looked closely at her teacher. "Do you?"

"Only indirectly. Frieda Schor taught her for six years before Lois won a scholarship to Juilliard. According to Frieda, she was an excellent technician but lacking in any true emotional depth, which is hardly surprising—the girl was practically ignored by her parents. In fact, in the six years Frieda taught her, she saw the parents only once. Apparently they didn't approve of their daughter's playing the piano. Also the mother suffered from such a severe bronchial condition that they spent less than half the year in New York, the rest of their time in Arizona. Without Lois," she added. "When Lois entered Juilliard, her parents bought her a co-op apartment on Fifth Avenue and moved to Arizona for good. She's ruthlessly ambitious, Kirishka, as well as being something of an isolate, and that makes her a rather formidable rival."

Gianna, who had been standing quietly by while Natalya was talking, was becoming impatient. She was far more concerned about Kirsten at the moment than some girl she had never even heard of before. "Come, *cara*," she said, trying to keep the impatience out of her voice as she helped her daughter to her feet. "I think it's time you ate something."

But Kirsten gently extricated herself and started for the door. "Later, Mama," she said. "Right now I want to hear Lois Eldershaw play."

She was too late; the other girl was already on her way out of the auditorium. Their gazes locked again, but only briefly this time because Lois turned almost immediately and started briskly down the corridor. She was met near the exit by an older man in a chauffeur's uniform, who draped a pale fox jacket over her shoulders, then held the door open for her. Kirsten stood with her eyes riveted on the door long after it had swung shut. Then in a voice only she could hear, she hurled a challenge at her now-departed enemy and steeled herself for battle.

Lois was gasping as she flung open the door of the penthouse and went inside. Switching on the lights in the foyer, she dashed through the living room and out onto the glass-enclosed terrace, with its unbroken view of Central Park. She sucked in a deep breath and held it, released it slowly, then repeated the exercise several more times. But concentrating on her breathing was only making it worse. Kirsten Harald seemed to be everywhere—in her nostrils, her throat, her lungs, polluting every inch of the apartment's carefully controlled and purified air.

Her next breath was accompanied by a dry rattle in her throat and a sharp whistling sound in her chest. She cautioned herself not to panic as she turned away from the windows and went back into the living room. Flicking on the antique brass lamp over the nine-foot Steinway, she sat down and immediately began playing one of her favorite sonatas by Mozart, hoping the music would work its usual magic and unlock the tightness in her chest. To her relief, it did. Little by little, the terrible tension inside her began to ease, and with it, most of the agonizing constriction.

Gazing down on the park as she played, she began to dream her favorite dream. She was a queen trapped high in a grand glass tower, waiting for the day when her music would set her free. And when it did, she would take full and victorious command of the world she had, for much of her life, observed only from the safety of distance. She would rule it with her talent and success, and she would move in the most rarefied of its social circles as its supreme and exalted center.

An image of Kirsten Harald flickered in front of her and quickly vanished. Her chest began tightening up again almost instantly. She missed a note, then an entire passage, her inner tension increasing with each mistake she made. She couldn't lose this competition, she simply couldn't. She was already twenty-two years old and her career was going nowhere. After giving up so much and having worked so hard to prove herself, she didn't dare consider the terrifying possibility of failing now. Without her music she had nothing. Worse still, she *was* nothing. How was she supposed to exist if someone like Kirsten Harald were to change the happy ending to the fairy tale she had written for herself so long ago?

Both Kirsten and Lois made it to the finals along with four other contestants. Kirsten was scheduled to play second to last on the program and Lois last, something Kirsten fretted about until the very moment she was called up onstage. When she automatically tested the damper pedal on the piano, she was surprised to find it slightly less flexible than she remembered. Lifting her foot, she waited a moment, then pressed down on the pedal again. In the silence she heard a man cough, followed by the sounds of restless shifting. But she refused to be hurried. Nibbling worriedly on her bottom lip, she pumped the pedal several more times and waited again. There was more coughing and more shifting. Hackles were beginning to rise on the back of her neck. She tried the pedal one last time, found it greatly improved, and blamed the entire episode on nerves.

Partway through her Schubert sonata it happened; the gasp from the audience only confirmed it. The damper pedal was stuck. The sound she was producing was now one elongated, cacophonous blur. Kirsten froze, her hands trapped in mid-air, and glanced helplessly in the direction of the judges. Within minutes a young man dressed in gray overalls, carrying a dark green metal toolbox, climbed onto the stage and crouched in front of the piano. It was another five minutes before he got up again and shook his head at the judges. The hobbled piano was immediately rolled away and a replacement wheeled out. While a formal apology was made over the loudspeaker, Kirsten sat down at the new piano and tried to prepare herself for the excruciating task of beginning the piece all over again.

She played with her heart splintering into fragments. Even with her hands breathing special life into every expressive note she carved out of the unfamiliar keyboard, she herself felt dead inside. Her mind was mired in agony, her body rooted in despair, knowing she had lost. When she rose from the piano, the applause was deafening, continuing long after she had left the stage and taken her place between her mother and Natalya again.

Two hours later the winners of the 1952 Wycliffe Trent Piano Competition were announced, starting with the third- and second-place winners, both of them British. When the first-place winner was finally announced, Kirsten was still so shaken that she didn't even hear her own name being called. Only her mother's insistent tugging succeeded in getting her to her feet. Stumbling into the aisle, she nearly collided with Lois Eldershaw, who was also on her way to the stage. Now Kirsten was completely confused; her mother had obviously made some terrible mistake. But there was no mistaking the accusatory look in Lois's cold blue eyes. It took Kirsten another moment to comprehend the situation. And then she didn't know whether to laugh or cry. Neither of them had won the competition. The two of them had tied for first place.

They stepped forward together to accept their checks of five hundred dollars apiece from Langston Foley, the music critic for the *Chicago Telegram* and senior judge of the competition. Then Kirsten surprised herself by extending her right hand to her rival. For the sake of propriety, Lois swallowed her pride and grudgingly accepted Kirsten's outstretched hand, giving it a light, perfunctory squeeze.

"My congratulations, Miss Harald," she said in a voice as cool as ice water.

"Miss Eldershaw." Kirsten inclined her head slightly. Then she released the other girl's hand, turned her back on her, and swept grandly from the stage.

"Kirishka, you were spectacular. And that exit, pure theatrics!" Natalya gushed as they headed for the door. "What happened with the pedal could have happened to anyone, yet you handled yourself like a true professional. I'm proud of you, Kirsten, very, very proud."

"And so am I, *mi amore*," Gianna said, her heart swelling as she hugged and squeezed her daughter all the way up the aisle.

"But I didn't win, did I?" Kirsten's voice was flat. She could barely look her mother in the eye. By tying for first place, neither she nor Lois Eldershaw had proven herself to be the superior musician, and that effectively defeated the whole purpose of the competition. If only they could run the competition over again. If only the pedal hadn't stuck. If only she hadn't been so tense when she'd had to start the Schubert for the second time. She gave her head an impatient shake. Indulging in if-onlys wouldn't change a thing. It was over. All she could do now was wait for the next time. And there would be plenty of next times, she would see to it.

She was so absorbed in her own thoughts that she failed to notice the middle-aged couple in the last row who had been monitoring all her movements with great interest. The man turned to the woman next to him and smiled. She returned his smile. Then the two of them shook hands. Their latest quest was over at last. They had finally found what they were looking for.

4

Eric Sheffield-Johns released his wife's hand to circle the name Kirsten Harald in his program. If Claudia's opaline eyes still seemed inordinately glazed, he could hardly blame her. He had seen it too—the girl's breathtaking resemblance to their dear friend Larry Olivier's own Vivien. Poor Vivien. Thank God, her Blanche in *A Streetcar Named Desire* which she had filmed last year had been such a critical success, because her health, mental and physical, had been and still was so precarious. Eric shook his head. Hopefully life would be kinder to the exquisite young creature they had just discovered.

Tucking his pen away, he stole a sideways glance at his wife and felt a rush of pleasure at the sight of her wonderfully aristocratic profile. What a superb team they still made, he and Claudia, as ever the perfect complements to each other, even after eighteen years of marriage. Beauty and the beast. Or, as she loved to call them, the prince and the pauper. That he had started life far poorer than she had ever been was the one secret he had successfully hidden from her all these years. He shuddered to think—and not for the first time either—that perhaps she had been just as successful at keeping some equally damning secret of her own hidden from him.

As he helped Claudia on with her coat—she always felt the cold, something he attributed to her whippetlike leanness, and every dress Norman Hartnell designed for her had a matching coat—he indulged himself in another luxurious moment of private speculation. Would anyone from his native Liverpool seeing him today recognize him as Eric Johnson, the postman's boy, he wondered. Humor, like a dark flame, brightened the blackness of his deep-set eyes. Even as a child he knew he had stood out, a conspicuous oddity, in Anne and Joe Johnson's mangy litter of seven. But it was more than just looks that had set him apart from his brothers and sisters. It was his ferocious ambition. A determination to see himself

43

catapulted from the life of degradation his family had meekly accepted as their due, into some great, grand world of his own creation.

Would the townspeople to whom he once delivered the *Liverpool Daily Post* or the blokes in the postroom at the *Liverpool Dispatch* remember him? Would the reporters remember that at twenty he was named publisher and managing editor of the *Dispatch*, a mere two years after his lifelong idol, William Aitken, had founded the *Sunday Express* at the ripe old age of forty-two? Would the swells in the boardrooms on Bond Street remember crowning him the undisputed king of the tabloids when he was only twenty-nine or that by then, his total circulation far outstripped Aitken's?

And what of Aitken himself, who had still managed to surpass him in terms of respectability, being knighted by King George V and given the title Lord Beaverbrook, Eric wondered. He grinned, remembering how, on the day he left Liverpool to take up permanent residence in London, he had retaliated by bestowing upon himself his own form of noble title. He shortened his surname from Johnson to Johns and borrowed the Sheffield from the city renowned for its manufacture of silverplate. What more appropriate appellation for a man who was himself a brilliantly successful fusion of so many disparate parts? What more fitting description for someone as comfortable in the salons of Bloomsbury as in the local pub, as relaxed at court as he was on the streets?

Motioning to their driver, Eric couldn't help but chuckle. He doubted anyone from his long forgotten past would recognize him today. Not this impeccably groomed and remarkably refined toff on his way to the Plaza and the most expensive suite his hard-won fortune could buy.

Emil and Gianna met with the Sheffield-Johnses first, then it was Kirsten's turn. She had been anticipating the meeting for two days, percolating all the while with an enthusiasm that made her feel there were millions of tiny pop bubbles living inside her. And as the appointed time drew nearer and nearer, the more deliriously excited she became.

"I've been dis-cov-ered, I've been dis-cov-ered," she chanted over and over again in a high, wobbly voice as she danced around her tiny bedroom. "I've been dis-cov-ered, I've been dis-cov-ered."

She spun herself dizzy then flopped backward onto her

bed. Lying there, spread-eagled and out of breath, her long black hair splayed around her like a gleaming silken fan, she stared up at the ceiling with an ear-to-ear grin on her flushed and perfect face. If what her parents had told her was true, she had found herself sponsors. No, she hastily corrected herself, patrons. She had recently decided she preferred the word patron to sponsor. It sounded far more romantic, much more . . . Renaissance. She repeated it aloud several times— pa-tron, pa-tron, pa-tron—dramatically elongating the first syllable, then allowing the rest of the word to linger in the air above her head like a gentle benediction. Michelangelo had had the Medicis; Hadyn, the Esterhazy family; van Gogh, his brother Theo. And she, Kirsten Harald, had Eric and Claudia Sheffield-Johns. She hugged herself and laughed out of sheer euphoric delight. One vital part of her cherished dream was about to come true. Unbelievably, improbably, but most assuredly about to come true at last.

She and her parents met the Sheffield-Johnses at the Russian Tea Room on Fifty-seventh Street at four, and as she slid onto the cool red leather banquette next to her mother, Kirsten couldn't contain her wide-eyed curiosity about her exotic surroundings. She felt like an impostor, sitting in a booth usually reserved only for the rich and famous, beside herself with excitement as she reveled in such a rare and unexpected privilege. To think that she was actually here, seated inside the fabled restaurant she had passed countless times without ever once daring a swing through its revolving glass doors for a coveted look at the interior.

It was as though she had stepped back in time to live out one single fragile moment in the history of Imperial Russia, when the Tea Room might just as easily have been the dining room of a Russian nobleman. Its walls, painted a deep forest green, were trimmed in gold and hung with elaborately framed oil paintings, all lavishly evoking the memories of a bygone era. The accents were brass: from the pots of brilliantly colored silk flowers to the edges of the chairs and booths to the giant, highly polished samovars, so similar to the one Natalya had. The subtle lighting was provided by red-shaded brass wall sconces, and in their rubious glow the atmosphere in the place was one of comfort, camaraderie, and hushed intimacy.

She felt a pair of eyes on her and immediately careened back into the present again. Flushing self-consciously, she laced her fingers nervously together in her lap, gave her hair

a light toss, and presented her brightest face to the man
seated directly across from her. A man whose large, coarse
features were somehow smoothed and softened by a wonderful gentleness, making him look, in Kirsten's eyes, every bit
the benevolent benefactor. In his three-piece gray pin-stripe
suit, his overall appearance would have been hopelessly intimidating were it not for his habit of winking appreciatively
whenever he or someone else at the table made a particularly
clever or irreverent remark.

"Having difficulty deciding, are you?" One of Eric's arched
black eyebrows indicated the menu resting on the table in
front of Kirsten.

She gulped, glanced at the menu she hadn't even begun to
study, and flushed again.

"May I make a suggestion?"

"Please."

Leaning across the table toward her and lowering his voice
so that only the two of them could hear, he winked at her and
said, "If you want something frightfully caloric, do try the
Black Forest cake." He rolled his eyes in wicked delight. "It's
sinful, positively sinful."

Kirsten giggled, her flush of embarrassment turning into a
flush of pleasure. Eric Sheffield-Johns, in spite of his grand
name, his illustrious reputation, and formidable presence,
was fun. A grown-up scamp who didn't seem to take life
particularly seriously. Easing quickly into the game he had
initiated, she leaned forward herself until their dark heads
were almost touching and whispered back,

"I will if you will."

He pretended to be scandalized. "Do you think I ought
to?" He patted his well-padded waistline and Kirsten joined
in his easy laughter. "Why the devil not? I'll simply compensate for it by having some lovely lean sole for dinner."

Kirsten made a face and Eric nodded in agreement.

"Too many bones," they said in unison, laughing together
again.

Eric beamed with pure paternal satisfaction as Kirsten
pretended to swoon after taking her first bite of the Black
Forest cake he had recommended she try. Turning a jocular
eye to Claudia, he gave his wife a wink that said "we've found
ourselves a treasure here," then concentrated on his own
generous slice of cake. How he envied Claudia her self-
discipline—she steadfastly refused all desserts and always

drank her tea with lemon instead of milk—and her single-minded adherence to the Duchess of Windsor's successfully proven principle that one can never be too rich or too thin. He watched her watching Kirsten and wondered if there would have been any Kirstens in their lives had they ever been able to have children of their own.

God knows they had certainly tried hard. But after three miscarriages and two stillbirths, even Claudia had conceded that her long, angular body, with its nonexistent hips and tiny breasts, was obviously an inhospitable home for a fetus. It was her suggestion to convert the third floor of their four-story town house in Belgravia into a self-contained flat and offer it each year to some young man or woman of rare talent.

Although they would never be parents themselves, at least this way they could act as surrogate parents, happily turning prodigies into protégés and then sending them into the world to live out their special promise.

Kirsten washed down a mouthful of the dark cherry-studded cake with some tea and glanced up to find Claudia watching her again. While Eric made her feel warm and protected, Claudia, on the other hand, had just the opposite effect. Each time their eyes met, each time she spoke, something in Claudia's expression made her uncomfortable and self-conscious. But that wasn't all. With her blue-gray eyes and silver-blond hair, which was swept back from her narrow face in a sleek chignon, the woman reminded Kirsten of Lois Eldershaw. Even their taste in clothes was the same: simple and elegant. And Claudia's fine royal blue silk dress, with its matching coat, made Kirsten even more uncomfortably aware of the stiff scratchiness of the homemade wool dress she herself was wearing.

"Kirsten, my dear." Eric laid a large, square hand on top of hers, effectively directing her attention back to him again. "How would you feel about spending a year with us in London?"

There it was at last. That simple question. One single sentence. Only a dozen words. But with enough power to alter the course of her life. Kirsten's head began to spin. She suddenly seemed incapable of drawing a full breath. Her throat tightened into a bottleneck of emotions and sensations while her heart dipped and soared like a roller coaster out of control.

"Commencing in the autumn of 'fifty-three to be more

precise," Eric continued. "Our year always seems to begin in September now."

"Much the way the regular concert season does," Claudia provided in her cool, bell-like voice, her gaze fastened unrelentingly on Kirsten's warm face.

"You'd be studying with one of the finest music teachers in Europe," Eric told her. "Magda Szabo."

Kirsten smiled when she heard the name. Natalya and the Hungarian-born Magda had been friendly rivals on the concert circuit.

"Not only would you be studying with Magda, darling," said Claudia, "but you'd also be performing at our Sunday afternoon salons and meeting some of the most influential men and women in the arts: composers, musicians, artists, writers, critics, publishers. The list is positively endless. I think you'll find our home to be a virtual Mecca for a young creative artist like yourself."

Kirsten gulped. Her eyes were stinging as she turned to her parents for guidance. Emil's face was carefully closed, but his expression seemed to assure her that whatever decision she made would receive his support. Gianna's emotions, however, were far more obvious, the internal battle she was waging all too apparent in the anxious shifting of her dark, tear-smudged eyes and the trembling of her bottom lip. She was a mother. And right now she was torn between wanting to keep her daughter near her and admitting that the time had come to let her go.

"This isn't something you need decide on the spot, you know." Eric was well aware of the turmoil, the tug-of-war raging in all three of them. Snapping open the antique gold pocket watch Claudia had given him the day their first spectacularly successful glossy women's magazine, *Lady Bountiful*, was published ten years before, he pretended to be studying the time. "I'd say another five minutes should just about do it."

"Eric!" Claudia slapped him playfully on the wrist.

"Just teasing, pet, just teasing." He tucked the watch back inside his vest pocket. Nodding at Kirsten, he urged her to continue eating. "There's more than enough time to decide, my dear, that I promise you."

Kirsten picked up her fork again and stabbed blindly at her cake. Her mind was crowded with images, all of them blending together, making clear thinking next to impossible. Red double-decker buses. Piccadilly Circus. Sir Thomas Beecham. Buckingham Palace. Wigmore Hall. The London Symphony. The Tower of London. The Sadler's Wells Ballet. She swallowed without tasting and speared a cherry. What she had just received was an official invitation to enter the exclusive world into which women like Claudia Sheffield-Johns and Lois Eldershaw had been born. An opportunity to meet others like them, to learn from them, to become one of them herself. A chance to return to New York one rung higher up the golden ladder, one step closer to the top of the mountain. It was a miracle, nothing short of a miracle.

But in order to take advantage of this miracle, she was being asked to leave behind everything that was safe and warm and familiar to her. Her parents. Her home. Natalya. Her own piano. Not just for a week or a month, but for an entire year. Three hundred and sixty-five days away from the only world she had ever known. With the width of the Atlantic Ocean to separate them.

"We didn't quite realize what we were getting ourselves into when we started all this fourteen years ago," Eric was telling Gianna, and Kirsten was only too happy to listen to something besides the frantic hammering of her own heart. "We thought we were simply enjoying a bit of beginner's luck with Michael, but that proved not to be the case at all. Every other aspiring artist since Michael has been equally gifted, equally ambitious, and equally successful."

"Michael?" Kirsten piped up, her voice hardly more than a strangled squeak.

Eric nodded. "Yes, Michael Eastbourne."

Her fork clattered onto the table.

"Michael Eastbourne, the conductor?" Her heart was now a kettledrum threatening to burst through the walls of her chest.

"The very same. Why?" One of Eric's eyebrows was arched again. "Do you know Michael?"

"Not really," she admitted, feeling a bit foolish. "I was at Carnegie Hall when he made his American debut." She hesitated. "I . . . I promised myself that one day he'd conduct me."

Eric couldn't have appeared more pleased. "Now, that's a noble ambition if ever I've heard one, isn't it, pet?" He was grinning as he turned to his wife for confirmation.

Claudia's own smile was surprisingly frigid. "It certainly is."

Kirsten glanced from Claudia to Eric, then back at Claudia again, wondering why the woman's mood had changed so abruptly at the mere mention of Michael Eastbourne's name. So he had been a protégé of theirs. The shock of it, the incredible coincidence of it, was almost too much for her to absorb. Was this a portent then, some sort of omen she should be heeding? Her breathing quickened. Suddenly, her dream of being discovered by Michael Eastbourne didn't seem quite so farfetched anymore. In fact, as Eric and Claudia's protégé, anything was possible.

"It's the opportunity of a lifetime, Kirsty," Emil told his daughter as the three of them sat until after midnight around the kitchen table, where all their serious family discussions took place. "What they're offering you is something your mother and I could only wish you to have."

Kirsten looked down at the worn linoleum and found herself wondering what the kitchen floor in the Sheffield-Johnses house looked like. Questions, so many questions. She reached for her parents' hands and gripped them with a fierceness she could feel all the way down to her toes. Here was love and loyalty and proven sustenance. Here was nurturing and caring and concern. Would they feel betrayed if she chose to live apart from them for a year in the home of two complete strangers? And what about Natalya? After eleven years of coaxing and encouragement and stubborn faith, would she feel she was being abandoned in favor of her onetime rival? Questions, questions, too many questions.

"I love you, Mama. I love you, Pappy." Kirsten turned from one to the other, her voice breaking, her chest tight. "And if I do decide to go to London, I want you to know that I'd be doing it for the three of us. Besides," she said with a shaky laugh as her eyes began to fill, "think of all the money you'd save in piano lessons and sheet music." Then before either Gianna or Emil could respond, she bolted from the table and closeted herself in her bedroom.

She walked over to the window in the dark and peered outside, marveling at how anything so ugly during the day could look so lovely at night. The battleground of the city had been turned into a magical fairyland, its scars and blemishes erased by the thousands of twinkling lights burning in their place. What would the view be like from the flat in the town house in London, she wondered. Once again she conjured up a vision of faraway London in her mind; only this time, instead of England's capital, she saw herself playing Brahms's Second Piano Concerto at the Royal Albert Hall in a royal command performance.

She laughed out loud at her silliness and blinked the tantalizing image away. Gazing across Ninth Avenue, she did what she did every night before going to bed: she followed the configuration of lights that formed a luminous arrow pointing east toward Seventh Avenue and the amber brick building sprawled between Fifty-sixth and Fifty-seventh Streets. Leaning her elbows on the dusty windowsill, she sighed a long, wishful sigh. If a year in London could bring her closer to her beloved Carnegie Hall, she would leave tomorrow.

Andantino

1953–1954

5

In 1953 England was a sleeping beauty being roused, not by a handsome and charming prince, but by a gradual return to the grand lifestyle it had enjoyed before the outbreak of World War II. The general election of 1950 had seen the end of the Labour government and the return to power of the Conservatives led by Winston Churchill. Sweets, eggs, sugar, butter, cheese, and meat were slowly being derationed, and white bread was available again in bakeries and grocery stores everywhere. In June the entire country had erupted in a joyous display of love and hope when Princess Elizabeth of the House of Windsor was crowned Queen of England. Remembering the golden reign of that first illustrious Elizabeth, the loyal and ever-fanciful British were quick to insist that another such golden era was about to begin.

Like America, England was also witnessing the start of the age of consumerism. An increasing number of people now owned their own homes, many began vacationing abroad for the first time, and horse racing was reinstated as the country's most revered and cherished pastime. Performances of Shakespeare resumed at Stratford-upon-Avon; opera returned to Covent Garden and ballet to the Sadler's Wells Theatre. All three major orchestras—the London Philharmonic, London Symphony, and Royal Philharmonic—began to tour again, and for the first time in years British designers received worldwide attention by declaring that men should take fashion as seriously as women did.

This was the England—invigorated and revitalized—awaiting Kirsten when her ship docked at Southampton on Labor Day. And the slate-gray door opening to welcome her to Eric and Claudia's imposing white stone town house invited her to take that next bold step out of the shabby familiarness of her own world into the breathtaking swankiness of theirs. In the large square foyer, with its brass lantern chandelier and its checkerboard floor of black and white marble tiles, she found the entire household staff lined up in silent precision to greet her. Flanked on either side by Eric and Claudia, she moved slowly down the line like a fledgling head of state reviewing her very first honor guard, while conscientiously trying to memorize each staff member's name at the same time.

Randolph was the butler, Gretta the housekeeper and Meg the cook. Alyce and Edna were the downstairs maids, Gwen and Valerie the upstairs maids. Megan was Claudia's personal maid; Gilbert was Eric's valet. She had already met Parker, the chauffeur, and the gardeners, according to Claudia, didn't really count.

"As soon as you're quite through pinching yourself to make certain you're awake," said Eric with one of his broad winks, "Claudia and I will be delighted to show you the rest of our little nest."

"Little nest?" Kirsten echoed. "Now I know how Alice must have felt when she tumbled into Wonderland."

To her, the house was just that: a veritable wonderland, a vast treasure-trove of delights to explore and savor. As they went from room to room, Kirsten was open-mouthed, enchanted, and completely overwhelmed. After a while everything began to blur, until it seemed she was viewing the house through one end of a kaleidoscope, as a series of continually changing, brilliantly colored patterns. That it was a study in such dramatic and dazzling contrasts made its impact on her all the more profound.

There were formal striped silks and lush velvets played off against casual glazed-cotton chintzes and fragile lace. Inlaid rosewood, heavy oak, carved mahogany, and glass. The icy prisms of glittering chandeliers and sconces, the waxen smoothness of ivory tapers, decorative china, heirloom crystal. Pastel-papered walls, cool marble floors, warm jewel-toned Persian rugs. Flowers, both silk and real. But most memorable of all was the art everywhere: oil paintings, watercolors, sculptures and statuary, tapestries, hand-painted scrolls, and miniatures carved out of ivory, ebony, coral, and jade.

As they entered the library, Claudia pointed to a large soapstone carving with a small rectangular brass plaque affixed to its black marble base, and told Kirsten, "This was done by the second of our illustrious houseguests, the Italian sculptor, Giorgio Rizzolini. It's become a custom of sorts for our guests to give us something indicative of their particular pursuit when they leave."

"And through the years, most of them have continued to

send us samples of their works," Eric interjected, pretending to be bored with the whole thing. "We now live inside a virtual museum, my dear Kirsten, with my lovely wife acting as its curator. She simply adores collecting things. Isn't that right, pet?"

"Look at the pot calling the kettle black," Claudia retorted. "You and your precious magazines. That's his true passion, darling," she said to Kirsten, her pale eyes dancing as she and Eric continued their little game. "He simply adores collecting magazines."

"I believe the proper term for it is *acquiring*, pet." Blowing his wife a kiss, he said, "We'll be back in a jiffy," and reached for Kirsten's hand. "I have something to show you that should be of particular interest to you, my dear. Heaven only knows why we didn't start with that room first."

Flinging open a pair of double glass doors, he led her into the conservatory. It was a large and airy room with a highly polished parquetry floor, dotted here and there with round brass planters containing miniature orange and ficus trees. Buttery sunshine spilled through an entire wall of windows and traveled across the floor to illuminate the satiny black finish of the Steinway set at an angle in the far corner of the room. At the welcome sight of the nine-foot concert grand, Kirsten clapped her hands in glee and raced over to it.

"Do you realize I haven't so much as touched a piano all week, and I haven't missed a single day since I was five?" She brushed her fingers back and forth across the top of the keyboard cover as though she were reestablishing contact with her only lifeline. "Now I feel I can start existing again after being completely invisible for seven whole days. Strange, isn't it?"

"Not strange at all." Eric's voice was surprisingly gentle, his smile comprehending. "Now, come over here a moment, will you? This should rather amuse you, I think."

Amused was hardly the word to describe Kirsten's feelings as she followed Eric's pointing finger to the narrow glass case set on top of a white marble pedestal. Inside the case, resting on a bed of red velvet, was a slender wooden baton. The small brass plaque on the pedestal read:

MICHAEL EASTBOURNE
1938–1939

She put out her hand to touch the case, then drew it back again and self-consciously tucked both hands behind her back. Staring down at the baton, she imagined him holding it, tapping it smartly against the top of his music stand to get the orchestra's attention, then using it to lead them, the way a general leads his troops, just as he had that wondrous night at Carnegie Hall.

"I should have known you'd be in here." Claudia's voice from the doorway made Kirsten jump. "Don't you have an appointment at your office at three, Eric?"

Hastily snapping open his pocket watch, Eric scowled when he noticed the time. "Bloody hell, I'm late." He squeezed Kirsten's hand, pecked his wife on the mouth, and headed quickly for the door. "See you anon," he called back with a jaunty wave just before he disappeared.

"Well then, what do you say I show you your flat now?" Claudia noticed Kirsten's wistful sideways glance at the piano and smiled. "There's more than enough time for that later. Let's get you unpacked and settled first, shall we?" She was halfway across the room before Kirsten had even taken a single step. "Coming, darling?" It was a question Kirsten would hear quite often in the coming months, because no matter how quickly she walked, she was never able to keep up with Claudia's long-legged stride.

"Tomorrow, darling, I'll take you shopping," she said as they climbed the stairs to the third floor. "I do so want to start you off with a decent wardrobe."

"But—"

"No buts, darling. It's all part of the package, so to speak. Eric gets to manage the business side of things while I have the divine pleasure of tending to the social side. You may be a musician, but you're also a woman, you know. And I intend to help you develop your wonderful femininity as best I can."

They had arrived at the third-floor landing and Kirsten's eyes began to widen.

"As you can see, darling, I redecorated with your marvelous eyes in mind."

The flat consisted of a spacious bedroom, sitting room, dressing room, bathroom, and tiny, modified kitchen, all upholstered and curtained in a glazed-cotton floral chintz of lavender, purple, and periwinkle blue against a white background. The walls and ceilings were painted lavender, the woodwork and plaster trim periwinkle blue. The furniture was Italian Provincial, delicate and curving, and painted white. Small white china pots filled with fully blooming African violets lined the ledges of both windows in the bedroom, and there was a velvety nosegay of purple violets in a sterling silver bud vase on the night table next to the large, canopied bed.

"Direct from Piccadilly," Claudia explained. "Eric thought it most appropriate."

"Eliza and her Professor Higgins?" asked Kirsten with a smile.

"That's exactly how we both feel at times, yes." Claudia gently emphasized the word *both*.

She then allowed Kirsten to continue exploring on her own, while she stayed behind in the bedroom. Leaning up against the doorjamb with her arms folded across her chest, Claudia gave in to the broad, contented smile that was already tugging at the outside corners of her slightly downturned mouth. Kirsten's very nearness, her unspoiled freshness, and tender innocence had so disarmed and humbled her that she felt like weeping for joy. The feeling was as intense as it was unnerving, for it was a feeling she thought she had buried long ago, together with her vanquished dreams of motherhood. Now she was alive as she hadn't been in years. She yearned to enfold Kirsten in her arms, to speak to her the way any loving mother speaks to the child she adores, and share with her everything she might have shared with her own daughter, had her treacherous body not betrayed her.

No doubt Eric would consider her a complete fool. Right from the start he had cautioned her to remember that these young men and women were theirs for one year and one year only. Out on loan as it were. Borrowed temporarily from their rightful parents, then returned. And through the years, she had remembered, considering herself safely beyond caring too deeply for any of them. Until Kirsten, whose breathtaking talent and bewitching beauty had conspired together so successfully to make her forget.

"Claudia?"

At the sound of Kirsten's voice the older woman's head snapped forward with a guilty start.

"This watercolor." Kirsten indicated the ten-by-fourteen-inch painting that was hanging above a dainty five-drawer chiffonier. "Didn't I see one just like it in the library?"

"The unerring eye of the artist." Claudia's smile betrayed

none of her rampaging inner emotions. "You certainly did, darling. In fact, if you look very carefully, you'll find nine of them in the house. I'm working on the tenth right now." She ran the tips of her long, graceful fingers over the decorative gilt frame and sighed. "It's become a hobby of mine, you might say. All I ever change are the colors, depending on the room I'm painting it for. I did this one while the flat was being redone."

"And they're all exactly the same?" Kirsten stared hard at the watercolor of the large country estate painted in tones of blue and lavender and wondered why anyone would want to paint the same scene over and over again. The longer she looked, however, the clearer it became. Claudia had obviously done it out of love. It was there in each tiny, precise brushstroke, each dollop of color, each exquisitely wrought detail.

Claudia seemed to have guessed what Kirsten was thinking because she said, "I always thought that if Monet could get away with painting the same haystack over and over again, I could bloody well get away with painting Wynford Hall as often as I liked."

"Wynford Hall." Kirsten repeated the name several times, liking the gentle sound of it.

"It was my home." Claudia said this so softly that if Kirsten hadn't been standing next to her, she wouldn't have heard her.

"Your home?"

"Or rather, my dear uncle's home," she spat, her abrupt change of mood taking Kirsten by surprise. She drew in her thin lips until they seemed to disappear, and a look of pure undiluted loathing hardened the rest of her sharply defined features. "Oh yes, darling, the home of the great Nigel Edmund Charles Bartholomew Bisham, fifth Earl of Wynford, and my father's older brother. In case you've never heard of Wynford, it's in Wiltshire."

Kirsten had never heard of Wynford, but she had heard of Wiltshire. Salisbury Cathedral and Stonehenge were in Wiltshire. She smiled to herself. Mr. Widemann had been wrong; she *had* learned something in his history classes.

"See those windows?" Claudia was pointing to the painting now. "That was the ballroom." Her finger moved slightly to the right. "That was the dining room." Her finger moved again. On and on she went, naming each room, square by tiny square, while Kirsten followed with the eerie feeling that she was being taken on a walking tour not only of Claudia's erstwhile home, but of Claudia's past as well.

"We lived in the cottage," Claudia explained, her hostility biting off the ends of her words. "All six of us. Dear father and mother and their four darling daughters, crammed into that wretched cottage, while the three of them, my aunt and uncle and my cousin, lived so splendidly in that magnificent house."

"I don't see the cottage anywhere," Kirsten ventured innocently.

"Why should I have painted the bloody cottage?" Claudia snapped. Seeing the startled hurt in Kirsten's violet eyes, Claudia instantly mellowed. "Oh, darling, I'm sorry. Do forgive me, please, you couldn't possibly have known." And with that she swept from the room, leaving Kirsten to stare after her, more confused than ever by the woman's strangely capricious behavior.

Before Kirsten climbed into the tester bed that was to be hers for the next year, she went over to one of the windows, parted the ruffled chintz draperies, and took her first look at nighttime London from her new room. How different it was from New York. There the sky, punctured by the jagged rim of so many illuminated buildings, never seemed to get truly black. Here the sky was one unbroken blanket of black, and the only lights she could see came from the houses across the street and the old-fashioned lamp standard just below her window. Here, too, the night was quiet and still, so quiet, in fact, that her ears hurt. Was this the sound of wealth and privilege, then, she wondered. No sound at all?

Slipping somewhat gingerly between flowered sheets as soft and smooth as silk, she turned onto her side and peered at the photograph of her parents in the plain metal frame from Woolworth's that she had set out on her night table. An ache rose from deep within her belly, tightened itself into a ball, and lodged itself firmly in her throat. Placing the photograph on the pillow close to her head, she stared at the faces of her beloved parents and pretended that the two of them were actually with her until she began to get drowsy. Only then did she finally reach up, switch off the lamp, and close her eyes.

*   *   *

In the morning, when she awoke to find herself afloat on a cloth sea of violets, peonies, and bachelor buttons, she did what Eric had jokingly suggested she do the day before: She pinched herself. Four times. Twice on each arm. Astounded to discover that she really was awake, she dressed quickly and hurried downstairs to the conservatory. Everything was just as she remembered it—the greenery, the baton in its clear glass case, the Steinway gleaming in the corner. Seating herself at the piano, she lifted the lid over the keyboard, worked the stiffness from her fingers with a few warm-up exercises, then launched into Schumann's "Carnaval." With her hands skimming over the keys and her soul taking flight, she was gloriously, ecstatically whole again.

She was still playing when Claudia came into the room an hour later and motioned for her to stop. "Why don't you leave that until this evening, darling?" she suggested. "I'm taking you shopping today, remember?"

Torn between her desire to please Claudia and her need to continue playing, Kirsten bargained for time. "Could I have two hours first before we go?"

"I'd much prefer if you made it one," Claudia replied.

"One and a half?"

"My God, darling, this isn't a market." Claudia looked aghast at Kirsten. "We don't usually haggle for things around here." But Kirsten refused to give in. "Very well, have it your way then. The last thing I want is someone with the sulks at Selfridge's."

Delighted to have won some additional time with her music, Kirsten tripped gaily through a Chopin mazurka, then decided to play the last piece that she and Natalya had worked on together—the majestic and intensely dramatic Grieg A Minor Concerto.

"Really, darling, we had an agreement, remember?"

Kirsten crashed to a halt, wondering how long Claudia had been standing over her. "I—I'm sorry," she stammered, closing the piano and getting up. "I always lose track of the time when I'm playing."

"Obviously." Claudia regarded Kirsten's flushed face with amusement. "Now, do come along."

"The look in fashion this year," explained the saleswoman in the dress salon at Selfridge's, "is sleek and slender. While it's rather a sophisticated look, there's a certain gaminlike quality to it that's delightfully young and fresh. But of course your daughter would look simply smashing in whatever she wears." Kirsten and Claudia exchanged smiling glances and said nothing. "Well then, ladies, shall we begin?"

Three hours later Kirsten was near collapse. "You don't actually expect me to wear all these clothes, do you?" she asked Claudia as they left the store.

"Of course I do, darling, and this is only the start."

"The start?" Kirsten watched as Parker made a second trip to the Bentley with his arms laden with boxes. "Do you realize we've already bought two cocktail dresses, an evening gown, two suits, three skirts with matching swea—"

"And we still have to buy shoes, purses, hats, gloves, lingerie, and so on. Darling, my list is far, far longer than yours." Claudia consulted her diamond wristwatch and steered Kirsten briskly toward the car. "We'll stop at Fortnum and Mason for tea, then continue our shopping there." As Kirsten sank into the backseat with a groan, Claudia gave her a light pat on the cheek. "You're supposed to be enjoying this, not suffering. It's part of a woman's nature to indulge herself; you'll learn to love it, I assure you."

"If Natalya could hear you, she'd order me back to New York on the first ship leaving Southampton," said Kirsten, trying unsuccessfully to stifle a yawn.

By six she could barely stand. Her back ached and her feet were swollen and blistered, yet she and Claudia had managed to buy her another gown, two dinner dresses, and three pairs of shoes with purses to match before the doors of Fortnum & Mason had threatened to close on them. Slumped beside Claudia in the Bentley again, Kirsten kicked off her shoes and began to massage her aching feet.

If ever she should have been pinching herself, it was now. She, whose mother had sewn almost all her clothes, now had an entire new wardrobe that would last her for years. If only her mother could have seen her posing in front of strange saleswomen and strange dressing room mirrors in outfits so glamorous that mere mortals should have been forbidden to wear them, while Claudia, with a casual flick of her wrist, pronounced the magic words: "Put it on my husband's account." The face of Lois Eldershaw rose in front of her, floating like a disembodied spirit through the air, and Kirsten found herself grinning. If only the girl from Fifth Avenue could see her now.

"You seem rather pleased with yourself," Claudia remarked as she opened the car's small bar and poured some sherry into two delicate crystal glasses. Handing one to Kirsten, she raised hers in a toast. "To a most propitious beginning," she said, clinking the side of her glass against Kirsten's.

It was the first time Kirsten had ever tried sherry, and although she didn't particularly like the taste, she liked the way it warmed her sore, exhausted body. Watching Claudia closely, she made certain she took the same tiny sips of her sherry that Claudia took of hers. It was with a bit of a jolt that she realized she had spent the entire day watching the older woman and carefully observing everything she did. Seeing the respect accorded Claudia by the people they met wherever they went made her feel miserably inadequate and gauche by comparison. She had so much to learn. So much.

Natalya had advised her once to live, truly live. And here in London, with two people as worldly as Eric and Claudia, that was precisely what she intended to do. She watched as Claudia refilled their glasses. Then she raised her brimming glass in the air, took a deep breath, and proposed a toast of her own.

"To life," she announced in a loud, clear voice.

"To life," repeated Claudia.

And they continued drinking to life as they drove all the way back to Belgravia.

6

"No, no, no!" Magda Szabo stamped her foot for emphasis. *"Piano,* Kirsten, *piano,* not *forte."*

"I don't agree," Kirsten replied, tapping stubbornly at the disputed passage on the page in front of her. "Schubert's building toward a climax here. If I'm still playing softly at this point, it'll lessen the impact of the entire crescendo."

"It will not." Magda was equally adamant. "I want this part of the passage subtle, please, and I do emphasize the word *subtle."*

"Natalya never would have—"

"Ach! Natalya again, always Natalya. Natalya Federenko

was a tempestuous peasant who should have played a bala-laika instead of the piano. She knew nothing about subtlety."

As usual, Kirsten rose nobly to her beloved teacher's defense. "She knew *every*thing about subtlety, especially where and when *not* to use it."

Magda Szabo, bright red curls bobbing, piquant features crinkled in defiance, made a great display of holding her ground. Yet in spite of her bold posturing, she knew her brilliant young pupil would inevitably win this newest battle just as she had won most of their other battles in the two months they had been working together. It was simply a question of timing. And to Magda, the truly good teacher never gave in too soon.

"So, *petite*, are you still convinced you're correct, or have you changed your mind and decided to follow the instructions of the poor, ignorant composer?"

Without looking up from her music, Kirsten's voice was firm. "I haven't changed my mind and I don't intend to."

At this point Magda capitulated. "Very well, play it your way if you insist. But don't be surprised if everyone covers his or her ears and walks out of your recital on Sunday."

At the mere mention of Sunday, Kirsten attacked the keyboard with a ferocity that startled even her. After two months of being a spectator and observer, she was finally going to be the featured attraction at Eric and Claudia's Sunday afternoon salons. And this Sunday marked her debut performance. She missed a note and began the entire passage over again. It was impossible for her to believe that two months had sped by; impossible, too, to recall even a single moment in all that time when her toes had touched solid ground.

Although her work schedule followed the same rigorous pattern as it had in New York—six hours of practice each day and lessons twice a week—almost everything else in her life was different. Thanks to Eric and Claudia, she could actually feel herself changing, evolving, undergoing a metamorphosis that affected each and every part of her being. She had become a human sponge, absorbing, then rapidly assimilating every facet of her newly expanded world into her system. She was malleable, curious, reaching out here, stretching there, and growing, all the time growing. Stimulated and challenged as never before, she was the most eager and responsive of students, with a voracious appetite for more, more, more.

The secretary in her sitting room had become the reposi-

tory for what Eric and Claudia chose for her to read, its four
narrow shelves crammed with books on world history, the
classics, biographies, plays, and poetry. No sooner had she
finished one than another would take its place. Then there
were her evenings out, experiences from which lasting memories are made. There were dinners at the homes of close
friends like Sir Stafford Cripps of the Board of Trade, the
Countess of Albemarle, BBC producer Hew Wheldon and his
wife, Jacqueline, and political commentator Henry Fairlie.
Cocktails with such assorted luminaries as author Kingsley
Amis and playwright John Osborne; stage personalities Sir
John Gielgud and Dame Edith Sitwell, dancer Moira Shearer
and photographer Norman Parkinson. Nights at the opera,
the ballet, and the theater—her two favorites being Drury
Lane, where Nell Gwyn made her stage debut in 1665, and
the Phoenix, known fondly by Londoners as Noel Coward
and Gertie Lawrence's theater. She didn't feel like Alice in
Wonderland anymore, but rather like Cinderella, who had
miraculously been allowed to stay at the ball.

Yet in spite of these head-spinning experiences, one thing
had remained maddeningly constant; everyone still referred
to her as Eric and Claudia's "latest." Sunday, she knew,
would change all that, and change it forever. On Sunday she
would so impress the sixty-five guests fortunate enough to
have been invited to her debut recital that none of them
would ever dare refer to her as the Sheffield-Johnses' "latest"
again. After Sunday her name would be as familiar to them as
their own; they would even consider it a privilege to pass it
on. Before the week was out, she was convinced that all of
London would know her name.

When her lesson was over for the day, she relaxed for a
while in a hot, lemon-scented bubble bath, then sat down at
her secretary to write her daily postcard home. Her first
project upon arriving in London had been to collect three
hundred and sixty-five different picture postcards—one for
each day she would be away—and number them consecu-
tively. Mailing one with zealous punctuality at the corner
post box every evening at six became the first of her two daily
rituals. The second, instituted a week later, took up a bit
more of her time. It consisted of walking through her bulging
clothes closet every morning—as if to prove that her clothes
were still real and hadn't vanished like some dream overnight—
selecting an outfit at random, then posing before the large

cheval glass in her dressing room just long enough to convince herself that the stunningly turned-out young woman in the mirror was truly she.

The salon was scheduled to begin promptly at two, but at one o'clock Kirsten was still standing in the middle of her closet in her underwear, unable to decide which gown to put on. She had never been confronted with this kind of choice before, and she didn't quite trust herself to choose correctly. She was just about to give up and ask for Claudia's advice, when one of the gowns suddenly caught her eye. It was as though she were seeing it clearly for the first time. How could she have been so blind, she wondered. The gown was lavender, the only color she had sworn ever to wear onstage. With her heart thumping excitedly, she reached for the floor-length crepe de chine gown cut along the lines of a Grecian toga, and pulled it on over her head. Just as she was emerging again, Claudia came into the room to see what was keeping her.

"We really must do something about your hair, darling," Claudia said by way of greeting as she watched Kirsten struggle into a pair of peau de soie pumps dyed the same lavender as her dress.

"Why?" Kirsten puffed, straightening up again. "What's the matter with it?" She blew a long, silky strand out of her eyes and studied her reflection in the mirror.

"A Pierre Balmain calls for something slightly more—" Claudia paused, fumbling for a word that wouldn't hurt Kirsten's feelings.

"Sophisticated?" Kirsten completed the sentence for her.

"That's it precisely, darling, sophisticated." Picking up a silver-backed hairbrush from the top of Kirsten's vanity, she motioned for her to sit down. "Now, let's see how clever we can be."

Claudia was positively purring inside; she had dreamed of brushing Kirsten's hair for weeks now. How she envied the girl her glorious hair, so long and so luxuriously thick. Her own hair had always been too fine to wear down; a chignon at least gave it some semblance of thickness. She brushed Kirsten's hair until it crackled, then used her fingers to separate and twist it into an elaborate cluster of plump ringlets, which she pinned into place with tiny black hairpins. She sighed a deep sigh of blissful contentment. Here at last was the daughter she had always wanted, to cherish and adore, to pamper and pet and perfect. She fixed one final curl in place, clasped Kirsten's bare shoulders lightly with both hands, and leaned down to plant a tender kiss on either side of her neck.

"Well, darling," she breathed softly into Kirsten's sensitive ear, sending shivers up and down her spine. "What do you think?"

"I can't believe it's me," she said.

"Believe it, darling." Claudia gave her another loving squeeze. "Because it most assuredly is you."

Her dramatic entrance into the conservatory would have made Natalya proud, and when she played Schubert's "Fantasia" the way she had warned Magda she would, she knew she had been far more than just correct in interpreting the piece so boldly; she had been inspired. And instead of clearing the conservatory, it brought the guests to their feet, clamoring for more. Their senses had been taken by surprise, their legendary British reserve totally undone, leaving them to react spontaneously and unabashedly to what far less distinguished audiences had been reacting to for years inside the church basements and community halls of New York City.

As an encore, she played what she had decided would be her signature piece. It was Claude Debussy's "Reflets dans l'Eau," a brief and delicate homage to the play of light upon the surface of a pond. Like the sunlight itself, the Impressionist piece was a shimmering illusion of sound, capturing with notes what the Impressionist painters had themselves captured with oil. Staggered by the almost delirious response to her playing by such a select and sophisticated audience, Kirsten rose on trembling legs to take her bows. Then she beckoned to Magda, just as she had beckoned so often to Natalya, feeling a pang of longing as the tiny redheaded Hungarian flounced across the room to join her.

Directly following the recital, tea was offered in the drawing room, champagne and sherry in the living room, and a light buffet consisting of tea sandwiches, miniature fruit tarts, French pastries, and English trifle in the dining room. With her own plate filled but left untouched, Kirsten was delighted to find she was the focus of attention. Everyone wanted to talk to her, pulling her this way and that, bouncing her back and forth among them. She was glowing, heady from so much extravagant praise, all traces of her usual reticence gone, as she moved from room to room with a new confidence in her step and a clearer awareness of her own growing power.

Just as she had known it would, her music had served as the battering ram to break down that barrier between simple curiosity and eventual acceptance. A space had been cleared for her on the perimeter of the exalted circle. She wasn't through the door to the inner sanctum just yet—she still had one foot poised tentatively on the threshold—but her performance today had at least opened that golden door for her. Today she knew how it felt to be a star, valued and adored, and she didn't need any champagne to feel like a thousand tickly, dancing bubbles all by herself.

"Come, darling, there's someone you've simply got to meet." Claudia had grabbed her by the elbow and was now steering her toward the far corner of the living room. "None other than his eminence, the almighty Clemence Treaves."

Kirsten's wide eyes grew even wider. "The impresario?"

"The very same."

Having Clemence Treaves here today was a rare privilege; he didn't dispense his social favors lightly. But with Kirsten as the lure, he had finally bitten, and it thrilled Claudia to be able to introduce her delicious child to the world-renowned Treaves. With his sleek brown hair, full mustache, and trim beard, he bore a striking resemblance to the late Edward VII. He capitalized on the resemblance by carrying himself with an arrogance worthy only of royalty, then effectively offsetting his haughty demeanor by dressing like a dandified country squire.

Being part of the influential Treaves family made him a member of an extended network that dominated the international artistic community, much the way Queen Victoria's family had once dominated the political one. On his own, he was a ruthless broker in talent. One kind word from him and a career took wing; one cutting remark carefully placed, and that same career swiftly plummeted. With offices in Vienna, London, New York, and San Francisco, Treaves was a cultural octopus, his influence unquestioned and unparalleled, his connections innumerable, and to those artists he favored, invaluable.

"You're every bit the treasure I was told you were," pronounced the illustrious Treaves, taking hold of both of Kirsten's hands. He released her after a moment with a slight twitching smile. "I'm delighted to find that such extraordinary hands are human after all."

Kirsten blushed with pleasure. "Thank you, sir, you're very kind."

"Not kind, my dear, merely truthful." His eyes began to narrow, and Kirsten had the uncomfortable feeling he was about to snatch his compliment back. "Tell me something, then"—he paused, his brown eyes practically slits now—"just how committed are you to your music? Please don't think it presumptuous of me, it's a question I ask every young artist I meet."

"Every young artist or every young *woman* artist?" Kirsten's guard was up and the words were out before she could stop them. "If I were a man, Mr. Treaves, would you really have asked me that?"

"Yes, I most certainly would have."

"Then let me assure you I'm as deeply committed to my music as any man, probably more so."

"And why is that?"

"Because as a woman I'm forced to work twice as hard as a man in order to be taken seriously. We're too quickly condemned, either for being emotional and unreliable, or timid and bland. If we play with any kind of power, we're considered masculine; if we play with any degree of sensitivity, we're criticized for being sentimental. It's unfair, Mr. Treaves, terribly unfair, but to tell you the truth, I don't really mind; it just makes me that much more determined."

"Determined?"

"Yes, determined." Kirsten's eyes were bright, her chin firm and proud. "To be the best pianist in the world."

Clemence Treaves snickered. "A rather tall order, wouldn't you say?"

"Not at all."

"Then you won't be abandoning your music to run off and get married?"

"Why should I?"

"What about raising a family?"

"Why couldn't I do both?" It was with an eerie sense of déjà vu that she recalled her similar discussion with Natalya.

Treaves rolled his eyes. "You couldn't possibly do justice to both. Something would have to suffer, and it would invariably be your career. Women are by birth nurturing creatures, my dear, wives and mothers, featherers of the nest, keepers of the hearth. Oh, they may rebel on occasion, but it's only temporary, I assure you. Full-time careers are much better left to men."

"Why?" Kirsten was fighting hard to keep her temper under control.

"Because unlike women, men put their careers first and their families second. They neither raise their children nor look after their homes. They have wives to do all that for them. Who's going to prepare your meals and lay out the proverbial slippers for you, my dear Miss Harald, when you return home after playing fifty cities in almost as many days? Who's going to bring up your children in your absence? Certainly not your husband."

"I still say I could do both; I'd simply balance my time between them."

Treaves looked positively apoplectic. "Impossible, utterly impossible. You can't give one hundred percent of yourself to two things, and to be the best means giving yourself over to it one hundred percent. If you think it can be otherwise, then, my dear, I'm afraid you're only deluding yourself."

At that point Claudia, the ever-watchful hostess, intervened, and skillfully guided Kirsten over to a less volatile corner of the room.

"Really, that man can be so bloody exasperating at times," she muttered through clenched teeth. "The supreme devil's advocate. He probably can't get to sleep at night if he hasn't successfully torn a strip off some poor person's back. Forget about him, darling. Today's your day, remember that. Now, go and glory in it."

But when Kirsten returned to their guests, some of her wonderful new glow was gone.

Turning up the collar of her navy blue cashmere coat, Kirsten thrust her gloved hands into her pockets and hunched her back to counteract the force of the wind. The late December air was biting, and the brisk wind had already stained her cheeks and the tip of her nose bright red. She shivered once, gave herself a vigorous shake, then quickened her pace, hurrying down Marylebone Road toward Portland Place. Walking around London remained her sole form of exercise, and this was her favorite route. At least three times a week she would ride the Underground to Regents Park, then walk the invigorating four miles back to Belgravia again.

She dropped by the tobacconist's outside Victoria Station, picked up a copy of *The Times*, and opened it to the entertainment section. Halfway down the first page, the sight of a familiar name made her catch her breath. There it was at last—at long, long last. According to the notice, he would be in London in February to guest-conduct a series of three concerts with the London Philharmonic. Her hands were shaking as she folded the paper and put it back on the pile next to the cash register. After all these months in London, she would finally have the chance to meet him. She would simply ask Eric and Claudia to invite him to tea.

But when she broached the subject that evening at dinner, she was met by a disconcerting wall of silence. Eric's face seemed to close up right in front of her, and Claudia's jaw became so taut that even her neck muscles were straining.

"Wasn't Michael Eastbourne your first protégé?" Kirsten continued uncertainly.

"He was," Eric admitted.

"And wasn't he also your favorite, the one you were closest to?"

"Correct again."

"Then I don't understand."

Eric glanced down at his wife, who was sitting stiffly and silently at the foot of the long mahogany table. "Well, pet, I think you should be the one to answer this, don't you?"

Claudia dabbed at the corners of her mouth with the edge of her white damask napkin, then carefully rearranged it in her lap. "Michael Eastbourne hasn't set foot in this house in over ten years," she said very quietly.

"But why?" Suddenly Kirsten was almost afraid to hear the answer.

"He simply hasn't been welcome here, that's why."

"What did he do?" she persisted in spite of her fears. "Did he do something wrong? Did he hurt you or—"

"Hurt me?" Claudia's laugh was laced with venom. "Yes, I suppose you could say he hurt me. You see, darling, ten years ago, our precious Michael married my uncle Nigel's daughter, my own dear cousin, Roxanne Bisham."

7

Scraping back her chair, Claudia rose swiftly to her feet. For one tense moment it appeared she might charge out of the room, but she didn't. Instead, she stopped just short of the doorway, where a small mahogany tea wagon stood. Above the wagon hung the first watercolor of Wynford Hall she had ever done. Her eyes immediately filled with tears. She managed to blink them away without much difficulty, but it was not quite as easy to clear her throat of that familiar clogging sensation. Then, as though giving in to a compulsion she was constantly forced to combat, she reached up and traced the outline of the country estate she herself had so faithfully re-created. To her dismay, all five of her pale long-boned fingers were trembling.

With her back still turned to the table, she said, "I loved this house."

It was a simple statement, but she made it sound like a benediction.

"When I was a child, my uncle Nigel allowed me the run of the place, and I used to pretend it was mine. Nigel was only eleven months older than my father, but those eleven months made all the difference. Being the eldest, it was Nigel who inherited everything when grandfather Bisham died the year before I was born. Everything, including the house."

There was a dreamy smile on her face as she glanced back over her shoulder at Kirsten.

"You never saw anything so remarkable. It was truly a marvel—steeped in history, crammed full of wonderful hiding places, gleaming with silver and gold and crystal, surrounded by the most exquisitely fragrant gardens. And Nigel, well"—the timbre of her voice softened, rippling outward with reverential tenderness—"Nigel was the most beautiful man I'd ever seen. I adored him and he adored me."

At this, Eric made a slight coughing sound, but Claudia paid no attention to him.

"He even swore that when I was old enough, he would

marry me and bring me up to Wynford Hall to live. He was teasing, of course, but children believe what they want to believe, and because I was a child, I believed him. Oh, how I believed him." Her throat was clogging again; she stopped and waited for the tightness to ease. "When I was nine, he married someone else. I was crushed; my beloved Nigel had betrayed me. But he obviously didn't think so, because he still invited me up to the house as though absolutely nothing had changed."

Her inner agitation was mounting and it was quickly reflected in her body movements. She dropped her hand from the painting to close it around her throat instead. And when she focused on Kirsten again, the clearness of her cool blue eyes had been marred by a mysterious pain.

"Five months to the day after their marriage, Nigel's wife, Constance, gave birth to an eight-pound girl they grandly named Roxanne Mary Victoria Elena Bisham. Because my father never missed an opportunity to point out the real reason behind Nigel's rushed marriage, I waited patiently for him to throw the scheming baggage out, thus freeing himself from a situation he couldn't possibly have sought in the first place."

She laughed at this, a shrill bark of a laugh that made the hackles rise on the back of Kirsten's neck.

"Of course that never happened. But fool that I was, I continued to go up to the house like some pathetic beggar desperate for whatever crumbs of his love he might dole out to me. I knew Constance and Roxanne resented me terribly, but I didn't care. I was determined not to let anything stand in the way of my being with Nigel." Her thin arms were now circling her waist as if to hold both her insides and her memories in. "Unfortunately, I underestimated dear little Roxanne. She took to throwing the most beastly temper tantrums whenever she saw me. The strategy worked. Constance was quick to inform me—in the most civilized tones imaginable—that I was no longer welcome in her house. *Her* house," she repeated bitterly. "It should have been my house. And Nigel"—she hugged herself more tightly as she uttered his name—"my beautiful, treacherous Nigel went along with her. After everything he had promised me, after everything we—" She broke off abruptly, took a deep breath, and said in a changed tone of voice, "Well, Nigel actually had the temerity to go along with her."

A moment of uncomfortable silence passed, to be followed by another and another. Finally, in the merest whisper, she said, "I was devastated. The gates of heaven had been slammed shut in the face of a true believer, and I knew it was finally time for me to stop believing. I was seventeen by then, and when I realized how much of my life had been wasted on sheer lunacy, I vowed not to waste any more of it. So I left."

After several more moments of awkward silence, it was obvious that Claudia had said as much as she intended to say, but Kirsten couldn't resist asking, "Did you ever go back to Wynford?"

The answer was a clipped no.

"Not even to visit?"

"Not even to visit."

"But you stayed in touch with your family, didn't you?"

Claudia looked surprised, as if the thought had never occurred to her. "Whatever for?"

It was Kirsten's turn to look surprised. She couldn't visualize a life without *her* family. "What about your uncle?"

Claudia actually grimaced. "What about him? The bastard's sixty-five. By now he's undoubtedly gone the way of all flesh, noble or otherwise. You know, pot-bellied and bald, with a definite stoop."

"And Roxanne?"

"We take great pains not to move in the same circles. She has her sphere of influence, I have mine."

Despite the brusque, offhanded manner she had adopted, there was a vein of agony in her so thick that if pain had had a color, Claudia's fine white skin would have been stained a bilious yellow.

"So you see, darling," the woman concluded with a tight little smile, "I have nothing whatsoever against Michael Eastbourne except the company he's chosen to keep."

This time she did walk out of the room, leaving in her wake two very surprised people—especially Eric.

He was staggered. So Claudia had had her own secret after all—a childhood crush on her dashing uncle. Hell hath no fury, he conceded, be it a child or a woman scorned. It certainly explained part of her lifelong obsession with Wynford, but he had the sudden sickening feeling that it did not explain it all.

Leaning back in his chair, he tapped his index finger thoughtfully against his chin as the germ of an idea took hold within his fertile mind.

"So you want to meet Michael, eh?" he asked Kirsten.

Still reeling from the effects of Claudia's story, all she could manage in answer to Eric's question was a vague, distracted nod.

"Let me think about it," he said. "I should be able to come up with something." Lowering his voice conspiratorially, he gave her one of his famous winks. "Trust me?" he whispered.

"Completely," she whispered back.

"Good girl. That shows extremely sound judgment on your part."

They finished a second cup of tea together, and when Claudia still hadn't reappeared, Kirsten decided to look in on her. Knocking softly on the door of Claudia's room, she went in to find the older woman stretched out on her pale blue velvet chaise, with her eyes closed and a washcloth draped across her forehead.

"Another migraine?" asked Kirsten.

Claudia turned her head slightly and opened her eyes. "I think I managed to catch this one in time," she said with a wan smile. "Don't worry, darling, this is definitely not the final act of *Camille;* I fully intend to recover." She patted the space on the chaise beside her and motioned to Kirsten to come and sit down.

"Are you sure? You wouldn't prefer to just try to sleep?"

"I'm positive. You know how much better I always feel when you sit with me awhile."

Kirsten hesitated another moment, then finally settled herself beside Claudia and peered curiously around the lavishly appointed room. With its pale blue moiré wallpaper and pale blue furnishings, it reminded her of a seascape, tranquil and remarkably restorative, the perfect retreat from the turbulence of the world outside.

"Why do you and Eric have separate bedrooms?" She blurted out the question she had been wanting to ask for months now.

Claudia's answer was surprisingly matter-of-fact. "Most couples do after a certain number of years."

"Really? I think that's kind of sad."

"Not sad, darling, realistic, not to mention bloody practical at times."

"I wouldn't want to have separate rooms," Kirsten said. "It would probably mean we'd be leading separate lives by then as well."

"Eric and I don't lead separate lives."

"But don't you feel you're missing out on something?"

"Not really."

"I know I would. And if that's what eventually happens to everyone, why bother getting married in the first place?"

"For any number of very valid reasons, darling, but mainly for companionship."

Kirsten made a face. "I'd rather marry for passion, thank you."

"And what happens when the passion dies?"

"I'd never let it die!"

Claudia laughed at the girl's earnestness. Removing the lukewarm washcloth from her forehead, she slowly sat up again. "You, darling, are such an innocent," she said, cupping Kirsten's face in her hands.

Feeling somewhat chastened, Kirsten would have turned away if Claudia hadn't begun gently stroking her hair. There was something so soothing and so hypnotic about the woman's touch that suddenly all she wanted was to curl up into a ball, and close her eyes.

"I thought I was supposed to be comforting you," murmured Kirsten.

"You are, simply by being here with me."

As her head dropped to Claudia's shoulder, Kirsten began to imagine that she was home again, nestled safely in her mother's arms, and she gave a long, contented sigh.

"Does that feel good, darling?" Claudia asked, brushing the hair back from Kirsten's face and kissing her softly on the forehead. Kirsten nodded in reply. "I'm glad." She kissed her on the forehead again, then dusted a series of tiny kisses all along her slender nose. "You're such a beautiful child," she crooned, "such a beautiful, beautiful child."

Kirsten shifted slightly. Claudia's kisses felt like butterflies, landing only for a moment, then darting off again. Playful and teasing. Whispery and delicate and strangely exciting. Making her turn all soft and warm and twitchy inside. It was a feeling she couldn't contain or control; it seemed to possess a will of its own. To her dismay, it began to spread, shooting out to every part of her body the way a flame travels down a length of lighted cord. The sensations it aroused were all too familiar. They were the same ones she had needed those sharp edges for, the ones she had crossed her legs to suppress. The ones that on occasion woke her from a deep sleep to throb and pulse like some independent heartbeat, until she thought she would go mad looking for a way to make it stop.

She didn't know whether it was the sudden involuntary moan she let out or whether Claudia's pills had finally begun to take effect. Whatever the reason, Claudia gave her one last peck on the cheek, wrapped her arms around her as though she were a pillow, and closed her eyes. It took some time for Kirsten's rapid pulse to slow down again and for the prickles of excitement all over her body to finally subside, but even then she found it difficult to breathe normally. Afraid of waking Claudia, she forced herself to lie there and wait a while longer, then she gently extricated herself from the sleeping woman's embrace and tiptoed out of the room.

Quietly closing her own bedroom door, she leaned up against it and groped suspiciously between her legs. A flush of shame spread across her face when she discovered the dampness that had seeped through her underpants and soaked the crotch of her heavy wool slacks.

"Ladies, ladies!" Eric clapped his hands to get Claudia and Kirsten's attention. They had taken refuge from the biting February cold in Claudia's sitting room, where they were sipping mulled wine and taking turns stoking the fire.

"You look like the proverbial cat that's just swallowed the canary," remarked Claudia, raising her face for a kiss. "Well, out with it, darling, before you burst your buttons."

"I have it on good authority that the National Trust is about to snap up your uncle Nigel's precious Wynford."

Claudia blanched, her cup of hot spiced wine tipping as she set it down.

"From what I understand, they're perched and all but ready to take over the cherished family manse and convert part of it into a tourist attraction. You know the type, pay at the door, red velvet ropes everywhere, sticky fingers all over the heirloom silver, cameras recording every private ancestral nook and cra—"

"Do stop, darling, you're making me drool." Claudia was like a woman transformed. Jumping to her feet, she grabbed hold of her husband's hands. "Eric, Eric darling, what do you say to selling off a paper or two and buying the place? Just think of it, my owning Wynford. Oh, Eric, I can't believe it, I simply can't believe it. Wouldn't Roxanne just curl up and die if I did? And Nigel. Hah! What heaven that would be, what sheer and utter heaven."

"It's a bloody marvelous idea."

"You really think so?"

"Don't look so astonished, pet, it is a damned good idea. I should have begun diversifying a long time ago; all I needed was the proper incentive. Now I've got it."

"Eric, you can't be serious."

"Oh, but I am, completely serious." He glanced over at Kirsten, who suddenly understood what he was about to do. "We'll consider it an exchange of sorts—I'll purchase Wynford Hall for you and in return you'll do something for me. What do you say?"

Claudia was immediately wary. "Am I going to like this, Eric?"

"I doubt it, pet, but it is rather a small price to pay for truly one-upping the family."

"Just how small is small?"

"All I want you to do is invite Michael Eastbourne to the salon on Sunday."

"I most certainly will not!"

"If you're concerned about Roxanne, you needn't be. She's in Wiltshire at the moment; Michael's here in London alone."

Claudia's hands were now clenched so tightly that the knuckles were turning white. She looked over at Kirsten, who seemed to be holding her breath, then back at her husband, whose expression was maddeningly unreadable. "All right, Eric," she said. "Wynford Hall for an afternoon with Michael. I'd say that was an equitable exchange, wouldn't you?"

Kirsten let out a shriek and flung her arms around Claudia's neck. Then she grabbed hold of Eric and waltzed him around the room. When he was finally able to catch his breath, he bent close to her ear and whispered, "Didn't I tell you I'd think of something?"

On Sunday afternoon Kirsten circulated among the guests like an automaton. In her mauve satin Jacques Fath gown, with its deep square neckline and full puffed sleeves, she looked like a royal princess, calm and self-possessed, but inside she was churning with contradictory emotions. Elation. Trepidation. Excitement. Dread. Anticipation. Outright incredulity. Each time Randolph announced the name of yet

another new arrival, Kirsten cringed. Michael wasn't coming.
He'd forgotten. He was sick. He'd been in an accident. Her
mouth was dry, her palms wet. She had been waiting for this
moment for nearly eight years now, and she couldn't bear it if
she had to keep on waiting. It was obvious he wasn't going to
show up. He'd changed his mind. He was dead.

"It's two, darling," Claudia whispered close to her elbow,
and Kirsten jumped.

"Couldn't we wait a few more minutes?"

"You know how punctual we are; we always start precisely
at two."

"But he's not here yet."

"If he chooses to be rude and arrive late, there's no reason
for us to be equally rude by keeping everyone else waiting."

"Claudia, please." Kirsten's voice was quavering. "Just ten
more minutes. Please."

"Five."

"Ten!"

"What, no seven?" Claudia observed wryly. "Am I to as-
sume then that there's to be no haggling whatsoever where
Michael Eastbourne's concerned?" Kirsten shook her head.
"All right, darling, ten minutes it is."

At exactly ten minutes past two Kirsten took her place at
the piano. Only one of the fifty chairs in the conservatory was
still empty. She touched the damper pedal with her right
foot, moved the bench back, then touched the pedal again. A
hammer was pounding inside her head, her arms were leaden,
and her heart was a heavy stone deep in the pit of her
stomach. Raising her hands, she struck the opening note of
Liszt's Sonata in B Minor. It sounded dull and uninspired. So
did all the notes that followed. Never had she played a piece
so colorlessly or lackadaisically before.

She was just completing the piece, when she sensed a
sudden change in the room. It began as a prickling at the
base of her neck, then spread throughout her body becoming
hotter and brighter, transforming all ten of her fingers into
slender streaks of living flame. Without even turning her
head, she knew he was there. She could feel his eyes searing
her back, melting the icy encasement around her heart, and
setting her spirit free. With his gaze enclosing her in a halo of
fire, she and her music finally took flight.

8

She was trapped inside a human maze with no way out. There were people all around her, holding her back. To her immense relief, Eric sensed her distress and hurried to her rescue. Firmly clasping her left elbow, he steered her away from the crush over to the door of the conservatory, where the tall figure in the dark business suit was waiting to meet her.

He was no longer simply a face on a poster or an album cover, or a compelling memory whose music had touched her the way no one else's had, but a man, real at last. Up close she saw that the hair falling in a soft wave across his high forehead was a warm chestnut brown, and that his eyes were hazel, flecked with green and gold. The set of his mouth was serious, but as he smiled at her, the fine-boned planes of his face gentled, relaxing into the poetic expression she remembered so well. He held out his hand and she felt hers dissolve inside his grip.

"To say you were magnificent would indeed be an understatement, Miss Harald," were Michael Eastbourne's first words to her, and Kirsten knew she would remember them always.

Her "thank you" sounded forced, the two words woefully inadequate by comparison, as she tried to free herself from the hypnotic pull of his hazel eyes and failed.

"Eric's invitation was impossible to turn down," he told her. His accent was part Boston, part London, his voice softly modulated and somewhat husky. "Considering the price of real estate in Wiltshire these days, I must admit I was extremely flattered."

Seeing that Kirsten was nearly paralyzed with shyness, Eric hastily stepped in and rescued her again. "Well, my dear, since we've finally gotten Michael to accept our hospitality, why don't you take advantage of his being here and show him around? I'm certain he'll find the place quite changed."

"Miss Harald?" Michael was gallantly offering her his arm.

"Please call me Kirsten," she finally managed to say. "I think Miss Harald makes me sound like a librarian." Tucking her arm somewhat gingerly through his, she allowed him to lead her out of the room.

It took all of her iron self-control just to breathe normally and keep her pace matched with his at the same time. She was incredulous. Not only was she walking beside Michael Eastbourne, she was touching him, actually touching him. The soft roughness of his wool jacket was a brand biting into her bare flesh, bruising her sensitive skin, and rubbing her nerve endings raw. She felt lightheaded and subdued, mischievous and serious all at once. Each time she spoke she was convinced she was shouting, but somehow the words coming out of her mouth sounded peculiarly muffled.

There was so much she wanted to ask, to learn, to confide, yet there they were, chatting with stilted politeness about Eric and Claudia's home. Instead of discussing the one vital thing they shared—their music—they were behaving like strangers on a guided tour of some foreign country. How absurd it seemed, how banal. She glanced at Michael and flushed crimson when she found him looking back at her. He smiled. She lost her footing and would have tripped over the hem of her gown if he hadn't steadied her.

Michael got a firmer grip on Kirsten's arm. He was amazed that such a slender arm could be so strong; astounded, too, that such a petite young woman could produce as powerful a sound as she did. Her stupendous virtuosity had staggered him—every note she had played remained inscribed on his brain—and her delicate beauty had stunned him. Gazing into her eyes was like losing oneself in pools the color of dew-kissed violets. What made her beauty all the more unique, its impact that much more dramatic, was her disarming ingenuousness, her utter lack of vanity. It was as though she were the only one unaware of and unimpressed by her own loveliness. In the presence of such a potent combination of talent and beauty, he felt awed and strangely discomfited.

They started up the stairs to the second floor, and Michael's right knee immediately stiffened. When Kirsten noticed the subtle shift in his step, she became alarmed and slowed down.

"It acts up like this when I'm tired," Michael told her. "Polio," he quickly added. "I had polio when I was fifteen."

"My God!" Her shocked response was instantaneous.

"It was probably the best thing that ever happened to me."

Kirsten looked doubtful. "It was?"

"If it hadn't been for my bout with polio, I might have ended up a pretty disgruntled second-class violinist or cellist instead of a conductor." Michael leaned against the banister and began to rub his sore leg. "My father was a musicologist and a cellist who had formed his own string quartet," he explained. "My mother played the viola, my uncle the violin, and my older brother the bass. Everyone naturally assumed I'd make it a quintet one day. But not me. I couldn't decide on which instrument to play. The truth was, I didn't really want to play any one of them; I wanted only to conduct. It became an obsession with me. I was always off someplace conducting some imaginary orchestra, using anything I could get my hands on as a baton. My father and I fought about it constantly, but I was stubborn, I wouldn't give in. Then, when I contracted polio, none of that seemed to matter anymore. I was faced with the prospect of being paralyzed permanently, and all I wanted to do was die." Michael shook his head, musingly sad at the memory of it. "One day my father walked into my hospital room and slapped an authentic wooden baton in my hands. He told me it was one of Toscanini's own batons and I believed him. That was the day I started fighting for my life."

"And was it really his baton?" whispered Kirsten, her eyes brimming.

"I have no idea, I've never wanted to find out."

Kirsten drew in a deep, shuddering breath, then let it out again slowly, very slowly.

"I haven't told anyone that story in years," Michael admitted, giving her a sincere but somewhat baffled smile. "Well, shall we?" He took her arm and they continued up the stairs.

All the time they were touring the second floor, Kirsten seemed far more relaxed in her role as official guide, and Michael appeared much more comfortable as the suitably impressed visitor. Yet nothing could have been further from the truth. Something was happening between them. It was as palpable as it was intangible. A thickening of the air. An invisible but powerful magnetization. A splendid energy force wrapping itself around them to insulate them from the rest of the world. And both of them felt it.

"Do you know that—"

"This was the—"

They both stopped in mid-sentence and started to laugh.

"Ladies first." Michael deferred to Kirsten with a courtly bow.

"Do you know that I was at Carnegie Hall when you made your American debut eight years ago?"

Michael's hazel eyes were twinkling. "And you decided to become a musician anyway?"

She was too caught up in the excitement of the moment to realize he was teasing her. "Not only that, I even taught myself the Rachmaninoff Second Piano Concerto."

"And how did it compare with Rubinstein's interpretation?"

She was totally guileless in her honest response. "I liked mine better."

"Did you get any second opinions?"

Unaccustomed to carrying on casual conversations with any man other than her father or Eric, Kirsten continued to take Michael seriously. "Just my teacher Natalya's," she said. "Natalya Federenko." He nodded when he heard the name. "Did you know her?"

"One of my greatest regrets was that she retired before I could ever conduct her."

Kirsten gazed up at him through the heavy protective veil of her dark lashes. "Would you consider conducting one of her pupils instead?" she asked, realizing to her horror that she was actually flirting with him.

"After what I heard this afternoon, I'd say it was a distinct possibility."

Kirsten's hopes soared. "Then you don't think I'm wasting my time?" Her question seemed to puzzle him. "You don't think I should consider playing the piano only until I find a husband, then give it up to keep house?"

Michael laughed. "It sounds as though you've been talking to Clemence Treaves."

"Actually, he was the one doing most of the talking."

"Let me tell you something about men like Clemence Treaves. The closest they ever come to creativity is when they're buying and selling it. They're no different from stockbrokers or salesmen, except that they deal in other people's talent. Their own lack of genuine creativity makes them envious and it makes them devious. Unfortunately, we, as artists, need them, and that makes us vulnerable. We have to protect ourselves from them at all times, because we're the ones with the dreams. And as you probably know, both the dream and the dreamer can be terribly fragile."

As Kirsten listened to what he was saying, she felt a oneness with him that was almost frightening. Looking at him was like looking at herself. They were kindred spirits, two dreamers with the same kind of dream. The only difference between them was that he was already living his.

"And now I'm afraid I've got to go." Without even consulting his watch, Michael knew he was running late. "I have a rehearsal in half an hour."

Panicked, Kirsten grabbed hold of his sleeve. "But I haven't even finished showing you the house."

"I liked whatever you did show me," he assured her.

"Eric will think I've been an awful guide if you leave now."

"No, he won't."

"Stay at least for some tea or a sherry," she persisted.

"Kirsten, I can't, I'll be late."

"Now Claudia will accuse me of being a terrible hostess."

"And the orchestra will accuse *me* of being a neglectful conductor."

He was slipping away from her and she was powerless to stop him. "I'm playing again next Sunday," she said hopefully. "Should I reserve the same seat for you?"

"Why, is another estate being put up for sale?" He saw his humor wasn't being appreciated and sobered immediately. "As much as I'd like to say yes, Kirsten, I can't. I'm flying to Vienna Sunday."

"Oh." Her stomach felt as though it were weighted with sand as it began sinking all the way to her feet. There was nothing left to do now but follow him back downstairs again. When they reached the front door, he took her hands and squeezed them gently.

"Protect these wonderful hands of yours, Kirsten," he said. "They'll take you right to the top one day; you have my word on that."

His good-bye sounded so final. After having just discovered a miraculous extension of herself in someone else, an added dimension to her wholeness, was she about to lose it all so quickly? The door closed and the impact of wood slamming against wood made her shake; the jolt of it reverberated through her body, the sound echoed inside her skull.

It was as though she had been invited to a banquet, then asked to leave after the appetizer had been served. Her brief time with Michael had been precisely that—a taste of something unique without the promise of anything more substantial to follow. There had been no talk of some future meeting, no mention of an audition. Nothing but the vague possibility of playing with him one day. Perhaps it would have been better if she had never met him, if she had kept him tucked safely away inside her head as an illusion. Forever a tantalizing possibility, and therefore never quite real.

She turned to find Claudia standing in the foyer, her expression undecipherable.

"Are you all right, darling?" she asked, and Kirsten nodded. "Then come, there are still plenty of other guests for you to talk to."

As she wrapped an arm around Kirsten's trembling shoulders, Claudia felt a sad, longing well up inside her. Seeing her precious child staring after the closing front door as if it were the door on her own life that was closing had torn her apart. Her first instinct had been to rally to Kirsten's defense. But then something else had taken over. Possessiveness. Jealousy. Urges she had long denied had begun to writhe inside her like a snake seeking release from the oppressive darkness holding it captive.

She took a sip of her sherry and swallowed it quickly. Then she drained the glass. The spiraling burst of heat forced the snake back into hiding, where it belonged. Putting on her best hostess smile, she returned Kirsten to their guests.

Kirsten was furious with herself. It seemed all she could do was think about Michael Eastbourne. The harder she fought it, the more insistent the memory of him became. She woke up every morning with his name on her lips. She found him inside every room on the first two floors of the house. She saw him leaning against the banister on the staircase and massaging his right leg. She felt the pressure of his hands on hers while she was practicing. She heard the front door close behind him and felt that same sweeping sense of desolation all over again. And at night, when she closed her eyes and tried to sleep, his was the face that followed her into her dreams.

Whenever she had needed a place of refuge in the past, she had always found it in her music, and this time was no exception. With desperate determination she flung herself at the piano, increasing her practicing time from six hours to eight each day. As Natalya had once pointed out, if treated well, her music would serve as her friend and ally, and she was counting on that being true now as never before. As the days dissolved into weeks, she was relentless; she used her piano mercilessly, driving herself to the point of exhaustion and blessed obliviousness. But even though she eventually succeeded in purging Michael from her active thoughts, he was still there in her music. In a tender and yearning poignancy that brought tears to the eyes of every guest attending her spectacularly successful Sunday afternoon performances.

As winter yielded to spring, the days grew longer, the air warmer, the times themselves gentler. Claudia had insisted Kirsten set aside the first Saturday in May so that the two of them could attend the official opening of Picasso's latest exhibition at the National Gallery, and she had grudgingly agreed. To compensate for the disruption in her daily practice schedule, she got up at six that morning and practiced nonstop until noon. Then she went looking for Claudia. She found her with Eric in his study where, to her consternation, they were embroiled in a fierce argument.

"I'm going upstairs to change," she announced cautiously from the doorway. "What time do you want to leave?"

"I don't know," Claudia snapped without turning around.

"We are going, aren't we?"

"That all depends on how quickly I can dispose of the matter at hand."

"Which is?"

"Murdering my beloved husband here."

Glancing over at Eric, Kirsten tried to turn the whole thing into a game. "Well, I hope whatever she's murdering you for is worth it," she said.

"*She* obviously thinks it is." His voice sounded strangely subdued. "She's even gone so far as to call me a traitor."

"That *is* serious," Kirsten acknowledged. "Punishable by hanging, no less."

"Hanging is too bloody good for the beast," snarled Claudia. "I think I'd much rather he be tortured to death."

"My God, Eric, what did you do?" All traces of teasing were gone now.

"I'm afraid it's what I *didn't* do, lamb." He sighed. "I didn't get Wynford for her.

"You probably never had any intention of buying it for me

in the first place," Claudia cried. "It was all a bloody ruse just to have me invite Michael Eastbourne over here."

"Is it my fault that Roxanne sold her own estate in Hampstead and gave her father the money to keep him afloat?" Eric demanded. "He did have the right to hold on to his own damned property, you know."

"But you fiddled and faddled all along, Eric. First, it was the newspaper, then—"

"Do you think it's easy to sell off a bloody newspaper just like that?"

"Then there was the business with the magazine."

"They reneged on the deal, you know that. Claudia, pet, I'm sorry, truly I am, dreadfully sorry. I did the best I could." He reached for her to calm her, but she was beyond calming.

"The hell you did, you bastard. Don't touch me!" she screamed. "Keep away from me, damn you!"

Eric allowed his arms to drop and went to stand behind his desk again. Kirsten stared at them aghast; she had never seen two people in such terrible pain before. In the face of so much hateful anger, all she could think of was trying to diffuse the situation. Going quietly over to Claudia, she touched her lightly on the arm and said, "Why don't you come upstairs with me and change? I'm sure that once we get to the exhibition you'll forget all about the house and—"

"I will not forget about the house!" Claudia practically flung Kirsten away from her in her rage. "I have no intention of ever forgetting about that house."

Kirsten and Eric exchanged helpless glances. "Then you don't want to go to the National Gallery at all today?" She gave it one last try.

"No, I most certainly do not."

"What would you like to do instead?"

"What I'd like to do and what I'm going to do are two entirely different things. Unfortunately, what I'd like to do is against the law; what I'm going to do isn't."

"And what might that be?" Eric inquired, a hint of a smile returning to his worried face.

"Go to my room and have myself a bloody good cry."

Kirsten was about to go after her, but Eric shook his head. "Best leave her be, lamb. I'm afraid I've let her down most horribly, and that's something I never intended to do, God help me."

Claudia remained in her room with the door locked for the rest of the day and even refused to come downstairs for dinner. That night the entire household slept fitfully, as though expecting something dreadful to happen. It was a house on edge, fearfully waiting, anxiously holding its breath. But the night passed without incident, and in the morning everyone heaved a great sigh of relief. The maids were the first ones to notice the difference; Alice and Edna discovered it only moments before Gwenn and Valerie did. Wherever a watercolor of Wynford Hall had been, there was now nothing but an empty space—a slightly lighter patch on the wall where each painting had hung. Every one of them had been taken down. When Meg put out the trash later that morning, she found all of the missing pictures in a large metal bin, the frames smashed, the watercolors themselves cut into thousands of tiny pieces.

9

"Tell me something, lamb." Eric looked up from his paper and fixed Kirsten with one of his most opaque stares. "What do you know about Wigmore Hall?"

Dropping her copy of *The Sun Also Rises* into her lap, Kirsten brought her knees up to her chin and smiled. "That's easy," she said, remembering the same kind of casually pointed question the long-ago Mr. Widemann was famous for. "It's a concert hall on Wigmore Street; it has near-perfect acoustics, a marble and alabaster interior, and Arthur Rubinstein gave his first recital there, when he was twenty-five."

Eric gave her a broad grin. How much she had learned, and in so short a time too. "Quite so," he nodded, "quite so." He glanced over at Claudia, who was seated next to him on the sofa, and winked. She actually winked back. Sometimes it seemed that their ghastly fight had never happened—their relationship was as warm and easy as ever—and no one in the house had ever once mentioned the destroyed watercolors. One by one they had each been systematically replaced by similar-size oils bought at auction from Sotheby's and Christie's. "How would you like to best Mr. Rubinstein by four years?" he directed his question at Kirsten again.

"I beg your pardon?"

"What Eric's attempting to ask in a mangled, roundabout way, darling," interrupted Claudia without raising her head from the latest needlepoint seat cover she was working on for one of the twelve dining room chairs, "is how would you like to give a recital at Wigmore Hall?"

"What kind of a question is that?" Kirsten was beginning to flush. "Of course I'd like to give a recital at Wigmore Hall. In fact, I'd love it; I'd adore it; I'd give anything to do it!" She was practically shouting now, and her exuberance made it extremely difficult for either Eric or Claudia to contain themselves any longer.

"Consider it done then," said Eric.

"What?" Kirsten blinked.

"Consi—"

"Eric!" Kirsten was on her feet, hopping around as though all ten of her toes were on fire.

"It's all been arranged, lamb. We've rented the hall for the evening of June twentieth."

"I don't believe it, I just don't believe it!"

"We've hoarded you long enough, darling," Claudia said. "It's time you made your official London debut. That's what all this has been about, remember. Think of it, if you will, as a form of musical coming-out party."

Kirsten was overwhelmed, shocked speechless. Then once the news had penetrated more completely, she let out a whoop of joy and reached for their hands.

"I'm going to play Wigmore Hall!" she crowed, coaxing them up onto their feet. "I'm going to play Wigmore Hall!"

All three of them linked arms and started careening wildly around the room to the sounds of Kirsten's ecstatic warbling and several priceless Ming vases rocking back and forth precariously on their carved wooden bases. The commotion brought Randolph hurrying up the stairs to the study. Peering in on the dancing threesome, he shook his head and wondered if the Sheffield-Johnses had finally gone stark raving mad.

The next four weeks whirled by in a merry, dizzying blur of activity. For the upcoming recital, Kirsten and Magda put together a program of compositions by Grieg, Rachmaninoff,

Liszt, and Chopin, which Kirsten then honed and polished and refined until each piece gleamed like purest gold. The gown she and Claudia chose for the occasion was a Christian Dior—a strapless lavender silk sheath with a long, trailing overskirt of chiffon in a slightly darker shade of lavender. Once that decision was made, they went to Asprey's, where, in spite of Kirsten's protests, Claudia insisted on buying her a pair of diamond and amethyst drop earrings to wear with the gown.

Her first official publicity photograph was taken by a tousle-haired twenty-three-year-old with the impressive-sounding name of Antony Armstrong-Jones, a recent discovery of Eric's whose work he considered refreshing and wonderfully innovative. Copies of the photo were dispatched, along with a suitable press release, to every major newspaper on the continent, and enclosed inside, the twelve hundred specially engraved invitations being issued. Kirsten didn't have to check the guest list to know whose name wouldn't be included on it, so she brazenly addressed an invitation to Michael Eastbourne on her own and posted it herself—almost as a dare.

The night of the recital, Kirsten stalked her small dressing room inside London's famed Wigmore Hall alone, half-wishing she were anywhere but there. She kept alternating between flashes of damp heat and icy chills, her stomach was pitching and tossing like a ship in a storm, and her knees were knocking under her long, rustling silk and chiffon gown. *Be calm*, she repeated over and over to herself. *This is the night you've been waiting for, your first public recital of any significance, that first real step up the ladder, that first firm toehold on the mountain. Be calm, be calm.* If only her parents and Natalya could have been there with her. Out in the front row, where she could have seen them when she made her entrance. Sharing the magic of a night that was as much theirs as hers. *Be calm, be calm, be calm.* She caught a glimpse of herself in the large mirror above the dressing table, and wondered who the woman with the ashen face and wide, wild eyes could possibly be.

She paced the room until she felt dizzy, catching briefer and briefer glimpses of her reflection as she paced and turned, paced and turned. Then suddenly she wasn't alone in the mirror anymore. She sucked in her breath and spun around, grabbing hold of the edge of the dressing table for support.

"I guess you didn't hear my knock," said Michael Eastbourne as he closed the door quietly behind him.

"Are you sure you did knock?" She was so stunned she could barely get the words out.

"As a matter of fact, it sounded something like this." Michael turned and rapped his knuckles lightly on the door.

Kirsten smiled in spite of herself. She couldn't take her eyes off him. Seeing him formally dressed in a black tuxedo with a pleated white shirt and black bow tie reminded her of the first time she had seen him—in tails at Carnegie Hall. She smiled again, this time at the remarkable irony of it all. He had been the one onstage then; now it was her turn.

"That was quite an exceptional photograph of you," Michael said as he slowly came toward her. "It managed to capture that very special look you have."

Kirsten frowned. Eric had mentioned something to her about a look, but she hadn't really paid any attention. "What look?" she asked.

Michael seemed surprised. "You mean you don't know?" She shook her head. "It's what lights up your entire face and surrounds you like an aura. But most of all, it's what lives in your eyes. It's the dream, Kirsten. It's the first thing people see when they look at you."

The dream. Something so intensely personal, buried so deep, so close to the very core of her that she had never once thought it might be visible to others. Knowing it was made her feel frighteningly vulnerable and exposed. And even a bit betrayed. She turned around and stared hard at her reflection, trying to see what everyone else had apparently been seeing all along.

"Is it there now?" Her voice was so low that Michael had to move closer to hear her. The satin lapels of his tuxedo jacket were cold against her bare back as he leaned forward to look for himself. Their eyes met in the glass and Kirsten shivered.

"Yes," he told her, "it's there."

Time froze. Neither of them moved or blinked; both were too reluctant to sever the tenuous connection between them. Against her back Kirsten could feel the rapid thump, thump, thump of Michael's heart, and her legs turned to jelly. Michael felt the beginnings of an excruciating ache deep in his groin, a treacherous heaviness, and abruptly stepped away from her. If Kirsten hadn't been bracing herself against the dressing table, she would have fallen, her knees were that weak.

"Mi—"

"Kir—"

Neither of them laughed this time, but Michael's curt nod indicated that ladies still went first.

"Eric and Claudia are holding a champagne reception for me at Claridge's after the recital," she said. "Will you come?"

He shook his head and her heart turned over once, then seemed to stop altogether. "Claudia was good enough to have put up with me that other time; I couldn't honestly expect her to do it again."

"But the reception's being held in the main ballroom. No one would even notice if you were there."

"The room's big, Kirsten, but not that big."

"You could always hide behind one of the potted plants," she suggested, and only half-jokingly at that.

Michael laughed. "I'm afraid there wouldn't be one large enough." Gazing down at Kirsten's flawless heart-shaped face, he almost wished there were. He felt torn between responding to what he read in her luminous eyes and continuing to keep a safe distance between them. From the very first she had been like a magnet drawing him toward her, her talent and beauty a double-edged temptation anyone would have found impossible to resist. But he *had* resisted. It had nearly drained his inexhaustible reserves of self-discipline and willpower to do so, but he *had* succeeded in staying away. He therefore found it difficult to believe it was his own voice he was hearing when he said, "Don't come back to your dressing room after the recital. Meet me at the stage door. We'll have a drink—a quick one, a half hour at most—then I'll drop you at the hotel." He quickly wished her good luck and hurried out the door before he had time to come to his senses and change his mind.

Tiny electrical charges of excitement were exploding inside her as Kirsten watched him leave. She hugged herself and grinned. She was glad he wouldn't be at the reception; now she wouldn't have to share him with anybody else. Taking one last look in the mirror, she gave in to the impulse and winked at herself. Then she started out the door.

All the way down the corridor she could hear Natalya warning her in that basso profundo of hers: "If you allow yourself to be distracted even for a moment, Kirishka, you'll

lose everything—yourself, your gift, but above all, your dream."
And on this all-important night she had indeed allowed herself to be distracted. Distracted by the promise of spending a half hour with a man who was as inaccessible to her as Carnegie Hall. A man who had his own career and obligations, his own loyalties and responsibilities. A man who was married to the cousin Claudia despised. An alarm began ringing inside her head, and she responded to it like the supremely disciplined performer she was. There was absolutely no room in her thoughts right now for anything or anyone—even Michael. There was room only for her music, because tonight the fantasy, which had seemed so remote on that spring night in New York two years ago, was about to come true.

She glided trancelike out of the shadow of the wings into the brilliant glare of the lights, a beautiful somnambulist, ethereal and exquisite, trailing clouds of softly billowing lavender behind her. Applause warmed her way as she swept past a blurred sea of expectant, upturned faces to the Steinway that glowed like a beacon in the midst of such unfamiliar surroundings. Behind the serene smile and graceful carriage she was alive with the tremulous fluttering of a thousand hummingbirds' wings. Each breath she drew absorbed the audience more deeply into her system, the sanctity of the occasion into her soul, until she and they and the moment had melded together into a glorious and indivisible oneness.

She began the program with Rachmaninoff's Sonata in B Flat Minor. One by one the familiar notes laid claim to her consciousness, twirling around her thicker and faster and lifting her up and out of herself. Leaving the possessive pull of earth, she hurtled skyward toward her own private infinity. When the time came for her to return, she knew she would find her world had changed, and that she need never question her privileged place in it again.

The air erupted all around her. She heard her name being called, soaring high above the applause and the exuberant shouts of Brava! Brava! Brava! Her heart urged her to respond immediately, but her head—and Natalya's training—held her impetuousness in check. She forced herself to count to ten before standing up and walking with regal stateliness to the center of the stage. Tears were pooling in her violet eyes as she dropped gracefully to one knee, pressed both hands to her chest, and bowed her head. Fantasy and reality had converged at last. She was the child pledging herself to her dream on the icy steps outside Carnegie Hall. The girl daydreaming her way through school. The young woman vowing to surpass them all whatever the price. Tonight, in the presence of an international audience of twelve hundred enraptured witnesses, musical history had been made, and a phenomenon named Kirsten Harald born.

"Tonight your performance went far beyond magnificent," Michael told her as they drove through streets whose names she would never remember. "It was inspired, Kirsten, transcendental."

His extravagant praise warmed her almost as much as the touch of his hand on her elbow as he guided her into the dimly lit cocktail lounge whose name she would never remember either. She was intoxicated, floating and free, adrift on a cloud so sumptuous and sublime, she doubted she would ever be as happy again. She had just captured the hearts of the cultural nobility of Europe and was about to share the glory of that triumph with the man who had been a secret part of her precious dream for so very long.

The hostess led them to a discreet corner of the room and seated them at a small round table covered by a square white tablecloth. In the center of the table a flickering red candle dripped hot red wax down the sides of an empty Chianti bottle and cast undulating shadows across their faces. Michael ordered cognacs, and after toasting her spectacular success, they lapsed into silence. Whenever one of them did speak, it was only about subjects superficial and safe. The rest of the time they simply sat and looked at each other, the way a man and a woman do when there's no need for conversation, when silence is the strongest unifying bond of all. As far as they were concerned, nothing existed outside the two of them. It was only Kirsten and Michael—Michael and Kirsten.

She began to memorize everything about him, registering her impressions with all five of her heightened senses and storing them away for those times when she would have only her memories to rely on. She watched the way his right hand closed around the bowl of his snifter. She noticed how the skin around his eyes creased whenever he smiled. How white his teeth were in the glimmering candlelight. How his forehead puckered when he was deep in some private thought. How green his eyes seemed one minute, how gold the next.

She marveled, too, at how the sound of his voice made her tremble, and how the intensity of his gaze made her weak.

"You're looking at your watch again," she chided him as she sipped the last of her cognac.

"Do you realize we've been sitting here for nearly an hour?"

"Impossible!"

"But true."

"It can't be." It was too cruel; the time couldn't have slipped away from them that quickly.

"Sad, isn't it," Michael commented, echoing her thoughts, "how time seems to govern our lives?"

"Only if we let it."

"We usually have no choice in the matter." He tossed several one-pound notes on the table and scraped back his chair. "Besides, if it isn't time, it's always something else."

She wondered if there were a message in there for her and the very thought of it suddenly made her feel clammy and cold. When he offered her his hand to help her up, she refused to take it.

"Please, Kirsten, we're really late."

"Good, there's nothing I love more than making a grand entrance."

"Well, you certainly can't make it sitting here."

Knowing it was senseless to argue, she gave in as gracefully as she could and followed him out to the car. All the way to the hotel she found herself praying for red lights. When that didn't slow them down enough to suit her, she began wishing for detours, traffic jams, even a minor accident—anything to make the ride take longer. But the ride was a short one, almost spitefully so. They pulled up in front of the entrance to Claridge's only moments later. Michael cut the engine and turned to face her.

Taking hold of her right hand, he fondled it gently for a moment, then buried his mouth in the soft, warm flesh of her open palm. Kirsten shuddered as his caress sent shock waves of pleasure through her body. With her free hand she reached up and touched his hair for the first time, feeling its wavy thickness, its silken smoothness. She followed the shape of his head in one continuous gliding motion, watching his eyes close as she neared the sensitive base of his neck. When he opened his eyes again, it was to look directly into hers, and she parted her lips expectantly. But he made no move to kiss her; he seemed quite content just to look at her. Then, before either of them could react, the hotel doorman had opened Kirsten's door. The spell was broken instantly.

She got out of the car with tears blazing in her eyes, then merely stood on the sidewalk. For one long, aching moment, all she wanted to do was fling herself back into the car and beg Michael to drive off. To drive so fast and so far that no one would ever be able to find them. To take them to a place where it would be only the two of them and their music, with no interruptions, no interference, no outside demands. But she didn't. Instead, she lifted her head proudly, squared her shoulders, and began walking slowly and deliberately up the front steps of the hotel, where the most celebrated people in Europe were waiting to welcome her and add her name to their golden list.

10

Michael Eastbourne was restless. He was a man looking for a comfortable place to put himself—both literally and figuratively—and failing miserably at it. Their Hampstead home was in a state of upheaval, with everything being boxed and crated for their move to the five-story town house he and Roxanne had bought in Belgravia. The start of the '54–'55 season was only weeks away, which meant he would soon be ripped from the comfortable pattern of family life that the summer had woven around him. And Kirsten Harald was under his skin. She had invaded his life, trespassed on his privacy, and laid seige to his every thought. Nothing he said to himself, nothing he did, was able to purge her from his system or from his mind.

One of the movers had begun dismantling the gallery of family photographs in the study, and Michael was outraged as he watched the faces of those he loved being touched by strange hands, wrapped in sheets of newspaper, then placed inside a deep wooden barrel. As if to spite them, he snatched one of his favorite photos from the top of his desk and gazed down at the three faces behind the dust-flecked glass: Roxanne, her smoky beauty as ripe and exciting now as the day

Clemence Treaves had first introduced them outside the Royal Albert Hall fifteen years before; Daniel, now ten, their oldest and the image of Roxanne; and Christopher, younger than Daniel by only fourteen months. Michael still maintained that the best thing Treaves had ever done for him and for his career was introducing him to Roxanne.

In eleven years of marriage, Michael had never once been tempted to cheat, either in thought or deed. His marriage bed remained as steamy a place of satisfaction as ever; he adored his boys; and when he was away on tour, it was his music, and only his music, that served him as constant companion, preoccupation, and passion. If ever two people had been created especially for each other, it was Roxanne and Michael Eastbourne. Everybody said so. Roxanne wasn't only his wife and the mother of his sons, she was also his manager—shrewd, ambitious, and fiercely protective of him. She was the one who had advised him to guest-conduct first before accepting any permanent positions anywhere, and her sage advice had quickly turned him into the most sought-after conductor in the world.

There was only one area in their otherwise ideal relationship that remained a mystery to him: he still didn't know why Roxanne and Claudia hated each other so much. Being ostracized so completely by his two former patrons was a pain that still rankled, even after eleven years. This year, however, the pain had been worse, far worse, because a dazzling musical talent named Kirsten Harald had twice granted him access to a part of the world that was no longer open to him.

The mover was waiting. Michael reluctantly handed him the photograph and watched bleakly as the man packed it away with the others. A knob of desolation hardened inside him. All traces of his family were now gone. It was as though the room itself had suddenly lost its soul, turning into a shell of a place, anonymous and barren and foreign to him. Even he felt anonymous now. Stripped bare, exposed and totally defenseless. He looked out of the curtainless windows to the garden, but her face intervened. Rubbing his eyes to clear them, he succeeded only in grinding her image farther and deeper into his head. In another two weeks she would be gone. Then hopefully, distance and the passage of time would finally set him free.

Kirsten counted to fifty, then dialed again. The line was

still busy. She slammed down the receiver in frustration and went to do some more packing. In precisely twenty-nine hours and fifteen minutes, she would be sailing from Southampton aboard the S.S. *United States* bound for New York. Her year was almost up. The three hundred and sixty-five days allotted her had trickled down to only one. She reached for a Kleenex, blew her nose several times, then added the soggy tissue to the growing collection in her bathroom wastebasket.

Opening the bottom drawer of her dresser, she took out the two scrapbooks she had kept during the year, and sat down cross-legged on the floor to look at them. She smiled when she saw the steamship ticket taped to the first page of the first book, but that didn't stop a wayward tear from rolling down her cheek and landing with a gentle plop right in the middle of the name S.S. *Queen Mary*. As she went through the books page by page, she automatically relived each one of the very precious moments she had so carefully and systematically preserved. All the bits and pieces she had collected to form a single montage of memories she would cherish forever. When she came to the pasteboard coaster from the cocktail lounge she had been in with Michael, she suddenly stopped. What was the point in lacerating herself this way? Closing the book, she got up, blew her nose one more time, then picked up the phone again.

Expecting nothing but another busy signal, she wasn't prepared for the phone to start ringing. Her mind immediately went blank and her hands began to shake so violently that she nearly dropped the receiver. What if *she* answered? She thought of hanging up, then quickly changed her mind. She was leaving in the morning; she had every right to call and say good-bye. When Michael himself answered, Kirsten turned mute. A moment later, the dial tone was buzzing angrily in her ear. Mortified, she dialed the number again.

"I just called to say good-bye," she blurted into the mouthpiece, cutting off his snappish hello.

"Kirsten?"

"Yes, I'm sorry, I hope I'm not disturbing you."

"Not at all. As a matter of fact, I was just about to call you."

"You were, why?" The moment she said it, she really wanted to hang up.

Michael chuckled. "For the same reason you called me. To

say good-bye and to tell you that I'll be looking for more rave reviews about you in the papers."

She began toying with the telephone cord, twisting it around her wrist. "Michael—" She stopped, wet her lips, and began again. "Michael, I've got something for you, a memento of sorts. Of course I could always drop it in the mail . . ." She allowed her voice to trail off suggestively and crossed her fingers. In the silence that followed she held her breath, prayed as hard and as fast as she could, and crossed a second pair of fingers for additional luck.

"Why don't I come by and pick it up?"

She slowly began to breathe again. "When?"

"Let's say in about an hour, in front of the house."

She had barely squeaked out her good-bye and hung up than she was rushing over to one of the new steamer trunks Claudia had purchased for her to choose a change of clothes.

An hour later she was standing outside the house wearing a flounced, cotton sundress in a muted Liberty print, looking more like an innocent schoolgirl than a young woman about to add a slight twist to the Tenth Commandment by coveting her neighbor's *husband*. Because in only a matter of days, that was precisely what the Sheffield-Johnses and Eastbournes were going to be: neighbors separated only by the civilized distance of two city blocks. When Claudia had learned of the pending move several weeks before, it sent her into such a tailspin that she barricaded herself in her bedroom and refused to come out for three days. Now whenever she left the house, she did so almost stealthily, steeling herself once she got outside as though she expected to be attacked at any moment.

Kirsten walked to the corner and back again six times, studiously counting every step she took. Then, just as she was convinced he wasn't coming, his silver-gray Jaguar drew alongside her with a furtive, staccato beep of its horn.

"Sorry I'm late," Michael apologized as she slid in beside him, "but there was quite a bit of traffic coming into the city."

She peered down at her hands and told him it didn't matter; he was there now. As always, that first moment of reestablished contact with him left her tongue-tied and slightly breathless. Each time was like the first time all over again; their moments together intensified by an unnaturalness that made her feel hurried and anxious, perched on some precarious ledge, with too much to cram into too small a space. She was reminded of a plant appropriately called an ephemeral, because it grows, flowers, and dies all within a few days. That was how she had come to see her relationship with Michael—as an ephemeral—except that its entire life span never lasted any longer than an hour.

"Are you looking forward to going home?" Michael, who was having difficulty grappling with his own seesawing emotions, was anxious to neutralize the highly charged atmosphere in the car.

"I have mixed feelings about it," she replied.

"Well, that's only natural."

"I haven't seen my parents in a whole year." She turned and looked out of the window. "A year ago I didn't think I could do it. For a while I even felt guilty for being able to have a good time without them. Then whenever I enjoyed myself without feeling guilty, *that* made me feel guilty. Crazy, isn't it?" His warm laugh told her there was nothing crazy about it at all. "Now that I'm going home, I can't wait to see them again, yet at the same time I'm a little bit scared. I keep wondering if they'll have changed, because I know I have." She told him about the postcards she had sent them every day. "I'm mailing the last one tonight," she said. "I wonder which one of us will get to New York first, the card or me."

"Judging by how slow the mails are, I'd put my money on you."

This made Kirsten smile. Turning toward him again, she scanned his face with eager eyes. "Do you know I already have three recitals lined up for October thanks to the reviews of my Wigmore Hall appearance? Natalya cabled me with the news yesterday."

Watching her face as she talked about her music was like watching a star. She shimmered with a luminosity that was as deeply spiritual as it was otherworldly. "It won't be long before your schedule's as busy as mine," Michael said, his own eyes tender and a touch moist.

"Do you really think so?"

"I don't only think so, I know so."

"And you meant it when you said the chances of my playing with you were good?"

"I meant it, Kirsten, you *will* play with me one day."

"Promise?"

"I promise."

And she believed him. She had to, otherwise she wouldn't have been able to leave him. Michael would never make a promise he didn't intend to keep. He wouldn't be another Eduard van Beinum. He wouldn't let her down, not when it was as much her promise as his that they would play together one day. And not just once either. But time and time again, with every major orchestra in every major city in the world.

"Now, what was this memento you mentioned over the phone?" Michael asked the question reluctantly, but the clock on the dashboard had already begun ticking away their few remaining minutes together.

Sensing the unspoken urgency in his voice, Kirsten quickly handed him a rolled piece of sheet music tied with a narrow lavender satin ribbon. The look she gave him told him that along with this souvenir came a part of her soul. "I've even signed it for you in lavender ink," she warned him, her impish smile deepening her single dimple.

"Now, that's what I call appropriate." In spite of his efforts to keep the conversation light, Michael's hands were trembling as he undid the ribbon and discovered she had given him a copy of Debussy's "Reflets dans l'Eau." He read the simple inscription and smiled, a gentle, bittersweet smile. "Thank you, sweet Kirsten," he murmured. The husky edge to his voice was pronounced, and Kirsten could feel her heart beginning to break.

When he leaned over to kiss the tip of her nose, she saw him glance at the clock and she tensed, consciously preparing herself for what she knew was coming. "You have to go, don't you?" she asked.

"I'm afraid so. We're in the midst of moving, you know. Ironic, isn't it? We're moving in just as you're moving out."

"Yes, ironic." Her voice was now as hollow as the rest of her; with all the feelings scooped out of her, the only feeling left was no feeling.

They took another moment just to sit and look deep into each other's eyes, trying to divine what the other was thinking. Then Kirsten cupped Michael's face in her hands and kissed him continental-style on both cheeks.

"Don't forget me, Michael," she whispered as she quickly let herself out of the car. Closing the door with a soft click, she walked away without once looking back. He had teased her before about her fondness for grand entrances, but too often lately it was her exits she was proudest of.

Directly after dinner that evening, Kirsten excused herself and went upstairs to lie down. She wasn't even aware of Claudia letting herself into the room sometime later; she simply looked up to find her sitting at the foot of the bed.

"I think *I'm* acting out the last act of *Camille*," Kirsten said with a sigh.

"You do look a trifle peaked." Claudia reached over and touched Kirsten's forehead. "You don't have any fever, do you?" Kirsten shook her head. "Then it's obviously nothing more than a temporary state of melancholia. It may be a tad painful for a while, but it's hardly ever fatal. Besides, darling, he's not worth dying for."

"Who isn't?"

"Michael Eastbourne, that's who. Oh, darling, don't bother to deny it. I saw you getting out of his car this afternoon."

Kirsten turned her face away. "I was only saying good-bye to him."

Claudia bit her lip and tried not to react, but her heart was contracting in anguished spasms as she studied the unhappy face of the girl she adored. "God, I'm going to miss you," she said. "I'm going to miss you dreadfully."

Kirsten gulped. "I'll miss you too."

She was crying as Claudia pulled her into her arms and began to rock her back and forth. "Have you ever thought of staying in London, Kirsten?" she asked gently. "Eric and I could find you a flat nearby; we'd even pay the rent on it until you were able to support yourself. Oh, think of it, darling, think of how wonderful it could be. You wouldn't really be leaving us at all then."

Kirsten wiped her eyes with the backs of her hands and made a soft snuffling sound. Claudia's offer was tempting, almost irresistibly so. She tried to imagine herself staying. Living close to the two people who had been her substitute parents all year. Continuing the enchanted storybook life they had opened up to her. Concertizing in a city where her name was already known. Being able to see Michael whenever he was in town. She stopped right there.

"I can't, Claudia," she said, the tears starting all over again. "I just can't."

Claudia was in agony. With the tip of her tongue she

lapped up both of the tiny crystalline tears trickling slowly down Kirsten's cheeks, absorbing their salty wetness into the very core of her being. Kirsten giggled. It was as though a kitten were licking her face, and the ticklish feeling almost made her want to sneeze. Claudia was more hopeful now. Emboldened by Kirsten's bubbly laugh, she began dabbing sweet pecking kisses all over her face.

Seeing Kirsten with Michael that afternoon had thrown open the shutters on her passion and allowed her yearning for this winsome creature to come flooding through at last. It was a desire so powerful and so all-consuming that if she had been forced to contain it a moment more, she feared it would have exploded and torn apart her insides. Until today, only her terror of alienating Kirsten had kept her rampaging feelings under some semblance of control, but now she was desperate. Her beloved Kirsten was leaving. After reviving in her feelings she had never thought to experience again, the child, the daughter, the woman she worshiped was leaving her.

Kirsten flinched. Something warm and silky had grazed her lips. Before she could discover what it was, it was gone. A moment later it was back, this time to nibble at the corners of her mouth. And then it was closing over her entire mouth. Soft and moist. A satiny pressure bearing down on her. Lightly sucking at her flesh. A gentle thrust. A tentative probing, plunging deeper, then deeper still. She nearly gagged. She was suffocating. Her eyes flew open and she stared in horror at Claudia's flushed and strangely contorted face.

"Kirsten, oh, my darling Kirsten." Claudia's voice was husky with desire, her eyes glazed as she tried to calm the frightened girl. "Darling child, don't look at me that way. I cherish you, Kirsten, I'd never do anything to harm you. Darling, please, you must believe me."

But Kirsten wasn't listening. "We . . . we shouldn't . . . you shouldn't have done that." She was so agitated she could hardly form a coherent sentence. "It was wrong, Claudia, wrong."

"It wasn't wrong," Claudia argued, "it was right, Kirsten. Right and beautiful. An expression of caring, nothing more." She reached for her again, but Kirsten recoiled, the revulsion in her eyes darkening the irises until they were almost black. Frantic, Claudia grabbed her by the shoulders. "Hold me then," she begged. "Hold me for just a little while. Please, Kirsten. Please, my darling, my angel, my own."

But Kirsten was equally frantic as she fought to free herself from Claudia's smothering embrace. "No, Claudia, don't," she panted. It seemed to her there were arms and legs, hands and feet everywhere. Thrashing. Flailing. "Claudia, please, please don't." She was strangling. Gasping for air. Trapped in a nightmare of someone else's creation. "Stop it!" she screamed.

Claudia froze. Her arms fell to her sides. Without saying another word, she stood up, adjusted her dress, and fixed Kirsten with a stare so chilling that she became frightened.

"Claudia, I'm sorry, I didn't mean to shout, but you were hurting me."

"Was I, darling?" Her voice was as icy as her look. "I thought I was loving you." Her mouth compressed in a taut, angry line, she marched out of the room.

The moment the door closed, Kirsten leapt up from the bed and ran into the bathroom. She turned on the cold water, squeezed some toothpaste onto her toothbrush, and began vigorously brushing her teeth. After rinsing her mouth with a full glass of mouthwash, she started brushing her teeth all over again. Then she soaped a washcloth and scrubbed her face until it was red and sore, but even after a second equally brutal cleansing, she still didn't feel clean.

She turned off all the lights and flung herself onto her bed again, curled her body into a tight little ball, and tried to cry herself to sleep. She gave up shortly after midnight. In her anguish and confusion, she began punching her pillow. Then she folded it in half and used its doubled thickness to muffle her sobs and absorb her tears. By two in the morning she was lying on her back exhausted, wept dry, her throat raw. Up until only a few hours ago her entire year had been like one exquisite, extended dream. Now the ending to that beautiful dream had been twisted out of shape. Corrupted and defiled. And she wondered how she was ever going to face either Eric or Claudia again.

But face them she did. She came down the stairs for the last time at noon with a smile on her face, the absolute picture of composure. If her eyes were red-rimmed and swollen, everyone simply assumed it was because she was leaving. The household staff was lined up in the front hall just as they had been on the day she arrived. After they said their good-byes and were dismissed, leaving her alone with Eric and a stiffly silent Claudia, Kirsten presented them with a second signed copy of her signature piece as a memento for their collection, and received a sealed envelope, along with a hug and a wink from Eric in return.

"Well, lamb, we'd best get started," he said after a hasty peek at the time. But Kirsten appeared not to have heard him. "Where the devil are you going?" he called after her as she darted down the hall in the direction of the conservatory.

Pushing open the double glass doors, she quickly crossed the floor to the case holding Michael's wooden baton. "Remember your promise to me, Michael Eastbourne," she murmured as she bent down and planted the lightest of kisses on the top of the clear glass case. She waited until the impression made by her lips had faded and disappeared completely, then backed slowly out of the room.

They were already waiting for her in the car by the time she got outside. She took one final look at the house that had been her home for a year and slid into the backseat next to Eric.

"This isn't good-bye, you know," he told her, misinterpreting the expression on her face as her eyes met Claudia's. "It'll never really be good-bye for the three of us anyway. The French have a marvelous expression for it; they don't say good-bye, they say *au revoir*, which means until we meet again. So let's think of it that way, shall we, lamb, simply as *au revoir*?"

Kirsten repeated the words softly to herself. *Au revoir.* Until we meet again. It did make the good-bye less final, the parting less painful, her feelings about going home less ambivalent. She had set out to conquer London and had wound up capturing most of England, even, perhaps, a part of the continent as well. Now she intended to return to New York and conquer America.

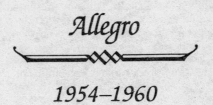

Allegro

1954–1960

11

"Do you want some coffee while you're waiting, Miss Harald?"

Kirsten glanced up from the scathing review *Time* magazine had given Tennessee Williams's new play, *Camino Real*, and shook her head. "You wouldn't happen to have any tea, would you?"

"Sorry."

"I just spent a year in London," she explained. "I got used to drinking tea while I was over there."

Nelson Pendell's secretary faked her best smile and tried not to let her disapproval show. To her, tea was a holdover from colonial days and tasted like something that had come straight from the Hudson River without being filtered first. As a patriotic American and diehard New Yorker, Eileen Harper considered it her sworn duty to end each working day in jangling overdrive from nothing but the caffeine in good old-fashioned java with cream. Tea. Yech! But she shouldn't have been the least bit surprised. After working for Nelson Pendell for seventeen years, she had pretty much heard it all. Artists. What a weird bunch they were.

Kirsten went back to her magazine with a fair idea of what the other woman was thinking and tried hard to keep a straight face. Coffee was the last thing she needed right now. Her nerves were stretched to the limit as it was. Even her scalp was tingling with anticipation. She had been home only a week, but she had wasted no time in setting up an interview with Nelson Pendell, the senior partner of Pendell and Rhodes, a management agency that could be described only as the most prestigious in New York City. In the black alligator handbag beside her on the low slung teakwood chair was the letter of introduction to Pendell that Eric had given her that last day in London. And on her lap rested a folder containing the newspaper clippings of her reviews.

Putting the magazine down on the teakwood table next to her chair, Kirsten leaned back in her seat, crossed her arms in front of her and considered the tips of her black alligator pumps. Had she really been home seven days? Sometimes it seemed like only yesterday, at other times it seemed she had never been away at all. Contrary to her fears, neither her parents nor Natalya had changed. There were a few more strands of white in her mother's thick black hair; the creases in her father's high forehead were slightly more pronounced, but their arms had felt as strong and supportive as ever, the force of their love as intense now as it had always been. And after her first lesson with Natalya, the Russian had enveloped her in a bear hug, planted a kiss on both her cheeks, and pronounced grandly that she was ripening well.

Her greatest shock, however, had been coming home to Ninth Avenue. To the scarred and battered tenements, the unrelenting blare of the streets, the sweat and garbage stench of another dying summer. It seemed to her there was more clutter in the back alleys. More limp clotheslines, more stray cats and broken bottles, more stumbling drunks and ragtag children running loose. The apartment looked even smaller and dingier than it had before she left, and she found it almost impossible to readjust to the tone and action of her aunt Sophia's piano after having played Eric and Claudia's superlative concert grand all year.

For the first time in her life she had clothes to give away. She cleared out her dresser and closet, gave everything to the Salvation Army, then crammed as many of her London clothes as she could into the meager space left behind. The hall closet accommodated some of the overflow, the rest went into the locker in the basement of the building. She wouldn't be needing as many clothes now. She had no cocktail parties or dinners to attend. No Sunday afternoon salons. No theater. No opera or ballet. No art gallery openings. She had no friends. Cinderella had finally returned from the ball. From the gilded palace back to the ghetto. If not as a complete stranger, then as a strangely awkward fit at best.

Her head snapped up at the sound of raised voices coming from behind the door to Nelson Pendell's private office. She glanced over at Eileen Harper as if for verification, but the woman didn't so much as blink or miss a beat. She continued tap-tapping blithely away on her typewriter, her obvious indifference to the situation indicating that she was as used to the temperamental outbursts of artists as she was to their odd requests. A moment later the door was flung open and a woman came storming out, handbag bouncing on her hip, hat in one hand, sheet music in the other. Kirsten gasped. The woman was Lois Eldershaw.

Lois was halfway across the waiting room when she noticed Kirsten. She stopped dead in her tracks. She was staring and she hated herself for it. Her chest tightened ominously. She had read in the papers where a wealthy British couple had been Kirsten's sponsors for the past year and here, right in front of her, was the proof. The ugly duckling had been transformed into a swan, wearing a suit almost the twin of her own, with a look of such self-confidence on her face that it was all Lois could do just to draw in a full breath of air without it whistling in her ears.

"Hello, Lois." Kirsten smiled sweetly at her erstwhile rival, watching as Lois ground her teeth together.

"Kirsten." Her abrupt nod bit off the end of Kirsten's name.

"Miss Harald?" Eileen Harper cut their interchange short. "He'll see you now."

"Thank you." Kirsten was every bit the serenely composed lady as she gathered up her purse and the folder of her clippings and stood up.

Lois didn't move. She remained exactly where she was, planted firmly in Kirsten's path, standing between her and the closed door to Nelson Pendell's office. Her pugnacious stance almost dared Kirsten to go through her, but Kirsten refused to be baited. She simply stepped around Lois as though she were nothing more threatening than a lamppost, knocked once on Pendell's door, and swept regally into the room.

The big, bulky man in the gray suit heaved himself up from his chair, extended his hand to her, then motioned for her to sit anywhere. She chose the middle of three chairs arranged in a semicircle in front of Pendell's surprisingly bare, oval desk. Nelson Pendell touched down himself only a second after Kirsten, with the sigh of a man who finds getting in and out of his seat an effort hardly worth the energy expended, and peered curiously at her through a pair of thick, black-rimmed glasses.

"Danish modern, what do you think of it?" He indicated the furniture, using it as he always did, as an icebreaker.

Kirsten glanced around the room and wondered how to reply without hurting his feelings. "I understand it's the latest thing," she said.

"It is." The ends of Nelson Pendell's bristly gray mustache twitched good-naturedly. "But I don't like it either, especially the wool they use on the chairs."

Kirsten cocked her head to one side, studied the man's face a moment, and took a chance. "It itches."

He beamed and Kirsten instinctively knew she had just passed some sort of test. She may not have liked his furniture, but she found herself liking Nelson Pendell. He scanned Eric's letter, flipped quickly through the newspaper clippings, then set them off to the side, as though the only thing that really mattered was who was sitting directly in front of him. She'd chosen the middle chair; he liked that.

"How old are you, Kirsten?" he asked, his speckled gray eyes unblinking behind the glasses. "You don't mind my calling you Kirsten, do you?"

"Not at all," she said. "I'm twenty-one."

"You know you're an incredibly beautiful young woman, don't you?" Kirsten merely smiled. "I can see you're used to hearing people tell you that. But I was saying it for a specific reason. I wanted to make a point. In the world of classical music, beauty, especially in a woman, can be a liability rather than an asset. Too many critics still subscribe to the old adage—all beauty and no brains. They see the surface and immediately assume what's underneath isn't substance but sawdust. They love crucifying good-looking performers; they hate having to take them seriously. To them, good looks belong in Hollywood, not in Carnegie Hall." He pushed his glasses onto the top of his head, where they all but disappeared in the thick waves of his iron-gray hair. "Tell me, Kirsten, are you as talented as you are beautiful? Do you think you can make them see beyond the surface to the substance?"

Kirsten leaned forward in her chair, her eyes snapping. "I'm a musician, Mr. Pendell, a very serious and very dedicated musician. Not a *woman* musician. Not a *good-looking* woman musician either. Just a musician, pure and simple. Let me play for you, let me show you just how serious and dedicated I really am. Don't judge me by the way I look, Mr. Pendell, judge me by the way I play."

Nelson Pendell was grinning as he shoved his glasses back onto the bridge of his broad, lumpy nose. The girl had guts. Pushing himself to his feet again, he came round the desk and gave Kirsten an unrestrained slap on the back.

"I like the sound of your conviction, Kirsten Harald, now let's see if I also like the sound of your music."

She was still reeling from the force of his slap as she seated herself at the Baldwin in the soundproofed studio two doors down from his office. "What would you like me to play?" she asked, warming up her fingers while he settled himself in a well-worn black leather armchair at the far end of the windowless room.

"It's entirely up to you," he told her, but he couldn't help adding with a saucy smile, "just impress the hell out of me."

Without hesitation Kirsten launched directly into Prokofiev's "Toccata."

Nelson Pendell leaned back in his chair and folded his arms across his chest. As he watched her small, nimble fingers crisscross the keyboard with such breathtaking facility and dexterity, he found himself cheering her on. He had been in the business of representing the great, the would-be great and the should-have-been great for twenty-five of his fifty-three years, but he still behaved like a kid when it came to discovering new talent. It turned his two hundred and thirty pounds of bulk to mush. It made the frustration of all those wasted auditions, one-hit stars and burned-out geniuses more than worthwhile.

It was his insistence on holding out for greatness that had made the early years so lean, but his stubbornness had ultimately paid off. He handled only the best, and because he did, men like Eric Sheffield-Johns sent him only the best. As far as he knew, he was the only shoe salesman from Brooklyn holding a Masters in music from Columbia. Although his passion had always been music, he had been astute enough to know that his real talent lay in selling the musical talent of others. Next to selling shoes, it was what he did best, and it had brought him the two things he had wanted most out of life: success for his clients and comfort for himself.

He still spoke with Brooklyn blocking his nose—and whenever he got excited, he would pepper his speech with the colorful street slang he had spent a lifetime trying to tame—but he dressed in custom-made Brooks Brothers suits and drove a sedate gray Chrysler sedan between his plush home in Westchester and his office on the twenty-first floor of the RCA Building. He had a son at Harvard, a daughter at Smith, and a wife named Bea, whom he adored almost as much as he adored spoiling her.

He pulled a white handkerchief from the breast pocket of his jacket and mopped his forehead. Kirsten had concluded the Prokofiev and was just beginning Chopin's Polonaise in F Sharp Major. Nelson Pendell held the damp handkerchief to his left temple. He could feel the pulse dancing beneath his fingers. The music was getting to him, making him feel as though he had just gone nine rounds in the ring with Jack Dempsey. He was open, wide open. The notes, like blows, kept jabbing away at him. A right to the jaw, a left to the gut. A fast hook caught him on the chin, a low cut slammed into his kidneys. Instead of defending himself against each new assault on his senses, he welcomed it. It was the only way he could tell if someone had it or not. And from the way his body was jumping and twitching, Kirsten Harald definitely had it.

One hour later he begged her to stop. With his handkerchief scrunched into a soggy ball in his hand, he lumbered toward her as though his shoes were too tight and the soles of his feet were blistered.

"Well, you did it," he said. "You impressed the hell out of me." The Brooklyn street boy in him was alive and on the rampage. "You've got it, Kirsten, you've got what it takes to go all the way to the top, and I plan to see that you do. Now, before you start thanking me, I have something to say. Don't look at me like that. I'm your agent now. Me you have to listen to, the others you don't."

"Yes, sir," Kirsten responded with mock seriousness.

"You already know the story: you're a woman, you're beautiful, and you're small. You look as though you need someone to take care of you. You and I know better, but no one else does, so I intend to trade on that three-way combination for all it's worth. Then, when everyone expects a nice little April shower from you, you're going to damn well give them Hurricane Harald. Okay, now you can thank me."

Lois was just finishing her second glass of iced coffee when she noticed Kirsten come down the steps and start across the plaza of Rockefeller Center. She consulted the discreet gold Piaget on her wrist and frowned. Kirsten had been with Nelson Pendell for nearly two hours. Digging into her handbag, she took out a sterling silver pillbox and hastily swallowed a small pink tablet with the last, watery remains of the coffee. She rested her head in one hand and massaged her chest with the other. She felt wretched, tired, and totally drained. Once again she had tried, and once again her talent had come up short. Once again she had been cut off, shunted aside, passed over. Was Kirsten Harald to be her nemesis for life now, she asked herself bitterly as her lungs ached and strained to deliver enough air to her body and brain.

Opening her wallet, she left a five-dollar bill on the table without even looking at the amount on the check, a gesture that would undoubtedly make some poor waitress very happy, she mused. She pictured Kirsten dressed as a waitress and smiled at the thought. As her parents had told her often enough, you can't buy class, you have to be born with it. Kirsten Harald had no class, she never would. In spite of her talent, her clothes, and her pretensions, she would never belong; she would always remain an outsider. All Lois had to do was be patient and wait.

"Well, pet, she did it, Nelson Pendell's agreed to represent her." Eric handed Kirsten's latest letter to Claudia and settled back in his favorite wing chair, his hands linked behind his neck, a smile of sheer fatherly delight on his face. "There'll be no stopping her now," he said.

He stared into the fire, feeling so lazy that he didn't have the energy to get up and throw on another log. It was cold even for October, yet he knew the cold had less to do with the start of another London autumn than with the coldness that had descended upon the house the day of Kirsten's departure. Claudia had become uncharacteristically withdrawn that day, and had remained so ever since. Not even the arrival from Paris of Guillaume St. Lambert, the brilliant nineteen-year-old cellist they were sponsoring for the year, had boosted his wife's flagging spirits. She was still behaving like someone in mourning.

Claudia pressed the four-page letter to her chest and closed her eyes, willing the absent Kirsten to spring to life from the flowing script that covered the lightly scented lavender notepaper, and soothe away her terrible loneliness. Her continuing sense of loss was all-pervasive—she slept with it, woke with it, moved through the day with it—and time had done little to blunt the pain.

If her love for Kirsten was, as Eric so naively chose to believe, purely and simply maternal, she would have been far more adept at dealing with her loneliness. But as only she knew, it went far beyond mother love to dwell in the murky realm of forbidden passion. It was a desperate and a helpless passion, made all the more devastating by its having remained unrequited.

To Claudia, Kirsten was a living scourge. A high fever affecting her brain, her heart, her groin. A constant and persistent nub of heat, as though some internal element buried deep within her soul had been left to burn.

Her one release from the torture was through orgasm, and even then it was only temporary. A momentary relief perpetrated by her own loving touch. One magical moment when, with the spilling of her precious liquids and the throbbing of her climax's restorative aftermath, she actually believed in the exorcism of demons. But all too soon she was in agony again. The snake had been freed at last, and it was working its way through her system with the stealthy sureness of a sharpened knife blade. Uglier and blacker than ever.

"Claudia?" Eric's hand on her shoulder made her jump. "You were rather far off just now."

"Sorry, darling," she murmured, wishing she could manage a more convincing smile.

"Would you prefer if we canceled the theater this evening?"

"Don't be silly. Peggy would never forgive us if we missed her as Hedda."

She loathed the very idea of having to sit through the newest revival of *Hedda Gabler*, even if Peggy Ashcroft was starring in it, but she would have agreed to anything at that moment in order to placate Eric and get out of the study. She fairly ran down the hall to her bedroom and bolted the door. The insides of her thighs were already damp, she herself tremblingly close to orgasm. Leaning up against the door, she cupped both hands between her legs and pressed. Once, twice, three times. She climaxed instantly, the shuddering spasms driving her back against the door over and over and over again. Her lips parted and she moaned. Then, biting back the tears, she whispered her beloved's name.

12

Kirsten's career as a concert soloist began the way it so often does for an unknown musician: through the cancellation of a scheduled performance by some other soloist. When pianist Lili Kraus was forced to cancel her upcoming concert with the Cleveland Orchestra because of pneumonia, Nelson Pendell immediately contacted the orchestra's manager and convinced him to allow Kirsten to fill in for her. Kirsten's fee: five hundred dollars less Nelson's ten percent commission. It was official. On January 5, 1955, Kirsten Harald would be making her American concert debut at Severance Hall with George Szell and the Cleveland Orchestra, playing the same piece Lili Kraus was to have played—Tchaikovsky's B Flat Minor Piano Concerto.

"Is it my imagination or does this note sound flat to you?" Kirsten stopped her run-through of the piece for the third time in fifteen minutes and glanced over at Szell. When she noticed the muscle in his jaw beginning to jump, she knew his reputation for sternness and precision was well founded; she fully expected him to bite her head off any minute now. But she refused to be daunted—she, too, was a perfectionist— and she stubbornly pounded away at the F until Szell was obliged to close his eyes and listen more closely.

"It is a bit off," he agreed somewhat testily, "but not so far off anyone will really notice." He scribbled something in the margin of one of the pages in his score, then glanced at his watch. "But just to be on the safe side, I'll have the tuner check it as soon as we're through here."

His message was clear; he wanted this pesky last-minute rehearsal over with as quickly as possible. Even the most mild-mannered of conductors could turn into a tyrant when it came to rehearsing replacement soloists, especially un- knowns like herself. Kirsten gritted her teeth and told herself not to take it personally. She hastily began where she had left off, but as soon as she saw Szell check his watch again, she promptly made two mistakes in a row. She winced at the glowering look he gave her and forced herself to concentrate more on the music, less on him. Then just as she was getting comfortable, he told her to stop.

"I didn't like what you did there." He backed her up in the score and hummed the passage the way he wanted it played. "Tone it down a little; you have a tendency to overdo things. No, don't bother going over it now. Let's get on with the rest of the movement."

The more he stopped her—usually to tone down her playing—the more frustrated she became. He was draining the life out of what was supposed to be a very rich and highly dramatic work. By the middle of the second movement she couldn't stand it anymore. She stopped playing altogether and told him what she thought. He skewered her with his eyes, and in a voice that was deadly calm said, "You're no Horowitz, Miss Harald. When you play with me, you play it my way."

She was so stunned, her mouth dropped open. It was never going to work out, she thought miserably, never. It was a disaster, a complete, unmitigated disaster. She was dangerously close to tears now. Was this what he wanted then, to see her break down? Have her prove women were everything they were supposed to be: unreliable, unstable, weak, overwrought? He was watching her too closely, and that more than anything snapped her out of her temporary helplessness. Her head came up proudly, she squared her shoulders, and clamped her mouth tightly shut. Then she began the second movement of the concerto all over again.

He didn't stop her once. By the time she hammered out the final chords of the piece, she was drenched in perspiration, her muscles were aching, and every one of her nerves was as tautly strung as a piano wire. But she remained completely expressionless while she awaited his verdict.

"Not bad," he said, closing his score and easing himself down from his stool.

Kirsten took this as her cue; she closed her own score and stood up too. For a moment their eyes locked. Szell was the first to look away, but not before she had seen something in his eyes she had never expected to see there—respect.

Not bad. Recalling his words, Kirsten grimaced as she started to dress in her cubbyhole of a room at the Sheraton-Cleveland later that evening. She had to be better than "not bad" tonight if she wanted people to know she even existed.

They certainly wouldn't know by their programs. It was Lili Kraus's name that was still on the cover, her photograph and her biography inside. The name Kirsten Harald would be nothing more significant than a last-minute insertion on a piece of mimeographed white paper.

If only her mother had come with her; she could barely zip up the lavender Balmain she had worn for her debut at Eric and Claudia's salon. Her hands were shaking so badly she nearly blinded herself with her mascara brush, and she had to reapply her lipstick three times before it was even. Then she dropped one of the diamond and amethyst earrings Claudia had bought her before her Wigmore Hall recital, and watched in horror while it narrowly missed going down the drain in the bathroom sink.

As she stood, rigid with stage fright, in the wings waiting to make her entrance, she tried to concentrate on what Natalya had told her just as she was boarding the train at Penn Station.

"Don't be afraid of being nervous, Kirishka," her teacher had said, "be grateful that you are. It's what makes the difference between an ordinary performance and an inspired performance. Confidence dulls, fear sharpens; remember that. Use your nervousness as you would any other emotion—to your advantage. Make it work *for* you, Kirishka, not against you."

The trembling began to leave her body; she pulled herself up straight and tall. Tonight she was being given the chance to prove herself, and that was exactly what she intended to do. She was determined to go out there and show George Szell, the orchestra, the audience, and the critics that Kirsten Harald was worthy of being more than just a last-minute replacement; she was worthy of being billed as a guest soloist in her own right. The stage manager cued her entrance and she stepped into the light girded for combat.

She swept across the stage, head high, to the sound of polite, if somewhat muted applause, and every pair of opera glasses in the hall trained on her. By their lackluster response, the people in the audience were sending her a definite message: she was an unknown quantity, and they were reserving judgment until they saw what she was capable of. By the time she had seated herself at the Steinway, Kirsten's nervousness was gone. In its place was defiance. She nodded once, brusquely, at Szell, signaling him that she was ready to begin.

With every note she played she was aware of the entire audience collectively holding its breath, waiting for her to make her first mistake. But she had made all her mistakes at rehearsal; she had no intention of making any now. As absorbed as she was in her music, she was equally absorbed in monitoring the mood in the hall. Bit by bit she could actually feel it changing—shifting from indifference to appreciation to admiration. The audience was losing some of its rigidity; people were bending, yielding. She could feel her own power growing and its effect on her was intoxicating. One by one they began to fall, transformed from skeptics into believers. By the start of the third movement she had converted almost all of them. She was now unquestionably in complete command. Lifting her willing suppliants out of their seats and out of themselves, she led them upward and set them high on a sweet, supernal plain.

People were on their feet, clapping, shouting out her name. They refused to let her go; they kept calling her back again and again. Even the man who had just conducted her was far different from the one who had rehearsed her that afternoon. This man was beaming. Reaching for Kirsten's hand, he kissed the back of it, then raised it triumphantly in the air. George Szell was among the converted, and his broad smile was the smile of someone whose reward for conversion has been an unprecedented glimpse of heaven. Kirsten was smiling, too, but for an entirely different reason. Tonight she had proven she could do it. And tonight was just the beginning.

"Mama, guess what? I've just gotten my first marriage proposal." Kirsten was howling with laughter as she handed the letter to Gianna. "I've never even been on a date, and now some man from Cleveland named Pat McIntyre wants to marry me."

Emil put on his reading glasses and peered at the letter over his wife's shoulder. "Hmmph. The man can't even spell properly."

Kirsten wiped her eyes and sat back on her heels. She was kneeling on the living room floor, going through the various letters and cables she had received in the two weeks since her spectacular Cleveland debut, and pasting them into the fat leatherbound album with her name stamped in gold on its cover that she had recently ordered from Mark Cross.

"I think I'd better have Nelson's office handle my mail from now on," she said. She had heard too many grisly accounts of public personalities being harassed by overly zealous fans.

"Good idea," Emil agreed. He was just about to crumple up the letter from Pat McIntyre, when Kirsten stopped him.

"How could you do that to my first marriage proposal, Pappy? Every girl should remember her first proposal."

Gianna rolled her eyes and watched as her daughter smoothed out the slightly wrinkled sheet of paper. "Just what do you intend to do with it, *carissima?*"

"Paste it in my album, of course. Who knows? It might be the only proposal I ever get."

Once the letter was safely pasted into place, she went back over her reviews, pretending to be reading each of them for the first time and singling out certain phrases to memorize:

". . . a welcome and refreshing breath of spring after a particularly long and dry winter . . ."

". . . combines the best in style, personality, daring, and above all, imagination . . ."

". . . a brilliant new interpreter of the lush sound and dramatic tempo fluctuations for which the Romantics were so revered . . ."

". . . masters the fine art of the legato, that exquisite singing quality which imbues even the simplest phrase with such haunting and lyrical beauty . . ."

When she was certain neither of her parents were watching, she stealthily withdrew a piece of neatly folded yellow paper from the pocket of her skirt, opened it up, and flattened out the creases with the palms of her hands. Her heart skipped a beat as she scanned the brief congratulatory message on the cable, but it was tripping excitedly by the time she got to the name taped at the bottom of the page. MI-CHAEL. The seven even capital letters didn't simply spell out his name, they shouted it out. A bold and vehement declaration. MICHAEL. A frank exclamation mark of a name. Signing off the sweetest and most tender of messages. She ran her fingers over his name, pretending it was his face she was touching instead. Then she pasted the cable onto a page of its own and closed the album with a sigh.

Her career began slowly and built quickly. Nelson Pendell put his vast international network of contacts to work ensur-

ing that every manager of every major orchestra in the world
knew Kirsten Harald's name. Whenever there was a cancellation, he made certain she was the soloist they considered
first; where there were no cancellations, he booked recitals
for her instead. He insisted she sit for a new publicity photograph and assigned Richard Avedon the task of immortalizing
the famous look Antony Armstrong-Jones had first revealed to
the world only eight months earlier. Kirsten posed for Avedon
in a gown by the American designer Nørman Norell, and the
eight-by-ten glossies were included in the press kits Nelson
made up and sent out by the hundreds. She was a manager's
dream, her talent and beauty forging the headiest and most
potent combination imaginable. Nineteen fifty-six marked the
bicentennial of the birth of Mozart, and with every orchestra
in the world scheduled to perform the legendary composer's
works that year, Nelson astutely suggested Kirsten add a
Mozart concerto and several of his sonatas to her repertoire,
which she readily agreed to do.

By the time the season ended in June, Kirsten had given
nine recitals and managed to fill in twice more as a soloist—
once with Eugene Ormandy and the Philadelphia Orchestra,
once with the Chicago Symphony under Fritz Reiner—playing
the Grieg A Minor Piano Concerto both times. Her schedule
for the coming season already included fifteen concerts and
twenty-seven recitals, but her summer promised to be busy
as well; Nelson had arranged for her to appear at eight noted
American music festivals, the most popular one being the
Berkshire Festival held annually at Tanglewood just outside
Boston.

Kirsten's state of mind could be described only as euphoric. She was ecstatic, gloriously alive, afloat at last on the
purling waves of her precious dream. Buoyed by its forceful
current and taken higher, always higher.

On her way to Patelson's one afternoon to buy some sheet
music, she was stopped on the street by a young violin
student who asked for her autograph. When she told him she
had no pen with her, he promptly produced one, which, to
her astonishment was an Esterbrook fountain pen filled with
lavender ink.

"I've been carrying it around with me for two months now,
hoping I might run into you," he admitted, blushing crimson
and staring down at his feet. "I read where lavender is the
only color you ever wear onstage." He shifted his violin case

from one hand to the other. "My name's Paul, by the way, Paul Bell." He peered nervously at the piece of paper he had given her to see what she was writing. Then, when she tried to hand him back his fountain pen, the young man shook his head. "Please keep it," he said. "I sorta bought it for you in the first place."

Before she could even thank him properly, he was darting up the street toward the studio entrance to Carnegie Hall. She was so touched by the thoughtfulness of his gesture that for a moment she couldn't move. She stared down at the pen she was holding and repeated the boy's name to herself several times to make certain she wouldn't forget it. Then she tucked Paul Bell's beautifully sentimental present in her purse and went on to Patelson's.

Kirsten's first fight with Nelson was over her refusal to accept a booking with the Los Angeles Philharmonic for November of '56.

"I told you before, I don't want to play with them then." She folded her arms and glared at Nelson, who was glaring back at her from behind his desk.

"But you didn't tell me why."

"Because Eduard van Beinum's going to be their guest conductor next year, that's why. I refuse to play with any orchestra he's conducting."

"Just because he slighted you as a kid?"

Kirsten's jaw tightened. "It was more than a simple slight. It devastated me, Nelson, and I'll never forgive him for making me feel the reason he could afford to treat me so cavalierly was that I was a nobody with an appointment to audition for a somebody. No, Nelson, I won't play with him, now or ever."

"It still doesn't make good business sense, you know."

"I don't have to make good business sense. I'm an artist, remember?" She said this with such a mischievous glint in her eye that Nelson couldn't help smiling at her as he gave in. "By the way," she said, standing up and reaching for her gloves, "were you able to get me the ticket I wanted?"

"You think you deserve it after all the aggravation you've caused me?"

In answer to that, she leaned over and kissed the top of his head. "It's about time we started arguing about something.

Poor Eileen was probably beginning to wonder about me.
You know, artistic temperament and all that."

"Some reasoning," he muttered. But that didn't prevent
him from opening the top drawer of his desk and taking out a
small white envelope. "I had one hell of a time, but here it is,
front row center. Enjoy."

She pocketed the ticket and left the office. Had she been a
dancer, she would have jumped up and clicked her heels à
la Gene Kelly or Fred Astaire. But being a musician, she
satisfied her urge to leap into the air by happily belting out a
series of arpeggios out loud while she waited for the elevator
to arrive.

That evening it was just as unseasonably warm for October
as it had been that memorable October night nine years
before. But the young woman sweeping grandly up the stairs
and into the imposing vaulted lobby of Carnegie Hall was a
far different person from the thirteen-year-old in the homemade blue rayon dress, who had climbed shyly up those same
stairs for the very first time that night. She thought of the
elderly Englishwoman with her diamonds and her chauffeur
and wished they could come face-to-face again now. This time
she would know precisely how to handle her.

Kirsten knew people were staring at her and she smiled to
herself. In her black silk brocade cocktail suit, black peau de
soie pumps, and matching clutch, she was the epitome of
exquisite, understated elegance. Composed, self-contained,
and provocatively aloof. A veritable magnet drawing everyone's attention to her—some because they recognized her,
others simply because of her astounding beauty. Even her
seat invited attention. And the way she sat in it, so proudly
erect, like a queen holding court.

A hush fell over the hall as the lights began to dim. Kirsten
sat taller in her seat, got a firmer grip on her program, and
tried to ignore the rapid acceleration of her pulse. The fingers
of her left hand closed around the pearl choker she was
wearing. Never had the word choker seemed more appropriate than at that exact moment: she could barely swallow. The
passing seconds were becoming intolerable, stretching tortu-
ously before her like some obstacle course she had to tra-
verse. Then, suddenly and mercifully, the waiting was over.

Michael Eastbourne strode onto the stage to the sound of
thunderous applause, but all Kirsten could hear was the loud,

staccato beating of her happy heart. This was the first time he
had been in New York in over a year, the first time she had
seen him since leaving London. Her hungry eyes feasted
greedily on the welcome sight of him, so slim and elegant in
his black tails, white shirt, and bow tie, his baton tucked
under his right arm as he bowed. His face serious, with only
a hint of a smile softening the firm line of his mouth. One
lock of wavy brown hair falling across his forehead as he
straightened up again, turned, and stepped nimbly onto the
podium. She held her breath and waited for him to raise his
baton. When he did, she released her breath slowly and with
a slight, approving nod, as the opening strains of Tchaikovsky's overture from *Romeo and Juliet* filled the expectant
silence.

She sat through the entire concert enclosed within a world
comprised of music, Michael, and herself, with guest soloist
Yehudi Menuhin's rendering of Brahms's only violin concerto
lifting her higher and higher. When the program concluded
with Ravel's "La Valse," she descended with such a pronounced thud, it took her another moment to realize it wasn't
the sound of her landing she had heard, but the sound of the
audience's wild applause.

She left while everyone was still standing and clapping,
and hurried outside to the stage door. To her dismay, a
number of photographers were already there waiting. Spot-
ting a row of black limousines lined up at the curb, she went
from car to car until she finally located the one reserved for
him. She hesitated. Speaking with him outside the stage door
was one thing; waiting for him inside a rented limousine was
something else entirely.

The crowd grew; members of the audience were milling
about and several of the musicians were already coming through
the door. She agonized for another minute, glancing anxiously at the crowd, then at the limousine, then back at the
crowd again. Finally, in a burst of daring, she pulled open
the back door of the car. Before the uniformed driver could
protest, she had slid all the way over to the far end of the
roomy black leather upholstered seat.

"What the—?"

"Oh, it's perfectly all right," she assured the man with her
warmest smile. She was beginning to enjoy this—her first
conscious attempt at vamping someone. "Mr. Eastbourne
asked me to wait for him here." She even went so far as to

lower her lashes suggestively and cross her legs, hoping his imagination would do the rest.

"Sure thing." The driver angled his rearview mirror to get a better look at her legs and envied the lucky man who'd be climbing in next to her.

As soon as he noticed Michael Eastbourne approaching, the driver sprang out of the car, leaving Kirsten only a moment—during which she had violent second thoughts about what she was doing—to compose herself. The back door opened and the overhead light flashed on, illuminating Michael in a dramatic flare of yellow whiteness.

"Limousine, sir?" Cocking an imaginary cap, Kirsten burst into a gale of delighted laughter when she saw the expression on his face.

But Michael didn't join in her laughter. He was so stunned he could hardly breathe, much less laugh. For one long, tantalizing moment, they did nothing but stare at each other. Taking stock. Looking for changes. When they finally moved, they moved at precisely the same moment. The distance between them narrowed, then disappeared altogether. Gently cupping Kirsten's face in his hands, Michael tenderly kissed her forehead, her eyelids, the tip of her nose and her chin. Then he kissed her mouth. It was their first true kiss, and it was as sweet and endless as eternity.

13

Kissing Kirsten had been as impetuous as it had been instinctive. A spontaneous reaction to her beauty, to seeing her again after more than a year. A year during which he had remained helplessly enslaved by her memory. But taking her up to his suite at the St. Regis was madness, utter madness. And yet, Michael felt mad. Out of control. His need for her had bucked and kicked inside him for far too long now. The time for control, for exercising restraint, had passed. But even as he capitulated, he remained tormented, knowing his unbridled desire for this woman defiled the sanctity of his marriage and endangered both of their careers.

Without turning on the lights he led Kirsten over to the window and caressed her with the night glow of the city as a backdrop. His hands were gentle with a restrained, underlying strength, her skin silken velvet as he began to learn her the way he would a piece of music. Slowly, patiently, perfectly. She was a single, sustained note, held in thrall by his touch. His mouth breathed life into her body, his fingers shaped and defined her entire being. She felt weak. Pliable and moist. Growing softer and warmer against his hardness, while the borders dividing them into two separate entities began to dissolve.

"Kirsten." He was drowning and she wouldn't save him. He murmured her name again and again; the last urgent pleas of a man already beyond saving.

"Love me, Michael," she whispered, clasping his buttocks and grinding her hips in a repeated demand against his. "Please, Michael, teach me, I've got to know. Please, Michael, please." She needed to know if there was an end to the restless feelings she had lived with so long. She needed to know if there was another plateau of pleasure besides the treacherous one Claudia had taken her to. And Michael, only Michael, had the power to show her.

Michael waged one last desperate battle with his conscience and lost. Scooping Kirsten up into his arms, he carried her over to the bed and laid her down with all the gentleness left in him. Together they peeled away their clothing, layer by tantalizing layer, until there were no further barriers between them. Then, flesh to flesh, they began the achingly delicate ritual of discovering how to love each other for the first time.

His maleness intrigued her: the span of his chest, his narrow hips, the dark, curling hair strategically matting his body in warm, brushy clumps. Her curiosity made her hungry; her need made her greedy. Whatever she saw, she touched and tasted, breathing in the scent of him and hearing by his deep, protracted groans just how much she was pleasing him.

It seemed she had barely begun to explore the uncharted territory of his wonderful body, when Michael turned her over onto her back and began an exploration of his own. He used not only his lips, but his tongue and his fingers, watching how his caresses changed the texture of her skin from silken smoothness to tiny goose bumps of aroused sensitivity. Her startled exclamations of delight, her sighs of sheer pleasure, made him search for even more imaginative ways to stimulate and satisfy her.

Lying with her legs spread and her arms flung outward, Kirsten felt wickedly, deliciously wanton. Michael's expert touch was unleashing sensations in her she never knew existed. The more he kissed and stroked her, the more she craved; she was insatiable. Opening herself up to him completely, she was alternately demanding and pliant, frenzied and yielding. No longer flesh but fire, she was an inferno of feeling—all tingles and shivers and an expectancy bordering on agony.

The sight of his dark head bending over her breasts to suck them, then moving slowly across her belly to the precise spot where her legs were parted made her giddy with anticipation. When he covered her with his warm mouth, she gasped. But a moment later her gasp gave way to a quivering moan as her entire body began to rise and fall in accordance with the rhythm that his tongue was setting deep inside her.

She thought she was as close to ecstasy as she would ever get, but she was wrong. No sooner had Michael, with his tongue, built her up to the point of bursting than he took her in his arms and gently, very gently, entered her. At the moment that she surrendered her virginity to him, he broke the most sacred of his marriage vows, and they both knew that nothing would ever be the same for either of them again.

Instinct made her wrap her legs around his waist to deepen his thrusts, and whatever stab of pain she felt as he penetrated her paled in the glory of their mutual submission. Using their bodies as weapons of tender combat, they were both ally and enemy, driven forward by a hunger as primeval as it was infinite, the joyousness of their union surpassed only by the heights to which that joy was taking them. Their completion was so violent, the sensations so extreme that Kirsten screamed as she experienced her first, exquisite climax, while Michael finally understood what it meant to die, and lost his fear of death forever.

She lay wrapped in his arms, sated and weak, her limbs trembling, her body glistening with a musky-scented film. She had been released at last, at long, long last from the torment of having hovered on the brink of womanhood for so many years. She had never felt such completeness before, not even those times when it seemed she had touched infin-

ity with her music. She was a woman now; Michael had made
her a woman.

Her wonderful contentedness lasted only a few moments
more. Then it was supplanted by something else—an overwhelming sense of uncertainty. And guilt. Guilt over what
they had done, what *she* had done. Had she been wrong in
allowing it to happen, wrong in encouraging Michael to make
love to her? What had seemed so right and natural before was
suddenly fraught with all kinds of questions and doubts.

She was no longer a virgin. She had given herself, willingly
and eagerly, not to her boyfriend, her fiancé, or even her
husband, but to someone else's husband. She pressed a fist to
her mouth to keep from crying out. Michael's being married
had never seemed to matter as much as it did now. Now that
they had crossed that forbidden line. Twisting around in his
arms, she looked at him closely. Had she hurt him, she
wondered. Had she hurt this man whom she barely knew but
whose soul had touched hers so long ago?

Michael smiled up at her and gave her a long, tender kiss.
If he felt a slight resistance in her response, he attributed it
to shyness, something altogether expected considering her
innocence and inexperience. He drew her head down onto
his chest and began stroking her hair while he tried to sort
out his feelings about what had just happened between them.

Suddenly the sweetness of the moment turned sour; all he
could taste was the bitterness of remorse. There had been an
inevitability about it, he knew; yet he cursed himself for
giving in just the same. Whenever he had been attracted to
another woman in the past, his love for Roxanne had made it
easy to resist. But with Kirsten it was different. Resisting her
had been torture.

While the moralist in him was demanding he be punished,
the man in him ached to make love to her again. But he
didn't. He couldn't. They had to talk. They had to put a
boundary around what had just happened between them, a
perimeter to define and protect them now and in the future.

"Do you know that when I'm holding you this way," he
began, "I feel as if we've melted together, become the same
person?" He paused a moment, then continued softly, almost
tentatively. "But we're not the same person, are we, Kirsten?" He felt her shake her head while her arms tightened
around him. "We're two very separate people, leading separate lives, with a great many people depending on us. I

can never give you any more than what we've just had, Kirsten, and I probably had no right to make love to you knowing I can't."

She took a deep breath and tried to keep her voice steady. "Did I ever ask you for more, Michael?"

"No," he answered honestly. "But you're entitled to more. And I'll never be able to give it to you. I'm married. I have two sons I adore and a wife I love too much to ever leave. She's a vital part of who and what I am, and we've been partners in every sense of the word for a very long time now." There were unshed tears in his voice, a thickening deep in his throat as though he were choking.

So he was in turmoil too; he hadn't expected this to happen either. Neither of them had been prepared for the act or the aftermath, and now it seemed they were both looking for a way back over the line they had crossed. Kirsten felt cold. Nothing, not even loneliness had ever felt this cold before. Yet she sensed this was how loneliness would feel from now on if she were never to see Michael again. The prospect was so terrifying, it instantly banished her doubts and vanquished her guilt. If the price for keeping him in her life—no matter how infrequent—was not to ask for anything more, then it was a price she would gladly pay. She would rather have some of him than none of him, and she told him that.

"Do you realize what you're saying?" he demanded, seizing hold of her face and trying to see her eyes in the darkness.

"Yes, Michael," she whispered fiercely, "I do."

"No, Kirsten, you don't." She tried to turn her head away but he wouldn't let her. "I don't think you fully understand just how much is at stake. We're very much at risk, you and I. If we ever got careless or greedy, we could lose everything we've worked so hard for. We live in a very small and very competitive world, Kirsten, where rivalry makes people do terrible things to each other. No one thinks twice about using something vicious against a rival if he feels it can further his own career. And if anyone found out about us, it could ruin us. Plenty of people have the power to do it too. Roxanne does, so does Clemence Treaves. We'd have to be careful, Kirsten, very careful, because there are a lot of extremely jealous people out there with their claws bared, just waiting for us to prove we're only human."

She digested everything he was telling her slowly and carefully, then she said, "Michael, when I was thirteen, I promised myself that you'd conduct me one day. Last year you promised me the same thing. Do you think either of us would have ever made that kind of promise if our music weren't so important to us? Michael, my music is my life. I've never known where my music ends and I begin, and vice versa. I *am* my music. And I won't allow anything, *anything* to jeopardize that, because if there's no music, there's no me." Propping herself up on one elbow, she reached out and lightly stroked his face, and when she spoke again, her voice was lighter too. "How often do you think about me?" she asked him.

"How often!" His muted laugh sounded more like a groan. "There's hardly a moment when I *don't* think about you."

"Really?" She looked as delighted as a child celebrating her first Christmas.

"Really."

She gave him a hug and burrowed deep in his arms again. "Will you promise me something then?"

"What?"

"That whenever you think about me, you'll hold me just the way you're holding me now."

"Even tighter if I can."

"And I'll do the same. That way we'll never really be apart, will we?"

Her simple logic made him smile. Drawing her down on top of him, he allowed the dark, silky spill of her long hair to fall like a curtain around them and seal them off from the outside world. "You make it all sound so easy, Kirsten," he said, "but it won't be, you know. You'll never be satisfied with moments snatched from here, hours stolen from there, with only thoughts to fill the gaps in between. You shouldn't even ask it of yourself. You're far too young to settle for an arrangement like this. It's not fair to you; you won't be happy."

She put a hand over his mouth to silence him. "I won't be happy *not* settling," she told him. "I can be satisfied with it, you'll see. And I promise I'll never ask you for any more than what we have right now."

"Don't make that promise yet," he warned. "When you have some time to think about it, you might change your mind."

"No, I won't." She bent down and kissed him gently on the lips.

"It's a promise you'll have every right to break someday."

"Never." She kissed him again. "Never. Never. Never," she vowed, punctuating each word with another kiss.

He buried his fingers in the thickness of her hair and prolonged this last kiss until the two of them were gasping for breath. Then he eased her slowly onto her back. Beginning with her forehead, he kissed his way down her entire body. Alternately nipping and sucking, biting and nuzzling her. Kirsten arched her back, twisting this way and that as she followed the path of his demanding mouth. Thrusting herself against his lips and questing tongue, she deepened his kisses and widened the rings of pleasure spreading outward from her core. She pleaded for him to take her, but Michael held off until he had succeeded in building the two of them up to the point where their need for release bordered on agony. Then as he pulled her back on top of him, he entered her at the same time, and began to make love to her all over again.

She awoke to the sound of the alarm clock shrilling in her brain. But as she switched on the bedside lamp, she noticed it was just past six. The alarm wasn't set to go off for another two hours. Something was wrong. She could sense it, much the way she always sensed rather than heard when one of the children was calling her. She began to shiver; goose bumps formed on her neck and arms as she slid quickly out of bed. Pulling on a long satin robe, she tied the sash around her waist and tiptoed barefoot from the master bedroom into the hall. She climbed silently up the stairs to the third floor of the house and looked in on Christopher first, then Daniel. Both boys were sound asleep, their breathing regular, their young faces so handsome, so touchingly innocent.

Roxanne Eastbourne ran her fingers anxiously through her short dark auburn hair and shuddered. Wrapping both arms around herself to keep warm, she returned to her bedroom and sat down on the edge of the bed. After having lived most of her life in the country, she still hadn't gotten used to the noise of the city. That was probably what she had heard: the background hum of early morning London. Either that or the ordinary creaking sounds every hundred-year-old house makes.

How she dreaded these times when it was almost impossible for her to fall asleep again but still too early to get up and start the day. This was when she missed Michael most. When she hated his being away so much, and regretted her insis-

tence that he guest-conduct awhile longer. Perhaps the time
had come for them to reevaluate the situation. She needed a
full-time husband again and the boys needed a father.

She looked over at the collection of framed photographs on
the night table nearest her and sighed longingly. How strange
that her table was covered only with photographs of Michael,
while his held photos of all four of them—taken together as a
family, in various groupings and combinations, and individually. She picked up her favorite photo of him, the one taken
just before their engagement had been officially announced in
The Times, and cradled it against her chest. His mouth was
centered directly on the nipple of her left breast. Closing her
eyes, she imagined him tugging on it with his lips and teeth
the way he so often did. An ache of such desperate yearning
seized her at the very thought of him touching her that she
opened her eyes, hastily put the picture back, and got up
from the bed. Knowing it was senseless to even try to fall
asleep now, she went into his study and did what she always
did when she missed him: she walked around the room,
touching everything that belonged to him. Then she sat down
at his desk.

It was authentic Chippendale, with brass mounts and ornate brass drawer handles, bought at auction at Sotheby's to
celebrate their first wedding anniversary. She adored this
desk; it felt so much like Michael himself—solid yet graceful,
strong and enduring. Pulling out the drawers one by one, she
leafed through his daily calendar, his bankbooks, various
musical scores, the notes he kept for the articles he intended
to write someday. Loose photographs, old telegrams, yellow-
ing newspaper clippings, letters he had forgotten to answer.
She opened the last drawer, riffled through a stack of old
theater programs, and was just about to close it again, when
something caught her eye. Something she had never noticed there before.

She lifted out a packet of newspaper clippings, all of them
neatly and precisely trimmed, and held together with a large
paper clip. A vise clamped itself around her windpipe and
began shutting off her air supply. The woman's face gazing
out at her from one of the clippings looked vaguely familiar.
The caption beneath the photo confirmed it: she was Eric and
Claudia's former protégé. Whatever air remained in Roxanne's seizing lungs quickly evaporated.

Why was Michael saving clippings of Kirsten Harald, she

asked herself as she searched frantically through the drawer
for any other surprises he might have hidden. The next thing
she discovered was the copy of a cable he had sent her,
followed by a rolled piece of sheet music tied with a lavender
ribbon. Roxanne's heart was slamming wildly against her ribs
as she read the inscription at the top of the first page of
Claude Debussy's *"Reflets dans l'Eau."* If she remembered
correctly, the Debussy was the young pianist's signature piece.

Her temples were throbbing, her insides roiling. There
wasn't a part of her that wasn't trembling. What if it were
happening all over again? She buried her face in her hands.

"Dear God," she whimpered, "please don't let it be happening. Please, God, please."

It couldn't be happening, it just couldn't. Michael would
never do that to her, he loved her. Surely she would have
known. He could never have hidden it from her; he was
terrible at hiding things. Taking her hands away from her
face, she sat up straight and tried to think more clearly. What
if nothing had actually happened yet? What if this was simply
a warning, the chance for her to prevent what might still be
only a possibility from ever becoming a reality? Suddenly
there was hope again. She immediately lunged for the phone.

"Clemence dear." She hated waking her uncle, but once he
understood the reason for her call, she was certain he would
forgive her. "Tell me what you know about Kirsten Harald,
and I don't mean the things anyone can read in the papers."

Clemence Treaves yawned loudly. He didn't dare glance at
the time, though, it was bound to upset him. But for his
niece to be calling him this early, she had to be in fairly high
dudgeon about something. He rubbed the sleep from his
eyes and tried to think. He could come up with nothing of
any particular significance. After admitting as much to her,
he yawned again and tried a bit harder. It was then that he
remembered.

"Do you mean to say Claudia actually invited Michael to a
salon when I was at Wynford?" Roxanne could feel the world
slipping away from her. "Of course. He would have met her
there then." Not only had Michael betrayed her, but Claudia
had also been involved in it. Claudia, always Claudia. She
was right to have called Clemence; there wasn't anything he
didn't know.

"It couldn't have been more than a perfectly harmless
coincidence," Treaves hastened to assure his niece. "Rox-

anne?" Puzzled by her sudden silence, he gave the receiver a shake. "Are you there, girl?"

Roxanne felt as though she had just stepped out onto a high wire with no safety net to catch her should she slip and fall.

"Yes, I'm here," she answered dully.

"What can you possibly be thinking?"

"I'm thinking, my dear Clemence, that I'd do well to see what might have begun as a perfectly harmless coincidence *remains* perfectly harmless."

"And just how do you propose to do that?"

"By making quite certain Michael never gets the chance to conduct dear cousin Claudia's famous protégé. And I do mean never."

Treaves let out a yelp of pain and held the receiver away from his ear. Nothing irked him more than having the phone slammed down on him, especially so damned bloody early in the day.

14

Over the next two years, while most critics called Kirsten a "brilliant new star in the musical firmament," and her virtuosity an "incandescent glow growing stronger and brighter with each performance," there were those who preferred criticizing her to praising her. The older ones found her "innovative to the point of arrogance"; the younger ones didn't think she was innovative enough. To some she was either too strident or too subtle, too wild or too tame, too bold or too muted. But in spite of their differing opinions, no critic ever described her in anything less than hyperbolic terms. It seemed Kirsten Harald was fated to inspire only the extremes in people.

It was to her harshest critics that Kirsten directed her performances, so intent was she on converting all of them into believers. It made her work doubly hard at perfecting her craft and her art. That, and knowing, as a musician, she was only as good as her last good note. She had to keep proving herself again every time she played. Far from intimidating her, the challenge invigorated her.

Sweeping onto the stages of every major concert hall in the United States, Canada, and Europe, she captured the hearts of her fellow musicians and the tens of thousands of concertgoers who made up her audiences. She belonged to the world now; she was idolized and adored. Sought after, pampered, and flattered. Imitated. Orchestra managers and conductors everywhere vied for her attention like jealous suitors, both in concert and in the recording studio; and the incredible demands on her professional time left her hardly a moment for a private life of her own. But she wouldn't have had it any other way.

Gowned by the most famous designers in the world—always in her signature shade of lavender—her black hair now cut into a gleaming cap that fell from a center part to just below her ears, her beauty remained as legendary as her talent. But while Kirsten Harald the performer was continually exploited by the press for an increasingly voracious public, Kirsten Harald the person remained an enigma. Her privacy was fiercely guarded by her parents and Nelson's office; no one, no matter how influential or prestigious, was ever granted access to her or permitted to interview her. And this only added to her allure.

The day she moved her parents away from Ninth Avenue was one of the most satisfying days of her life; the large three-bedroom apartment she had rented for the three of them on East Eighty-first Street was the fulfillment of one of her most important promises to herself. She had New York decorator Billy Baldwin furnish the apartment for her, and at her insistence he had done it entirely in white. Kirsten knew that white was an impractical choice as a color, but after the filth and clutter of the old apartment, what she craved most now was a sense of pristine and open space. The very antithesis of what she had grown up with. She wanted their new home to be a haven for her mother and father, and a place of tranquility for her to counteract the frenetic pace of her own life. And this was precisely what Baldwin had created.

"What are we going to do with so much room?" Gianna griped good-naturedly as Kirsten took her parents on their first tour of the completed apartment the day before they were scheduled to move in.

"Get lost in it, of course." Kirsten gave her mother a hug and pointed her toward the large modern kitchen.

"At my age, I need less room, not more. Look at all the extra cleaning I'm going to have to do."

"I've already hired a woman for that," Kirsten replied. "She's coming in three mornings a week, so don't you dare do anything more strenuous than make your bed."

"You've hired someone to do *my* cleaning!" Gianna looked indignant. "What do you think *I've* been paid for all my life?"

"That's another thing I intend to change. I want you *going* to concerts at Carnegie Hall, Mama, not cleaning up after them anymore."

"Listen to the star!" Gianna grasped both sides of her daughter's face and kissed her noisily on the mouth, but there were tears in her dark eyes when she let her go. *"Grazie, mi amore,"* she said, her voice hoarse as she kissed Kirsten again, gently this time on both cheeks. "You're not only the most beautiful and talented daughter in the world, you're also the most generous."

Kirsten's own eyes were beginning to fill. Turning quickly to her father, who had been silent all this time, she linked her arm through his and smiled up at him. "Well, Pappy, what did you think of the doorman downstairs? Do you think you can get used to having someone open the door for you for a change?"

"If a person puts his mind to it, he can get used to anything. Isn't that right, Gianna?" His wife's glare dissolved into a look of pure adoration as he slipped his arm around her waist and gave her a tight squeeze. "Your mother agrees with me, Kirsty," he said.

Gazing tenderly at her parents, Kirsten felt a stab of envy so sharp it startled her. They fit together so well—his tall fairness and her small darkness the perfect dramatic foils. They looked as though they truly belonged together. That made her think of Michael. Did they fit together as well as her parents did, she wondered. Could anyone tell by looking at them that they *didn't* belong together? That Michael belonged to someone else? She gave her head an impatient toss. She never allowed herself such destructive thoughts; they brought her nothing but pain.

She was almost relieved when she noticed the time on the electric clock on the stove. Dropping a set of keys into her father's hand, she said, "Take as much time as you want here, but I have to leave. I've got a date with a very special man in exactly twenty minutes." Emil and Gianna exchanged hopeful glances. "Sorry to disappoint you, it's purely professional."

She walked into the showroom of Steinway & Sons as though she were walking onto a stage. And when she located Ralph Bowers and told him she was there to purchase a concert grand, he grabbed hold of her hand, pumped it up and down, and appeared never to want to stop.

"So Miss Mozart made it after all." He was beaming, his wide proprietary smile announcing to the rest of the world that he was the one who had originally discovered her. "I suppose you'll want to try them all out first."

"Not all of them, Mr. Bowers." Kirsten was grinning too. "Just the ones in the basement this time."

Ralph Bowers nodded his approval. She really had made it. Only the ones who had made it knew about the pianos in the basement.

"Then if you'll please follow me, Miss Kirsten Harald with two a's," he said, pointing the way with a grand, exaggerated flick of his wrist.

Kirsten could have sworn there were tears in the man's eyes as he extended his arm to her, humbly, almost reverently, as though he were offering it to royalty.

As exciting as these two years were for Kirsten, 1956 and 1957 proved to be especially exciting years for the music world in general. Both the Berlin and Vienna philharmonics toured the United States for the first time since the start of the war, the Boston Symphony became the first American orchestra ever to visit the Soviet Union, and violinist Isaac Stern was the first American concert artist in ten years to perform in Moscow's Grand Conservatory. Twenty-three-year-old Toronto-born prodigy Glenn Gould's recording of the "Goldberg Variations" of J. S. Bach made musical history by becoming the first classical record ever to be a best seller. The seventy-fifth birthday of composer Igor Stravinsky was celebrated throughout the world, with his newest ballet, *Agon*, performed in concert form in Los Angeles in honor of the occasion. Conductor Arturo Toscanini died in New York at the age of eighty-nine, and Michael Eastbourne accepted his first permanent position with an orchestra when he was appointed conductor of the London Symphony.

Although Lois Eldershaw was in mild demand for concerts, she and Kirsten seldom crossed paths. There were veiled references made to a simmering rivalry between the two women in the more sensationalist press, but because neither Nelson nor Lois's personal manager, Carey Dundonald, would ever comment on the supposed feud, it remained for most little more than titillating speculation.

Kirsten and Michael managed to see each other only a total of eleven times, meeting however briefly, and gorging themselves on every delicious morsel of togetherness allowed them. It was time borrowed from rehearsals and social functions, shared in airport lounges and limousines, stolen in concert hall dressing rooms and hotel suites. They found strength in each other's arms, drew sustenance from their closeness, and stored up as many memories as they could for all the barren times between meetings. But what they indulged in private they took great care to disguise in public—both of them wary of the hovering press, the sycophants, the potential informers—careful to keep their true feelings concealed, treating each other with only the most proper deference and respect. Acting as professional colleagues, nothing more.

Every parting was a painful wrench, a devastating blow. At first Kirsten doubted she could ever keep her word about not asking him for more. Yet, where instinct would have had her cling to him, reason loosened her grip. She carried him with her everywhere, his image was tattooed on her flesh and superimposed on the world around her. Every face she saw and every voice she heard was his; she could even feel him holding her when she was alone in bed at night. There were times, however, when she saw their relationship as tragic. Hopeless. Like some terminal disease where the patient languishes and waits and prays for remission. Those were the times she wanted to either end it or ask for more. But she did neither.

Because she had her music.

She learned to prolong the wondrous afterglow from their brief encounters by using her intense feelings to energize her playing and enrich her already remarkably rich sound. And she learned to have faith. To believe the in-between times were simply that—intervals not endings. She even came to think of their relationship in musical terms. As a series of beautiful preludes. Because, like the prelude, each meeting and every parting was an exquisitely self-contained and unique experience. It was good this way, she finally concluded. And

safe. Something she found as surprising as it was reassuring.
With Michael in her life so sporadically, she was free to keep
all of her energies funneled in one direction and one direction only: her music.

"Are you sitting down, Kirsten?" Nelson's voice came over
the wire with a boom, and Kirsten held the receiver away
from her ear for a moment to recover. "Because if you're not,
you'd better be." She obligingly plunked herself down on the
white silk chaise next to the telephone table in her bedroom
and told him she was ready. "Congratulate me, my girl, I
finally did it."

"Did what?"

"Booked you with the New York Philharmonic."

"What!" Kirsten was up on her feet again.

"He wants you, Kirsten, Lenny wants you."

"My God."

"You'll be replacing Gary Graffman for the season closer in
five days. You know Liszt's E Flat Major Piano Concerto,
don't you?"

Kirsten swallowed hard. "Yes, I know it." It was a spectacular piece, difficult and flamboyant, and part of the repertoire
of every pianist specializing in the Romantic composers.

"I'm sorry I couldn't do better than a replacement for
you, Kirsten, but at least it's Carnegie Hall."

Carnegie Hall. When Kirsten hung up, she began repeating those two sacred words over and over again. Carnegie
Hall. Carnegie Hall. Finally. For reasons neither she nor
Nelson could fathom, Dmitri Mitropoulos had never once
asked her to play with the Philharmonic. It was a slight that
had hurt her deeply, an open wound that still rankled. But
now Leonard Bernstein, that master showman with an unparalleled flair for the dramatic, wanted her. And his wanting
her more than made up for his predecessor's snub. She
hugged herself tightly and danced around the room, humming the opening bars of the Liszt. Then she danced herself
over to the telephone again and called Nelson back.

"Get the three best seats in the house and reserve them for
my parents and Natalya," she blurted out even before saying
hello.

"That's already been taken care of." Her manager sounded
extremely pleased with himself. "Next?"

"Have someone from your office deliver a complimentary

ticket to a salesman at Steinway & Sons by the name of Ralph Bowers."

"Ralph Bowers," he repeated, jotting it down. "Next?"

"Cable Eric and Claudia in London. No, never mind, I'll call them." She paused, knowing there was one more thing. "Oh, yes, contact Carnegie Hall and see if they have an address for a Paul Bell, who rents a studio there"

"And if they do?"

"Send him a ticket."

"Anything else?"

Kirsten laughed. "Isn't that enough? Thank you, Nelson, thank you a million times over." She blew him a kiss and hung up again. Then she strolled calmly into the den, where her father was reading and her mother was curled up on the couch next to him knitting. They both looked up at the same time.

"Pappy, is your new tuxedo pressed?" she asked her father in a tone she hoped would pass for nonchalance.

"Of course it's pressed," Gianna answered for him. "I pressed it myself after he wore it to Anna-Marie's wedding last month." Anna-Marie was Aunt Sophia's youngest daughter.

Kirsten sighed as if to say some things would never change. And they wouldn't. Her mother still refused to have the dry cleaner press her father's suits.

"And you, Mama, you haven't worn that new cocktail suit yet, have you?" Gianna shook her head. "Well, it looks as though you'll be wearing it sooner than you expected. Be-cau-au-au-ause"—she stretched the word out until she was breathless, then paused for effect, and flung her arms wide—"five days from today," she shouted, "your daughter, Kirsten Harald, is going to be playing Carnegie Hall!"

Inside the acoustical paradise that had been the official home of the New York Philharmonic since 1892, Kirsten paced her private dressing room and waited. When she got tired of pacing, she practiced awhile on the Steinway concert vertical in the anteroom. But practicing only made her more nervous. Quickly giving that up, she went over to the tiny window looking out onto the red, white, and gold horseshoe-shaped hall, and watched the audience file in. She still couldn't believe that tonight she wouldn't be one of them, that tonight she would finally be performing for them instead.

If only Michael were there, she thought. If only she could walk out onto the stage knowing he was watching her, applauding her, cheering for her. But tonight he was guest-conducting in Prague. Tonight of all nights he was a whole world away from her. Her bottom lip began to quiver. This was the most difficult part of their arrangement, adding yet another triumph to the growing list of triumphs they hadn't been able to share.

She wouldn't be sharing her triumph with Eric and Claudia either. When she called to give them the news, Randolph, the butler, told her the couple was in Manchester and gave her the number of their hotel. Eric's disappointment was as great as hers, but he was embroiled in final negotiations over the purchase of a small local shipping line, and because the talks had reached a critical stage, suspending them even for a day was virtually impossible. He then confided in typical Eric fashion that given his disastrous experience with Wynford Hall, he was dealing only in commercial matters again—not personal ones—where his success rate was infinitely higher, and that, as part of his diversification program, he had already acquired a chain of small hotels in Brighton, a canning factory in Liverpool, and a pottery works in Stafford.

"It's time, Miss Harald," the stage manager called out, and Kirsten's entire body turned to jelly. She tried to move and couldn't. Catching sight of her reflection in the mirror above the dressing table, she almost didn't recognize the apparition staring back at her. She drew in a deep breath and willed Michael to be there in the room with her, to calm and steady her, just as he had the night of her recital at Wigmore Hall. She whispered his name and felt his arms close around her like a cloak. She whispered it again and felt his kisses on her forehead, her eyelids, the tip of her nose, her chin, her mouth.

"Miss Harald?"

The image disintegrated. Turning slowly away from the mirror, she took her first, unsteady step toward the door.

She was a vision of majestic calmness, in full command of herself once more as she swept onto the stage, the fine pleats of her lavender crepe gown swirling around her body and giving the impression that she was floating, not walking. The applause crescendoed with each step she took, each step that brought her nearer the Steinway whose upstage leg rested on a tiny screw in the highly varnished blond wood floor known as the Horowitz mark—the precise spot where the legendary pianist had once declared the hall's already perfect acoustics to be their most perfect.

She gazed out toward the audience and saw only the refracted glare from the lights. She felt isolated, elevated, as though some celestial beacon were lifting her up and carrying her off, allowing her to hear everything, yet see nothing. The diffused light began to solidify. She became its focus. Its radiant epicenter. Like a human halo, all the light now emanated from her. She looked around and instantly knew where she was. She was standing alone at the top of the golden mountain, where even the air was golden.

She took her place at the piano and gazed up into the handsome face of Leonard Bernstein. In his black tails, he appeared more darkly sensual than ever, his thick black hair forming a dramatic frame for his generously molded features. But when he trained his famous smile on her, it was someone else's smile she saw. The baton he raised was someone else's; the nod he cued her with was someone else's too. It wasn't Bernstein steering her through all three dramatic movements of the Liszt—the allegro maestoso, quasi adagio, and allegro marziale animato. It wasn't even Bernstein who kissed her hand and led her closer to the edge of the stage at the grand and glorious conclusion of her performance. It was Eastbourne. For Kirsten, it would always be Eastbourne.

She exited in triumph, her arms filled with the flowers they had tossed onstage to her, her ears ringing with the sound of their adulation. When she sailed into the Stork Club on Nelson's arm, with her parents, Gianna clutching a half dozen programs, Natalya and her father following, the acclaim continued. Many of the people in the club had also attended the concert, and one by one they all rose to applaud her again. The word was quickly passed around, spreading from table to table, until everyone in the place knew she was there. Flashbulbs exploded in her face. She was asked to sign everything from autograph books and programs to matchbooks, napkins, and handkerchiefs. One man even had her sign the cuff of his formal white dress shirt.

Setting down what seemed to be her tenth glass of champagne, she used the table for support and pushed herself to her feet; she desperately needed to use the ladies' room. Knowing everyone was watching her, she tried to walk with as much dignity as her advanced state of inebriation would allow, but the path she wove through the crowded club was still a shaky one. She had the feeling that she was battling a strong wind—the harder she tried to move forward, the harder the wind tried to force her back. When she finally reached the ladies' room, she pushed the door open and heaved a loud sigh of relief.

The tall man at the mirror immediately stopped trying to readjust his tie and turned to stare at her. "I believe you want the other door," he said in a clipped voice that spoke of old money, position, and Yale.

Kirsten blinked. "I do?"

"You do."

She didn't understand. "Why are you in the ladies' room?" she asked him.

"I'm not in the ladies' room."

"You're not?"

"No, I'm not." He seemed to be looming over her, blocking the light, so that all she could see were twin images of herself reflected in his close-set black eyes. There was a compelling arrogance about his lean, handsome face. His narrow features were drawn in spare and precise detail, and the slightly cynical curl to his mouth lent him an almost sinister appeal. "You, my dear"—one black eyebrow was arched in amusement as he said this—"happen to be in the men's room."

"Oh, no." Kirsten's cheeks were beginning to blaze. "I don't think I feel very well."

The stranger laughed. "I'm not surprised, not with all the champagne you've been drinking."

But Kirsten hadn't heard him. She was staring at his hands. They were large and broad, their backs covered with fine black hair. His fingers were beautifully shaped, strong and disturbingly seductive. She shivered as a pang of something exciting and unexplainable shot through her.

"Are you all right?"

She didn't know why, but she shook her head.

"Here, let me have a look at you."

"Why?" She took an uneasy step backward. "Are you a doctor?"

"Yes, as a matter of fact, I am." He seized her by the elbow, and before she could protest he was guiding her out of the door toward one of several chairs located near the cloakroom. He saw her safely seated, then crouched down in front of her. "Do you feel faint?" he asked, and she nodded. "Then put your head between your knees. That's right. Now, hold it just like that."

He obviously didn't trust her to follow his instructions, because the moment she bent forward, he placed his hand on the top of her head and kept it there. His touch was as surprisingly gentle as it was authoritative. Comforting and paternal. Yet something more, far more. It suddenly made being in his presence a strangely disquieting experience.

"Would you like to try raising your head now?" he asked.

"Not particularly," she answered truthfully.

He chuckled. "All right, then, just let me know when you're ready."

She didn't think she would ever be ready; she wished she could go on sitting there with his hand warming the top of her head forever. But she knew she couldn't. She was being ridiculous. And so, long before she really wanted to, she forced herself to raise her head again while he gently supported the back of her neck.

"How do you feel now?" he inquired. "Better, worse, or the same?"

Kirsten blinked several times and gave her head a cautious shake. "Better, I guess."

"But not perfect."

"I think better is as good as I can expect to feel right now."

He waited another few minutes, then helped her up. Wagging a stern finger at her, he said, "No more champagne now, all right?"

The thought of another glass of champagne made her want to gag. "No more, I promise." She was far less secure standing up than she had been sitting down, and although she was tempted to have him wait and walk her back to her table, she restrained herself. Holding out her hand, she gave him a brave smile. "Thank you, Doctor . . ." She paused, waiting for him to fill in his name.

"Oliver," he promptly supplied. "Jeffrey Powell Oliver."

"I'm Kir—"

"I know who you are, Miss Harald," he said with a smile that made her pulse quicken. "I heard you at Carnegie Hall this evening. You were extraordinary." His dark eyes seemed almost sad as he released her hand. "And now, if you'll excuse me, I have some people waiting."

Kirsten felt abandoned as she watched him head back

toward his own table. Her disappointment at his abrupt departure shocked her; the lingering effects of their brief encounter astounded her. But even more unsettling was the realization that while she was in the company of the icily attractive Dr. Oliver, she hadn't thought about Michael once.

15

Jeffrey Powell Oliver was possessed. His entire six-foot frame had been taken over by a diminutive spirit—black-haired and violet-eyed, with a devilish innocence and a pair of magical hands with the power to spin musical floss into gold. The impact of his first encounter with Kirsten Harald had exploded like a grenade inside him, shattering his usual upper-class reserve and turning his aristocratic insides to mush. Impulsiveness—never an Oliver trait—had squared off against caution, and the resultant battle was sending him on a rocketing, gut-clenching roller-coaster ride. Where reason had once ruled all of his baser instincts, chaos now reigned. Yet sanity, as diminished a capacity as it was, still prevailed long enough to make him wait an entire day before calling and inviting her to dinner.

Kirsten was finally going out on her first official date. As unlikely as it seemed, the acclaimed concert pianist who was embroiled in a secret and sporadic transatlantic affair with one of the world's greatest conductors was still very much that same naive girl who had once asked her piano teacher about love. And just like a teenager getting ready for her first date, she was nervous and giggly; she talked incessantly and couldn't decide what to wear.

"What do you know about this man anyway?" Gianna couldn't help asking as she watched her daughter spray herself with perfume.

"Not very much really." Kirsten set the atomizer down and leaned closer to the mirror on her vanity. "Do you think I need some more eye shadow?"

"You could be going out with a masher, and all you're worried about is your eye shadow?"

"Mama, please. Dr. Oliver comes from one of the finest families in New York; he lives on a Long Island estate and heads the Powell Oliver Institute for Medical Research. Does he sound like a masher to you?"

Gianna shrugged. "Well, you said it yourself, this is your first date."

"Mothers." Kirsten rolled her eyes in a perfect imitation of Gianna. If her mother were reacting this way to a simple date, how would she have taken the news that her dateless daughter was no longer a virgin? The very thought of it brought a flush to her cheeks and with it a twinge of guilt. As though by accepting this date with Jeffrey she was somehow betraying Michael. She tried to shake off the uncomfortable feeling by telling herself that nothing could ever affect what she had with him. Their relationship was too special. Separate and apart from everything else in her life. The secret she shared with no one. Besides, he was married, wasn't he? He had a wife and family. Surely she could be allowed one date. She was almost belligerent now. But when the door chimes rang, announcing the arrival of that date, she felt uneasy all over again.

"We have your usual table as you requested, Dr. Oliver." The mâitre d' at Lutèce gathered up several menus and a wine list, and led them through the restaurant as famous for its fine food as it was for the people who dined there.

Kirsten was well aware of the stir their entrance had caused; there was hardly a table where Jeffrey wasn't stopped by someone he knew. And each time he introduced her, it was with the possessive pride of a winning bidder in a high-stakes auction.

"You're positively glowing," Jeffrey remarked when they were finally seated. "You like attention, I see."

"You seem to handle it quite well yourself," she tossed back at him with surprising ease.

When the waiter arrived to take their drinks order, instead of ordering for both of them the way Michael always did, Jeffrey asked Kirsten what she wanted. For a moment she was at a loss.

"What are you having?" she asked.

"A martini with a twist."

"Then I'll have the same." But she wondered what a twist was.

"Two martinis with a twist, Anton," Jeffrey told the waiter, "but keep the vermouth down to a whisper."

Kirsten stared at him. He made a martini sound like something you could order only if you knew the secret code. She could hardly wait to try it. But when she took her first sip of the mysterious concoction, she was disappointed. It reminded her of nail polish remover. Except that it slammed into her stomach with the force of a sledgehammer, making her gasp and her eyes start to tear.

"Would you prefer something a little less potent?" Jeffrey was watching her with a tender smile on his face. "A sherry or some Dubonnet?"

"No, thanks." Kirsten's voice came out sounding slightly raspy. "It's not that bad once you get used to it."

"You don't have to get used to it, you know."

"Oh, but I want to." She swallowed some more of the foul-tasting drink. "This is a challenge."

"It's really an acquired taste more than anything else."

"Like asparagus."

"Or caviar."

Kirsten considered the contents of her glass. "I don't think I'll ever like martinis as much as I like . . ." She hesitated somewhat coyly.

"Caviar?"

She grinned at him and shook her head. "Asparagus."

As he watched her take another sip of her drink, Jeffrey found himself becoming hopelessly infatuated with her hands. They were such perfect hands. Small and delicate, yet strong and capable and commanding. How he envied her such gifted hands. He gazed sadly down at his own hands. They were take-charge hands to be sure. But they were still only the hands of an administrator. Not the surgeon he had wanted to be.

"A penny for your thoughts."

Jeffrey started. He felt something cold pressing against the back of his right hand.

"As I said"—Kirsten's glass was empty and she was giggling— "a penny for your thoughts."

"I was thinking about how beautiful you are."

"Liar."

"You're right." He tossed the penny in the air, called out heads, and watched it land on tails. "I was really thinking that we should order dinner before you ask for a refill."

Kirsten made a face and twirled her empty glass between her thumb and forefinger. "Not much danger of that," she assured him. "I think I'll stick to—"

"Asparagus?"

"Uh-uh. Caviar."

During dinner Kirsten decided that one of the most intriguing things about Jeffrey Powell Oliver was his insatiable curiosity about her. No sooner had she answered one of his questions than he promptly asked her another. She barely touched the coquelet à la crème aux morilles she had ordered and concentrated on her wine instead. It wasn't long before her head was spinning. Whether it was because of the wine or because of the man, she didn't know. What she did know was that she felt wonderfully intoxicated and thoroughly relaxed.

Leaning her elbow on the table, she rested her chin in her cupped hand and peered blearily at Jeffrey, who was just finishing the last of his rognons de veau au vin rouge. "Are you sure you're not really a reporter who's going to make a fortune by selling everything I've been telling you to some magazine?"

"Damn, you've found me out." Jeffrey sighed as he patted the breast pocket of his jacket. "As a matter of fact, I have the world's smallest tape recorder hidden right in here."

"I thought so." Her head wobbled and nearly slipped out of her hand. "In that case, it's your turn now. Tell me about you. If you're Jeffrey Powell Oliver the second, there must be a Jeffrey Powell Oliver the first out there somewhere."

Jeffrey's smile was rueful. "There was. My parents are dead though. They drowned in a boating accident off Long Island Sound seven years ago."

"Oh, Jeffrey, I'm sorry. I shouldn't have—"

"Don't be silly. How were you to know?" He held his hands out, fingers splayed, and scowled. "My father always maintained it wasn't what a man did that counted, it was who he was and who came before him. I wanted to be a surgeon; my father just wanted me to be an Oliver. According to him, Oliver men were meant to serve the world in a more indirect way—through endowments, charities, foundations, trusts, those sorts of things. All very noble and generous, of course, but hardly involving. It didn't even seem to matter to him that the man who started the illustrious Oliver dynasty in the first place was an illiterate fur trader who was once jailed for stealing a horse." Kirsten put her hand over her mouth to stifle a laugh, but Jeffrey was smiling too. "My mother wasn't much better. She believed the main obligation of every proper

Long Island gentleman was to satisfy the demands of the
purse first, the heart second. In other words, marry for
money and keep your own money safe. I suppose I let them
both down." His voice grew serious again. "I always thought
of myself as special, you see. I wanted to be more than just
another proper Long Island gentleman; I wanted to be a
savior. Unfortunately, these hands of mine weren't the brilliant instruments every self-respecting savior needs." His
hands abruptly disappeared into his lap. "So I became a
cardiologist instead. I built up a fairly solid practice for myself
on Park Avenue, but I still couldn't help feeling I was really a
savior in disguise, waiting for the day when my hands would
turn into the masterful healing tools they were supposed to
be."

Over coffee and mousse chocolat au rhum, Jeffrey finished
his story. "My older brother Charles was originally supposed
to have headed the institute. But five months before its
official opening six years ago, he suffered a stroke." Here
Jeffrey's voice suddenly quavered. "It left him without speech
and completely paralyzed on his right side. He was thirty-
seven when it happened, exactly one year older than I am
right now." He set his cup down and Kirsten saw that his
hand was shaking. "So now, instead of a scalpel or a stethoscope, I wield a pen." Some of his former humor returned
as he added, "And it's a pretty weighty pen at that. We've
already begun our second expansion program in three years."
Then with a snap of his fingers he not only signaled their
waiter for the check but put an end to their conversation as
well.

What he didn't tell Kirsten was that in spite of his best
intentions, he had, however, become very much his late
father's son. As the titular head of the Oliver family these last
six years, he had evolved into a perfect example of how every
head of an old family with old money should behave. He
attended all the right social functions, supported all the right
causes and charities, befriended all the right people, and
voted respectably, right-thinking Republican. The only area
in which he had continued to rebel was marriage. While poor
Charles had married correctly several years before his stroke,
he himself had remained blissfully free. Free to select and
discard, refusing to spend a lifetime being bored by the same
women who had bored him as girls. Seeking that one special
female who was different. A challenge. Who stimulated,

amazed, and amused. Who could offer him more than simply her pedigree. He signed his name to the check with a flourish and added "II" after the Oliver, something he seldom did. Because suddenly—and perhaps not so inexplicably—he had found himself thinking about sons.

It was one-thirty by the time Kirsten tiptoed into the apartment. Her mother had turned down the bed for her, but thankfully, neither of her parents was up. She was exhausted, and she knew the effects of her late night with Jeffrey would show when she had her lesson with Natalya at ten. She groaned and rubbed her eyes with her hands. They didn't feel like her hands at all; they felt limp and rubbery. Just like the rest of her body. Tumbling into bed still half dressed, she tried to untangle her muddled feelings: Was it Jeffrey or the alcohol or both?

She trembled when she thought of how he had kissed all ten of her fingers individually as his way of saying good night at the door. It had aroused a terrible yearning in her. Turning onto her side, she drew her knees up to her chin. She was ashamed of the sensations Jeffrey had been able to stir in her, ashamed and very much afraid of them. She thought of Michael and her eyes began to fill. She felt like a traitor.

Jeffrey Powell Oliver had touched her as only Michael had ever touched her before. He fascinated her—this scion of wealth and power with the heart of a humanitarian, haughty and proud, yet poignantly tender and self-effacing at the same time. And the way he looked at her made her feel light-headed and giddy, and gave her a renewed sense of herself as a woman. A beautiful and desirable woman.

She didn't remember falling asleep. But she woke up at four to find the lower half of her body jerking spasmodically to the irregular rhythm of a dream-induced orgasm. Wave upon wave of tingly heat washed over her, flooding her with a soothing warmth, until she shuddered violently one last time, then lay still. Her heart was pounding, her thighs were damp, her nipples stiff, and there was a satisfied throbbing deep inside her. But when she realized whose phantom strokings had brought her to orgasm, she buried her face in her pillow and wept.

Following their first dinner together at Lutèce, Kirsten and Jeffrey began seeing each other twice, sometimes three times a week. It was summer, Kirsten's schedule was light, and

Jeffrey slipped into her life with an ease that astonished her. He was something she had never permitted herself before: a diversion. And she took great pains to ensure he remained a diversion. Nothing more. Nothing that might ultimately threaten her equanimity or subvert her fierce loyalty to her music. But in spite of her efforts, it was undeniably a battle, one that Natalya made even more difficult.

"Since when do we release the pedal in the middle of a phrase?" she would demand. "Again please, from the beginning, and try to concentrate on the music, not on that man you're seeing."

"How stupid of me, I thought Beethoven wrote that particular concerto in the key of B flat."

"*En animant*, Kirishka!" One long, scarlet-tipped finger would stab impatiently at the page. "It means livelier, remember? You couldn't possibly have gotten more than five hours sleep last night."

"Congratulations, Kirishka, you've just played eight wrong notes in a row. And he's been out of town for only two days. What's going to happen to you in September?"

And so it went. Up and down like the proverbial seesaw—Jeffrey on one end, Natalya on the other, and Kirsten herself in the middle, fighting hard to keep everything in perfect balance. With Jeffrey, she had the one thing she never had with Michael: the luxury of time. Of spending hours with him undisturbed. Of seeing him two evenings in a row. Of knowing he was as close as Long Island. As near to her as a telephone call or a limousine ride.

He treated her with a tender reverence that made her feel like a priceless piece of porcelain. His kisses were almost tremblingly sweet, as gentlemanly as he was himself, and in his arms she felt cherished and adored. He would caress her the way one caresses an animal that's not fully tamed, as though he were afraid she might jump up and bolt if he were the slightest bit rough with her. And yet, he was unreservedly ardent about her hands. He couldn't seem to get enough of them—of holding them, stroking them, kissing them. He would suck each of her fingers into his mouth in turn, lightly clamp his teeth around it, and circle it over and over again with the moistened tip of his tongue. With his eyes closed and a gentle half smile on his face, he looked as content as an infant suckling at his mother's breast.

But above all, Jeffrey was courtly; he wooed her. And she

allowed him to spoil her shamelessly. He sent her boxes of cut flowers, never the same variety twice. He gave her gifts—a mother-of-pearl compact, a jeweled evening bag, a pair of carved ivory combs to wear in her hair, a signed Tiffany paperweight, an antique silver and amethyst brooch. Fully cooked dinners would arrive unannounced from "21" for her parents and her. He mailed her greeting cards for no other reason than to let her know he was thinking of her. He took her for open carriage rides through Central Park at sunset.

As the weeks passed, she couldn't think of Jeffrey without thinking of the word *security*. He made her feel anchored, protected, and safe, just as her father always had. But he also presented her with a problem. She was now a woman with two men in her life, two very different men with very different claims on her. And she was confused. Conflicted. Afraid that her growing dependency on Jeffrey would affect her relationship with Michael. Afraid that her feelings for one would negate what she felt for the other. She began each day in fear of being asked to choose between them; she even started waking up in the morning with her fists balled, her entire body braced for a possible confrontation.

For the first time in her brief career she watched September approach with a mixture of anticipation and dread. It was nearly time for her to withdraw, close the doors on the temptations of the outside world and channel all of her energies back into her music again. Now she found herself faced with a new dilemma. Jeffrey wasn't just a diversion anymore, he had grown far beyond that. She knew she would never be able to contain him the way she contained Michael. He was free, he could give her what Michael couldn't: all of himself. And the thought of it terrified her.

Her season opened in Pittsburgh, and the night before she was scheduled to leave she practiced until ten, called Jeffrey to say good-bye to him, then went straight to bed. The phone woke her up at two.

"Kirsten, it's Michael."

The receiver slid out of her hand and banged against the edge of the night table before landing on the carpet. She fumbled around for it in the dark.

"I—I'm sorry," she stammered. "I dropped the phone."

His laugh sent chills running through her. "I know, I have the ringing in my left ear to prove it. Sorry if I woke you; sometimes I forget all about the time difference." He lowered his voice, making it almost impossible for Kirsten to hear what he said next. "I'm calling from home, so I'll have to make this brief. Glenn Gould just canceled his appearance with the Berlin Philharmonic on the ninth of October. I'm guest-conducting that night and I need a replacement. The moment I realized what concerto he was supposed to play, I knew it couldn't be anyone but you."

"Rachmaninoff's Second?" Kirsten ventured, holding her breath.

"Rachmaninoff's Second."

Her heart began to swell until it was filling her entire chest and all of her throat.

"Check your schedule and get back to me as quickly as you can. To me personally, remember that."

As groggy as she was, she didn't miss the urgency in his tone. It even sounded slightly ominous. And then she understood why. Roxanne obviously didn't know. She shivered apprehensively. She didn't even realize Michael had hung up until she heard the hum of the dial tone in her ear.

The Rachmaninoff. *Oh, God,* she prayed, *please let me be free that night. Please, please, please.* She lay down again with her eyes wide open in the darkness and saw herself playing the exquisite concerto with Michael just the way she had imagined herself playing it with him that first night at Carnegie Hall. She immediately forgot about her upcoming concert in Pittsburgh. She even forgot about Jeffrey. All she could think of now was Berlin. And Michael. Michael, whom she hadn't seen in seven long months. Michael, who would be waiting there for her; waiting to make their promise to each other finally come true.

16

"I never thought I'd mind this part so much," Jeffrey grumbled. He and Kirsten were sitting hand in hand in the back of his black Lincoln limousine on their way to Idlewild Airport. "All these comings and goings, how can you stand it? It plays havoc with the system, not to mention what it does to a normal relationship."

Struggling with her own conflicted emotions, Kirsten tried to keep her tone light. "Whoever said a relationship with a musician was normal?" He grunted in response to this, and she moved closer to him on the seat and rested her head on his shoulder. He kissed her tenderly on the forehead.

"I'm going to miss you, Kirsten." His voice sounded hoarse, almost gruff.

"I'm going to miss you too." And she was, much more than she wanted to admit. "But look at the bright side," she said with forced cheerfulness. "It's for only five days this time."

"Only." He groaned. "A vagabond says only."

"Yes, but the true vagabond probably wouldn't come back at all."

She could feel him tense. "Don't even joke about it, Kirsten, please." He turned her toward him and kissed her fiercely. "Don't *ever* joke about it. Promise me that."

"I promise." He kissed her again, softer this time, but the intensity still remained.

As though to hold her to that promise and safeguard her return to him, Jeffrey pressed a small velvet box into her hands when she got out of the car and told her not to open it until she was on the plane. She kissed him one last time, then broke away from him before he could see the tears in her eyes. And when she opened his gift just prior to takeoff, fresh tears instantly welled up and began spilling over the tops of her bottom lashes. He had given her a gold pin in the shape of a forget-me-not, its petals formed out of marquise-cut sapphires, its heart a small round diamond.

She tossed in and out of a restless sleep all the way across the Atlantic. Her dreams were fragmented and disorderly. Concert grands that shrank and then grew larger again. Flash-bulbs popping, the sound of applause. Oversize headlines. Photographs torn in half. Seesaws in the shape of triangles going up and down, up and down. Tears turning into diamonds, then back into tears again. Her name spelled backward in lavender ink.

She woke up gasping for breath, her pulse racing, her upper lip beaded with perspiration. She rang for the stewardess and asked for a glass of water. Then she glanced anxiously at her watch. In another three hours they would be landing in Berlin. Her pulse started to race all over again, but this time it had nothing whatsoever to do with the jumbled dreams.

Michael had booked them into the Hotel Kempinski, but

in separate suites on separate floors of course. Stopping off at the hotel just long enough to shower and change her clothes, Kirsten hailed a taxi and arrived at the Philharmonic exactly one hour before rehearsals were scheduled to begin. She was panting by the time she finally managed to locate Michael's dressing room. There were only fifty-three minutes remaining now, yet something made her hesitate before she knocked. Out of the corner of her eye she could see the gleam of one of the sapphire petals on the brooch she had fastened to the collar of her jacket. She felt an eerie tugging sensation in the pit of her stomach; her body swayed uncertainly. Grabbing hold of the doorjamb for support, she took a deep breath to steady herself, then rapped gently on the door.

Even as Michael pulled her into his arms, she continued to waver. This was the first time she had seen him since meeting Jeffrey, and the confusion she had considered safely dealt with was surfacing all over again. The definite boundaries that usually kept both men clearly separated were hazy now; the images were overlapping. Jeffrey was as much a part of their embrace as she and Michael were, and the fit was extremely awkward.

"Kirsten?" Michael was regarding her quizzically.

She smiled to cover her ambivalence. "I'm sorry."

Jeffrey's had been the last lips to touch hers, but Michael's were beginning to erase the imprint of them. She felt a familiar stirring deep inside her. Jeffrey was fading, his hold gradually weakening as Michael reasserted his prior claim on her. When he took her face in his hands and began covering her features with tiny kisses, she opened her eyes to watch him. His eyes held hers for a fraction of a second before he kissed her on the mouth again—kissed her with a yearning that melted her resistance and dispelled whatever conflict remained.

Their kisses grew hungrier as they themselves grew needier. Seven months of separation had left them starved and greedy. They tugged and tore at each other in an attempt to appease their hunger and assuage their need, but nothing helped. Whatever they did only inflamed them further.

"Tonight," Michael whispered to her between kisses. His whole body was so engorged with desire he could feel it bursting through his clothes. "We'll have all night together."

Kirsten dug her fingers deeper into his scalp and rotated her hips against his. Tonight. All night. What a sweet and wonderful thought. So full of delicious promise. The first whole night they had ever spent together. At last. They would have time to make long and luxurious love. Time to fill in the spaces the seven intervening months had created. Time to wake up in the morning in each other's arms and make love again. Time on their side for a change.

Michael glanced uneasily toward the door, as though he expected someone to come hurtling through it at any moment, then led Kirsten over to the worn green velvet couch that faced his dressing table. Drawing her down onto his lap, he cradled her in his arms and pressed his lips against her forehead. After the tempest, this was the calm, yet the feeling was no less intense for either of them. Stirring contentedly in his embrace, Kirsten asked him as gently as she could how he had finally been able to arrange for them to play together. The way his body immediately stiffened told her more than his words ever would.

"I simply presented it to Roxanne as a fait accompli."

His abrupt answer fell short of the actual truth. He still couldn't comprehend Roxanne's continued resistance to his playing with Kirsten. He had spent months arguing that it made no sense for him to be the only conductor in the world—with the exception of Eduard van Beinum—who wasn't playing with her. But as he recalled the look of sheer terror on Roxanne's face when he informed her of the first business decision he had ever made without her, he shuddered. She had reacted to the announcement as though he had just told her he was leaving her. And the unexpected violence of her reaction had torn him apart.

"Herr Eastbourne?" It was the concertmaster at the door.

Kirsten and Michael sprung apart like a pair of startled deer. After hastily straightening their clothes, they presented themselves to the man as a calm and united front and followed him onto the stage. But Kirsten's composure failed her the moment she took her place at the piano. She suddenly forgot the entire Rachmaninoff.

"Are you all right?" Michael called down to her from the podium.

She nodded, waving away his concern with her hand, and took a series of long, deep breaths.

"Kirsten, are you sure?"

At that point she wasn't sure of anything, but she told him she was anyway. He gave her another minute, then started the rehearsal. To her complete amazement, she found she hadn't really forgotten the concerto at all, and the rehearsal proceeded exceptionally smoothly. But that evening, while she was waiting in the wings to make her entrance, the panic returned in full force. She tried to tell herself it was only natural. This was the first time she and Michael had ever played together; she had every right to be nervous. All she needed to do was focus on him and she would be fine.

When she swept onto the stage, no one was aware of her inner turmoil. Not even Michael. He saw only what everyone else saw—a spectacularly beautiful young woman in a flowing lavender gown, whose smile outdazzled the diamonds she was wearing, and whose luminous presence caused everything around her to fade into insignificance. Once she was seated, with her hands clasped lightly in her lap, she looked up from the keyboard just as she always did before they began. She had been pretending for so long that she was actually shocked to discover Michael himself standing there, looking back at her. In his eyes was a tender kiss and the silent acknowledgment of the specialness of this night.

He raised then lowered his baton with a deft flick of the wrist. The opening chords were hers alone. The strings followed. The rest dissolved into a dream. In spite of her fears, she had never played more expressively or poignantly or with more lyrical clarity. Michael may have been conducting an entire orchestra, but to Kirsten he was conducting only her. Their eyes met from time to time, and the energy generated by each glance elevated them and their music and swept them upward on one continuously building harmonic wave.

As she began the third movement's final and most dramatic series of crescendos, Kirsten could feel an exquisite tension swell inside her. It was a bittersweet plea, reaching out from her soul to his, begging him to prolong what was coming and never let it end. But she knew only too well that the end was inevitable. Each minor chord she was playing now was a chord plucked on the strings of her weeping heart. As she reached that final, brutally romantic peak, the tears in her eyes obscured the keys. Her arms fell numbly to her sides while the orchestra sounded the dramatic four-note finale. It was over.

She and Michael took their bows together, their hands tightly locked in secret triumph. It had finally happened. They had played together at last. Their special magic had been witnessed by thousands and recorded live for millions by Deutsche Grammophon, preserving the concert forever. Kirsten was floating, her head grazing heaven, her feet cushioned by marshmallow clouds. When Michael left her at the door to her dressing room, his parting words to her were, "Remember, we have the whole night." But they had a reception at the home of the American ambassador to get through first.

The reception rooms of the imposing gray stone mansion were ablaze with dozens of glittering crystal chandeliers and alive with hundreds of formally attired men and women. Waitresses in crisp black uniforms and white aprons passed among the guests with silver trays of assorted canapés and hors d'oeuvres; waiters offered domestic white and red wines or imported champagne. In a corner of the living room a string quartet was playing selections from Johann Strauss. Michael took two flutes of champagne from the tray of a passing waiter and handed one to Kirsten.

"To us," he said, clinking the rim of his glass against hers. "May tonight be only the beginning."

"To us." She raised her own glass and gulped down half its contents.

They were the center of attention and Kirsten was as warmed by everyone's effusive praises as she was by the champagne. How much longer would they have to stay and continue to exchange polite conversation with complete strangers, she wondered. How long before they could steal away without being missed? She glanced over at Michael, who was talking to the ambassador and his wife. He looked up and met her gaze. A shiver of anticipation ran through her as she watched him excuse himself and start toward her. Taking her by the elbow, he steered her out of the living room into the less crowded adjoining dining room. Her heart lifted expectantly, but quickly plummeted when she looked closely at his expression. He was staring at something over her left shoulder, his features a frozen mask. She turned her head and followed his stare. Coming toward them was a woman wearing a russet brocade cocktail dress that was so superbly draped it merely suggested rather than stated the voluptuousness of the body it concealed. Her thick dark auburn hair was cut short and framed her startlingly sensual face in feathery points. The diamonds and topazes blazing at her ears and throat dramatically accentuated the ivory translucence of her flaw-

less skin, and as she got closer, Kirsten could see that her
eyes were a clear and perfect bottle green.

"No, darling, it's not a ghost." Roxanne Eastbourne's lovely
eyes were growing misty at the sight of her husband. "I know
it was beastly of me, but I wanted to surprise you."

Kirsten could feel herself growing smaller and smaller,
fading first into obscurity, then into total oblivion. To her,
Roxanne Eastbourne looked like the human embodiment of a
brilliant copper flame, warning anyone who dared to threaten
her and hers to stay away or risk being burned alive.

"May I congratulate you on your performance this evening,
Miss Harald?" There was a slight duskiness to Roxanne
Eastbourne's voice, unlike the sharper bell tones of her cousin
Claudia's. "You really were marvelous. My husband was quite
right about you." Turning to Michael, she smiled and lovingly rubbed the side of his face with the back of her hand. "I
would have been here sooner, darling, but after the concert I
went back to your hotel room to change. I don't know why
you booked yourself into the Kempinski when you always
stay at the Savoy."

Kirsten couldn't look Michael in the eye. Instead, she
gulped down the last of her champagne and signaled for
another. Terrified that her face might betray her, she concentrated on the dancing bubbles in her fresh champagne and
tried to get a tighter hold on her stampeding emotions. Then,
once she trusted herself more, she looked up and gave Roxanne what she hoped was an open and friendly smile.

Roxanne's insides were threatening to rebel. It was taking
all of her self-control to stand there and try to keep her glass
of red wine from spilling down the front of her dress. While
the three of them bravely attempted to make idle conversation, all she wanted to do was pull Michael away from the
gloriously gifted Miss Harald and make love to him—if only
to prove to them both that there really was nothing more
between him and the beautiful pianist than their music.

"If the two of you will excuse me, I think I'll get myself
something to eat." Kirsten couldn't bear the thinly disguised
tension another moment. Her skin was burning, her stomach
was an icy, yawning pit. There would be no first night together for them after all. No time to make love. No time to
revel in the joy of their first shared triumph. No time at all.
That she was even thinking this way in the presence of
Michael's wife made her feel ill. Desperate. Guilty and grief-

stricken. Roxanne Eastbourne had a face now. She was real. Kirsten's hand moved involuntarily to her stomach. She didn't want anything to eat; she wanted to lock herself inside the first bathroom she could find and throw up.

As Michael watched Kirsten walk away, he finally understood what it meant to be torn in two. His treachery was a bitter taste on his tongue. He had betrayed his wife and disappointed his lover. He felt trapped. All three of them were. He should have anticipated this; he should have been better prepared.

Kirsten came out of one of the bathrooms on the second floor to find Michael waiting for her. Without saying a word he tugged her back inside and locked the door. Pulling her up against him, he pressed her head to his chest and wrapped his arms around her.

"Kirsten, I'm so sorry," he whispered into her hair. "I had no idea she'd be here tonight, none whatsoever. And I'd wanted the whole night to be so perfect for you."

"Don't talk," she pleaded with him, her voice quivering. "Hold me, just hold me."

When he knew he wouldn't be able to continue holding her without wanting to kiss her too, he gently took her arms from around his neck, squeezed her hands once, and backed away from her. "I have something for you," he said, clearing his throat to take some of the hoarseness out of it. Placing a small brown leather pouch in the palm of her right hand, he closed her fingers around it and smiled at her. "I know it won't compensate for tonight, but it might help a little." After giving her one more hug, he unlocked the door and left.

She waited another few minutes, then she left too. But instead of returning to the party downstairs, she went back to the hotel. It wasn't until she had undressed and climbed into bed that she finally loosened the narrow leather drawstring on the pouch Michael had given her and opened it. She dipped her hand inside and took out a delicate gold-link bracelet with a single flat gold charm hanging from it. No larger than a nickel, it was shaped like a grand piano. She turned it over and her eyes began to swim. On the back of the charm, engraved in a light script, was the word "Berlin" and beneath it, the date: 10/9/58.

Blinded by a rush of helpless tears, it was nearly impossible for her to see clearly enough to fasten the bracelet around her left wrist, but she eventually managed. Then she switched off the light and lay down in the dark. Using the thumb and index finger of her right hand, she caressed the gold charm until she had memorized its shape. The longer she rubbed its smooth, cool surface, the warmer it became, while the space reserved for Michael beside her in bed grew colder and colder.

He should have been there with her. They should have been allowed to spend this special night together. She should have known better than to expect a miracle. Should, should, should. There were too many shoulds. She was getting tired of all the shoulds. The hours ticked by with agonizing slowness; she couldn't fall asleep. The emptiness was too intense.

She nearly knocked over the lamp in her haste to get to the telephone. She gave the operator the number and waited, breathing heavily, impatiently counting off the rings one by one. And then he was on the line, and the operator was telling her to go ahead, please.

"Jeffrey?" she shouted into the receiver across the thousands of miles that separated them. "Oh, Jeffrey, I'm so glad I got you. I just needed to hear your voice."

Two floors above Kirsten, Michael and Roxanne were still awake, lying stiffly in each other's arms, a shaky wall of fearful and embarrassed silence between them. Although neither of them had mentioned Kirsten by name, she was a lingering presence in the room nonetheless, a presence they tried to deny and couldn't. Roxanne turned onto her side, away from Michael, and allowed a pair of silent tears to trickle down her cheeks into her pillow. She didn't dare close her eyes though. Each time she did, she could see the two of them together. First Michael and Kirsten Harald. Then—she coughed, choking on the sordidness of the memory—her father and her cousin Claudia.

Claudia as a child, receiving the love she herself was consistently denied. Seeing him holding her hand, taking her for walks, sitting with her on his knee. Sharing with his niece what he refused to share with his own daughter. Claudia as a budding woman. Reaching for his hand on her own. Seeing the two of them whispering and laughing together. Discovering them by chance in the secret room behind the wine cellar, the one room in the house she had thought was her own private hideaway. Watching her naked father bounce a grown and naked Claudia on his knee. Staring as her cousin moved up and down like one of the carved wooden horses on her carousel. Seeing Claudia banished from their home, but not from their lives, because the love her father had reserved solely for Claudia was never diverted to her.

She moaned, and Michael pressed himself up against her, flinging one leg across her cold, trembling body to warm and protect her. But Roxanne didn't respond. She continued to lie there motionless, rigid with fear. Was she supposed to share Michael with Kirsten Harald now, the way she had once shared her father with Claudia? She squeezed her eyes shut to staunch the flow of her tears, but it didn't stop them from pouring out of her. She was in so much pain that she almost wanted to die. And she would too. Because if Michael ever stopped loving her, she knew that was precisely what would happen.

Desperate in his concern for her, Michael innocently misinterpreted the reason for his wife's anguish. He couldn't blame her for crying; he felt like crying himself. It wasn't her fault, it was his. For the first time in all their years of exquisite lovemaking, he had been impotent.

17

"You're spoiling us, *carissima*," Gianna protested, although not particularly strenuously, as Emil closed the last of their three suitcases and set it down on the floor alongside the others. "Last year it was the trip to Scandinavia, six months ago it was the cruise of the Caribbean, and now you're sending us off to Europe for a month. It's too much."

"Is it now?" Kirsten's eyes were sparkling with delight. "Since I was the one who finally got you both to quit work, I had to find something to keep you busy, didn't I?"

Emil put his arms around his daughter and kissed the top of her dark head. "You're wonderful to be doing all this for us, Kirsty, and we thank you for it, we truly do," he told her in the gentle voice she loved. "But like your mother said, it really is too much."

"No, it's not, Pappy. It could never be too much as far as

I'm concerned." She reached up to pat him tenderly on the cheek. "Besides, this isn't just *any* trip, it's an occasion. You're celebrating your fortieth wedding anniversary next week, remember?"

But Gianna wouldn't be deterred. Wagging a playful finger at Kirsten, she said, "You can't fool me for a minute. The real reason you want us to take this trip is so you can be alone here with Jeffrey."

"Mama!" Kirsten actually started to blush.

"Gianna, you're embarrassing her." Emil grabbed hold of his wife's pointing finger and gave it a quick shake, but she persisted anyway.

"Who's going to clean up the place and take care of all your clothes while we're gone?"

"Marta will." Marta was the woman she had hired when they had first moved into the apartment. "But I'll be away most of the month myself, so please, Mama, stop worrying about me. Right now you should be sounding less like a mother and more like a bride leaving on her honeymoon. Pappy"—she made an imploring gesture with her hands— "please phone for the limousine before you end up having to take this trip by yourself."

By the time they finally left—after much hugging and kissing and last-minute instructions from Gianna on how to defrost and cook all the food she had left in the freezer— Kirsten was twenty minutes late for her lesson with Natalya. She arrived apologetic and distracted, and got no further than the middle of the first movement in the Mendelssohn concerto they were working on before Natalya made her stop.

"So the good doctor's out of town again, is he?" Kirsten's jaw dropped. "It's obvious, I could hear it in your playing. This isn't like you, Kirishka, and I'm worried." Kirsten began toying with the heart-shaped amethyst ring Jeffrey had given her and said nothing. "How much does he mean to you, Kirsten, I think I have a right to know."

Kirsten abruptly stopped toying with the ring and gazed up at her teacher with a dreamy look in her eyes. "He's my best friend, Natalya." She said it in such a quiet voice that the aging Russian just barely heard her. "My first date and my first friend too; strange, isn't it? Oh, Natalya, please don't scowl. You of all people should understand, you know how excruciatingly lonely it can be. Jeffrey adores me, Natalya, he makes me feel I'm the most important person in his life. Did you know that he always asks me to play something for him before we go out? And when I do, he sits there with such an enraptured look on his face that you'd think he'd never heard a piano before." Her own face was glowing as she spoke, her eyes as bright as the stone in her ring. "Playing for Jeffrey isn't the same as playing for an audience; no one's real to me when I'm performing. Jeffrey is very real. At the end of my concerts everyone else always has someone to leave with, while I always leave alone. But after I've played for Jeffrey, he's right there waiting for me. He's also there at the end of every one of my tours, and just knowing I have him to come home to makes all the difference in the world."

Natalya fingered the heavy gold chains that were looped around her neck and thought very carefully about what Kirsten had just said. Then she leaned down and cupped her treasured pupil's chin in her hand.

"I do understand, Kirishka," she said, "believe me, I do. But I'm begging you not to lose sight of your goal. You willingly closed out the entire world in order to reach the top, and you succeeded. Let the world in now and you've no place to go but down. There's no room at the top for distractions, Kirishka, no room for sloppiness. Audiences are cruelly unforgiving of those they've elevated to greatness; they don't tolerate mistakes. Don't siphon the passion out of your music and give it to Jeffrey. Let it be just the reverse; flood your music with your positive feelings for *him*. Use him, Kirishka, use him to enhance your wonderful gift, not detract from it. I implore you again, please don't jeopardize your brilliant career; don't lose what you've finally won."

By the time she left Natalya's two hours later, Kirsten was exhausted. Her teacher had forced her to think about the one thing she had been trying *not* to think about for months now: that awful choice. Either music or a man, but never both. Her thoughts turned inadvertently to Michael. With Michael, the question of a choice had never arisen. Michael. Her lips trembled as they formed his name. She hadn't even heard from him in the six months since Berlin. Her resentment over what had occurred that terrible night had gradually mellowed, fading into a dull, lingering sadness. She closed her fingers over the solitary charm on the gold bracelet he had given her, wishing that by simply rubbing its smooth surface she could magically rub away some of the ache inside her. The sun caught the facets of the ring she was wearing on her right hand, and she gasped as a searing shaft of pain went through her.

She suddenly felt weighted down, as though even her hands were at war with each other now. Michael on the left, Jeffrey on the right. When he had asked her about the bracelet, she had admitted only that it was a gift from Michael, and that they had been friends a long time. Jeffrey, being the gentleman he was, hadn't pursued it any further, but the very next day he had gone to Van Cleef & Arpels and bought her the two-carat heart-shaped amethyst.

Before she even realized what she was doing, she had taken off both the ring and the bracelet and buried them inside her purse.

"Why won't you let your nails grow?" Jeffrey asked while he nibbled lightly on one of Kirsten's thumbs. They were curled up on the sofa in her den, sipping cocktails, and waiting for one of Gianna's frozen lasagnas to heat. "Hmm, why won't you? Give me one good reason."

"You know *all* the reasons." She tried to reclaim her thumb and failed. "I'd lose too much of my control and my reach, not to mention making the most godawful clicking sounds on the keys."

"Just a little?" He indicated the precise length he had in mind with his thumb and forefinger. She shook her head. He reduced the amount. She shook her head again. When the space had gradually been whittled down to a single hair-breadth and she was still shaking her head, he finally conceded defeat. She rewarded his defeat with a kiss, then snuggled up against him and put her head in his lap.

Jeffrey shifted slightly to relieve the growing pressure in his groin. Sitting with her this way was torture, sheer torture. He wanted her more than he could remember ever wanting anyone before. Her exquisite face, the delectable curves of her small body, drove him to distraction. He longed to rip off her clothes, throw her down on the carpet, and ravage her. He longed to take her in every possible way imaginable, possess her completely—her body, her mind, her genius— and absorb them until they became as much a part of him as they were of her. But he didn't. He couldn't. In a corrupt and evil world she represented purity and goodness. In the midst of so much ugliness she was beauty. Surrounded as they were by imperfection, only she was perfect. She demanded not ravishment, but reverence.

Although baptized an Anglican, Jeffrey had entered manhood as an avowed atheist—disillusioned and cynical. Now, to his supreme astonishment, his discovery of Kirsten had helped him rediscover the faith he had lost. Because of her, he had been born again. She was the newer deity he worshiped, the sole source of his salvation; and as penance for his past transgressions, he had taken a vow of celibacy. For he believed that in abstinence lay atonement. And when he had atoned sufficiently, then and only then would he be clean enough and worthy enough to claim her as his just reward.

Kirsten was so happily ensconced in Jeffrey's arms that she didn't even know the phone had been ringing until he handed it to her. At her quizzical look, he merely shrugged. It turned out to be Nelson.

"I just got a call from Thomas Beecham in London," he said. "De Larrocha is sick. How does Tuesday with the Royal Philharmonic sound? That way you can fly directly to Brussels from London instead of leaving from New York on Thursday as originally planned."

"It sounds fine to me." She wondered fleetingly whether or not Michael would be in London then.

"Oh, and something else. *Time* wants to do a cover story on you."

"You know I don't give interviews."

"But we're talking about the cover of *Time*, Kirsten, not a tabloid or some fan magazine." He could almost see her shaking her head. "Are you listening to me?"

"Yes, I'm listening to you."

"If the cover of *Time* was good enough for Charles de Gaulle when they named him Man of the Year in January, don't you think it's good enough for you?"

"The truth?"

"Please, do me a favor. Stop thinking like an artist and try thinking more like a businesswoman."

But thinking of any kind was becoming increasingly difficult; Jeffrey had started kissing his way up her neck and was now moving in the general direction of her mouth.

"Kirsten, you can't buy this kind of publicity."

"I don't need any more pub—"

Jeffrey had reached her mouth and was running the tip of his tongue along the inside rim of her bottom lip.

"Everyone needs publicity."

She closed her eyes and opened her mouth wider.

"Kirsten, are you still there?"

She tried to shake herself free of the feelings inundating her and couldn't. "All right," she gasped, the receiver half-sliding out of her hand.

"Good girl. They'll be sending their cover artist over at two tomorrow." All he got in response to that was something that sounded like a moan, followed by a click.

"Do you know who you remind me of, pet?" Eric was trying hard to keep the edge out of his voice, and only partially succeeding. "Miss Haversham in *Great Expectations*. All we're missing is the tattered wedding gown, the rotting cake, and the bloody mice scurrying about. You can't keep this flat as a monument to Kirsten forever, you know, forcing one unfortunate young man after another to spend an entire year with us surrounded by fading chintz. If you don't want another girl in the house, all well and good; but for God's sake, redecorate the damned place."

Claudia looked up from her watering can and said nothing. After plucking a withered blossom from one of the African violets that lined the windowsills in the bedroom, she went to refill the empty watering can in the bathroom sink.

"And you could at least see her when she comes to town next week." Kirsten had phoned only moments before to tell them of her concert on Tuesday. "How much longer do you think I can go on inventing excuses for you? It isn't fair, pet. It's as if you're punishing her, and you've no earthly reason to do that."

Claudia set the watering can down on the rim of the sink and peered at herself in the mirror of the medicine chest. She looked old. Bloodless. Empty. Sucked dry. She had the face of a spinster, all bitter and pinched. Proof that she was leading a frustrated, sexless life. Pushing herself up against a corner of the sink, she drew some comfort from the increased pressure of the cold, hard porcelain between her legs. Without even closing her eyes, she could see Kirsten standing right in front of her. Kirsten, with her exquisite face and perfect body and seductive innocence. Kirsten, her cherished darling, at the top of the world, where she herself had helped to put her. Claudia could feel the tears beginning and she angrily batted them away. Kirsten, her treacherous angel, daring to reteach her love and then abandoning her. Leaving her without any place to put that love and no one to give it to.

"So, pet?" Eric was standing in the doorway, his face a picture of concern. "Are you going to come with me to the Dorchester on Tuesday or will I be seeing her alone again?"

Claudia's eyes were cold as they met his in the mirror. "You needn't make such a fuss about it, darling. Simply tell the child I've got one of my ghastly migraines, she'll understand."

When Kirsten put the phone down after speaking to Eric, she felt the same stab of homesickness she always felt when she talked to him. She never stopped missing him—his wonderfully wry wit, his generosity and warmth, the way he winked at her, his easy hold on the world. Although she continued to write every week and call at least once a month, the time between visits seemed to stretch longer and longer with each passing year. Idly wrapping and unwrapping the telephone cord around her wrist, she thought briefly about Claudia. They hadn't seen or spoken to each other since her last day in London. But then, perhaps it was better that way. A sudden shudder of revulsion went through her. It was as intense and uncomfortable a feeling as ever, the one nerve-jangling sensation that even time had been unable to deaden.

The sound of the door chimes ringing brought her to her feet with an anxious start. She glanced at the clock on her night table. It was two. And out in the hall was some stranger who was being paid to invade her privacy. If only Nelson hadn't badgered her into this. If only he had agreed to cancel the sitting after she had called him that morning and begged him to. The chimes sounded again. Gritting her teeth, she stomped angrily through the apartment to the front door, where she purposely waited another thirty seconds before finally opening it a fraction of an inch.

"Miss Harald?"

Kirsten blinked. She knew she was staring, but it seemed to take forever to trace the source of his richly timbred voice.

"Six feet three," he said by way of introduction as he extended one large, long-fingered hand to her.

Remembering that he was the enemy, she refused it. The broad-shouldered shrug that told her it didn't matter set her teeth on edge. Doubling her fists, she readied herself to do battle with what was unfortunately promising to be a charming and impressive opponent. It wasn't only the man's height she found awesome, it was the sheer masculinity of him. The muscled strength that shaped and defined his powerful body. The shaggy thickness of his sunstreaked blond hair. The ruggedly modeled features and the smoky green of his eyes as they narrowed to appraise her. It was the way he was dressed—in a pale yellow crewneck, blue jeans, and cordovan loafers—that made him look more like a college student than *Time*'s youngest and finest cover artist. But above all, it was her profound reaction to him—this magnificent and intimidating obelisk of a man—and how her heart continued to pound loudly long after it should have slowed again to a more normal, steady beat.

"I'm Andrew Beaton," he said while she continued to use the door as a safety wedge between them. "I'm from *Time* mag—"

"I know who you are." She was determined to make this as uncomfortable for him as it was for her.

"May I come in?"

It was her turn to shrug.

"Please?"

She grudgingly opened the door a few more inches, and he eased his large frame inside with a grace that astounded her.

"We did have an appointment at two, didn't we?"

Her hostile glare told him nothing.

"Would you prefer if I came back some other time then?"

Kirsten cleared her throat, but when she spoke, her voice still came out sounding strained and artificial. "What I'd really prefer is not to have to do this at all."

One blond eyebrow arched speculatively. "And failing that?"

"I'd like to get it over with as quickly as possible."

"You make it sound like torture," he said. "I suppose I should be insulted, but I'm not." The harder his grin worked to win her over, the more stubbornly Kirsten resisted it. "You've never sat for a portrait before, have you?" She didn't answer him. "It's really pretty painless, you know. After a while you'll forget I'm even in the same room."

She doubted it. She couldn't imagine ever forgetting Andrew Beaton was in the same room. Even now he seemed to be using up all the available space in her foyer.

"Is it me or what I do?" he asked as his eyes continued to scrape and dig at her defenses.

Once again she had to clear her throat, hating herself for her skin's sudden clamminess. "Since I don't know you personally, Mr. Beaton, I'd have to say it's what you do. I don't particularly like the idea of being dissected and exposed to the entire world."

"It's not my job to dissect anyone, Miss Harald, I leave that to the reporters."

Kirsten cracked a vague smile and crossed her arms in front of her.

"I'm an artist, Miss Harald; I create, I don't destroy," he told her in a voice improbably gentle for such a big man. "My sole intention is to capture the essence of my subject, not either to judge or to betray. I consider a sitting to be a form of mutual trust, and trust isn't something I take lightly."

His words—as gently enunciated as they were—were as effective a rebuke as a slap on the wrist, but Kirsten refused to acknowledge them as such. Doing an abrupt about-face, she turned and led the way into the living room with her shoulders squared and her jaw set in a belligerent line.

"Where would you like me to sit?" she asked while her back was still turned to him.

"Wherever you'd feel most comfortable."

Without giving it much thought, she promptly settled herself on one of the two white three-seater damask sofas that faced each other in front of the white marble fireplace, folded her hands in her lap, and stared directly ahead of her.

"You don't look particularly comfortable to me," was Andrew Beaton's comment as he leaned up against the mantelpiece, his sketchpad still tucked under his arm, unopened.

"How can I be comfortable with you staring at me?" Kirsten retorted. Crossing her legs, she carefully readjusted the folds of her skirt, then clamped both hands around one knee.

"I'd have thought you'd be used to having people stare at you by now, Miss Harald. You are a performer, you know."

Still gazing straight ahead of her, Kirsten made an impatient clacking sound that reminded her of her mother. "This is different."

"Why?"

"Because when I'm onstage, I'm so absorbed in my music that I'm never fully conscious of anyone actually watching me. But you"—she paused, her eyes darting momentarily in his direction—"you're too close to me. It's much too personal this way. I don't have anything to keep me distracted, so the only thing I'm aware of is your standing over there and examining me."

"Then why don't we make it easier for both of us?" He pointed to the piano with one of his pencils. "Play something for me; pretend I'm just another faceless member of your audience."

Kirsten couldn't seem to get to the piano fast enough. But then, as she was limbering up her fingers, the most peculiar thing happened. For no apparent reason she found herself wanting to impress Andrew Beaton. It was as though she actually *needed* to impress him. To show him that here at the piano she was the one in control again. As she had for her audition with Nelson Pendell, she chose to begin with Prokofiev's "Toccata," and attacked it with savage delight, raking and strafing the keyboard with all ten of her highly charged fingers. It didn't take long before she was back in full command of herself.

No sooner had he started his preliminary sketches of her than Andrew Beaton could already visualize the finished oil. His hands were barely able to keep up with his mounting excitement; he couldn't recall ever being as intrigued or stimulated by a subject before. Kirsten Harald was an artist's dream, a spectacular study in contrasts and contradictions, the ultimate challenge. Photographs had captured only what she had wanted them to capture—the polished surface with only a hint of that special underlying dreaminess of hers. But what she had unknowingly revealed to him before sitting down at the piano and drawing the protection of her music around **her** was something entirely different. It was an unobstructed view of the passionate and unabashedly sensual woman who lived in turmoil beneath the carefully guarded surface.

Kirsten stumbled over the most elementary phrasing in a Schubert sonata and hastily improvised to disguise her mistake. She had sailed through the "Toccata," Beethoven's "Pathétique," two Liszt preludes, and a Chopin mazurka without a single blunder, yet all of a sudden her mind was wandering and her hands were behaving like willful children she couldn't discipline. She felt restless and uncomfortable, aware again of a pair of relentlessly probing smoky green eyes stripping her bare. Angry at herself for weakening, she played the rest of the sonata in strident forte and ended it with a series of blaring arpeggios.

Glancing up from the keys for a moment, she found Andrew Beaton staring down at her, a look of total amazement on his face. "I've never had such a negative effect on anyone before," he told her. "And if poor Schubert had ever heard his piece throttled to death that way, I'm sure he would have given up composing."

"Didn't I say you made me nervous?" Kirsten slammed the lid shut over the keyboard and sat there with both arms folded.

"You're doing it again."

"Doing what?"

"Closing yourself off by crossing your arms in front of your chest."

Kirsten just glared at him without saying anything.

"Well, you can relax now." Andrew closed his sketchpad and tucked his pencil back inside the spiral binding. "I'm all through tormenting you."

The moment he started out of the room, Kirsten jumped up and hurried after him. Suddenly and inexplicably, she didn't want him to leave.

"You certainly seem to know your music," she said, taking small running steps to keep up with his giant strides.

"I minored in it at college."

"Where did you go to school?"

"Northwestern. I'm from Chicago."

"Would you like a cup of coffee?" she asked just as he reached the front door.

"Thanks, but I'm already late for another appointment. Excuse me." He was indicating the doorknob. Her hand was covering it as though she were hoping to hide it from him. She instantly jerked her hand away, feeling utterly ridiculous, while a red-hot flush spread across her face.

Andrew watched the emotional tug-of-war taking place in her magnificent eyes and was almost tempted to change his mind about leaving. She was fascinating to watch—this electrifying enigma, this challenging composite of diametrically opposed extremes. All fire and ice, earth and air. A woman one moment, a child the next. Her calculated control offset by flashes of fiery pique. Pulling him toward her, yet pushing him away, both at the same time. He watched her internal struggle intensify; he didn't envy her that struggle. It was with a sharp pang of regret that he finally opened the door.

"Good-bye, Kirsten Harald." The husky edge to his voice surprised him. "And thank you. You're really what true art is all about."

Although the door had definitely closed behind him, it was as though he hadn't actually left at all; she could still feel him in the room with her. After spending less than two hours with him, she was convinced Andrew Beaton had learned more about her than anyone else ever had. She felt violated, as though by simply sketching her he had physically assaulted her. Was she reacting to Andrew Beaton the artist or Andrew Beaton the man, she wondered as she tried to force herself through the rest of the day with some modicum of equanimity. By the time she got into bed that night, she had her answer. She had completely forgotten about the artist; what she couldn't forget was the man.

18

Kirsten opened one end of the large brown envelope and gingerly eased out her complimentary copy of *Time*. With both parents peering curiously over her shoulder, she nervously narrowed her eyes until they were no more than slits before she even dared peek at the red-bordered cover of the magazine. What she noticed first was the name Beaton curving in bold black capital letters around her left shoulder with all the possessiveness of a lover's hand. To her chagrin, a tremor of excitement rippled through her. But the feeling was instantly cut short when her father suddenly began clearing his throat and her mother started making those familiar clacking sounds with her tongue. Bracing herself for the worst, she opened her eyes fully and tried to see her painted face the way her parents were seeing it.

The Kirsten Andrew Beaton had portrayed was a far different Kirsten from the one photographed by either Antony Armstrong-Jones or Richard Avedon. His Kirsten was a twenty-six year old enigma—vulnerable yet aloof, innocent but sensual too. A bewitching blend of the come-hither and the stay-away in her luminous violet eyes, an ambiguous promise in the upward tilt of her parted lips. The totality of it, however, came as a devastating shock to her. Andrew Beaton had seen the same face she herself saw each time she looked in the mirror after she and Michael had made love.

The issue of *Time* carrying the cover story on Kirsten had the highest number of newsstand sales in the magazine's thirty-six-year history. That it was the first in-depth interview Kirsten had ever given was in itself history. Everyone had an opinion about the cover, everyone had an opinion about the article. But whatever their opinions were, no one could dispute the fact that Nelson had been right. Kirsten was in demand everywhere. It was as though the entire world had suddenly discovered classical music, and the American press immediately capitalized on it by turning Kirsten into something the classical music world had never had before: its first true media personality.

"It's unbelievable, absolutely unbelievable!" Nelson was chewing on an antacid tablet and trying to speak at the same time. "You're doing for classical music what Elvis Presley has done for rock and roll." He looked hard at Kirsten sitting so serenely across from him, grabbed a thick batch of papers from his usually impeccable desk, and rattled them at her. "Do you know what these are? They're requests for interviews. Every major newspaper and magazine, every TV and radio show in the country wants to interview you. Every institution you can name, from schools to penitentiaries, wants to have you play for them. Every soloist from here to Tokyo wants to accompany you in recital. Some town in Oklahoma wants to name their main street after you, and a music school in Atlanta's already changed its name from the Haydn School of Music to the Harald School of Music."

Dropping the letters, he asked benignly, "So, tell me, how do you feel about all this?"

Kirsten's grin was so wide she could feel it warming both her ears. "I love it. I think the classical music world could use a little airing out, don't you?"

By the following April, Kirsten had added another four charms to her bracelet and four more rings to her ring collection. Their significance, however, far outweighed their number. The only times she had seen Michael that entire year were the four times they had played together, and the total number of days she had spent with Jeffrey barely added up to four weeks.

To Kirsten's utter dismay, Roxanne had accompanied Michael to all four cities for the sole purpose, it seemed, of standing guard over her husband. Her ominous presence had prevented them from spending even a moment alone together, intensifying not only their desperate need for just such a moment, but further underscoring the precariousness of their impossible situation. What their bodies had been denied, their music transmitted instead—a sound so impassioned and bittersweet, that it was heartbreaking.

They no longer phoned each other, nor did they write. With an increasing sense of despair Kirsten was forced to acknowledge that they were losing their hold on each other. The memories they had shared were dimming, growing stale; no newer ones were taking their place. The mutual ties that had once bound them together so fiercely were fraying. Whenever she thought of him now, her thoughts were edged with a gentle regret; and when she dreamed about him, his image would dissolve just before she woke up.

If Michael was dissolving, Jeffrey was becoming the one source of constancy in her constantly changing world. He was her rock and her refuge. Seemingly content with whatever bits and pieces of her he could have, just as she had been content with only bits and pieces of Michael. Didn't he ever feel cheated, she often wondered. She knew she did, but it seemed bits and pieces of people were all she was ever destined to have.

Jeffrey was panic-stricken. He had lost control of his emotions. And all because of a woman who continued to dart in and out of his life with the capriciousness of a flickering candle flame. Light one minute, dark the next. Her absences every bit as alluring and provocative as those times when they were actually together. Their hide-and-seek relationship had kept him living alarmingly close to the edge, in a constant state of arousal for nearly two years now. But as exciting as it had been, it had finally gone on long enough.

He was ready now. Ready to save her from her demanding public, a public nearly demented in their all-consuming need for her. What about *his* need? His need to possess her completely had ceased being a need months ago; it was now an obsession. He had served her sacred image long enough, ejaculating into enough washcloths and staining enough sheets with the outpourings of his deflected passion to last him the rest of his life. It was more than time.

He thought of the gold bracelet Michael Eastbourne had given her and tasted bile. He could hear those five gold charms jangling their defiance of his patient pursuit of her and ached to crush each one of them and silence their mocking sound forever. But there was still the matter of the man himself. Jeffrey smiled. Michael Eastbourne was a demon he could purge her of in time. All he needed was time.

The night before Kirsten was scheduled to leave for a three-week concert tour of Europe, Jeffrey took her to dinner at the Four Seasons. Almost from the moment its doors had been opened the preceding year, the Four Seasons had been one of the top two or three restaurants that the rich and famous frequented. Jeffrey sat next to her rather than across from her, and for the first time since she had known him, ordered for both of them. Then over a second cognac he took hold of her left hand.

"How would you feel about letting only one of your nails grow, this one for instance?" As he was speaking, he gently rubbed her ring finger with his thumb. Kirsten hastily moistened her lips with her tongue and tried to remain calm. "I've given you how many rings now, five?" She nodded. "None of them were diamonds though, were they?" She shook her head, feeling a curious numbness steal over her. Gripping her hand so tightly that it nearly made her wince, he whispered, "I want you, Kirsten. I want you and I need you. I need to know that each time you come home, you're coming home to me."

"But I do come home to you." Her voice was no more than a whisper.

"Not really. You come home to your own apartment and to your parents. I get to see you for only a few hours at a time. I want days with you, Kirsten, weeks whenever possible. I'm tired of having to share you with everyone else in the world."

"You're not asking me to give up my career, are you, Jeffrey?"

"God, no! I'd never ask you to do that, never."

"Then what are you asking?" Her heart was pounding so loudly she could barely hear herself speak.

"I'm asking you to marry me."

She knew she should have anticipated it happening eventually, but hearing Jeffrey actually propose to her still caught her unprepared. She sank against the back of her chair, her eyes wide, her mouth opened slightly, while her temperature rose and fell like a thermometer gone berserk. Her mind was dazed, her thoughts scrambled. Warnings sounded like blaring sirens in her head. The candlelight glanced off one of the gold charms on her bracelet and shone painfully into her eye. Jeffrey saw her flinch, give her wrist a shake, and felt his chest seize up. She trapped him with her eyes as though the answer lay buried somewhere inside his, and smiled, a watery, tremulous smile.

"Yes, Jeffrey," she said. "I'll marry you."

He responded to her answer in a way no proper Long Island gentleman would ever dream of responding: he kissed her in public. As their kiss deepened, the warnings in Kirsten's head receded farther and farther into the distance, until only a faint echo remained. They had told her countless times that she couldn't have both her career and marriage, that she would have to choose. She intended to prove them wrong. She wanted both and she would have both.

There were moments when Michael was convinced he was a masochist. How many more of the same stories would he have to read before he'd finally had enough pain? For the past week, even the London press had seemed bent on fueling his morbid preoccupation, happily printing everything they possibly could about the plans for what was being called the storybook wedding of the decade between pianist Kirsten Harald and millionaire physician Jeffrey Powell Oliver II. Folding his latest copy of *The Times* neatly in half, he placed it faceup on top of his desk and put his head in his hands.

They had one more concert to play together—in Houston on the fifth of June, exactly thirty-five days before she was scheduled to be married. How could he face her, he asked himself. How could he look into those wonderful eyes of hers while he wished her happiness and have it sound sincere? He did wish her happiness, of course; he wasn't that selfish. But part of him was dying on account of that happiness—the part of him reserved solely for her, the part of him she had kept so vibrantly alive.

"Michael?" Roxanne peeked in from the doorway and he

started guiltily. "You look as if you could use a drink, darling. Shall I mix you one?"

He shook his head. "What I could really use is a hug."

She rushed over to him like an eager schoolgirl and happily curled up on his lap. Seizing hold of her face, Michael kissed her long and hard, grinding his mouth against hers and hungrily beating her with his tongue. Roxanne moaned and pressed herself even tighter against him, her own tongue lashing back at his, her fingers tugging insistently at his thick wavy hair. The ferocity of their kiss left them both breathless and slightly stunned, and when it ended, Roxanne gave a soft, contented sigh and rested her head against Michael's chest. But her contentment was only momentary; her peacefulness shattered by the intrusive sight of Kirsten Harald's picture in the paper on Michael's desk. And she wondered if she would ever have the luxury of feeling entirely secure about anything again.

Kirsten's flight from Kansas City into Houston was delayed due to severe thunderstorms. As a result, she went directly from the airport to rehearsals, arriving late, hungry, disheveled, and feeling uncharacteristically cranky. Michael, in an unusual display of impatience, nearly snapped his baton in half trying to get the rehearsal going. The tension in the air was so patently obvious that no one was immune to it.

At the Steinway, Kirsten was battling a sensation akin to seasickness, and nothing she did seemed to make the slightest difference. In a vain attempt to quiet her screaming nerves, she began to play Schumann's spirited A Minor Piano Concerto like a funeral dirge. Michael immediately stopped her and had them start again. After that, they continued stopping and starting with the irritating regularity of a milk train, and Kirsten could feel herself gradually coming unglued. She stumbled through the second movement, making one jarring mistake after another, until partway into the third movement Michael finally slammed his baton down in exasperation and told them all to take a break.

"I ought to scratch you from the program right now, dammit!" he shouted, following Kirsten into her dressing room and banging the door shut. "Just what in God's name are you doing?"

"Nothing unusual," she snapped back. "I'm just trying to play the piano."

"Trying, ha!" he snorted. "Trying *not* to play would be more like it."

Kirsten had never seen Michael angry before. And she didn't have to ask why. He couldn't seem to take his eyes off the glittering three-carat emerald-cut diamond on her left hand.

"Michael, I'm sorry."

"For what, trying to sabotage this concert?"

"I am not trying to sabotage this concert." She put a hand on his sleeve, only to have him jerk his arm away. "For not telling you about Jeffrey and me personally."

"You don't owe me any explanation." His voice was rough, almost gravelly. "I wish you well, and I mean that." There, he had said it. He had gotten the words out. Yet he could still feel them sticking together like a solid lump in the middle of his throat. He noticed she wasn't wearing the bracelet he had given her, but just as he was about to comment on it, he remembered she never wore it when she played. His head was beginning to throb, so was his right leg. He was falling apart, losing control. Of all the times for Roxanne not to have been there with him, but two days ago her father had suffered his second coronary in three years, and she had rushed home to Wynford.

"Michael?"

He couldn't look at her. He didn't dare. She was coming toward him, one hand outstretched, and while he wanted nothing more than to take her in his arms, he managed to find the strength to back away. She stopped then, standing so perfectly still she didn't even appear to be breathing. He could look at her now. As long as there were those few feet between them, it was safe for him to look at her. She hadn't moved, she hadn't so much as blinked, yet suddenly the entire room seemed to be tilting. She hurtled toward him, and he instinctively held out his arms to catch her.

The collision of their bodies sent them tumbling to the floor. They were a tangle of arms and legs neither dared sort out, so fearful were they of tearing the fragile web that had spun itself around them. They made love without undressing; their passion was so intense it all but dissolved their clothes. Their kisses, hot and wet, were like splashes of kerosene added to a fire already threatening to burn out of control. Their mingled breaths combined to whip the flames higher still, until their desire became an inferno that consumed them both. And in the heart of the fire was their damnation and their absolution. One final hello, one last good-bye.

They straightened their clothes as best they could, neither of them speaking, neither one looking too closely at the other. No doubt everyone was already waiting for them. Kirsten made the first move to leave. Her hand had only just touched the doorknob when Michael called her back. Cupping her face in his hands, he kissed her forehead, both her eyelids, the tip of her nose, her chin, and finally her mouth.

It was only after he had released her that she realized what they had done. She thought of Jeffrey and was immediately stung by her own treachery. She threw open the door and heard it slam against the wall. Michael's footsteps were close behind her as she started running down the corridor in the direction of the stage. He called her name, but she refused to slow down or turn around. If she looked back now, she would be lost.

What this final encounter had proven was that Michael would always be a part of her, a part of her music, a part of her precious, living dream. A steady incandescence, lighting the same private corner of her mind that had been his for fourteen of her twenty-seven years. More than one-half her life. And nothing would ever alter that—she knew that now—not even time. But Michael was her past; Jeffrey was her future.

Allegretto

1960–1972

19

July tenth was a day dipped in confectioner's sugar and draped around Kirsten like a fine lace mantilla. It was irridescent with silk and satin and pearls. Fragrant with gardenias and stephanotis. Ethereal as a dream; as permanent as a moment stolen from heaven.

The wedding of the decade, as the press called it, was held outside on the sweeping back lawn of the Oliver estate, with its commanding view of Long Island Sound. It was a celebrity watcher's treat: all five hundred of the invited guests were either members of the Social Register or luminaries from the music world. They sipped Dom Pérignon and feasted on an elaborate cold buffet—the men in summer white, the women in pastels—moving like a gently flowing stream between the round tables with their fluttering white cloths and shade umbrellas, the rockeries and two ornamental goldfish ponds.

At the heart of the festivities was Kirsten; she was the pulse by which the five hundred celebrants measured theirs. She was as radiant as the sun, resplendent in a wedding gown designed especially for her by the aging master of high fashion himself, Cristobal Balenciaga. Its sculpted white lace bodice was embroidered with seed-pearl rosettes and fitted to just below her hips, where it flared out into a billowing double skirt of tissue thin white satin. Her headdress was a stiff lace cap, coming to a point in the middle of her forehead, with a spray of pearl-trimmed tulle fastened to the back of it. Understated in its exquisite elegance, it set off her own exquisiteness to perfection.

"Well, lamb, you've certainly tipped this creaky bastion of tradition on its ear." Eric Sheffield-Johns slid his arm around Kirsten's waist and squeezed her tightly. "You've absolutely dazzled them, you know, and I can't imagine why." Kirsten giggled and leaned closer to him. Giving her one of his famous winks, Eric pecked her on the nose and whispered, "Much happiness, dearest one; much, much happiness indeed."

Eric's presence at the wedding had brought with it a cascade of memories—most of them wonderful, some of them painful—but Kirsten couldn't have conceived of getting married without him there. If it hadn't been for Eric and Claudia—who was cruelly conspicuous by her absence—she might never have gotten that initial toehold on the mountain, never have climbed as high as she had. Jeffrey certainly wouldn't have come courting her on Ninth Avenue either. Thanks to the Sheffield-Johnses, her precious dream had been given the chance to live.

"So, Eric, what do you think of my bride?" Jeffrey joined them and clapped a friendly hand on the older man's shoulder. His face was flushed, his eyes glittering like black diamonds as he gazed worshipfully at Kirsten. "There isn't a man here who wouldn't trade places with me today," he told her, "and I can't say I blame them. If they weren't such proper gentlemen, half of them would probably have slipped you their private telephone numbers by now."

"Jeffrey!" Kirsten pretended to be shocked, and gave him a playful slap on the wrist.

"Anyone ask you for your autograph yet?"

"Yes, dozens of people."

"Really now?" One of Jeffrey's black eyebrows shot up. "Which ones? I'll have them thrown off the premises for impropriety." He only barely managed to get the word out correctly, and Kirsten and Eric exchanged amused glances.

"Why, Jeffrey Powell Oliver the second"—Kirsten put both hands on her hips and continued her imitation of an indignant Scarlett O'Hara—"I do believe you're drunk."

"I do believe you're right." Jeffrey executed a low but wobbly bow in front of her. "And why shouldn't I be? It isn't every day a mere mortal gets hitched to a star." A self-satisfied grin spread across his face. "Hey, I think that's pretty damned clever, don't you?"

"Damned clever, old man," Eric concurred. Patting Kirsten fondly on the cheek, he gave Jeffrey the thumbs-up sign and left the two of them to their bantering.

As soon as they were alone, Jeffrey raised what remained of his champagne to Kirsten in a toast. "To us," he said. She felt a momentary pang recalling a similar toast made by Michael that night in Berlin. "And to the newest branch on the Oliver family tree." His bloodshot eyes were devouring as he fastened them on the flatness of Kirsten's belly beneath the pearl-encrusted lace. It was a look she missed entirely.

While Jeffrey went in search of some more champagne, Kirsten joined her parents, who were standing off by themselves, holding hands, and gazing up at the huge house that would be their daughter's home from now on.

"It's like something out of a fairy tale," Gianna told Kirsten with a shake of her head. "I get weak just thinking about having to clean a place like that." She shook her head again. Both Kirsten and Emil burst out laughing; a moment later, Gianna joined in.

Her parents eventually drifted off, leaving Kirsten to stand looking up at her new home alone. It reminded her of the great manor houses of England. Built of gray fieldstone, the forty-room mansion was Tudor in style, with gothic stone gables, leaded windows, and hip roofs crested with clusters of clay chimney pots. Four generations of Olivers had lived and died in that house; its very solidness seemed saturated with the past as it rose haughtily from its protective ring of densely planted spruce trees, a proud monument to tradition. To her it was *Jane Eyre* and *Wuthering Heights* combined. But instead of desolate moors and jagged cliffs, there was Long Island Sound and the distant Connecticut shore.

"It's really quite remarkable, isn't it?"

As Kirsten turned, the sun illuminated the face of the woman who had spoken to her, lining her elegantly patrician features in gold and brightening the gold streaks in her artfully streaked light brown hair.

"Yes, yes, it is." Kirsten gave Dierdre Oliver, her new sister-in-law, a dazzling smile.

The older woman's returning smile was more practiced than warm. Shielding a pair of pale gray eyes from the glare of the sun, she nodded toward her own home, set high on the same hill, a discreet distance from Kirsten and Jeffrey's. "That's why I urged Charles to build us one just like it," she said. She took her hand away from her face and fixed Kirsten with a superior stare. "And speaking of homes, my dear, our men need to feel they reign supreme in theirs, even if they don't." After dispensing that bit of social advice, she walked away.

In spite of her supreme snobbishness, Dierdre Vaughn Hamilton Oliver was a woman Kirsten couldn't help but admire. It had been eight years since her husband Charles's stroke, yet the thirty-seven-year-old former debutante from

Philadelphia was still regarded as the undisputed leader of
Long Island society. She was its favorite martyr, standing
proudly alone among the elite community's otherwise comfortably paired couples. A striking combination of the quali-
ties they revered most, she was an indefatigable fund-raiser,
the consummate hostess, the acknowledged arbiter of fashion. But more important, she hadn't once been touched by a
hint of scandal.

"Kirsten?" It was Jeffrey again, tugging gently on her elbow. "I don't think you've met the Holdens yet."

Her smile faltered, then froze. She hardly noticed the man
Jeffrey was introducing to her as Alec Holden; she was too
busy staring at his wife.

"Mrs. Oliver." Lois Eldershaw Holden pronounced the
Oliver with a derisive curl of her upper lip, turning it into a
question. Unlike her more gracious peers, the fact of Kirsten
Harald's marriage to one of their own was something she
refused to sanction or accept.

Time had obviously made Lois more prickly than ever, but
Kirsten still tried to be cordial to her former rival. "I was
sorry to learn you'd stopped touring," she said, genuinely
meaning it.

"My doctors thought it best," Lois replied stiffly. "I'm
teaching now."

After that there didn't seem to be much left to say. The
moment they were gone, Kirsten turned to Jeffrey and asked
him what he knew about Lois. He seemed surprised by her
question and shrugged.

"Very little, why?"

"Did you ever date her?"

"The ice maiden?" He pretended to shiver. "Never. She's
Dierdre's friend, not mine. Actually, it was Dierdre who introduced Lois to Alec Holden. Both Lois's parents died a few
years ago, leaving her a small fortune; and since Alec always
did prefer playing to working, and because Lois was in the
market for a husband, they pooled their resources and got
married last August."

"Where do they live?"

"Here on the North Shore." Kirsten groaned. "Alec raises
polo ponies, Lois does charitable works like every other good
Long Island wife, and together they make a perfectly respectable team. Don't look so skeptical. They're both getting ex-

actly what they want. Alec now has a generous bank balance and Lois has a full-time paid escort."

"It sounds pretty awful to me," Kirsten said. "Poor Lois, she seems like such an unhappy person."

"I'm sure she wouldn't agree with you. I doubt she'd know a genuine feeling if it jumped up and hit her."

Emil and Gianna were the last to leave the reception, and it was with a bit of a jolt that Kirsten realized she wouldn't be going back to the apartment on Eighty-first Street with them. Tonight she wouldn't be sleeping in her own familiar bed or even in a bed in some strange hotel room. She would be sleeping in Jeffrey's bed, in his house. Their house now. She studied the thin circle of emerald-cut diamonds on her finger and blushed uneasily. It wouldn't be long before the man who was now her husband came to claim his bride for the very first time. And what would he find? A bride who had already given herself to someone else.

The newlyweds were ensconced in the large bedroom suite once occupied by Jeffrey's parents. Furnished entirely in oak, draped and swagged and upholstered in an elaborate but faded maroon, green, and ivory brocade, the rooms looked as though they had been transported intact from some drafty castle in seventeenth-century England. Their bed was an ornately carved oak four-poster, complete with canopy and matching side draperies, and as Kirsten settled herself in it somewhat apprehensively, wearing the lavender silk negligee Jeffrey had bought her—after teasing her that it was only fitting she wear lavender for her debut performance as his wife—she began to mentally redecorate the room.

The door to his bathroom opened and Jeffrey emerged, swaying slightly, smelling of men's cologne and wearing a maroon silk robe with a green, white, and gold crest embroidered on the breast pocket, looking every bit like the lord of the manor prepared to exercise his conjugal rights. Kirsten gazed up at him expectantly, lips parted, heart thumping, praying to God that by some miracle he would be oblivious to her lost virginity. But she needn't have worried. Jeffrey was too preoccupied with the glory of the moment. After two years of self-cleansing deprivation, he was about to claim his just reward. The rare jewel coveted by the entire world was his now, his to cherish, worship, and possess, to set in the center of his faded family name and watch as it restored that name to its former brilliance.

"My beautiful Kirsten," he said, cupping the back of her head with one hand and untying the sash on his robe with the other. "Do you know how long I've been waiting for this?" He kissed her lingeringly on the lips, then used his tongue and teeth to explore every succulent part of her mouth. Lowering himself onto the bed beside her, he continued to kiss her. His desire began to grow, stretching into a greedy living thing; throbbing and clawing and raging to be released from captivity. It was wild and exhilarating, torching every part of his body and turning him to flame.

Her gown came apart in his hands as he peeled it away to get his first glimpse of her nakedness. She was the perfection he knew she would be. Smooth alabaster, like a statue in an ancient Greek temple. Warm marble, growing hot beneath his hungry touch. He explored her body with the awed reverence of a loving disciple, wishing he could prolong the beauty of what he had just discovered forever. He heard her moans of pleasure and reveled in his power, but when she tried to touch him, he tugged her hands away.

"Let me do it," he whispered, "let me do everything. I want to adore you." Pressing himself against her, he rubbed the lower half of his torso back and forth across her moistness until the friction became unbearable. He couldn't hold back any longer. He gripped himself with one hand and the shock nearly sent him reeling. He was limp, soft. His flaccidness a grim and silent accusation, proof once again that he had failed. His abstinence hadn't purified him, his penance hadn't absolved him. Nothing had changed at all. Nothing.

In despair, he retreated into the safety of the past, conjuring up the only image capable of arousing him. It was the image of his own boyish hands stroking himself to orgasm while he knelt inside the linen closet in his mother's bathroom and watched through the keyhole as she took her bath. He could feel himself stiffening. And when he was big and hard, he wasted no time; he mounted Kirsten quickly. So intent was he on maintaining his erection, he didn't notice how easily he slid inside her. All he knew was relief.

He came almost immediately, exploding in great, helpless spurts, then instantly went soft again. Lying on top of her, he began to tremble, less from exertion than from guilt. And self-loathing. He balled his hands into fists, but stopped himself just before he could pound them into the pillows beneath Kirsten's head. His poor, cursed hands. How he despised them. His onetime allies, now his longtime enemies. They had turned against him years ago, punishing him for the unnatural act he had performed in secret all during his adolescence, keeping him out of the operating room and trapping him behind a desk forever. Was his marriage to be cursed, then, too?

Kirsten stirred uncomfortably; she was nearly suffocating beneath Jeffrey's weight, and there was a feeling of such incompleteness inside her that her entire body itched. After having aroused her so skillfully, Jeffrey had left her hanging in midair, dissatisfied and restless; her ardor unrequited, her need unresolved. He hadn't even allowed her to touch him. Why, she wondered. Had he realized right away that she wasn't a virgin and been disappointed and angry, even repulsed?

For the second time on her wedding day she found herself thinking about Michael. With him the lovemaking had been glorious, satisfying, and fulfilling. But he wasn't her husband, Jeffrey was; it was Jeffrey she would be sleeping with from now on. The memory of her few stolen times with Michael had no place in her thoughts now; none whatsoever.

As Jeffrey collapsed beside her with his back to her, Kirsten began to shiver. It was July, yet she felt cold. She pressed herself up against him, wishing he would roll over and put his arms around her. But he didn't move. From the sounds of his deep, regular breathing, she knew he had already fallen asleep.

She had tried telling herself it could only get better, that they were still strangers to each other, especially in bed; but she was wrong. It didn't get better. In spite of her continued efforts to participate actively in their lovemaking, Jeffrey wouldn't allow it. He would make a game of brushing her hands away, sometimes even pinning them above her head while he kissed and fondled her and begged her to let him adore her. Her own pleas went unheeded. He would stimulate her until she was ready to burst from the exquisite tension, but before she could ever reach orgasm, he would have already climaxed and rolled away from her.

She became a practiced dissembler, making certain no one could tell from outward appearances that her marriage wasn't perfect. Her first task was to redecorate the house, which Jeffrey—after some delicate cajoling on her part—grudgingly permitted her to do. Once again she called on the services of Billy Baldwin, ordering him to strip away the ancestral gloom and open up the place to the gardens, the Sound, and the sky. Once again they chose an all-white palette, but this time they added a different accent color in every room. The result was an ice-cream-colored world, as refreshing as a dollop of snowy white sherbet, tinted by the tail of a rainbow. And to his complete surprise, Jeffrey loved it.

With the household staff of fifteen under the capable thumb of the Olivers' longtime housekeeper, Thelma Joyce, Kirsten was free to enjoy being the estate's ornamental chatelaine. Free to be swept along on a gathering tide of social and cultural activities that reminded her of the wonderfully rich life she had led in London. While the members of the old guard treated her with suspicion and reserve, the younger women found her fascinating. If she was different from other Long Island wives, they seemed to think it lent her an added cachet. It was an accepted rule that she devoted six hours of every day to her practicing, six hours during which she was accessible to no one. And as a result, her admirers were doubly grateful for whatever time they did get to spend with her.

At Dierdre's suggestion, she joined the Junior League, an organization her sister-in-law had pointedly told her was not merely a social club but dedicated to doing good works, and the Victorian Picnic Club, whose members met on alternate Sundays to arrange for the restoration of Long Island's many abandoned gazebos. She and Jeffrey divided their time between the theater, private dinners at the homes of his friends, and dances at the Piping Rock Club. They attended parties of every possible description: cocktail parties, costume parties, theme parties, fund-raising parties, and anniversary parties.

To her surprise, the conversation at many of these parties went beyond the usual exchange of predictable banalities and surface chitchat to focus on the one subject about which she knew very little: politics. She had never been particularly aware politically. Her full-time preoccupation with her music was as much to blame for this as was her outright disinterest in the subject. Lately, though, she had begun to have second thoughts about it. And apparently she wasn't the only one.

Politics, as practiced in the fifties, had indeed been boring. But a new decade had begun; so, it seemed, had a new era. The entire country was finally emerging from a lengthy period of self-imposed isolationism, and she was emerging with it. People weren't changing entirely on their own, however, they were being asked to change. To leave complacency behind them, to become involved and committed, to take a chance—on themselves, on their nation, and on the world at large.

And the one doing the asking was a forty-three-year-old senator from Massachussetts with the ruddy good looks of a movie star, who had captured the Democratic Party's presidential nomination at their national convention in Los Angeles in July. His name: John Fitzgerald Kennedy. The young and the hopeful had found themselves their first real hero, while, for much of the rest of the country, it was a case of love at first sight.

"Well, he's certainly handsome, I'll grant him that much," Dierdre remarked to Lois Holden over cocktails at the home of the Buckleys one night in late August.

"Handsome, shmandsome," Jeffrey snapped. "The man's a Catholic. Elect a Catholic and you're as good as inviting the pope into the White House."

"Not necessarily," Kirsten interjected. Her husband rolled his eyes. He was getting tired of hearing her run on about John Kennedy as though he were her own personal discovery. "He's stated emphatically that his Catholicism would never make him beholden to the Vatican if he were elected, and I believe him."

"Forget him." Lois dismissed Kirsten's defense of the man with an imperious wave. "Have you seen *her* clothes?"

"You mean Jackie?" Dierdre appeared ready to swoon. "She buys only European, darling."

"And apparently Givenchy's her favorite."

"She's bowlegged." This from a scowling Jeffrey, who scooped up another flute of Moët & Chandon champagne from the silver tray of a passing waiter without asking if anyone else wanted any.

Alec Holden laughed. "Bowlegged or not, anyone would be a distinct improvement after eight years of Mamie."

Jeffrey put a finger to his lips and indicated their host, who was as staunchly conservative a Republican as one could find. "Don't be blasphemous, Alec," he warned sotto voce.

But Alec wasn't the least bit intimidated. "I'll admit I'm not that crazy about Nixon." Eisenhower's vice-president, Richard Nixon, had just won the Republican nomination for president in Chicago. "But Henry Cabot Lodge, on the other hand." He arched his eyebrows approvingly at Nixon's choice for his vice-presidential running mate. "Now, that man has class."

Kirsten recalled what Kennedy had said about the Republicans—namely, that they were a party of the past—and she tended to agree with him. She repeated his words now, and everyone around her groaned.

"It looks like you've got a rabid Democrat on your hands, old boy." Alec raised his glass to him in sympathy.

"And all this from someone who, up until two months ago, couldn't tell politics from a polonaise." Even Kirsten had to smile at her husband's quick-witted response. But it still didn't change her mind about anything.

"What about his ideas?" she persisted, undeterred. "Aren't you the least bit stimulated by them?"

"The New Frontier." Jeffrey gave a derisive snort. "It sounds more like a cattle drive heading west than a potential administration. And he's certainly chosen the right man to help him with the roundup." He was referring to Kennedy's running mate, Lyndon Baines Johnson from Texas. Everyone but Kirsten laughed appreciatively.

"Why are you taking him so literally?" she demanded. "He means new frontier in the widest sense of the word. He's talking about every frontier imaginable—science, technology, medicine, space, ecology, civil rights, world peace. He's touching people, Jeffrey, he's waking up an entire nation. He's making everything sound not only feasible but possible, and I find it exhilarating. Exhilarating and challenging and exciting."

"If I were you, I'd save all that fervor for music, darling." Jeffrey put an end to their discussion by giving her a peck on the nose and a slightly condescending smile. "Passion and politics simply don't mix; they never have, they never will."

That's where you're wrong, she retorted, but this time she did so only to herself.

Jeffrey's snide suggestion to the contrary, her music was the one place where her fervor seemed to be lacking these days, and Natalya, as astute as ever, was quick to point this out to her.

"What's the matter, Kirishka?" The aging Russian stopped her favorite student in the middle of the new piece, a Mendelssohn sonata that she was mangling, and laid her hand on top of hers. Kirsten thought back to the previous night, when Jeffrey had been impotent, and tried not to grimace. "Aren't you happy?"

Keeping her eyes carefully trained on her sheet music, she nodded. "Of course I'm happy; I'm just tired, that's all. I have a forty-room house to look after now and—"

"Stop it!" Kirsten jumped.

"You don't lift a finger to run that place and you know it. It's not housework I hear in your playing, it's hollowness. Something's missing."

Kirsten had no quick answer for her this time. "I'm sorry," she said. "I'll try a bit harder."

"It isn't a question of trying harder; you can't produce what you're just not feeling."

Kirsten turned to her teacher with a look of loving tenderness on her face and smiled. "All I'm feeling is tired, Natalya, nothing more serious or more dramatic than that. And I *am* happy, really I am. I've just never been anyone's wife before."

Natalya sighed. She knew Kirsten far too well to be entirely convinced. But she also knew Kirsten's stubbornness; she would never admit defeat in anything. It was that very same stubbornness that had helped take her to where she was today—the top—but it certainly wouldn't be enough to keep her there. Only her unique and remarkable sound could do that. She rubbed her chest to quell the worried ache inside her, kissed Kirsten gently on both cheeks, and pointed her to the start of the sonata again. Then she settled back, hoping to hear a difference. She wasn't disappointed.

Kirsten received her schedule for the upcoming concert season from Nelson on the same day her doctor received the results of her lab tests. She was pregnant. In all probability, she had conceived on her wedding night. She was horrified. It was too soon, too soon. She wasn't ready. She had been a wife for less than two months, a role she still didn't feel completely comfortable in. Now, suddenly, she had to start preparing herself for another new role. As a mother.

She waited until the shock subsided, then reached for the

phone to call Jeffrey. It rang just as she was about to pick it up. The moment she heard her mother's voice, she began blurting out her news.

"What?" Obviously her mother hadn't heard her, because she was still talking herself. Kirsten stopped and listened. The blood seemed to drain from her face; her knees grew weak and the room began to tilt. "I don't believe you."

Natalya, her precious, beloved Natalya, had collapsed and died of a heart attack that morning directly across the street from Carnegie Hall.

20

"Who's Mommy's favorite girl, hmm, who is she, Meredith? Who's Mommy's own precious darling?" Kirsten crooned as she pecked soft little kisses all across the top of her daughter's dark head. "Who does Mommy love? That's right, my angel, Mommy loves you." Reaching for a strand of Kirsten's own dark hair, Meredith tugged the ends into her mouth and began to suck on them. "You like Mommy's hair, don't you? Well, one day your hair will look just like Mommy's and you'll be able to brush it all by yourself." She kissed her daughter on the forehead and continued walking up and down the nursery floor. "Do you know what else you'll be able to do, my darling? You'll be able to play the piano just like Mommy does, maybe even better. And I'll teach you, my angel, I'll teach you to be the best in the world."

This was her dream now, to instill in her daughter her own love of music, and to be to Meredith what her beloved Natalya had been to her. Would she be a worthy substitute, she wondered, her bottom lip quivering. It had been nearly a year since her mother had called her with the news of Natalya's death, yet her sense of loss was as devastating now as then, a dull, chronic ache buried deep within her heart.

Sometimes she found it impossible to believe Natalya was gone—that flamboyant Russian flame extinguished, that deep voice silenced forever. She still looked up from her practicing expecting to see her teacher beside her, head shaking, finger pointing. She still reached for the phone to dial Natalya's number whenever she was having difficulty with a new piece she was trying to learn. And she still refused to work with someone else; it seemed like sacrilege to her. She much preferred teaching herself, hoping Natalya would have approved of the results. Her audiences obviously did, because she was even more wildly acclaimed than before.

Nearly a year. And what a year it had been. Natalya had missed so much.

Much to Jeffrey's chagrin and her delight, John F. Kennedy had succeeded in capturing the hearts and imaginations of the American people and had been elected the country's thirty-fifth president in November. Although his margin of victory over former vice-president Richard Nixon had been less than one hundred thousand votes, it had still been enough to sweep him up and set him down at 1600 Pennsylvania Avenue. And it was there that the eyes of the entire country had been focused ever since.

The New Frontier had been officially launched on a brilliantly blue but bitterly cold January morning, in a snow-blanketed capital, in a blaze of sunshine. Vigor was the watchword of the young administration, and it was contagious. It made people feel young and vigorous too. It made them feel vital and energetic.

Like so many of her fellow artists, Kirsten was also looking to the First Lady now. For them, she was the embodiment of culture. She represented grace and refinement; she was elegant, urbane, well-educated, and sophisticated. And she had already begun to turn the once staid and provincial White House into a gathering place for the distinctive, the creative, and the cultured.

With John as their leader and Jackie as their patron, even the impossible didn't seem impossible anymore.

Meredith had fallen asleep. Gently, so as not to waken her, Kirsten lowered her into her crib and covered her with the pale yellow hand-crocheted blanket that had been a christening gift from Dierdre. There was nothing Kirsten enjoyed more than watching her daughter sleep—the dark lashes closed over eyes that promised to be as inky as Jeffrey's in a small, heart-shaped face that was entirely hers. Every moment they spent together was a gift to treasure because of all the time they spent apart.

Now, as she gazed down at her cherished child, Kirsten

was filled with a contentment she had never known before. She had the best of all possible worlds: she had a career, she was a wife, and she was a mother. She hugged herself and grinned, a wide, triumphant grin. She was doing it, actually doing it; she was proving all of them wrong.

The one blemish in an otherwise flawless Oliver family portrait was hers and Jeffrey's sex life. It remained as frustrating and dissatisfying for her as ever. The few times she had tried making love to Jeffrey—always against his protests—he hadn't been able to maintain his erection. In spite of her patience, her tenderness, and skill, he never stayed hard long enough to enter her. In the end, she had given up; it had hurt her to see him so humiliated. As long as he was the one to initiate their lovemaking, he could perform, however inadequate that performance might be. If the price for an otherwise contented life was an occasional half hour of frustration in bed, it seemed to her a small one to pay.

But as stoical as she was about it, she was also vulnerable, frighteningly vulnerable to the intrusion of the past upon her consciousness. Never was she more susceptible to memory's invasion than in those final moments before falling asleep. It was then that she would think about Michael, the sweetness of their times together all the sweeter now that they were over. And because she was so vulnerable, she made certain to stay away from him. Nelson had strict instructions not to book them any concerts together, and for the first time in their business relationship, he didn't argue with her. In his own canny way, he probably knew.

What they did argue about, though, was her adamant refusal to accept any further engagements in the South. Fear played a small part in her decision, but outrage played the greater part. The South was a powder keg of racial injustice ready to explode. By refusing to play there, she was adding her voice to the growing chorus of voices protesting the continuing inequity of segregation.

Starting quietly and sporadically, the movement had been gathering impetus over the past year. As in the rest of the country, the South was awakening too; only many of its people were keeping pace with a far different drummer, one who was preaching a much different message.

Demanding what Abraham Lincoln had promised them, but which they had never fully gotten: freedom. And equality under the law as provided for in the Constitution. Suddenly, new words were being invented to describe what was happening in the South—words like "sit-in" and "stand-in" and "jail-in." And when groups of blacks and whites joined together in hiring and riding buses throughout the South to protest segregated bus terminals, they, too, were given a name: freedom riders.

It was the horrifying sight of one of these so-called "freedom buses" being fire-bombed and its occupants beaten by a mob of angry whites while she was being driven to a recital in Savannah in May that had finally led to Kirsten's decision to boycott any city still supporting segregation.

"You can't just eliminate the entire South from your schedule," Nelson had protested. "Since when have you become so political anyway?"

"Since I took a look around and saw a lot of things I didn't like."

"But Kirsten, do you realize how many states you're talking about here?" He began ticking them off on his fingers.

"Call it my own war of secession in reverse," she quipped, and her agent groaned. "I'm sorry, Nelson, but I simply won't play in any city where half the population isn't even allowed to sit at a lunch counter let alone attend one of my performances."

"I thought I'd find you in here." Jeffrey came up behind her, locked his arms around her waist, and nuzzled her neck with his mouth. Kirsten leaned back against him and, sighing, closed her eyes. His hands moved up to cup her breasts and desire instantly sprang to life inside her. "How about playing hooky and skipping the dinner at the club tonight?" he asked, nibbling lightly on her earlobe. "Better still, why don't we just crawl into bed right now and stay there all weekend?"

Kirsten could feel him stiffening as he talked. "We can't play hooky tonight," she told him in as casual a voice as she could manage. "I'm the honorary chairman of the benefit, remember?" She turned in his arms, gave him a quick peck on the lips, and wriggled away from him.

She ran the water for a bath, changed into a long, quilted satin robe, then sat down at the vanity in her dressing room and began to file her nails. Hearing a noise at the door, she looked up and found Jeffrey standing there.

"I like watching you do that," he said, leaning casually against the doorframe, his hands in the pockets of his trousers.

"You do?" Kirsten immediately stopped filing and stared at him. "Aren't you the one who's always after me to let my nails *grow*?"

"A man can change his mind, can't he, or are only women allowed that prerogative?"

Kirsten laughed. "I don't think either gender has a monopoly on anything."

"Don't let the purists hear you say that; it could get you into trouble."

They continued chatting comfortably that way until Jeffrey surprised her by suddenly turning off the water in the tub. The only sound in the room now was the gentle scratching made by the emery board as it moved rhythmically back and forth across Kirsten's nails. A moment later it was superseded by another sound: breathing, rapid and slightly ragged. Startled, Kirsten looked over at Jeffrey again and gasped.

"Kirsten." His voice was hoarse as he came toward her, the huge bulge in his trousers almost level with her wide, staring eyes.

He took the emery board out of her hand and put it down on the vanity. Then he began to kiss her. He was rough in his haste, his breath hot against her cool skin, his hands tearing what they couldn't unbutton, tugging when they met resistance. Lowering her onto the carpeted floor, he unzipped his trousers.

She thought of the diaphragm hidden inside an empty stationery box in her writing desk, and panicked. Determined not to be caught unprepared again, she had been fitted for a diaphragm immediately following Meredith's birth. She felt slightly underhanded about it at times—taking great pains to hide the plastic case and contraceptive jelly—but she didn't want to risk either another pregnancy or Jeffrey's anger if he knew what she was doing.

"Wait, Jeffrey, wait." She struggled to break his hold on her, but he wouldn't let her go; he pinned her down with the full weight of his body as though she were a protest he had to stifle.

He was so aroused he hadn't even bothered to take off his trousers, and the cold metal of his open fly bit cruelly into her thigh. She wasn't ready; she was dry and tight, but he was bursting. Closing one hand around his engorged penis, he tried to ram it inside her.

"Please, Jeffrey," she cried. "You're hurting me. Stop, please stop. Jeffrey!"

He silenced her with a kiss, plunging his tongue so deep inside her mouth that she gagged. She felt herself tear as he finally succeeded in entering her, and she nearly passed out from the pain.

"Good, so good," he said, gasping, battering away at her. "Oh, God, yes . . . so good, so good . . . yes . . ." His voice trailed off; his frenzied breathing took over.

Closing his eyes, Jeffrey rode the feeling that was miraculously sending him on his first extended journey to paradise in over twenty years. In her failure to redeem him from his past, she had become its reincarnation instead. If he still wasn't free, if he was still enslaved, it no longer mattered. Not when this newest bondage held such glorious promise.

Even after soaking in the tub for nearly an hour Kirsten was still in pain. Everything hurt; her whole body felt swollen and raw and sore. She herself felt violated, stunned. Confused. Was the madman who had brutalized her the same one who professed to adore her? Was the stranger who had gasped obscenities in her ear the same gentle man who once courted her so gallantly? She wanted answers to questions she didn't dare voice aloud. She had, for all intents and purposes, been raped. And by her very own husband.

But no one would ever have guessed the truth as she and Jeffrey made their entrance at the Piping Rock Club later that evening. Kirsten was smiling and serene, wearing a sapphire-blue satin gown by Dior and a fortune in diamonds and sapphires; Jeffrey was the same attentive escort he always was, sporting his celebrated wife with possessive pride, like the rarest of roses in the black silk lapel of his tuxedo. The only difference between them was that while Jeffrey's glow permeated his entire being, Kirsten's went no deeper than the surface.

It became a ritual of theirs whenever Kirsten was home between tours for her to sit at the vanity in her dressing room, wearing only her robe, and file her nails, while Jeffrey would stand in the doorway fully clothed and watch her. But she was always ready now—her diaphragm snugly in place, some extra jelly keeping her moist and at least physically prepared. Mentally, it was a brief state of siege; she didn't dare resist. The one time she had tried to fight him off he had slapped her so hard she had lost her balance and fallen, narrowly missing hitting her head on a corner of the vanity. After making love to her anyway, he had been contrite, almost pathetically so; he had even bought her a spectacular amethyst and diamond pendant at Van Cleef & Arpels as a conciliatory gesture. He had never struck her again, but then, she had never tried resisting him again either.

She almost dreaded coming home now. But home also meant Meredith, and staying away from her precious child even a moment longer than necessary was a torture far worse than what Jeffrey subjected her to. If he had his favorite ritual, so did she. Hers was setting up Meredith's playpen in the conservatory so that her daughter could be close to her even when she was practicing. Much to the consternation of Meredith's nurse, Agnes MacLaughlin—who had also been Charles's and Jeffrey's nurse—the child thrived on the arrangement. Lying happily on her stomach, her thumb in her mouth, she would ignore everything around her—even her favorite stuffed animals—and stare raptly at her mother while she played.

"You're a regular Pied Piper, Kirsty," remarked Emil, who was sitting cross-legged on the floor beside the playpen. "She hasn't blinked once." Gianna left her chair and sat down next to her husband, smiling as he draped his arm around her shoulder. From her place at the piano, Kirsten watched them wistfully. Would her father ever have dared treat her mother the way Jeffrey had begun treating her? She gave a brief, involuntary shiver of disgust and looked away. "It could be you'll have some serious competition from this little beauty one of these days," her father concluded, and Kirsten smiled.

"Don't let Jeffrey hear you say that, Pappy," she warned him. At the moment Jeffrey was attending a medical convention in Boston. "He'll tell you one vagabond in the Oliver family is enough."

"Is that what he calls you, *cara*, a vagabond?" Ever the protective mother, Gianna was instantly on the alert for possible signs of trouble.

Without missing a note of her mother's favorite, "Moonlight Sonata," Kirsten laughed off her own remark. "That's just

Jeffrey's pet name for musicians, Mama, because we come and go so much and never stay in one place for long."

"I know what the word means, Kirsten," Gianna snapped, ready to pursue the subject further; but the appearance of Micah, the butler, in the doorway, prevented it.

"Dinner is served, madame," the elderly retainer announced in his usual funeral monotone, even though dinner was their regular Sunday cold buffet.

A moment later Agnes MacLaughlin came bustling into the conservatory, all Scottish efficiency, as humorless as always. "I'll take the wee one from you now, ma'am," she said. "It's way past her bedtime as it is."

No sooner had the nurse left the room with Meredith howling loudly in protest than Kirsten ambled over to her parents—her walk an excellent imitation of the stocky little Scotswoman's bandylegged gait—and linked arms with them. Then in a perfect parody of Micah's proper English accent, she pronounced, "Dinner is served," and led them, laughing, into the dining room.

"Well, she's late again," Lois whispered to Dierdre after a hasty peek at her watch. "But they'll forgive her; they always do." She was referring to the other members of the Long Island Historical Society attending their annual Christmas luncheon at the Palm Court of the Plaza Hotel.

"In their eyes our Kirsten can do no wrong, can she?" Dierdre was frowning as she took a small, ladylike sip of her Bloody Mary.

"A star is a star is a star."

"And if that star had been you?"

"Don't be a bitch, Dee." Lois took a sip of her own drink to keep from saying more.

"I know, I know." Dierdre gently patted her friend on the sleeve. "What galls you is the fact that she's gate-crashed and people are still tripping all over themselves to hold the door open for her."

Lois could hardly quarrel with the truth. To think the urchin had climbed so high and so far while she herself had gone nowhere. Nowhere. There wasn't a day when the enormity of that injustice didn't flagellate her. She glanced at Dierdre, a quick, furtive glance, and smiled to herself. For all her offhandedness, Dierdre was every bit as resentful of Kirsten Harald as she was.

Dierdre had caught Lois's covert look and now *she* was seething inside. Lois could afford to be smug; after all, Kirsten Harald wasn't *her* sister-in-law. She wasn't the one in perpetual danger of losing the only socially acceptable escort she had, namely Jeffrey. Without Jeffrey she, Dierdre, would never have been able to hold on to her exalted position at the head of Long Island's closed social list. Her husband's younger brother had proven himself not only useful these last ten years but utterly indispensable; and that was something she didn't want changed.

As if reading Dierdre's mind, Lois leaned across the table and gave her hand a light squeeze. "Look on the bright side, darling; with your career-minded sister-in-law away most of the time, Jeffrey's just as available to you now as he ever was. It could be worse, you know."

"And speaking of career-minded sisters-in-law." Dierdre had just noticed Kirsten coming in.

Lois turned to follow Dierdre's pointed stare. There wasn't a head in the posh and discreetly elegant Palm Court that wasn't turning to do the same. And nearly every one of those heads sported a new bouffant hairdo topped by a small, round pillbox hat. They may all have been staunch Republicans, but they all looked like replicas of the First Lady, whether the style suited them or not. It seemed Jackie Kennedy wasn't only the First Lady of the land but the First Lady of fashion as well. Everyone, including Dierdre, wanted to look like her. And as Lois had so astutely pointed out, copying Jackie was even patriotic now that she had switched her allegiance from European couturiers like Hubert Givenchy to Americans like Oleg Cassini.

In classic Jackie tradition, all the women were wearing either two-piece dresses with blouson tops or suits with semi-fitted jackets ending just below the waist and the requisite oversize button closing it at the neck. Their skirts were A-line, the hems reaching to mid-knee; their shoes were low-heeled pumps, and their handbags were quilted with long gold chains.

As usual, Kirsten was the only one daring to be different. She wasn't wearing a hat; her dress was a one-piece Mary Quant in a lip-smacking shade of raspberry, and she was carrying a black lizard clutch.

"Sorry I'm late," she apologized, stripping off her black kid gloves and pulling out a chair for herself. "But Meredith had a bit of a cold and I wanted to wait until Dr. Browning had seen her."

"And what did he say?" Dierdre inquired politely.

"That she has a slight cold and I'm an alarmist."

"It's only natural, I suppose, you're away from her so much."

Kirsten bit back a retort and replied to her sister-in-law's caustic remark with a gentle, "Perhaps."

Dierdre and Lois exchanged knowing glances. Neither of them said a word; neither one had to.

When the luncheon was over, Dierdre and Lois headed across the street to Bergdorf's, while Kirsten took advantage of being in the city to stop by Patelson's for some sheet music. Then she spent the next two hours happily browsing through a number of the art galleries and antique stores along Fifty-seventh Street. Just as she was about to cross Park Avenue, the portrait of a young woman in one of the gallery windows caught her eye. She immediately stopped and went to take a closer look at it. The style of the large oil was unmistakable, its sensitive perceptiveness unique. The beauty of the young woman's features was heightened by a breathtaking tenderness. And the signature, curving lovingly around the wavy blond hair that curled past her left shoulder read Beaton.

Kirsten shivered, her throat constricting painfully. She was hypnotized by the painting and couldn't look away. If ever an artist had captured the face of love, Andrew Beaton had captured it in the face of this woman. It was clear that she was far more to him than a simple subject—as she herself had been—she was obviously the very object of the love he had so touchingly depicted. *His* love. Kirsten winced as something sharp twisted inside her. Was it envy, she wondered. Jealousy? Regret? Was it a combination of all three?

A pair of eloquent eyes the color of moon-drenched lapis held hers a moment longer, then let her go. The name on the tiny wooden marker set directly in front of the portrait read Marianne. Marianne. Her name, Kirsten decided, was as lyrical as her face. Marianne and Andrew. Andrew and Marianne. Their two names went well together. Even their golden good looks were well matched.

She had one hand on the gallery door, when she suddenly changed her mind and started up the street again. She heard a man call her name, but she didn't stop until his strong hand grabbing hold of her by the elbow forced her to. Even after nearly three years, Andrew Beaton's initial impact on her senses was no less shattering than the time she had opened the door of her apartment to find him standing there. His overwhelming physical presence was an obstacle she still had to circumvent before she could look directly into his handsome face.

"So you were actually going to run off without saying hello to me." His grin was as maddeningly appealing as she remembered.

"I didn't know you were there to say hello to," she retorted, just managing to retrieve her elbow before he crushed it. He seemed to be waiting for something. Cocking her head to one side, she gave him a grin almost as wide as his own. "Hello," she said.

"Hello yourself." He dug his hands into the back pockets of his navy blue cords and rocked back and forth on the balls of his feet. "Did you hate it?" he asked.

"Hate what?"

"The cover I did of you."

"No, I didn't hate it." She could feel herself beginning to blush and hoped he would think it was due to the wind.

"But?"

"But I was a bit surprised," she admitted.

"Why? I painted only what I saw."

"Maybe that's what surprised me."

Andrew laughed, "The truth can do that to people, I suppose, especially when they're not prepared for it."

"And you said you never judged anyone."

"The truth's not a judgment," he said, "it's a statement. It's only what you do with the statement that makes it judgmental."

Just as she was bracing herself to ask him about the woman in the portrait, a man in a dark business suit came out of the gallery and beckoned impatiently to him. Andrew nodded and waved the man away. Turning to Kirsten again, he spoke quickly.

"My show officially opens tomorrow night at seven; we're just setting everything up now. I'd love it if you and your husband could come."

But Kirsten had to shake her head no. "I'm flying to Los Angeles in the morning," she said. The way he was studying her made her feel he was trying to see whether or not she was telling the truth.

"Too bad. Maybe some other time then." He gave her elbow another tight squeeze. "I know you're not one for shaking hands," he said with a smile as he left her and headed back toward the gallery. He turned around once to wave, and Kirsten waved back at him.

It was true about her flying to Los Angeles in the morning, but even if she had been in town, she doubted she would have had the courage to attend his opening. She didn't want to risk having her questions answered; it was far safer for her never to know.

21

Eric was seated at his desk, his hands steepled together, both thumbs pressed firmly against his bottom lip as he contemplated the two newspaper clippings spread out in front of him. One was crisp and fresh, a brief announcement snipped from the business section of that morning's edition of the *Liverpool Daily Post;* the other was brittle and yellowed, the words nearly indistinct, a somewhat longer story from the front page of the *Liverpool Dispatch* dated August 4, 1916. The head on the story from the *Post* read: MAGNATE BUYS LAST NEVILLE HOLDING; the one from the *Dispatch* read: BOTULISM KILLS FIFTEEN AFTER CHURCH BAZAAR. The tears in Eric's dark eyes turned the print into a complete blur; even after forty-eight years, those six telling words had that same devastating effect on him. It had taken him a long time, all his adult life in fact, but he had finally done it.

He had stalked them one by one, each of the five Neville brothers, until he had bought all of them out. The Manchester shipping line. The Brighton hotels. The Stafford pottery works. The Liverpool canning factory. The wool mills in Leeds. Over the years his list had been determinedly whittled down, their holdings systematically pared away. And now, the last of them—the Sunderland iron smeltery—was gone. It was over.

Eric got up and poured himself some sherry. Then he raised his glass in a silent toast to this, his long-anticipated moment of victory. His eyes stung as he tossed back his drink in a single, bittersweet swallow. But the stinging had nothing to do with the sherry; it had to do with a tired young woman named Anne Johnson and her daughters, Sara and Hester. And the pickled beets the three of them had sampled at the monthly bazaar held in the basement of St. Mary's, while Joe Johnson and his four sons had kept to the apple cider.

Now, after forty-eight years, Eric was ready to lay the ghosts of his mother and two sisters to rest. The son of humble Anne and Joe Johnson had finally bested the sons of high-hatted Glenda and Wesley Neville. Little Eric Johnson, the postman's boy, had finally paid back the mayor's five boys. They all worked for him now. They were nothing, but then, they deserved to be nothing. Because it was their mother Glenda's batch of tainted beets that had cost fifteen of their almighty father's ordinary townspeople their common but decent lives.

"Eric!"

Claudia's sharp voice from the doorway crackled through his reverie, instantly jolting him back into the present.

"There's some man downstairs who claims he's here to paint the third-floor flat. Is that true?"

Rankled by his wife's belligerent tone, Eric slammed down his glass and turned to look at her. "Yes, it bloody well is true."

"Well, you needn't have bothered, because I'm only going to send him away."

"Not this time, you're not."

"The hell I won't."

"The hell you will!"

Claudia pursed her lips together until they seemed to vanish inside the creases lining her pale, thin face. "I've told you before, Eric, I simply won't tolerate strangers mucking about up there."

"And I've told you before I want that bloody place redecorated." Try as he might, he was finding it increasingly difficult to keep his temper under control and make his wife see reason at the same time, especially when it was obvious that Claudia and reason had parted company long ago.

"You know damned well I don't want it redecorated." Her voice was growing shrill. "I want it kept just as it is."

Eric began to clench and unclench his fists. "You're obsessed, Claudia. Do you hear me? Obsessed. You were obsessed with Nigel Bisham, you were obsessed with Wynford

Hall, and now you're obsessed with Kirsten Harald. Well, it's time we called a halt to all this bloody madness, because that's exactly what it is, you know, madness."

He was unprepared for the peal of shrill laughter that greeted his pronouncement, and its piercing sound set his teeth on edge.

"Poor Eric, what a burden you're carrying. Call it whatever you like, I don't mind. If the term madness pleases you, then so be it, consider me mad." She let her face go all slack and vacant-eyed, and Eric turned away in disgust. "But mad or not, I absolutely forbid you to touch that flat. I'd see it sealed over first. Have I made myself clear?" When Eric failed to answer, she kept repeating the question until he did. "Good, now we finally understand each other."

"Hardly," he snapped. Reaching for the crystal decanter in which he kept his sherry, he hastily refilled his glass. "Oh, by the way," he said, lowering his voice in an effort to sound nonchalant, "I've asked Alan Jessop to drop by the house tomorrow at eight."

The mention of their longtime family doctor's name immediately put Claudia on guard. "Alan Jessop, whatever for? Are you ill?"

"I'm perfectly fine. I thought it might be nice to have him over for a drink, that's all. We haven't seen much of him since Molly died." Molly was Alan's late wife. "Nothing grand, mind you, just three old friends getting together to—"

"Oh, no, you don't," Claudia shouted. "Precisely what kind of fool do you take me for? Did you honestly believe I wouldn't see right through this latest ploy of yours? If I haven't spoken to any of the other esteemed doctors you've trotted out here over the years, what makes you think I'll speak to Alan? If I were you, Eric, I'd tell the good doctor not to come. That way you'll be spared the embarrassment of watching me slam the door in his face." To emphasize her point, she grabbed hold of the study door on her way out of the room and slammed it shut with a nerve-jarring bang.

Eric stared balefully at the closed door while he finished his sherry, then poured himself another. His ongoing battle with Claudia was wearing him down. Having long since passed the point where his anger, pain, and frustration had fused, it was now virtually impossible for him to tell where one emotion left off and another began. Claudia was destroying herself, and while she seemed perfectly content to do so, he was still resolved to make it as difficult for her as possible.

Clutching the decanter of sherry by the neck, he carried it over to his desk and sat down again. What he needed right now was surcease. Perhaps if he got royally drunk . . . Squiffy. Blotto. Blind. Drunk as a lord, falling-down drunk. He poured himself a fourth sherry, then proceeded to work his way through the entire decanter.

But the surcease he so desperately needed continued to elude him.

"My God, I'm so nervous, my hands won't stop shaking," Kirsten whispered to Jeffrey.

"How do you think I feel?" Her husband brushed an imaginary speck of dust from the satin lapel of his tuxedo jacket. "I'm the one in the enemy camp, and I'll probably never be forgiven for it."

In spite of her nervousness, Kirsten couldn't help but smile. Jeffrey, the diehard Eisenhower Republican, had just been forced to share a dinner table in the Red Room of the White House with Secretary of State Dean Rusk and his wife, speechwriter Ted Sorenson and his wife, New York City Ballet choreographer George Balanchine, and contralto Marian Anderson, one of the thirty-one recipients of the new Presidential Medal of Freedom awarded in July.

"I still can't believe this is real," she whispered to him again. Jeffrey merely grunted.

It was true, none of it did seem real: the embossed invitation they had received a month ago; the East Room crowded with various dignitaries and guests, all of them eagerly awaiting the appearance of the President and First Lady; the martial music announcing their arrival; the long receiving line; the President's easy smile and affable warmth; Jackie's whispery voice and touching shyness; the guests being ushered into dinner; the endless round of toasts. Until now, when here they were, back in the East Room again, seated in long rows of gilt-backed chairs, listening to actor Frederic March read a selection from Ernest Hemingway's *A Moveable Feast*.

"How can you be so blasé about it?" Kirsten was frowning as she studied her husband's arrogant profile. "In the last three years they've turned this place into a cultural Mecca." Mecca. Claudia had once used that very same word to describe their town house in London to her. The thought gave her some pause. But Claudia aside, the Kennedy White House had indeed become the gathering place for the great that it had always promised to be. Scores of internationally renowned performers had played here; every form of entertainment imaginable had been featured here. And tonight it was her turn. "Don't you realize that the Kennedys have been to America what the Medicis were to Italy?" she continued. "This has been our own creative renaissance, Jeffrey, our cultural Eden, our—"

"Camelot?" he interrupted, turning to her with a sarcastic smile. Camelot was what everyone had begun to call the administration because the President apparently loved to play the sound track from the Lerner and Loewe musical about King Arthur and his court every night before he went to bed. Was that how Kennedy saw himself, Jeffrey wondered, as the legendary Arthur surrounded by his loyal Knights of the Round Table. He scowled. He had no use for romantic fluff like that or for any man who indulged in it.

But Kirsten stubbornly refused to let the matter drop. Recalling that even Spanish cellist Pablo Casals had played for the President after years of refusing to perform at all in the United States because of the government's support for Generalissimo Franco, she mentioned it to Jeffrey, who looked totally unimpressed by the information.

"Don't you think it says something about the Kennedys when someone like Casals agrees to perform for them?" Jeffrey yawned. "God, the last time the man played here, it was for Teddy Roosevelt." That perked him up instantly.

"Now, *there* was a president for you!"

Kirsten sighed. Jeffrey was impossible. But he still couldn't dampen her spirits or dull her enthusiasm about tonight; nothing could, not even the chill November night air that hovered about the edges of the large formal reception room. The First Lady had worked wonders with the presidential mansion, transforming it from something that resembled the lobby of a grand hotel into a homey showplace for the best of America's rich heritage. Then, once the extensive renovations were completed, she had graciously invited the TV cameras inside, and for an hour she had taken the country on a personal tour of the place.

Kirsten herself had seen Jackie in person only once before. It was the previous September, and she had come to New

York for the dedicatory concert formally opening Lincoln
Center's new Philharmonic Hall. Kirsten had performed two
selections from Schumann and one from Liszt that evening as
part of the opening festivities, and she had found out sometime later that the First Lady had so loved her playing that
she had gone out and ordered every one of her recordings.

Now, as she watched Jackie sitting silently between news
commentator David Brinkley and Washington columnist Art
Buchwald, she felt a slight catching in her throat. Exquisitely
gowned by Cassini in a sheath of shell pink satin, its Empire-
style bodice heavily encrusted with clear bugle beads, her
only jewelry a pair of large diamond drop earrings, she seemed
so serene and composed in her beauty. Yet she had recently
buried her infant son, Patrick Bouvier—only two days after
his premature birth—and had then set vicious tongues wagging when she embarked on a two-week recuperative sail
through the Aegean aboard the yacht of Greek shipping magnate Aristotle Onassis.

"Kirsten?" Jeffrey nudged her with his elbow. Frederic
March was walking back to his seat; the applause was dying
down. She was next on the program.

She swept over to the piano, a nine-foot concert grand,
accompanied by a fresh burst of applause. The spectacular
diamond and amethyst choker she was wearing caught the
light of an overhead chandelier and encircled her throat in its
glow; the long train of her lavender silk-chiffon evening gown
curled into a graceful semicircle at her feet as she seated
herself at the keyboard and waited for the room to grow silent
again. At dinner she had overheard someone making the
comment that these performances honored both the guests
and the artists, and she agreed. They had honored her with
their invitation here this evening; now it was her turn to
honor them with her playing.

For her performance she had chosen selections from Grieg,
Schubert, Chopin, and Rachmaninoff; and then to everyone's
delight—especially the President's—she concluded with a med-
ley of songs from his beloved *Camelot*. Only after she had
played three encores, including, of course, Debussy's "Reflets dans l'Eau," did the wildly appreciative audience finally
let her go. There were tears in the First Lady's eyes and her
lovely face was radiant as Kirsten took her seat again. She
herself was breathless and flushed with excitement, but she
felt her breathing stop altogether when the President himself

got up and came over to her. Taking hold of both her hands, he said, "Thank you, my dear," in that distinctive Boston twang of his. Then he returned to his own seat again and sat down. Kirsten stared after him, stunned, her hands warm and tingly, while Jeffrey simply stared at her.

One week later, Camelot came to an end.

Like everyone else, she would always remember where she was when she heard the news. It was three o'clock in the afternoon on the twenty-second of November, and she was being driven by limousine to the Drake Hotel in Chicago. The driver turned up the volume on the radio as soon as the program he had been listening to was interrupted for the bulletin, and Kirsten let out a shriek. Kennedy was dead. Shot while he and Jackie were traveling in an open motorcade through the streets of downtown Dallas. He had flown to Texas with Jackie only the day before, ostensibly to heal a rift between the state's liberal and conservative Democrats, and now, suddenly, he was dead.

It didn't seem possible.

She put her face in her hands and started to sob. The dream as he had dreamed it had ended; coldly and calculatedly shattered by a madman's bullets.

Had it been only a week since she had played for him in the East Room of the White House? Even that didn't seem possible now. The feeling of loss was so intense it made her feel weak. It went far beyond simple grief to encompass a dozen other emotions, the strongest ones being anger and helplessness and the birth of a terrible kind of cynicism.

Suddenly, she was afraid for the country. Had this been the isolated act of some solitary madman, she wondered, or had the country itself become tainted somehow.

The scene inside the lobby of the Drake was one that was being repeated all over the world. Whoever wasn't walking around looking dazed was either bent over a transistor radio, staring at a TV screen, or crying openly. Strangers clung desperately to other strangers, seeking not only comfort, but answers. After years of priding themselves on being one of the few civilized countries left in the world, no one was quite as certain about that anymore. Murder had touched the White House, the highest, most respected office in the land; everyone, no matter what their political beliefs or their party, had been touched too. It was a nightmare, and two hundred million people were all having the same one.

Alone in her hotel room, Kirsten, like millions of other Americans, sat for hours, bleary-eyed and sick at heart, in front of the TV. After a while she was no longer able to register anything she was seeing particularly clearly; all she would ever remember of that day and of the three that followed would be a series of gruesome, almost surrealistic images.

Suddenly she didn't want to be where she was, she wanted to be at home. With Jeffrey. And her parents. But most of all with Meredith. To know she was safe.

Watching the man who had awakened her interest in the world around her pass from her eyes and into history, she found herself believing that perhaps complacency was better after all. Indifference didn't hurt, neither did disinterest. Only caring hurt. And suddenly she didn't want to care anymore; she wanted to pull the covers of her music back over her head again and wait until the pain and the madness went away.

22

"Mommy, it's time to play."

Kirsten put down her pen and looked up at her three-year-old daughter in bewilderment. "Play?" she repeated, continuing Meredith's favorite new game. "Play what, darling, play with your dolls?"

"No, Mommy, not with my dolls."

"The puppy?"

Meredith shook her head. "No, not the puppy."

"With Cook then?"

"Uh-uh, not with Cook."

"Outside in the garden?"

"You're wrong again, Mommy, only one more guess. Try hard now, really hard."

Kirsten waited another moment while she pretended to be thinking, then snapped her fingers. "I know," she said, watching her daughter's glowing black eyes grow wider and wider. "You want to play the piano."

"Ya-ay, ya-ay, ya-ay!" Meredith shouted, jumping up and down excitedly. "You're right, Mommy, I do want to play the piano." Flinging herself at Kirsten, she wrapped her arms tightly around her mother's waist. "You're so smart, Mommy," she said. "I love you so, so, so much."

"And I love you, my precious." Kirsten bent down and scooped her daughter up into her arms. "My goodness, but you're getting heavy. Soon you'll be strong enough to carry me."

"Oh, Mommy," giggled the little girl, "I'll never be *that* strong."

Kirsten set Meredith down on the piano bench and started her off at middle C. Then while she watched her daughter's small hands work their way through her growing repertoire of nursery rhymes, she indulged in one of her favorite fantasies: Meredith in concert at Carnegie Hall, playing Rachmaninoff or Brahms or Liszt, not "Three Blind Mice," as she was playing now. Meredith basking in the golden limelight of success. Meredith standing at the top of the golden mountain, breathing in the rarefied air reserved only for those precious few.

A few, like Kirsten herself, who was now ranked among the finest pianists of the twentieth century. Hailed as one of the most gifted interpreters ever of the Romantic composers. Her name linked reverently with a handful of other pianists: Horowitz, Rubinstein, Serkin, Richter, and Ashkenazy. Not surprisingly, all five of them men. She had toured the entire world many times over, her records were always listed among the top-selling recordings anywhere; her career was still a glorious, golden arc of triumph.

But like Horowitz and Ashkenazy and the others, she paid a price for her glittering success. Except for July and August—which she had been taking off since the summer of her marriage to Jeffrey—she was seldom home for more than three days in a row at any one time. She missed her family and they missed her; together they missed sharing what other families normally shared. Matters grand and matters unimportant. As a result, whenever she *was* home, the three of them crammed a week's worth of missed moments into every hour, a month's worth into every day, an entire year into every summer. And they learned to be content with what they did have.

"Was that good, Mommy?" Meredith was tugging impatiently at Kirsten's sleeve, trying to get her attention.

Kirsten kissed the back of the small, warm hand and smiled. "It was wonderful."

"I don't think I want to play anymore right now."

"Are you tired, darling?" Meredith shook her head. "What then?"

"Sad."

Kirsten felt a sudden stab of concern. "Sad, Meredith, why?"

"Because you won't be here for my Halloween party next week." She looked down at the tips of her black Mary Janes and her bottom lip began to quiver. "You're never here."

"Meredith, that's not true." Kirsten lifted her daughter onto her lap and started stroking her long, dark hair. "I was here all summer, remember, and I'm here now, aren't I?"

"I know, but I still miss you. Don't you want to be here?"

"Of course I do, my darling." But Meredith didn't seem too convinced. "You know what Mommy does, don't you?"

"You play the piano."

"That's right. And a lot of people want to hear me play. But because they can't come to New York to hear me, I have to go to the cities where they live and play for them there."

"And do all those cities have pianos?"

"Yes, my precious, all those cities have pianos." This seemed to impress Meredith. "Would you like to see some of those pianos one day?"

"Oh, yes, Mommy, yes, I would." Suddenly, the small heart-shaped face was glowing.

"Then one day when you're a bit older, you can come on tour with me and see as many of them as you like."

Meredith tried to think of the highest number she knew. "Even a million?"

"Even a million."

She sighed happily and wrapped her arms around Kirsten's neck. "Now I'm not sad anymore," she said.

But Kirsten wasn't ready to let it go at that; she had an idea. "Darling, why don't you ask Miss MacLaughlin to help you put on the costume you're going to wear to the party?" Meredith sat up straight and gave her mother a funny look. "I'll wait right here, then as soon as you're ready, you come downstairs again and surprise me. Okay?"

Now Meredith understood. "Okay." Sliding down from her mother's lap, she scampered out of the room.

She returned fifteen minutes later looking like a miniature gypsy. She was wearing a red, purple, and white satin dress, a headdress of matching satin flowers and trailing ribbons in her hair, and carrying a small, beribboned tambourine. Tiny gold hoops swung from her ears, and when she moved, the dozens of small silver bells sewn around the neck and hem of her costume started to jangle. Kirsten made a great production out of her daughter's entrance, then began pounding out a lively mazurka at the keyboard. Meredith immediately joined in. Banging loudly on her tambourine, she improvised the steps to a gypsy dance and danced until she was breathless. Then she climbed up onto her mother's lap again and collapsed.

"You're the most beautiful Gypsy I've ever seen," Kirsten said as she bounced the little girl on her knee. "The most beautiful in the whole wide world."

"But I can be even more beautiful," Meredith told her, still slightly breathless from her dance, "if you let me wear your bracelet."

"Which bracelet, darling?"

"You know, the one with the bells on it."

The day Meredith had discovered the gold charm bracelet in the bottom drawer of one of Kirsten's dressers, she had found herself a plaything. There was nothing she enjoyed more than holding it close to her ear and shaking it just to hear the musical sounds it made.

"So, can I wear it, Mommy, can I, please?"

"It's too big, darling, it might fall off."

"No, it won't."

"Yes, Meredith, it will."

"I'll be careful."

"Meredith—"

"Please, Mommy, I'll be careful, I will, I will." Her face was darkening, tears were threatening, and her voice was rising in a wail.

"Hey, what's all the commotion about?"

At the sight of her father coming toward them, Meredith's mouth instantly snapped shut. Jeffrey bent to kiss Kirsten hello, then gave his daughter a hug.

"Well, now," he said, stepping back for a better look at her costume, "what have we here?"

"A gypsy," she mumbled, keeping her head down.

"A gypsy, my, my, my."

As Kirsten watched Jeffrey trying to coax their daughter out of one of her rare black moods, she felt wonderfully warm and happy inside. Moments like these were all too infrequent for the three of them, and she reveled in them.

"Now, can you tell me what you're pouting about?" she heard Jeffrey say. Meredith muttered something under her breath, which he had her repeat.

"Mommy won't let me wear her bracelet," she said, looking him directly in the eye for the first time. "The one with the bells on it."

"The bells?" Jeffrey glanced over at Kirsten. Suddenly, she could feel her heart start to pound. "She means the charm bracelet, doesn't she?"

"Yes, Daddy, that's the one," Meredith piped up. "The charm bracelet. Could you ask Mommy to let me wear it? Could you, Daddy, could you?"

But Jeffrey was no longer listening to her; all he could hear was the blood rushing to his temples. Giving his daughter a couple of absentminded pats on the back, he said, "Go upstairs to your room now, Meredith."

"But—"

"No buts, just do as you're told."

"Then you won't ask her?"

"No, I won't ask her."

With her large black eyes welling, Meredith ran out of the conservatory and up the stairs to find Miss MacLaughlin. At least her nurse loved her.

As Jeffrey glared at Kirsten, his own face was as dark as his daughter's had been only moments before. "So you still have the bracelet," he said.

Kirsten met his hardened gaze without flinching. "Yes, I still have it."

"Why?"

"Because it means a great deal to me, that's why."

"And does *he* still mean a great deal to you?" She didn't answer him. "Well, does he?"

"Michael Eastbourne was and is a part of my music, the way every other conductor I've ever played with is a part of my music."

"Now, that's a safe answer if I've ever heard one. Have you seen him?" He watched through narrowed eyes as she got up from the piano to put some distance between them. "I said, have you—"

"No, Jeffrey, I haven't seen him."

"I've got only your word on that though, haven't I?"

Kirsten rolled her eyes impatiently. "Why would I lie?"

"Why wouldn't you?"

"Jeffrey, stop it. You're getting upset for nothing. I haven't seen Michael and I haven't played with Michael since before you and I were married."

"And of course the only place you ever played with him was onstage, right?"

"Now you're being crude." She refused to be baited any longer and started to leave. But Jeffrey grabbed her by the wrist and spun her around to face him.

"You're gone over two hundred days a year, dammit, how the hell do I know who you are and aren't seeing?"

"Jeffrey, you're hurting me. Please let me go."

But instead, he grabbed hold of her other wrist and bent both of her hands back so far she screamed out in pain. "Sometimes I think I'd like nothing better than to snap these precious hands of yours in half, Kirsten. Maybe I should. It would be one sure way of keeping you here, now, wouldn't it?" He released her as abruptly as he had seized her and strode from the room.

Kirsten watched him leave, anxiously rotating and rubbing her throbbing wrists to make certain he had done nothing more serious than just threaten to harm her. Once again his flashfire temper had caught her off guard; once again his violent side had surfaced, consuming him and rendering him unrecognizable. The flare-up had been brief, but it had shaken her, upset the balance between them, and made her wary of him all over again. She was married to a man cursed with the irrational and uncontrollable temper of a child. And as with all children who throw tantrums, she had learned it was best to leave him alone until the anger had burned itself out completely.

She took a quick shower, changed into the new two-piece black lace Valentino she had bought on a whim the week before, and was just fastening the diamond clasp on the double strand of opera-length baroque pearls Jeffrey had bought for her thirty-first birthday in June, when Jeffrey himself tiptoed into her dressing room looking shamefaced and contrite. Bending down, he gripped her shoulders with both hands and kissed her on the neck.

"I'm sorry, Kirsten," he said. "I was jealous, forgive me." He took her hands, turned them over to examine her wrists, then kissed the soft insides of her palms, his touch once again the gentle, caring touch of the concerned healer. Kirsten closed her eyes for a moment and willed her tense body to relax. "Not a mark on you," he joked, and she cracked a slight smile. "Say you'll forgive me, Kirsten, please." The plaintive urgency in his voice made him difficult to resist.

"It's over, Jeffrey, I'm fine," she told him. "Let's just forget about it."

He watched her clip on a pair of pearl and diamond earrings, then study herself briefly in the mirror above her vanity.

"Perfect," he said, and Kirsten rewarded him with a genuinely warm and appreciative smile. "Should I be getting jealous again?"

"Of Eric?" She laughed. "Hardly."

"But you are standing me up in order to have dinner with him."

"He's going to be in town only overnight, remember?" She tapped him playfully on the nose with her finger. "Besides, he sounded so completely miserable when he phoned from London last week, I didn't have the heart to tell him I couldn't see him." Her playfulness turned tender as she stroked the side of his face. "I'm sorry it had to be tonight, really I am." There was to be a black tie reception at the Waldorf-Astoria at seven for Republican Senator Barry Goldwater, who was campaigning for the presidency against the incumbent president, Lyndon Johnson. But what Jeffrey didn't know was that a dinner was being given at the same time at the St. Regis in honor of Robert Kennedy, who was running for the United States Senate from New York. If she had had her druthers—and Eric hadn't been in town—she would have much preferred going to that one.

Despite her contradictory feelings immediately following John Kennedy's assassination, she hadn't given in to her emotions and retreated from the world. On the contrary, she had remained as curious and as interested as before, and, much to Jeffrey's consternation, just as diametrically opposed to his political views and those of his wealthy and influential friends. She couldn't help herself; she found them all so smug and so insulated, far more insulated than she had ever been, so eager for things to return to the way they were before the idealistic young senator from Massachussetts had come along and occupied the White House.

Their supreme indifference to the plight of others bordered on callousness, and that appalled her. What they gave to their trendy charities was, in her opinion, merely conscience money; they gave nothing of themselves in the form of genuine empathy or true concern. When the sweeping Civil Rights Act was signed into law by President Johnson in July as his personal tribute to his slain predecessor, their reaction to its historic passage had been no reaction. When race riots broke out in both Rochester and the Bedford-Stuyvesant section of Brooklyn during the summer, they had simply ignored them. When Martin Luther King, Jr. was awarded the Nobel Peace Prize in October, they had shrugged it off as another example of liberal tokenism. The longer she lived on Long Island and saw how isolated the people around her were from the rest of the world, the more isolated from *them* she became.

Totally unaware of what his wife was thinking, Jeffrey gave her a light peck on the cheek and thanked God that at least Dierdre would be at the reception tonight. Although he would never have admitted it to Kirsten, he found these functions extremely dull. Telling her to give Eric his best, he left her and walked slowly back to his own dressing room. But instead of changing into his tuxedo, he simply stood in front of the heavy oak-framed cheval glass that had been his father's and considered his reflection. Inside he was a turbulent mass of contradictory feelings, the most dominant one being desperation. It was almost impossible for him to make love to Kirsten now. His erections were rare; each one was a miracle, a cause for jubilation. Nothing worked anymore. His own fertile imagination was dried up and barren, a wasteland of failed fantasies. He was desperate for a newer one, one that would make him whole again.

To his horror, when he had grabbed Kirsten's hands and bent them back, the very thought of breaking them had made him hard. Her hands, her perfect hands. Her allies, his enemies, keeping them apart. If he was impotent, she was the cause. It was her fault. He had believed in her, worshiped her, and she had failed him. She had proven herself to be not a diety, but merely mortal, just as he was. Not divine at all, but human—disappointingly, cruelly human. And for that he despised her.

He thought of Dierdre, his glacial and unapproachable sister-in-law, and wondered how she had managed all these years. Did she have a secret lover somewhere? Was the unimpeachably perfect Dierdre in reality a closet Lady Chatterley? He laughed as he pictured her with her elegant mane of hair all tousled, and one of the gardeners or the pool man pumping away at her while she yawned and checked her social calendar for the time of her next luncheon date. Tossing the image off as nonsense, he removed his jacket and unzipped his trousers.

He could barely get the zipper past the enormous erection that was protruding, like a roadblock, through the fly of his undershorts.

At their corner table at La Caravelle on Fifty-fifth Street, Eric had just finished telling Kirsten about Claudia. She felt sick, utterly sick. The Claudia he had been describing was nothing like the vibrant, witty sophisticate she had last seen in London ten years before. That she herself was the object of Claudia's unnatural obsession made it all the more painful. She thought of the woman's attempts to seduce her and inwardly cringed, but her face reflected only her very genuine concern.

"Has she seen anyone?" she asked. Eric shook his head. "Have you spoken to anyone yourself?"

"Several people. But my talking to them won't help her. She's the one who needs the help, not me."

"Is there anything I can do?"

Eric's eyes were filled with gratitude at her offer, but once again he was forced to shake his head no. "I thank you, lamb, but nothing either of us does will make the slightest bit of difference, I'm afraid. Claudia seems to think she's perfectly fine. She's frozen time at the year 1954 and that's precisely where she intends to keep it."

Kirsten found eating almost impossible after that. She picked and poked at her slice of poached salmon, feeling slightly nauseated by the sight of the pinkish-colored fish on her plate and by the smell of Eric's blood-rare roast beef. She nibbled on a bread stick instead and hoped he wouldn't notice. He didn't, he was far too preoccupied.

She made it home just in time. Bolting the door to her bathroom, she dropped to her knees in front of the toilet and threw up. When it was all over, she washed her face and hands and brushed her teeth. Then she took her temperature. It was normal. Obviously it wasn't the flu; more than likely it was something she had eaten at lunch. She cast her mind back—all she had had for lunch was an omelet. Worried, she went looking for Jeffrey and found he hadn't come home yet.

She got undressed and slipped into bed, but she was still

feeling slightly nauseated. Turning gingerly onto her side, she let out a yelp of pain. Her breasts were so sensitive she couldn't bear to put any pressure on them. A moment later she was sitting bolt upright in bed, shivering. She had missed her period this month.

She nearly tripped in her haste to get to the empty stationery box in the middle drawer of her writing desk. Carrying the box back into the bathroom with her, she quickly locked the door again and took out the pale blue plastic case containing her diaphragm. Her stomach was tied in an excruciating knot of pure panic as she snapped open the lid and lifted out the broad rubber disc. Holding it up to the light, she narrowed her eyes and scrutinized it carefully.

Six tiny holes, no larger than pinpricks, had been punched through the heavy rubber.

23

> "Happy birthday to you,
> Happy birthday to you,
> Happy birthday, dear Je-eff,
> Happy birthday to you."

Only Jeffrey's deep voice had extended the Jeff to Jeffrey, and his smile was almost sheepish as his eyes met Kirsten's. Dierdre, who had been put in charge of holding her one-year-old godson while Kirsten lit the two bright blue candles on his cake, moved closer to the head of the table as Jeffrey called out, "All together now, blow!"

The two candles went out with a whoosh and a flourish, and everyone clapped appropriately.

"Are we cutting the cake right away, Mommy?" asked five-year-old Meredith, letting go of her grandmother Gianna's hand long enough to grab onto Kirsten's.

Gazing down adoringly at her beautiful young daughter, Kirsten said in an undertone only Meredith could hear, "Haven't you forgotten something?"

"Oops, you're right, I did forget." Signaling the others to follow her, she led everyone out of the dining room and down the hall to the conservatory.

While the thirty-two adults and twelve children were busy
assembling themselves around the piano, Meredith sat down
at the keyboard and waited until she had their full attention.
Then, after a last anxious glance at her mother, she launched
into her own version of "Happy Birthday," followed by "For
He's a Jolly Good Fellow," and concluding with a short song
she had composed herself especially for the occasion. At the
end of the brief recital there was a spontaneous burst of
genuinely appreciative applause, which Meredith acknowledged the way her mother had taught her to: she pressed
both hands to her chest, dropped gracefully onto one knee,
and bowed her head.

"Brava, my princess, brava!" Jeffrey shouted, applauding
louder than anyone else in the room. "That was marvelous,
darling, absolutely marvelous."

Meredith looked up at her father and smiled, but after
taking her final bow, it was to her mother that she ran, not
him.

"Now can we cut the cake?" she asked, her small face
flushed and shining with pleasure.

"Yes, darling," Kirsten told her, "now we can cut the
cake." Turning to her sister-in-law, she said, "I'll take Jeff
from you, Dierdre. He must be getting heavy."

Dierdre sniffed. "Not so much heavy, dear, as damp."

Kirsten couldn't help laughing. "That's the best part about
being a godmother; it's the real mother who gets to change all
the diapers." She had meant it as a joke, but Dierdre didn't
crack a smile. Addressing the others, she said, "If you'll all
excuse me a moment, our birthday boy here needs some
special attention." She started for the door with Meredith
trailing after her.

"You come with me, Meredith." Jeffrey was beckoning to
his daughter, but she just shook her head.

"I want to go upstairs with Mommy," she said.

"Meredith!"

Hearing the threatening tone in Jeffrey's voice, Kirsten
urged the resistant child to do what her father wanted.

"Please go with Daddy, darling, he needs your help in
cutting the cake. Don't you, Jeffrey?"

"Yes, yes, I do, princess. I'm really not very good at that
sort of thing."

"Oh, all right." She submitted almost meekly and took the

hand he was holding out to her. "It's pretty easy, you know; the only hard part is getting all the pieces the same size."

With peace temporarily restored, Kirsten hurried upstairs to the third-floor nursery. It was Agnes MacLaughlin's Sunday off and she was thrilled to be looking after her son alone.

"Hi there, my darling," she called softly to the little boy whose luminous eyes were the same clear blue as her father's but whose other features were a striking blend of both hers and Jeffrey's. "Hi, my angel." Bending over him on the changing table, she planted two noisy, smacking kisses right in the middle of his tummy. He giggled, and she kissed him again. Then she put him down in the crib that had once been his sister's. "I have such a good boy, yes, I do," she crooned, brushing back the fringe of dark hair falling in a straight line across his forehead, "such a good, good boy."

God, how she adored her children. They were her center, the reason she returned from whatever corner of the world she happened to be touring, the focus of every moment she spent at home. What she now shared with Jeffrey was a kind of friendly but guarded truce. The night she had discovered those six insidious punctures in her diaphragm, the last of the trust and hope had gone out of their marriage. When she had confronted him, accusing him of sabotage, he in turn had accused her of trying to cheat him out of the sons he wanted. Each of them had been right in his own way, and the result of that realization had been a standoff of stony silence lasting several weeks.

Although Jeff's birth the day before her own thirty-second birthday had closed a bit of the distance between them, some residual bitterness and mistrust still remained on both sides. They were undeniably united in one area, however—they both cherished the child they had created together in spite of the painful circumstances surrounding his conception. And that made the truce between them tolerable.

She smiled as Jeff slipped his thumb into his mouth and began to make gentle sucking sounds. There was nothing quite like the sleep of the young. How she envied them sometimes. She closed her own eyes for a moment, but all she saw was a collage of turmoil. What she was convinced had had its start with the murder of John Kennedy had been continuing over the years: that maddened spiral downward toward the abyss.

The country was out of control. The watchword had changed

from vigor to violence. For her, turning on the TV had become a sheer test of nerves; every newscast these days was an assault on the senses. People were getting accustomed to the sight of their cities burning in the summertime—last summer it had been Watts, a black neighborhood in Los Angeles. Of federal troops marching in to restore order. Of fire hoses being used to disperse mobs. Of attack dogs and billy clubs. Of riot gear and tear gas. Confrontation had become commonplace. Alongside the voting rights marches, there were peace marches now. Antiwar demonstrations. All of them directed at bringing an end to the undeclared war that was raging in an obscure Southeast Asian country called Vietnam. With every passing day, the death toll climbed steadily higher, and the number of protests climbed too.

"Kirsty?" She turned to find her father standing behind her, his blue eyes troubled. "Are you all right?"

"I'm fine, Pappy," she assured him. "Just a bit tired, I guess."

"I shouldn't wonder. But the season's nearly over now, you'll have the whole summer to rest."

Tucking her arm through his, she laid her head against his shoulder. "He has your eyes, you know." Emil nodded, but said nothing. "I wish one of them could have had your hair though. Another blond in the family would have been nice, don't you think?"

"Perhaps the next one."

How could Kirsten tell him there probably wouldn't be a next one? Jeffrey hadn't made love to her since before Jeff was born. She really didn't mind about the lovemaking, but he seldom held her or even kissed her anymore either, and that was the part she missed most.

"Do you think you're ready for some birthday cake?" Emil patted his daughter on the cheek and told himself to stop behaving like a father. "I happen to be on especially good terms with the young lady who's cutting the cake, and I'm sure I can convince her to give you an especially big piece."

Kirsten grinned. "In that case, Pappy," she said, "I'm positively starving."

She would never know the real reason behind it. Or even the combination of reasons. She refused to stop to analyze it, to ask herself why now, why not a year ago, two years ago, or even next year? Maybe being ready or simply wanting to was reason enough. Or maybe it was her fear of their crazy world ending before she got to see him again. But whatever the reason, the day after she closed out the season with a concert at Montreal's magnificent Place des Arts, she called Nelson and told him to book her something, anything, for the up-coming season with Michael Eastbourne. She half-expected him to drop the phone, but he didn't. He simply popped two antacid tablets into his mouth instead of the usual one.

"Congratulations." It was the only appropriate word he could think of; he even repeated it while he waited for what she had told him to sink in. Then he let out a giant-sized sigh. "I can't tell you how many times that man has called me personally these past few years and asked—no, make that begged—me to arrange either a concert date or a recording session with you. You should have heard some of the excuses I had to invent. Now, stop it, please, I can feel you blushing over the phone."

Kirsten pressed her hand to her cheek; it *was* warm. "You know me too well," she chided playfully. But she was secretly thrilled. Michael had wanted to conduct her, and knowing that was making her giddy. Suddenly she was angry with herself for having taken so long to reach this decision. Suddenly she couldn't wait to see him again.

"He's just been named permanent conductor of the Boston Symphony replacing Erich Leinsdorf," Nelson hastened to inform her.

But she already knew that. She also knew that he and Roxanne had rented a house in Beacon Hill for the duration of his appointment. There was very little about him she didn't know—thanks to the news media. It seemed ironic somehow. She, who was adored by millions of faceless, name-less fans, was herself an adoring fan.

Whether to celebrate the decision that had been so long in coming or to assuage the pang of guilt associated with it, she nevertheless had Lawrence, the family chauffeur, drive her into the city, where she spent the entire afternoon shopping for Jeffrey—at Burberry's, Mark Cross, and Tiffany's—and the children—at F.A.O. Schwarz—returning to the house shortly before dinnertime with the trunk of the black Lincoln completely filled with gift-wrapped boxes. She was humming as she burst into the front hall, a shopping bag in either hand, only to stop short at the sight of Jeffrey standing there, silent and grim-faced, waiting for her.

"Kirsten, I'm afraid I've got some bad news," he began somewhat hesitantly. "Your mother called about an hour ago. Your father—" he paused, and Kirsten began to lose her grip on the handles of the shopping bags she was carrying. "He's had a stroke, he's at Bellevue."

She didn't feel the bags slipping out of her hands; she didn't even hear them hitting the floor. All she could hear was the deep wail of agony spilling out of her mouth and filling the air around her. Jeffrey grabbed hold of her by the shoulders and started shaking her, but the terrible sound continued to pour out of her, growing higher and louder and stronger.

"Stop it," he pleaded, "stop it, Kirsten, the children." He tried to pull her rigid body back in the direction of the front door. "Please stop, Kirsten, please. I'll take you to him right away. Just come with me now, that's it, just come with me. Shh, shh, shh, good girl, calm down, that's it. I'm taking you to see him now." He held her close to him as they walked, speaking to her as though she herself were a child, in simple repetitions a child could understand, until he had her safely settled beside him in the backseat of the car. Then he cradled her in his arms and stroked her hair and talked to her all the way to Bellevue.

She found her mother, looking tiny, helpless, and frail, huddled alone on a long wooden bench just inside the doors to the emergency room, and ran to her.

"Mama!" she cried, flinging herself onto the bench and holding out her arms. "Oh, Mama, Mama, what happened?"

Gianna only had the strength to whisper. "We were talking, just talking in the kitchen. I was making a pitcher of lemonade. All of a sudden he wasn't talking anymore. I looked at him and . . . and . . ." She gulped and shook her head. "The way he was watching me, *carissima*, so helpless, he couldn't speak, he . . ." She buried her face in Kirsten's shoulder and started to sob.

"Can I see him, Mama?"

Gianna shook her head again. "They won't even let me see him; he's unconscious."

"What?" Thinking her mother was still speaking to her, Kirsten tilted her head to the side and listened more carefully. But she quickly realized it wasn't talking she was hearing, it was praying. Shifting her body slightly, she took a close look at her mother's hands. She was so stunned she gasped. A gleaming rope of ruby-colored glass beads was moving rhythmically through Gianna's fingers. It was a rosary. Not once in her entire life had Kirsten ever seen her mother use a rosary.

"Mama?" The woman smiled faintly as Kirsten pointed to the beads.

"Your father gave them to me," she explained. "On our wedding day. He told me every good Catholic had to have a rosary." She laughed, a hoarse, ironic kind of laugh. "I was never a good Catholic, *bella*; I married out of the faith, and now I'm being punished for it. I'm losing your father because I sinned."

"No, Mama, that's not true," Kirsten argued. "To have had a love as strong as yours could never be considered a sin, by anyone."

Gianna's shoulders slumped and fresh tears began coursing down her cheeks. "He's been my life, Kirsten, my whole life. If I lose him, I'll be only half a person from now on. I'll have nothing, *carissima*, nothing. If he dies, I want to die too."

Kirsten was adamant as she grasped her mother's face with both hands. "Listen to me, Mama, Pappy has *not* been your whole life, and you're *not* only half a person either. You're a complete person all by yourself. Yes, you are, Mama, you are. And if something should happen to him, you wouldn't be left with nothing. You'd still have a daughter who loves you and two beautiful grandchildren who need you. So, please, please, don't you dare say you'd have nothing. Don't you dare say you'd rather be dead too."

"Mrs. Harald?"

Startled, both Kirsten and Gianna glanced up at the same time. The expression on the young doctor's face who was standing over them was filled with sympathy and compassion, tinged by a vague helplessness, and edged in regret. A look translated into speech by those two most dreaded of words: "I'm sorry."

Kirsten shuddered as the pain pierced her entire being in a single vicious thrust.

"May we see him?" She rose slowly and pulled her mother up with her.

"Yes, of course."

He led them over to a cubicle and parted the heavy white

curtain. Draping one arm protectively around her mother's shoulder the way her father had done hundreds of times, Kirsten edged them both closer to the bed and peered down into the face of death for the first time in her life. It may have been her father's familiar face, but it wasn't her father lying there. This man was a stranger to her; it was the other man who was still real.

He was the one who had carried her when she was small and who had walked beside her while she was growing up. His was the soft voice filling the empty spaces of her lonely childhood with wonderful words. His were the hands that swept the pathway leading to her dream clear of so many of its obstacles. His was the gentle smile of unquestioning acceptance. He had been her life's first anchor. Her first love. There for her, always there for her.

She didn't cry when it was time to leave him. She didn't cry at his funeral. What her mind continued to reject, the rest of her didn't have to accept yet either. But the morning after the funeral she couldn't get out of bed. She simply lay there on her side with her knees tucked under her chin, staring vacantly at the emptiness all around her. It was then that the tears began.

She had lost both Natalya and her father now. Two of the main supports upon which her life had been built, upon which so much of it had rested. She felt strangely off balance, listing first to one side, then the other, like a ship foundering at sea, its rudder missing, its compass smashed, all sense of direction gone. Over the next few days she tossed in and out of a delirious sort of sleep while her grieving spirit and exhausted body worked to heal themselves. And Jeffrey helped her through it.

He brought her meals to her on a silver tray, sat with her while she talked about her father for hours, then held her in his arms until she fell asleep. Whenever she woke up, she found him there, waiting to comfort her; and as soon as she was ready to face the outside world again, he took her by the hand and led her back. He remained equally solicitous and caring all summer, and she basked in the renewed warmth of their relationship. The glow carried them right through until September, and then, regrettably, it began to fade. By the time she was ready to leave on her first scheduled concert tour of the new season, it was gone completely.

She had never wanted to believe Jeffrey was the kind of

man who could be threatened by an independent woman, but she finally had to face the truth about him. What he was doing, what he had been doing for some time, was punishing her because of her career. What he had so revered, he had come to repudiate; he resented her music and he resented her. As long as she was dependent on him—as she had been all summer—he felt needed; he was the strong one, the one in control. To him, her leaving meant she no longer needed him; it diminished him, stripped him of his power.

She couldn't bear to have him believe that. She had to make him see that her music was in no way a denial of him, that she wasn't choosing *it* instead of him. Eager to preserve what they had so recently recaptured, she went to him and tried to explain, but she came away knowing it hadn't made the slightest bit of difference. Jeffrey had closed himself off to her again. As long as she had her career, she would be punished.

She left New York with a heavy heart and flew to Stockholm. Checking into her suite at the Grand Hotel, she noticed the flashing red light on the telephone on the night table beside her bed, and immediately rang the hotel operator for her messages. Jeffrey had called, called to apologize, she was certain of it. She was surprised at how excited that made her feel. But no. Her heart slowed down almost immediately. The message was from Nelson. Disappointment gave way to elation, however, the moment she heard what the message was. He had arranged for her to replace pianist Bella Davidovich in concert on October second in Los Angeles. Conducting the Los Angeles Philharmonic that evening would be Michael Eastbourne.

The next twelve days were swept from the calendar like leaves before an autumn wind. On the afternoon of October second, Kirsten walked into the Dorothy Chandler Pavilion feeling very much like an ingenue who's finally accepted her first blind date. Nervous. Excited. Frightened. Not knowing what to expect. Afraid of being disappointed, even shocked. She hadn't seen Michael in over six years. Six years and four months to be precise. Her mouth was dry, her knees knocking as she approached the door to his dressing room. Stopping to compose herself, she checked her face in the mirror of her compact, straightened the jacket of the gray raw silk

Lanvin suit that needed no straightening, then knocked, briskly and sharply, on the door three times.

When it opened, she stepped inside a room that was no more than a blur. He, too, was a blur. An indistinct wash of color. A hazy shape. Growing clearer as the seconds ticked swiftly by. He came together in bits and pieces. As images out of joint and disconnected. The fading gold of a summer tan. A camel's-hair jacket. Brown trousers and a brown and camel striped tie. Silver threaded through his wavy chestnut hair. Delicate lines etched in his forehead and radiating outward like tiny fans from his hazel eyes. The gentle smile that brought a responsive rush of heat to the surface of her skin.

He was Michael as she remembered him. The changes were subtle, his effect on her was the same. She was once again the smitten thirteen-year-old piano student gazing up at the poster of the twenty-seven-year-old conductor outside Carnegie Hall. Except that this was twenty years later, almost to the day.

Neither of them moved; they simply continued touching each other first with their eyes. Then they reached out with their arms, feeling in that first electrifying moment of contact as though they had never been out of each other's arms at all. The boundaries between them dissolved; they were once again one inseparable being, drawing life only from each other.

"Damn you, Kirsten Harald," Michael breathed into her ear. "Damn you for keeping me waiting so long."

She had always wondered how she would feel when he held her again; now she knew. She expected to feel guilty because she was married to another man but she didn't feel guilty at all. She felt the same way she had always felt with Michael—at one with a kindred spirit.

He startled her by suddenly breaking their embrace. But he didn't release her completely, he simply stepped back a bit to study her while he kept both hands cupped around her face.

"I never did get a chance to kiss the bride," he said. "Do you think I might have the honor now?"

She nodded her consent, but when his kiss proved to be nothing more than a gentle brush of his lips across hers, she was the one who deepened it, who locked her hands behind his neck to intensify it, who refused to let him end it until they were both breathless. Even then she raised her lips again, expectantly, eagerly, hungrily, awaiting a second kiss.

But he pulled away from her, and a cold wind rushed in to chill the space in her heart that had only just begun to grow warm. Suddenly self-conscious and ill at ease, she fumbled awkwardly for something to say.

"How do you like living in Boston again?" she asked, choosing the safest topic she could think of.

"It's been wonderful so far." He shoved his hands into the pockets of his trousers and began studying the tips of his shoes. "It really *was* coming home again in every sense of the word."

"And the boys?"

"They're both at Harvard."

"My God." She was amazed. "Where has the time gone?"

"You have two of your own now, don't you? A girl and a boy, right?" Kirsten nodded. "And are either of them going to follow in their mother's illustrious footsteps?"

"Not if their father has anything to say about it, they won't." She noticed a faint flickering in his eyes when he heard her snappish reply. "What about *your* children?"

Michael's laugh sent shivers up and down her spine. "I'm afraid we've raised a mathematician and a marine biologist. To them, music means the Beatles, Bob Dylan, and Simon and Garfunkel."

"Their taste is eclectic, to say the least," Kirsten commented with a smile. "Does it bother you that neither of them wanted to become a musician?"

"I suppose the same way it bothered *my* father when I wanted to conduct rather than play an instrument. I've adjusted to it though. As parents, we give our children only their start; we have no right to expect them to grow up to be just like us."

It seemed so odd, she thought, to be talking about their children now, when there hadn't been any talk of children the last time they were together. In fact, there had been no talk at all, only the sound of their lovemaking. Kirsten could feel herself fading in and out of the room, in and out of their continuing conversation, in and out of her own body. It was frustrating, almost absurd. She felt tempted and teased, permitted to look but not touch, restrained by a barricade not hers to hurdle.

"We'd better go," he was saying, and she started guiltily. "We're already five minutes late for rehearsal." Still she didn't move. "Kirsten?"

"I heard you, Michael." He was already heading for the door; she began to panic. "Michael, wait!"

He turned instantly and hurried back to her. "What is it, Kirsten, what's wrong?"

She should never have asked to play with him again, never. She wanted to run, but she remained rooted to the spot, unable to move. There was so much lost time to make up for, so many huge gaps that needed to be filled in. She felt cheated, cheated, cheated.

Michael was miserable as he looked at her. Once again he was a man torn in two. The part of him that still belonged only to her yearned to crush her in his arms and make love to her, but the part of him that belonged to the wife he still loved and wanted absolutely forbade it. What he offered her instead was a compromise.

"Maybe this will help," he said, pressing the gold charm he had had engraved for her only that morning into the palm of her icy hand. "I'm giving it to you now because I doubt there'll be time after the performance tonight." Kirsten braced herself for what she knew was coming next. "Roxanne's here in Los Angeles. With both boys in college, she travels with me most of the time now."

He had his hand on the doorknob when Kirsten called him back again.

"Hold me, Michael," she whispered hoarsely. "Just for a minute, Michael, please?"

The tortured look on his face as he walked toward her told her everything she needed to know. He pulled her into his arms and felt his resistance crumble.

"Oh, Kirsten, my Kirsten." He buried his mouth deep in her dark, smooth hair. "If you only knew how much I've missed you. There hasn't been a day these past six years when I haven't thought about you, when you haven't been a part of everything I've done. If you only knew what it's taken for me to stay away from you, to let you lead the kind of life you were meant to lead. Oh, Kirsten, you'll never know how complete I feel just being able to hold you this way."

When they kissed this time, it was the rest of the world that dissolved, not them. And Kirsten knew nothing could ever dull the glory of this moment or keep her from playing with Michael again. And again

24

To Kirsten's dismay, the early promise Meredith had shown at the piano gradually faded, as did much of her interest in it. When Jeffrey enrolled their daughter at Greenbriar, a private school on the North Shore that had once been a Vanderbilt mansion, it wasn't long before Meredith began turning her considerable energies toward the new and exciting business of making friends. Suddenly the piano seemed too solitary a pursuit for her. She much preferred what every other girl her age preferred—the very thing Kirsten herself had been denied at that age—fun.

The thrill of sharing secrets, of skipping rope, playing jacks and pick-up sticks. Of trading stickers and swapping dolls. Of riding bicycles, roller skating, and playing tag. Now there were bruised knees and blistered heels, broken fingernails and scratched hands to contend with. Meredith was fearless; she never stopped long enough when she was playing to think about her hands. And as time went by, she lost all interest in pursuing the dream that had been more her mother's than hers. Although the emotional side of Kirsten bitterly regretted her daughter's decision, her more realistic side didn't blame her one bit.

It was Jeff who kept Kirsten company now whenever she practiced, and who played the same nursery rhymes his sister had once played. If Meredith disappointed, then Jeff astounded. Were someone to ask Kirsten what his favorite word was, she would have answered "more." More was never enough for him. He demanded more of hearing her play, more of her helping *him* to play, and more of showing her how well he could play on his own. Jeffrey Powell Oliver III couldn't get enough of the very thing Kirsten had been almost reluctant to encourage in him. It was becoming increasingly clear to her that her two-year-old son, with his serious blue eyes and his look of perpetual concentration, might ultimately prove to be the most gifted of the three of them.

For Easter that year, she and Jeff worked hard at perfecting

"Here Comes Peter Cottontail" the same way she and Meredith had once worked on Christmas carols together. And just
as with Meredith, she and Jeff had their favorite game too.
Whenever she seemed ready to lift him off the piano bench,
he would gaze up at her with baleful eyes and say very softly,
"More, Mommy, more."

While Kirsten pretended to be giving the matter a great
deal of thought, Jeff would wriggle around on the bench,
anxiously opening and closing his hands, pleading "More,
Mommy, more" until she finally gave in. His way of thanking
her never varied. First, he would wrap his arms around her
neck and hug her, then he would hammer a noisy path up the
keyboard with both fists, striking every white key with his
left hand and every black key with his right.

But on Easter Sunday, Kirsten and Jeff performed "Here
Comes Peter Cottontail" before a subdued audience of three,
consisting of her mother, Meredith, and Agnes MacLaughlin.
Jeffrey's brother, Charles, had suffered another stroke in the
early hours of the morning and died even before the ambulance arrived. Kirsten managed to keep the holiday spirit
intact for the children—she even sent them on an Easter egg
hunt—because to them their uncle Charles had been an in-
valided stranger they barely knew. As much an absence in their
lives as their aunt Dierdre was a presence.

At the funeral, Kirsten noted with a cynicism unusual for
her that Dierdre wore the black of widowhood with a hauteur
as shockingly declarative as it was sensual. There was an
intriguing new air about her, one that was mildly disconcerting and subtly indefinable, but potently obvious nonetheless.
Where she had once been merely a candidate for martyrdom
as the invalid's loyal and uncomplaining wife, it seemed
Charles's death had not only liberated her, it had practically
elevated her to sainthood.

Jeffrey noticed it too. It was so palpable he could almost
smell it. And he knew that if he held out his hand, he would
be able to touch it. When he should have been focusing on
his dead brother, all he could do was stare at Dierdre, and
thank God for the topcoat he was wearing. The heat in his
groin made standing still an ordeal, and made thinking solemn thoughts all but impossible.

He glanced beside him at Kirsten and felt his chest constrict. For one horrible, fleeting moment, he wished she were
the one being lowered into the ground instead of Charles. She

had become the bane of his existence; no longer his reward, but his retribution. If she had had her way, he would never have had a son. God, how he hated her for what she had tried to do; oh, how he hated her. She had deceived him, and now she was betraying him. She was playing with Michael Eastbourne again; for all he knew she was sleeping with him too.

Dierdre was looking directly at him. Jeffrey's face grew warm. Could she tell, he wondered. Could she tell just by looking at him how badly he wanted her? He thrust his hands into the slash pockets of his coat and pressed down as hard as he could. Dear God. He was beginning to panic. What if he came right now? What if he disgraced himself in front of the entire Social Register of New York? The fear of being discovered, of being humiliated publicly, became so intense, his shoulders hunched forward, his entire body began to shake, and he started to sob.

Everyone who saw him break down thought it only natural under the circumstances, and their hearts went out to him in sympathy.

"Dierdre suggested we name the new research facilities we're building at the institute after Charles," Jeffrey told Kirsten in a rare burst of conversation over dinner one night about a month after Charles's death.

Kirsten remained silent as she studied the contents of her wineglass, wondering if she was expected to respond in some way or simply listen.

"Did you hear what I just said?" he prompted her.

"Yes, I did."

"Well, what do you think?"

Kirsten set her glass down and smiled at him. "I think it's an excellent idea."

"Good, then we're all agreed." Wiping the corners of his mouth with his napkin, he tossed it aside and got up from the table. "Since I'm going over to Dierdre's anyway, I'll tell her in person." Kirsten's look made him feel he had to explain. "She's still going through Charles's papers," he said, giving her a shrug and a bit of a grin that reminded her of the old Jeffrey. "I guess I'm just indispensable to her."

She waited for him to leave, then sat down at the piano to practice awhile. She felt strangely disquieted. There were so many instances when the old Jeffrey flashed through the hardened surface of the new one that she still grabbed on to each promising glimmer and held on for as long as she could. But whether it lasted a moment, an hour, or a day, it invariably disappeared again. And the new Jeffrey would reemerge, more closed to her than ever.

His way of punishing her for playing with Michael again had been to move out of their bedroom into the room he had slept in as a boy. When he did, she couldn't help recalling the conversation she had had with Claudia about separate bedrooms all those years ago. And she couldn't help but feel disillusioned and terribly, terribly sad.

She was still at the piano when she heard Jeffrey come in. He had been gone less than an hour; she was surprised. But what surprised her more was the way he hurried straight upstairs without first stopping to say good night to her as he usually did.

"Dear God, it's happened again."

Kirsten was ashen-faced as she looked over at Jeffrey. He immediately got up from the sofa and snapped off the TV. She turned it back on. Switching it off wouldn't change anything; it couldn't undo what was already done. Robert Kennedy had been killed. Shot, just like his brother before him, shortly after winning the Democratic presidential primary in California.

Only three months had passed since he had announced his candidacy. Three months, too, since a beleaguered Lyndon Johnson had told the nation that he would neither seek nor accept his party's nomination for another term as president. The ongoing, bitterly divisive war in Vietnam had finally cost one of the most brilliantly successful domestic legislators in history his job.

And now the man who had sought to take his place was dead.

Kirsten shook her head in utter helplessness. Had it finally happened then, she asked herself. Had the world finally crashed into that waiting abyss? Was there to be nothing from now on but death, death, and more death?

"I suppose this means we should brace ourselves for number three," Jeffrey said. Kirsten just looked at him. "Well, it's only logical. First Jack, then Bobby, next up little Teddy. After him it'll be on to the next generation. Christ, we'll have Kennedys around to haunt us forever."

"How can you talk that way; it sounds so inhuman!" Kirsten's beautiful face was a contorted mask of pain. "This is a tragedy, Jeffrey, another ghastly national tragedy. Do you realize it was only two months ago that Martin Luther King was murdered? They're systematically killing off all the men with dreams and ideals, and the fearlessness to stand up for them. If this continues, there won't be a single person left who'll be willing to take a stand on anything, not if the penalty for it is death."

"Did it ever occur to you that perhaps idealism doesn't work, that the only thing that *does* work is good old-fashioned pragmatism?"

"I refuse to believe that."

"You wouldn't," he scoffed. "Talk about dreamers, you've always been the biggest dreamer of them all."

"And what's wrong with that?" she demanded. But Jeffrey chose not to answer her; instead, he walked over to the small mahogany bar he had had built into one of the bookcases in the library and poured himself a scotch, neat. Kirsten stared dolefully at her hands. "Our leaders are dead, Jeffrey," she whispered, her voice breaking.

"Your leaders maybe, they were certainly never mine."

"Oh, yes, I forgot." Her tone was caustic now. "You're the one who loved Ike, so naturally you'd be delirious at the prospect of having Nixon in the White House."

"If we'd had him in there eight years ago instead of your golden boy Kennedy, we wouldn't be in the mess we're in right now."

Kirsten gave her husband a disgusted look. "We started out with so much hope," she said more to herself than to him. "Who'd have thought it would end so horribly?"

As she sat there grimly and watched the stricken face of newscaster Walter Cronkite, she suddenly couldn't take any more. She leapt from her seat and turned off the TV herself this time. It had all come full circle. What had begun with the end of Eisenhower would, more than likely, end with the beginning of Nixon. There was no doubt in her mind now that he would win both the Republican nomination in August and the election in November.

She felt weighed down and worn out. Despair was sitting heavily on her shoulders as she walked out of the room and up the stairs. She needed to be alone for a while, to mourn everything she and the rest of the country had lost. Perhaps it was their innocence. But whatever it was, it was gone now. And she had the feeling they would never get it back.

*   *   *

The lid on the keyboard came crashing down, and Jeff pulled his hands back with a frightened yelp.

"I will not have him spending all of his time at this damned piano!" Jeffrey shouted at Kirsten as he hauled his protesting five-year-old son up from the bench and set him on his feet. "I want him either outside playing with his friends or riding his bike or in the playroom I built for him and stocked with every conceivable toy and game known to man. Have I made myself clear?"

Kirsten faced her irate husband with all the calmness she could muster and waited for his anger to wear itself out. But it didn't; it got worse.

"You still won't take me seriously, will you, Kirsten? You're still determined to turn my son into a carbon copy of yourself. Well, no son of mine is going to spend his life traveling the globe like some godforsaken minstrel. Any traveling he does he'll do as a representative of the Oliver family, and he'll do it with the same sense of duty as every other Oliver son before him."

Glancing over at Jeff, whose gentle eyes were regarding his father so solemnly, Kirsten wondered what he must be thinking. This was the first time Jeffrey had ever erupted in front of him, and she could see he was deeply shaken by the vehemence of his father's outburst. In an effort to reassure him, she placed her hands gently on his narrow shoulders, looked her husband in the eye, and in a carefully modulated voice said, "Our son's been given a tremendous gift, Jeffrey, the same unique and precious gift I was given. It isn't something you can ignore, you know, it isn't going to go away. He was born with the kind of talent that will surface and persist no matter how hard you try to stifle it."

"He's an Oliver, Kirsten, not a Harald," Jeffrey countered. "I'm his father, and sons obey their fathers or suffer the consequences."

"The only real suffering you can cause him is to try to deprive him of his music," she retorted heatedly. "I'm warning you, Jeffrey, don't ever ask an artist to choose between his art and someone else's plans for him, because he'll always choose his art."

"As you should know."

"You knew it too. You knew when you asked me to marry you that I'd never give up my music, yet you married me anyway."

"And what a mistake that was. You've never been a real wife to me, you've never been a real mother to our children; in fact, you've never been anything more than a boarder around here."

"Jeffrey!" His viciousness had actually made her flinch. But he was oblivious both to her hurt and to the changing expression on his son's face. With one last disdainful look in her general direction, he left the room, calling back over his shoulder, "I want that boy out of here. Now!"

"I hate him," muttered Jeff as soon as his father was gone. "I really hate him."

"No, you don't, my darling," Kirsten said, trying hard to sound convincing. "You don't hate him. You're just disappointed and a little frightened, that's all."

"I do hate him," Jeff insisted. "He won't let me play the piano."

"Of course he will, but he wants you to enjoy doing other things too."

"But I like the piano best, Mommy, I can't help it."

Kirsten smiled as she brushed back the shock of dark hair that was constantly falling across her son's forehead. "I know you do, sweetheart, and you don't ever have to apologize."

"I don't?"

"No, you don't."

"Are you sure it's all right?"

"I'm sure."

"And you're still our real mother then?"

Kirsten stiffened. "Of course I am, darling, why?"

"Because he just said you weren't."

"He meant it in a different way."

"What different way?"

"Jeff." His questions were making her uneasy. "Jeff, darling, why don't you go upstairs and play with the wonderful building set your father bought you last week?"

But the boy refused to be put off so easily. "What's a boarder, Mommy?" he persisted.

"Jeff, please. Do what your father wants, darling. Go upstairs to the playroom for a while."

"I will if you let me play the Beethoven again later."

Kirsten laughed and tousled his hair. "Now, that's what I call a fair trade. Okay, it's a deal."

"Honest?"

"Honest."

"Ya-hoo!" he shouted, and off he went.

Kirsten watched him go with a sigh. Her prediction was coming true; her beloved son *had* been touched with genius. He displayed not only an astounding musical ability, but the necessary determination and singlemindedness that went with it. Her dreams were for him now. He, not Meredith, was the one she would teach and guide and support. He was the one she would lead upward to greatness. He would be her extended legacy to the world. But with Jeffrey as her adversary, she knew it would be a long and tortuous uphill fight.

Her mother would have been so proud of Jeff. But Gianna had been dead nearly two years now—a withered shadow who had stolen away peacefully in her sleep one night. Sometimes Kirsten was certain she had done it on purpose, to prove she really couldn't live without the man she had claimed had been her whole life. Although she had pleaded with her mother continually, Gianna had stubbornly refused to move in with them after Emil's death. Her subtle way of refusing was to say that since she'd finally gotten used to such a large apartment, it made no sense to leave it. And so, Kirsten had realized painfully, the third support from her past was finally gone. Her parents and Natalya. All three of them gone.

She went upstairs to read, one hand holding her book steady as she reclined on the chaise in her sitting room, the other deep in the pocket of her slacks, curled tightly around the bulging brown leather pouch containing the gold charm bracelet. Following her reunion with Michael in Los Angeles, she had added another six charms to the bracelet. It barely fit inside the pouch anymore, but she carried it with her everywhere. It was her amulet and her talisman, her only way of keeping Michael with her at all times.

Suddenly she could feel herself starting to blush. Only two weeks before, Michael had called her from the Air France terminal at JFK. He was on his way to Paris—Roxanne was already over there—and had a two-hour stopover between flights. He had asked her to meet him, which she did, taking the precaution of going to the airport by taxi. It was the first time they had been alone together since their Los Angeles concert, and they had sequestered themselves in the VIP lounge, sipping cocktails and talking until they were both ready to burst. Then, laughing and shushing each other like a pair of delinquent teenagers, they had scouted around until they located a deserted cloakroom.

For the next twenty minutes they had indulged themselves wickedly, kissing and fondling each other with an abandon made all the more exciting because they knew anyone could walk in on them at any moment. She shivered as she recalled how he had slid his hand underneath her dress and inside her underpants while they stood there kissing. And how he had barely begun to stroke her when she came with an explosion so fierce they nearly lost their balance. And how he had refused to stop touching her until she had climaxed a second time, then a third.

"Mom, may I come in?" Meredith called out, rapping softly on the closed bedroom door.

Kirsten hastily pulled her hand out of her pocket. "Of course, darling, it's not locked." She was just setting her book down when Meredith skipped into the room to show off the new dress she was wearing. "Don't you look lovely," she exclaimed as her daughter spun around on tiptoe in front of her. "Now, tell me again where you're off to."

"Oh, Mother." Meredith stopped her twirling, put her hands on her hips, and pretended to be annoyed. "It's Veronica's birthday party, remember?"

"Veronica Hauser?"

"Harewood."

"I'm sorry, darling. I never *can* keep their names straight. That's what comes from having such a popular daughter."

"I'll bet you were popular too," Meredith volunteered loyally. "I'll bet you were the most popular girl in all of New York when you were growing up."

"I had no time to be popular, except with my piano teacher."

"You mean you never had friends or went to birthday parties or anything?" Kirsten shook her head. "Poor you." Meredith looked positively stricken. "Now you can see why I want to play the piano only for fun. I couldn't stand being a musician if it meant being alone all the time."

Eager to switch the subject, Kirsten turned to more mundane matters and asked her daughter if Lawrence was driving her over to the Harewoods. Meredith promptly made a face.

"I suppose so," she said, "although I don't see why I can't walk. Daddy's such a fusspot about these things."

"No, he's not, darling, he's just concerned."

"But it's only two blocks from here."

"Meredith." Kirsten's voice was gently chiding.

"I know, I know. I'll go with Lawrence, don't worry."

"Good girl. Now, give me a big kiss and go have yourself a wonderful time." Meredith bent down and kissed her mother, then added a hug for good measure. "I love you, my angel," Kirsten whispered.

"And I love you, Mom." Meredith kissed her again. "I love you more than anyone in the whole world."

"Even more than me?" Jeffrey remarked rather caustically from the doorway, and Meredith jumped.

"Daddy," she gasped. "You scared me."

"Sorry, princess, I didn't mean to." He glanced at Kirsten. "Am I interrupting something here?"

"No." She smiled. "Just mother and daughter talk."

He looked almost relieved. "In any case, I just came to tell Meredith that Lawrence is outside in the car." When his daughter seemed to be hesitating, he became impatient. "Well, what are you waiting for? Go on, go on."

Meredith gave him a nervous little smile and darted out of the door.

"She's certainly turned into the frightened little rabbit, hasn't she?" Jeffrey was gazing after his nine-year-old in amazement. "You'd think I was some sort of ogre just because I insist Lawrence drive her places. Ah, well." He sounded so wistful and looked so forlorn, Kirsten was half-tempted to put her arms around him. But his mood didn't last. It turned promptly to anger as the strains of Beethoven's "Moonlight Sonata" began filtering up through the house from the conservatory. "Damn that boy anyway!" he snarled, charging out of the room and leaving Kirsten staring sadly after him.

Roxanne looked through the entire packet of photographs one last time before slipping them back into the large brown envelope they had come in. Then she scanned the note that had been clipped to the first of the photos and forced herself to read the hateful words she already knew by heart. Such choice words, mocking and mean. So smugly self-satisfied. So vengeful. She slid the note inside the envelope, thrust the bulky package back into the small wall safe hidden behind the Constable in the library, and went to pour herself a drink.

She should never have given in to Michael's pressure and let him perform with Kirsten Harald again. She should never have been so naive as to feel safe, to believe the pianist's highly publicized society marriage would have made a differ-

ence. The two of them had probably been seeing each other
all along, in spite of the fact that they hadn't played together
for six years.

She clamped her teeth around the rim of the crystal glass
and pretended it was the neck of her enemy. No, she corrected herself, enemies. They were all her enemies now. She
had loved Michael slavishly, she had devoted her life to him
and to his career, and he had repaid her by dishonoring her
in the most clichéd and timeworn way a husband can dis-
honor his wife. He had betrayed and humiliated her. What
she had feared most, dreaded most, had happened. She had
been forced to share him too.

Slamming her empty glass down, she stared at her reflection in the mirror behind the bar while she traced the con-
tours of her body with the flats of her hands. The voluptuous
curves were alien to her now. Her eyes began to fill, and the
pain inside her became so intense she had to grab hold of the
edge of the bar to keep from falling.

Damn Michael. Damn him for what he had done; he had as
good as killed her. She had already begun to die, just as she
knew she would, and she would continue to die in stages,
until there was nothing left of her. She touched herself gingerly, touched the flatness that had once been her full left
breast, and shuddered in revulsion. She could hardly blame
him for what he was doing; she was no longer the woman she
once was. With the palm of her left hand still pressed against
her disfigured chest, she picked up the phone with her right.

25

"Why are we meeting at La Grenouille instead of at your
office?" Kirsten asked Nelson suspiciously as soon as their
drinks arrived.

He didn't answer her directly. He reached for his glass
instead, grateful to have something to do with his hands, and
took a quick gulp of his Chivas. "Is there a law somewhere
that says an agent can't take his favorite client out to lunch?"

"Of course not. I'm asking only because you never stay in
town on Fridays during the summer."

"There's a first time for everything, so they say." Had the air-conditioning gone off or was it just him, he wondered, grabbing his drink again.

Kirsten wrapped both hands around the Bloody Mary she hadn't even started yet and watched the sides of the glass grow foggy with condensation. Something was wrong. She studied Nelson's face; it looked gray. She felt a stab of panic. Was he sick? Was that what he wanted to tell her? Was that why they were here?

Nelson reached for his glass again and found it empty. He considered ordering another one but didn't; that would only prolong things. He cleared his throat, folded his hands on the table, and cleared his throat again. What he was about to say to Kirsten was the hardest thing he'd ever had to say to anyone. That she was someone he loved like a daughter made it worse, a thousand times worse.

"Nelson, please." Kirsten was practically beside herself with worry. "If you clear your throat one more time, I'm going to strangle you. Whatever it is, you've got to tell me. Now."

Behind the thick glasses, his speckled gray eyes were beginning to tear. "Kirsten," he began, only to stop again. He desperately needed to clear his throat, but settled for swallowing hard several times instead. "Kirsten," he started over, "most of your dates for next season have been canceled."

"What?" She was half out of her chair before he pulled her down again. "Are you mad, what are you telling me?"

"All week I've been getting phone calls and cables—"

"From whom?"

"Just about everyone."

"Everyone?"

Nelson looked down at the tablecloth. "Conductors, orchestra managers, hall managers, agents."

"Why?" she demanded, using her fist to punctuate her words. "Why, why, why?"

"I don't know why. What I do know is that they've canceled three quarters of your concerts and half your recitals."

Kirsten gripped the sides of the table and tried to take a deep breath. But she couldn't. The best she could manage was a series of tiny, inadequate gulps of air that were starting to make her feel light-headed.

"No," she whispered, "it isn't true. I don't believe you, I *can't* believe you." Her voice began to rise; Nelson reached for her hand. "Do you know what you're saying, do you know what this means? No, Nelson, I won't believe it, I won't!" It was a nightmare; it wasn't happening, it couldn't be happening. Not to her. And then, "Michael." She could barely squeeze out his name. "What about Michael, did he cancel too?"

Nelson nodded. He watched her wince. He felt sick inside. Sick and angry and totally helpless. But he had to know more. "Do you have any idea who might have started this?"

"Started this?" She looked at him blankly.

"Spread the word." He gestured with his hands. "Did someone want to get back at you for something?"

"You mean like van Beinum?"

She had actually cracked a smile, but he was being serious, deadly serious. "I mean anyone who might want to hurt you, to punish you for something."

She tried to think, but thinking, like breathing, was next to impossible.

"Kirsten, please, I know how hard this is for you, but you've got to help me. Think back."

The first person she thought of was Jeffrey. Then she felt guilty. No, it couldn't be he. She couldn't believe it of him; he would never be that cruel. He didn't have that kind of power, he didn't have the right con— She stopped in the middle of the word. Her head came up with a sharp snap and her eyes turned hard.

"My God."

"What, Kirsten, what?" Nelson leaned forward expectantly.

Contacts. The only person she knew with the right contacts was . . . Again she stopped herself, put her head in her hands. No, dear God, no. He had warned her they could do it. And obviously they had. Somehow they had found out.

"Kirsten?"

She took her hands away from her face. "Treaves." It came out so softly, he didn't hear her. "Clemence Treaves," she repeated. "Treaves and Roxanne. Roxanne Eastbourne."

Nelson sucked in his breath. Clemence Treaves and Roxanne Eastbourne. Now, that was an invincible combination if ever there was one. Kirsten was right; they did have the power. He'd seen that sort of blackballing done before by Treaves and people like Treaves. Their network was so extensive, it required nothing more strenuous than a number of well-placed phone calls. Anyone owing a man like Treaves anything—especially his own career—didn't dare refuse, and did whatever was asked of him.

Nelson ordered himself that second drink. He needed it now. His gut feeling about Kirsten and Michael Eastbourne had been right all along.

"They can't do this to me, Nelson. They can't. They simply can't." Kirsten was as pale as death as she watched the distraught man gulp down his fresh drink. "We've signed contracts with these people, they can't just arbitrarily break them."

"Every contract has a cancellation clause in it, Kirsten." He suddenly sounded weary, very weary. "We can cancel, they can cancel."

"Will you talk to Clemence Treaves?" she demanded.

"As soon as I'm certain it *is* Treaves behind this, yes."

"And what about your own contacts?"

"What do you think I've been doing all week?"

She was now so agitated, she could barely sit still. They were out to ruin her, destroy her career, put an end to her precious dream. How dare they do this to her? They had no right, no right at all to try to steal what was hers and had been hers for a very long time.

"Book whatever you can for me, Nelson," she told him. "Book me twice in the same place, three times even, I don't care. I'll play the most obscure concert halls in China, I'll go back to playing in church basements if I have to; only just book me. Keep me busy until we can straighten out this mess."

By the time she got home, the initial shock had worn off; anger, cold and directed, had taken its place. She was committed now, committed to fighting them—including Michael if she had to—until they agreed to return to her what was rightfully hers. She told no one about what had happened, nor did she wait for Nelson to act. She simply charged ahead on her own. She began by phoning everyone who had canceled either a concert or recital with her. The results were frustratingly the same each time: no one accepted her calls, no one called her back. She followed each phone call with a first cable, then a second, but no one answered any of them either. She tried unsuccessfully to reach Clemence Treaves by telephoning his various offices in London, Vienna, and San Francisco. She even visited his New York office on Madison Avenue and found it closed for the summer. They had certainly timed their campaign well, she noted with increasing bitterness; no one was ever available during July and August.

As a last resort she called Michael's house in Boston. She wasn't surprised when there was no answer. She was beginning to despair. She felt trapped. She was going round and round in circles, chasing her own shadow, and getting nowhere. All she was getting was dizzy. And frightened; she was finally getting frightened.

Michael was cold. It was getting late. He had been walking the beach at Hyannis Port for hours. His fingers and toes were numb, and he could no longer feel the tip of his nose. The only other time he had ever felt this numb was when he had polio. It was a deadness he had hoped never to experience again. And yet, ever since the night Roxanne had confronted him, shown him the incriminating photographs and told her what she and Clemence were doing, dead was the only way to describe how he felt.

"I love you, Roxanne," he had told her over and over again. "I've always loved you, I always will. What Kirsten and I share has nothing to do with you and me. It hasn't diminished what you and I have had together all these years; it's never been a threat to our marriage. She's never asked me for anything or expected anything from me. She doesn't deserve this; she doesn't deserve what you're doing to her."

"Would you like to trade places with her, Michael?" Roxanne had demanded. "Would you prefer to exchange your career for hers?"

They were safe questions to ask of him and she knew it; they both knew it. He wished he had had the courage to say yes—even if it were only a bluff, something to use as leverage—but he didn't. He couldn't. What artist could? What artist would sacrifice himself for someone else, even if that someone else were as special as Kirsten? He knew he was a coward, but he couldn't help it. He loved his music more than he loved life itself; without it, he really would be dead.

But that hadn't kept him from trying to change Roxanne's mind. He had begged, cajoled, badgered, even threatened, but to no avail. Roxanne remained convinced that he and Kirsten were lovers, and nothing he said to dissuade her made any difference. She loved him and she was terrified of losing him, especially now. In spite of everything, he loved her too. If he had occasionally fantasized about leaving her and running off with Kirsten, it had been sheer whimsy, nothing more. He hadn't left Roxanne before this, and in the face of her recent illness, he had no intention of leaving her now.

He skirted the side of the road as he headed back toward the cottage they had rented for the season. Stopping at the first mailbox he came to, he dropped in the small, padded brown envelope he had been carrying around with him all afternoon. He was mailing Kirsten another charm, but unlike the others, this one hadn't been inscribed. And the card he had enclosed with it read simply: "Until we play together again. M."

By noon of the following day he was on his way to Bonn, West Germany.

He had let her know where to find him. The postmark had made it easy, a few inquiries in Hyannis Port had done the rest. Timing had been the least of her considerations, but when she found herself walking in on a formal dinner party, she knew it wouldn't have mattered if she had interrupted a coronation. She was an artist fighting for her artistic life, and any time was the right time to confront those who would see that life ruined. It didn't matter to her that the faces around the table were those the average person would see only on the cover of a magazine; it didn't matter that she recognized several politicians and their wives, a composer, a Broadway actor and his wife, a French playwright, and a British novelist and her husband among them. She had been on more magazine covers than all of them combined. She was one of them, and she was here to make certain she remained one of them.

She was immediately ushered into the library, both wooden doors sliding shut with an ominous crack. She had expected Roxanne and Michael; she hadn't counted on it being Roxanne and Clemence Treaves instead.

"If you're looking for my husband, Miss Harald," said Roxanne in the low-pitched voice Kirsten remembered so vividly, "I'm afraid you're out of luck. He's in Europe for the Beethoven festival."

Slightly shaken but undaunted, Kirsten looked over at Treaves a moment, then back again at Roxanne. "Why?" she asked, keeping her own voice pitched low. "Why are you doing this to me?"

Clemence Treaves answered for his niece. "The reason's rather simple, my dear. You should have chosen someone else's husband to dally with. More's the pity that you didn't; you were quite a unique talent, you know."

"*Were?*" The word exploded out of Kirsten like a bullet. "Don't you dare talk about me in the past tense!"

"You *are* the past tense, my dear Miss Harald."

"I am not," she countered heatedly, "and you've no right to do what you're doing, no right whatsoever."

A brown eyebrow lifted as Treaves considered her with undisguised contempt. "We have every right," he said. "Surely Michael must have explained to you the folly of trying to bend the rules. You not only bent them, Miss Harald, you broke them. And in the process, you hurt someone I happen to love very much. Roxanne isn't only my niece, you know, she's also my godchild; and I've protected her all her life the way her lout of a father never did. I never could tolerate seeing her hurt; I still can't."

He put his arm around Roxanne's shoulder and she rewarded him with a smile that was almost blinding. Kirsten could taste bile as she watched the two of them together.

"Do you think Michael and I are having an affair?" She again directed her question at Roxanne, hoping this time Treaves would allow her to answer it herself. "Is that what this is all about?"

"How very perceptive of you." It was all Roxanne would say.

"But we're not having an affair, I swear we're not. Didn't Michael tell you the same thing himself?" When the woman didn't respond, Kirsten kept pushing.

"What if he did?" It was Treaves again. "Technicalities, my dear," he said with a flick of his wrist, "merely technicalities."

He was dismissing her the way one dismisses a servant or sends back a bottle of wine that hasn't been chilled properly. Kirsten could feel her hackles rising and her temper flaring as she turned for the third time to Michael's reticent wife.

"Roxanne, I'm a musician. If you deprive me of my music, you'll not only be cutting off my livelihood, but my lifeline with it."

Roxanne was unmoved. "If you'd thought more about your music and less about my husband in the first place, you wouldn't be faced with that problem now."

"Roxanne, please, don't go through with this."

"It's too late."

"No, it's not. One word from you and—"

"The word came from me," Treaves interrupted.

"Then you—"

"Then I nothing. What's done is done."

"I'll go to the press," Kirsten threatened. "I'll tell them you're deliberately trying to sabotage my career for no other reason than some misguided personal vendetta."

"I wouldn't if I were you, my dear. I'd hate to see you slapped with a libel suit on top of everything else."

"Libel? What would you call what you're doing to me then? I'd call it slander, wouldn't you?"

"I'd hardly call the truth slander." Treaves's tone was bonded in steel. "We have photographs to substantiate our claim, Miss Harald. What, pray tell, do you have?"

"Photographs?" Kirsten's heart skipped a beat.

"Yes, photographs, dating back quite a ways, I'm afraid. All saved up with great care and delivered to my niece when they were sure to do the most damage. Would you like to see some of the most recent ones? They were taken at the Air France terminal at JFK Airport, I believe." Kirsten could feel the blood draining out of her face. "And speaking of husbands, do you think yours might be interested in seeing the photos? We could always have another set made for him. No? I didn't think so."

Kirsten was reeling. Her temples were pressing in on her brain, causing thousands of tiny green dots to explode in front of her eyes. Someone had known about them all these years. Shared what she had thought to be their own special secret. Taken something beautiful and made it ugly. Profaned something sacred.

Michael had been wrong when he warned her about Roxanne and Clemence Treaves. They may have had the power to ruin both of their careers, yet they hadn't used that power to ruin his, only hers. The injustice of it, the double standard by which she, and only she, had been judged and condemned made her wish she could hate him, but she couldn't. He hadn't done this to her, they had.

Roxanne tasted victory as she watched her enemy disintegrating in front of her. It was time to deliver the final cutting blow.

"Aren't you the least bit curious as to who sent me the photographs?" she inquired. "Oh, but of course you are." She paused dramatically. "It was Claudia, Miss Harald, my dear cousin Claudia."

"God, no!" The two hateful faces staring at her dissolved into a blur as Kirsten fought to hold herself together.

"And now, if you're quite through, Miss Harald, I've left my guests alone long enough."

Treaves himself saw Kirsten out. When the front door closed quietly behind her, it wasn't the door of the house she was hearing, but the door on her glorious career slamming shut. Her mind turned again to what Roxanne had told her. Claudia. It had been Claudia. Claudia, who had claimed to love her, who had followed her life with the obsessiveness of a fanatic. Vengeful, vindictive Claudia. Not only paying her back for rejecting her advances, but paying Roxanne back at the same time for having had her banished from Wynford.

She recalled the woman's capricious behavior, the locked bedroom door, the rages, and the silences. The slashed watercolors. The shrine she had made out of the third-floor flat. She started to shake and couldn't stop. Poor Eric. Her poor beloved Eric. He was married to a madwoman.

She opened her purse and took out the tiny blue box containing the single gold charm Michael had sent her. If it had been engraved, it would have read: "Amsterdam. 11/18/70." The concerto she had been scheduled to play that night: Brahms's Second. The irony of it all was like a band clamped around her heart.

Closing her fist around the charm, she made a solemn pledge to herself to see it engraved one day. She would never give up. She *would* play with Michael again. She would, she swore she would.

How she survived the rest of the summer with her desperate secret intact she didn't know. Her family would learn the truth soon enough; all she could hope to do was postpone it as long as she possibly could. Thanks to Nelson's untiring efforts, she had fourteen concerts and thirty-one recitals to play. That alone gave her hope. Her first three recitals had been scheduled back to back the last week of September in Pittsburgh, Baltimore, and Washington, D.C. Although the reviews of her first two recitals were disappointing, almost critical, she paid no attention to them. She would prove herself more than worthy of hyperbole again at her recital in Washington.

She never got the chance. An hour after she checked into her suite at the Mayflower Hotel, she received a telephone call from Jeffrey.

"Kirsten, I want you to catch the first flight home," he said without preamble. "Meredith's disappeared."

26

It could have been a scene from *Naked City*. The living room dotted with blue-uniformed police officers and several men in beige trench-coats, notepads open, pencils scribbling; the small, dark-haired woman sitting grim-faced on a sofa; the tall, dark-haired man and thin brunette standing together near one of the windows; several of the servants hovering silently in the doorway. The curved drive leading up to the large stone house choked with squad cars, some with their red lights still flashing in the noonday sun. The front lawn mottled with more uniformed policemen, two of them holding the leashes of German Shepherds. Other officers fanning out across the estate to search the grounds. To Kirsten, who was still deeply in shock, it had to be an episode written for the TV series; it couldn't have been a page in the story of her own life.

"Why don't you go upstairs and lie down awhile, Mrs. Oliver?" suggested Lieutenant Robert Donaldson, the Nassau County police officer in charge of the search. Kirsten glanced up at him, startled and somewhat disoriented. He repeated his offer and motioned for one of his men to assist her.

"I'll take her upstairs myself, Lieutenant." Jeffrey waved the other officer away and helped Kirsten to her feet. "Come, darling," he said. His smile was solicitous as he led her toward the stairs and up to her bedroom, but no sooner had he closed the door than he discarded his civil pose and turned on her viciously. "This is your fault, you know, yours and no one else's. If you'd been here, this never would have happened. If you'd *ever* been here, you might have raised a daughter who obeyed instead of rebelled all the time. Did you know she's the second young girl from the North Shore to have disappeared this month? Of course you didn't, you're never here. Well, would you care to hear what happened to that first girl?" He jammed his hands into the pockets of his jacket to keep from wrapping them around her throat. "Damn you, Kirsten. If you'd been home all the time instead of only during the summer like some lousy camp counselor, this wouldn't have happened. If you'd been a full-time mother instead of a full-time musician, Meredith would be here with us right now."

Kirsten was shaking as she nervously put the chaise between them as a buffer. She was so distraught, she could barely think a clear thought or form a coherent sentence. Her daughter was missing. Her beautiful, adored little girl was missing. It was as though she had misplaced a part of herself and didn't know where to find it. Meredith was gone and Jeffrey was telling her that it was her fault. She twisted her handkerchief in her hands. Was he right, she asked herself. *Was* it her fault?

"What was that, I didn't quite hear you."

She wasn't even aware of having spoken. "I've been a good mother," she said through lips that felt frozen. Jeffrey greeted her statement with a loud snort of derision. Kirsten winced. Her daughter had disappeared; this was hardly the time to be defending herself as a mother. But she knew she had to try. If for no other reason than to convince her*self*.

"I *have* been a good mother." Jeffrey's response to that was to turn his back on her. "I'm not the only working mother in the world either, you know. This is 1970, Jeffrey, not the Middle Ages. A lot of women are dividing their time between their families and their careers, and I'm no different from any of them. Have I ever hurt my children? Have I ever abused them or neglected them? No, Jeffrey, I haven't. I've done nothing but love them and be supportive of them. I've given them the best of myself." She approached him somewhat warily and laid her hand on his sleeve. "Please, Jeffrey," she whispered, flinching as he yanked his arm away, "we shouldn't be fighting, not now, not when we're both in so much pain. This is our daughter we're talking about, yours and mine, and arguing about who's right and who's wrong isn't going to make the ordeal any easier for either of us."

But Jeffrey wasn't in a conciliatory mood, he was still hostile and combative. "Why did she always have to be so stubborn," he demanded, "so damned resistant? If I wouldn't allow her to walk to the Harewoods on her own, what the hell made her think she could walk home from Greenbriar alone?"

He left with both questions still hanging in the air unanswered, and Kirsten collapsed weakly onto her chaise. Closing her aching eyes, she began to rub their swollen lids with the tips of her fingers. Images of Meredith were all she could see. Her precious Meredith. As a baby, smiling and gurgling contentedly all the time. All lightness and joy and laughter—her dark hair and dark eyes in direct contrast to her sunny disposition. Meredith. As a child, seated at the piano. Her tiny fingers dancing across the keys, her feet dangling high above the pedals, her small body swaying with the music. Meredith. As a young girl, snuggled next to her in bed. The two of them giggling together, whispering, sharing the secrets only mothers and daughters share. Meredith saying she loved her more than anyone else in the world.

Kirsten began to cry again. If Meredith had said she loved her more than anyone else in the world, she must have done something right. She must have been a good mother for her daughter to have told her that. Suddenly she was on a seesaw, with Meredith's love for her on one side and Jeffrey's accusations on the other. Up and down she went, up and down, up and down, convinced she had been a good mother one minute, uncertain and guilt-ridden the next.

"Oh, Meredith, Meredith," she sobbed, covering her face with her hands. "I love you, my precious, I love you. Please be safe, my darling. Please let this be a mistake. Please let them find you at Jane's or Veronica's or Gillian's. Please, my angel, please phone us. Please let us know this was only a joke, that you did it only to frighten us. Oh, please, Meredith, please."

But Meredith didn't phone. Not that day or the next day or the day after that. When no demands for ransom were received, Lieutenant Donaldson began to rule out simple kidnapping as the reason for the nine-year-old's disappearance, but he said nothing to either Kirsten or Jeffrey. Both of them were strained nearly to the breaking point as it was. And to further compound their anguish, they were under constant siege by the media, their horrific ordeal chronicled daily in minute detail, then blasted from radios, flashed on TV screens, and splashed across the front page of every major newspaper in the world.

Kirsten existed on nerves, black tea, and hope. She even

had Nelson cancel all of her scheduled appearances for the rest of the year. Everything—including her own threatened career—had paled into insignificance beside the enormity of Meredith's disappearance. To stay sane, she remained in constant motion all day; only by keeping busy was she able to keep from thinking. She greeted each new shift of police officers with plates of sandwiches and pots of freshly brewed coffee, then she washed and dried every dirty dish and piece of cutlery herself. She answered the doorbell and the telephone. She took messages, delivered messages, and asked more questions than anyone had answers for.

Jeffrey and Dierdre observed Kirsten's frenetic activities with carefully veiled contempt. Although neither of them verbalized it, they were both thinking precisely the same thing. There was great truth to the old saw about a crisis bringing out the true nature of a person. To them the peasant in Kirsten Harald had finally surfaced.

Jeff was the most frightened and bewildered of all of them. Pulled from his kindergarten class at Greenbriar as soon as Jeffrey had reported Meredith's disappearance to the police, he spent all his time following after Kirsten. He wouldn't let her out of his sight. He followed her everywhere, trailing behind her like a mournful little shadow, his solemn blue eyes more solemn than ever in his small, pale face.

At night he agreed to go upstairs to bed only if Kirsten went with him and stayed with him until he fell asleep.

"You'll never leave me, will you, Mommy?" he would ask anxiously while she rocked him in her arms and kissed him.

"No, my precious, I'll never leave you."

"Promise?"

"I promise. I love you too much to leave you."

"And *I* love *you*, Mommy, so you'd better not leave, all right?"

"All right, my darling."

It would continue like this until his voice eventually faded and his grip on her relaxed. But even after he had fallen asleep, Kirsten always stayed with him awhile longer. For her, the nights were the worst. With nothing to keep her occupied, her thoughts invariably took control. All the unhappy, accusatory thoughts the daylight kept safely at bay. This was when she was her most vulnerable. These were the times she longed to be held, to be comforted, to be reassured that it wasn't her fault, and that everything would be all right. But there was no one to hold her. Her son was asleep and her husband now took the precaution of locking his bedroom door before retiring. She was alone, utterly, devastatingly alone. Alone with her pain and her guilt.

What she did was prowl the house, tiptoeing past all the closed doors, drifting in and out of every empty room, and gliding silently from floor to floor. A stealthy, soundless presence. The self-appointed guardian of all those fortunate enough to be able to sleep. Every noise she heard was Meredith knocking on the front door, every errant bit of moonlight was Meredith peering through one of the windows. She lost track of the number of times she opened the front door each night or ran to some window just to check.

Toward dawn she would wander into Meredith's room and touch all the things Meredith had ever touched—the furniture, the flounced curtains on the windows, the large tester bed, the antique dollhouse, her collection of miniature glass and china animals, her books and records, her clothes. Then she would sit down in the white wicker Victorian rocker they had bought her for her seventh birthday, and rock herself back and forth until she gradually became drowsy. When she was barely able to keep her eyes open anymore, she would curl up, fully dressed, on top of Meredith's bed, put her arms around her daughter's favorite Raggedy Ann doll, and fall into an exhausted sleep.

Ten days passed and the press was beginning to grow weary. And bored. So far there had been no sensational leads to track down, no intriguing clues to follow up, no spectacular breaks to report. It was difficult to make silence sound exciting. Dead-ends were dull. Even the occasional crank call and phony ransom demand wasn't particularly newsworthy anymore. The police were weary too. And frustrated. Jeffrey was a spent man, with no place to deposit the residue of his helpless rage, while Kirsten herself was fast losing what remained of her abundant supply of hope.

But on the twelfth morning of Meredith's disappearance, Kirsten awoke to find her hope renewed. Someone was downstairs playing the piano, playing "Clair de Lune," one of Meredith's earliest and most favorite pieces. Her fingers were trembling with such nervous excitement, she could barely button her robe. She finally gave up and left it open. Running barefoot down the stairs, she didn't stop running until she reached the conservatory.

"Meredith!"

The music crashed to a halt. Jeff looked up from the keyboard, and in a heartbreakingly tiny voice, said, "I'm sorry, Mommy, it's only me."

Kirsten's overwhelming desolation quickly turned to denial. "*Only* you, what do you mean, *only* you?" She ran to her son and gathered him up in her arms, whispering his name while she kissed away the hurt she had inadvertently caused him.

"Mommy?"

"Yes, my darling?"

"Let's play duets, okay?" His face brightened instantly when he saw her nod her head. "Oh, goody," he exclaimed, "just like me and Meredith." He promptly began "Chopsticks," the first duet his sister had ever taught him. Kirsten came in only a fraction of a second later than she should have. "What's wrong, Mommy?" Jeff asked without taking his eyes off the keyboard. "You're not playing."

"Of course I'm playing, darling."

"No, you're not, I can't hear you."

She pressed down a bit harder on the keys. "Now can you hear me?"

"No."

"Jeff, darling, really." It was then that she happened to glance down at her hands. "Oh, my God!"

Jeff immediately stopped playing. "Mommy?"

Kirsten stared at her hands in utter disbelief. They were poised over the keyboard like two frozen claws. Stiff. Unyielding. No longer supple flesh, but petrified stone. She tried to touch the keys again and couldn't. Her hands refused to move. They stayed exactly where they were, trapped in a rigid pose two inches above the keyboard. She tried flexing her fingers, one at a time. Not one finger responded.

"Mommy?" Jeff's blue eyes were wide with fright. "Your hands are stuck. Why won't they play?"

Kirsten shook her head. "I don't know." She tugged her hands back, rested them in her lap, and waited, her heart pounding, her forehead beaded with perspiration, until full circulation had been restored to them. Then she calmly placed them on the keys again and banged out ten loud notes at once.

"Mommy, there's still no sound."

Kirsten pretended she hadn't heard him. She tried again

and again and again. But her hands remained stubbornly
fixed, like a pair of arched talons belonging, not to her, but to
some primeval bird. Recalcitrant. Refusing to submit to her
higher will. She hammered away soundlessly at the keys until
Jeff burst into tears and begged her to stop. Her arms dropped
like leaden weights to her sides.

"She's dead," she whispered. "Meredith's dead. She's dead
and I've been punished for it. Dear God in heaven, I've
killed my daughter."

The following afternoon a drenching autumn rain finally
accomplished what the police, the tracking dogs, and hundreds of local volunteers had failed to do. It washed away part
of a shallow grave in a densely wooded area five miles from
the Oliver compound. Two boys playing hooky from school
discovered Meredith's nude body buried only a short distance from the ruins of Knollwood, a vast estate bought years
before for a bucket of rubies and diamonds by an exiled
Albanian king who never even lived in it. What Kirsten
dreaded most was confirmed when the Nassau County medical examiner released his findings. Meredith had been raped
before she was murdered. Her neck had been broken. She
had been dead at least a week.

The vigil was over. The press and the police began leaving
the grounds almost simultaneously. Where Juvenile left off,
Homicide took over. What had begun as a possible kidnapping had ended as murder. What was formerly a search now
evolved into a manhunt.

Draped heavily in black, her face further concealed by a
pair of oversize dark glasses, Kirsten stood motionless between Jeffrey and Dierdre and watched as her beloved daughter was buried in the Oliver family plot. Perhaps it was
absurd, but she couldn't help thinking of those other three
women she so admired—Jackie and Ethel Kennedy, and
Coretta King—women who, like herself, had all lost loved
ones to some murderer. She remembered their veiled faces,
their dignity, and their courage as they had stoically endured
having to share their grief with an entire nation. Her world
may have been smaller than theirs, but her own grief was
being made just as public.

Tears she couldn't feel ran down her ashen cheeks. With
both hands resting heavily on the narrow shoulders of her
son, she leaned against his back for added support without

even being aware of it. She was in such agony that she had transcended all feelings and now existed only in a waking state of somnambulism.

Yet she remained haunted. Haunted by the horror of her daughter's brutal rape and murder. Haunted by the doubts and questions and guilt that gave her no peace. Could she really have been a good mother if the daughter she loved was dead? Had she been fooling herself all these years when she thought she was dividing herself equally between her two separate worlds? Had she let her children and her husband down, cheated them, and deprived them just as Jeffrey said she had? If she had been home that last day, could she have prevented what had happened from happening? The police had assured her no, that in murders like these, the targets were usually random, not planned. It was simply and unfortunately a matter of being in the wrong place at the wrong time. Knowing this helped a bit, but not much. She still remained haunted.

She was barely aware of the service ending, barely aware of the brief drive home. She had lost all sense of time; she gauged its passage now by the ebb and flow of her pain.

"Can I make anyone some coffee?" she automatically asked of the two dozen people who had returned with them from the cemetery and who were now gathered in their living room. She had to keep busy, she had to, or she would go mad. She saw them exchange hasty glances, heard them whispering among themselves as one by one they shook their heads. "Dierdre?" She turned to her sister-in-law, who immediately pursed her lips and sniffed as though she had detected a bad odor.

"The servants will take care of it, dear."

Her contemptuous reply had been made in the softest tone imaginable, yet she might just as well have been shouting. The effect on Kirsten was the same: she recoiled. Dierdre had more than made her point these last few weeks, but now she had driven it home in front of everyone most effectively. *Kirsten, my dear,* she was saying, *you don't belong. You never have and you never will.* She watched as the woman turned and whispered something to Lois Holden. Lois smiled, then she laughed.

It was the laughter of her classmates in the school yard, the haughty stare of the elderly woman outside Carnegie Hall all over again. All of them letting her know she didn't belong.

Everyone was watching her, waiting to see what she would do. What she did was square her shoulders proudly and survey them with a cold contempt of her own. She was Kirsten Harald, her look told them, she didn't need them in order to belong. She belonged to the world.

27

And the world proved it to her.

Two months after Meredith's funeral, Kirsten was still being inundated with cards and letters and cables. In an outpouring of affection and support, tens of thousands of strangers had sought to give something back to the extraordinary woman who had, over the years, given them so much of herself. That the mail even reached her at all was a miracle—most of it had been addressed simply to Kirsten Harald, New York City. It was a loving tribute that astounded and humbled Kirsten and warmed a small part of her frozen heart.

Yet her grief remained unassuageable. She clung tenaciously to her dead child and refused to let go of her in any way, no matter how small. She began each day by putting fresh flowers on Meredith's grave and ended it by curling up on top of Meredith's bed with the Raggedy Ann doll in her arms. She scarcely ate, she barely slept, and when she did sleep, her nightmares were so violent and so graphic, she was soon afraid even to close her eyes. She took to lying down with a night-light on, the same little yellow plastic-covered light she had used in the nursery when Meredith was an infant, and that helped brighten some of the terrible darkness for her.

She missed her daughter and she wanted her back. She wanted a second chance; this time she would do it right. She wanted to turn the clock back and begin all over again from the beginning. She made all kinds of pacts with God, promising Him anything, if only He would return her daughter to her. But either she wasn't promising Him enough or He just wasn't listening, because Meredith continued to remain lost to her.

Natalya had told her long ago that she would always have

her music; Natalya had been wrong. Where was her music now? Lost to her, as lost to her as Meredith was. She was crippled, her hands hobbled. She couldn't get any closer to the keyboard now than on the day she knew for certain her daughter was dead. No matter what she did, no matter how long she sat at the piano and willed her hands to move, they wouldn't.

At last, she consulted a specialist in secret. He diagnosed her condition as a form of hysterical paralysis. She consulted a second, then a third. All three reached precisely the same conclusion: hysterical paralysis. She blamed herself for Meredith's death and considered her music to have been the cause of it. What she had done was translate her emotional grief into something physical. By being unable to play the piano, she was, in effect, punishing herself for what had happened to Meredith. Where she had once thought of her musical gift as a blessing, she now saw it as a curse. Unless and until she absolved herself of her guilt, she would remain paralyzed, unable to play a single note. All three specialists recommended she see, not a physiotherapist, but a psychotherapist.

She returned home from the latest consultation exhausted and more disheartened than ever. To think that her own mind had turned against her and cut her off from the wellspring from which she had been drawing sustenance all her life. It was ludicrous, inconceivable, incomprehensible. A pianist who couldn't play, what kind of a pianist was that? Without her music she was a musician committed to a living death.

She held her hands out in front of her and examined them closely. She studied the backs of them first—the fingers slender and delicately boned, the nails short and smooth, the surface veins fine and faintly blue—then she turned them over and studied her palms—the pads of her fingers lightly callused, the flesh of her palms softly firm. They looked exactly the same; they looked as though they were still her hands. Yet they weren't her hands at all anymore.

How long she continued to stand in the middle of her bedroom floor examining her hands, she didn't know. But it took the sounds of a violent argument coming from somewhere on the first floor to finally rouse her from her trancelike stupor. Careening down the stairs, her heart in her mouth, she came to a dead stop at the bottom and let out a shriek. Jeffrey was having her piano moved and Jeff was running alongside it, shouting and pounding away defiantly on the keyboard.

"Jeffrey!" she cried above the playing and the squeaking wheels of the large wooden dolly that three workmen were trying to maneuver through the front hall. "What are you doing? What in God's name do you think you're doing?"

She might just as well have been talking to herself for all the attention her husband paid her. His face was red as he kept trying to pull his crying young son away from the piano with one hand and direct the three movers with the other.

"Jeff, stop that infernal howling of yours," he demanded. "This piano is going, so you'd better get used to the idea. Now, take your hands away from the keyboard. Did you hear what I just said? Take your hands off those keys, dammit, do what I tell you to do."

Catching sight of Kirsten at the foot of the staircase, her face white with shock, Jeff called out to her in desperation.

"Mommy, make him put the piano back. Please, Mommy, make him put it back."

But Kirsten didn't need any extra urging from her son, she was already starting across the hall on her own volition.

"Jeffrey!"

She kept shouting his name and he kept ignoring her.

"Jeffrey, that piano's mine, it doesn't belong to you. You have no right to touch it." She grabbed hold of his arm with fingers of steel and wouldn't let go. "Put that piano back where it belongs, damn you," she screamed, sinking her fingers even deeper into his arm. "I said, put it back."

He turned on her viciously and backhanded a slap across her face. Jeff shrieked. Kirsten gasped, releasing her husband's sleeve as she reeled backward and fell, landing on the cold marble floor of the hall with a bruising thud. Whimpering in terror, Jeff ran toward her, throwing himself at her feet and wrapping his small arms around her waist in a child's anxious attempt to protect the mother he adored. The movers exchanged glances but said nothing.

Kirsten was more stunned than hurt. But the fall had temporarily winded her, giving Jeffrey the few extra seconds he needed. The piano was rolled out of the house with a final, deafening screech of the dolly's wheels, and the door slammed shut behind it. That done, Jeffrey marched determinedly down the hallway toward the conservatory without so much as a sideways glance at his wife and son, who were still huddled together on the floor.

"Mommy, what's he going to do now?" Jeff asked in a tiny, frightened voice.

Kirsten shook her head. "I don't know, my angel, but I think I'd better find out." She struggled to her feet, raised a cautious hand to her stinging cheek, and winced when she felt how hot and very tender the flesh was. Her legs were shaky, the first few steps she took were uncertain, but outrage stiffened her stride almost immediately. She reached the conservatory with both fists clenched and her whole body girded for combat. What she saw turned her blood cold.

"It's finished, Kirsten, finished!" Jeffrey shouted as he savagely shredded the pages of her sheet music, flinging whatever he tore into the air. "It's over and done with, now and forever. No one, and I mean no one, will ever play the piano in this house again. Your goddamned music's already cost me my daughter; it's not going to cost me my son as well. Because if you think he's going to grow up to be like you, you're wrong, bitch, dead wrong."

Kirsten watched him, momentarily transfixed. He was standing in the middle of a paper snowstorm, the area around him blanketed by thousands of tiny pieces of sheet music—sheet music that formed a veritable chronicle of her entire career. Before her horrified eyes he was attempting to destroy some of the very vital proof of that career: the simple pieces she had played as a child, the more complex works she had mastered as a teenager, the concertos that had marked her debut as a soloist and heralded her triumphant reign as one of the world's most respected classical pianists. By his hateful actions Jeffrey was debasing her music, defiling her dream, and effectively annihilating *her*.

With a howl of rage she hurled herself at him, nearly knocking him over. "You bastard!" she screamed. "You goddamned bastard!" Still cursing, she began tearing at his face with her fingers. "Damn you, Jeffrey, damn you to hell!" She was so incensed, all she could think of was ravaging him the way he had ravaged her music.

His superior strength enabled him to put an abrupt end to her furious rampage. Clamping both hands around her wrists, he shook her until she was nearly senseless, then flung her away from him. She was dizzy, her ears were ringing, she could barely stand upright, but she was dauntless as she came at him again.

"Do you know something, Jeffrey?" She was panting as they continued to grapple with each other. "This is the one time in my life when I wish I had long nails."

Upstairs in her room later, Kirsten paced the floor and tried to think rationally, but her mind was in such a chaotic jumble that clear thinking was next to impossible.

When she asked herself what her options were, the answers she came up with were scarcely more than fragmented and hostile images. Images of her murdering Jeffrey because of what he had just done. Images of her bringing another piano into the house, and continuing to do so every time he ordered one taken away. Of her divorcing him on grounds of physical and mental cruelty. Of her picking Jeff up and leaving. Of her going to the newspapers and telling them all about her respected husband's many well-concealed peculiarities. What a field day the press would have; what a tarnishing the illustrious name of Oliver would suffer.

Her pacing could barely keep up with her feverish thoughts as they continued to career from the ridiculous to the desperate to the absurd, then back again. Of all the options open to her, only one made any real sense: she would take Jeff and leave. Instantly buoyed by her decision, she half-ran, half-tripped to the cupboard in her dressing room where her luggage was stored. Flinging two large Vuitton suitcases and a matching garment bag onto her bed, she quickly began to empty out her dresser drawers. Then she went to work on her clothes closet.

She was just about to zip up the overstuffed garment bag when she suddenly stopped. Almost immediately her exuberance began to give way to despair. What she was contemplating was madness, sheer and utter madness. She would never get away with it, Jeffrey would see to that. Because of her, their daughter was dead, and he would sooner see *her* dead than be deprived of his only son.

For the moment she was trapped. But as she slowly began putting everything away again, she vowed she wouldn't stay trapped for long.

On Christmas morning Kirsten woke up to find Jeff cuddled beside her in Meredith's bed, watching her with his gentle blue eyes softly pensive. Greeting him with a big kiss, she wrapped her arms around him and whispered in his ear, "Are you my Christmas present this year, my little darling?"

This made him laugh; it was the first time she had heard her son laugh since before Meredith's disappearance.

"Are you my present, my angel?" she continued to tease him, "Are you, Jeff, hmm, Jeff, are you?"

But instead of answering her directly, he squirmed free of her embrace and scampered out of the room. He returned a few minutes later, slightly breathless, with a fat red bow looped around his neck, and flung himself back into bed.

"Now I am," he announced gleefully, burrowing deep inside her arms again and pressing his cheek against hers.

Kirsten sighed. What a precious respite this was. With Jeff's warm little body nestled so close to her, she felt safe and content—even though she knew the feelings were only temporary.

In the ten days since Jeffrey had had the piano taken away, she had been feeling anything but safe and content. There was such turmoil inside her, she no longer knew where one emotion left off and another began. Her music had been cruelly silenced, her once satisfying marriage was a disastrous shambles, and her sadly diminished family was in chaos, trapped in an ugly civil war: she and Jeff on one side, Jeffrey on the other. Both sides distant, hostile, and unyielding.

Even the house felt different. It was unnaturally still; the atmosphere was tense and expectant, like the deadly warning calm before some terrible storm. Everyone knew that one was imminent, but no one knew precisely when it would strike. All they could do was wait. And while they waited, the level of anxiety continued to rise, minute by minute, hour by hour, day by day.

She and Jeff were still snuggling comfortably together when Jeffrey came barging into the room uninvited and ordered his son to leave. When the boy resisted, Jeffrey hauled him roughly out of bed by one arm and pointed him toward the door.

"Out!" He emphasized his terse command by giving Jeff a light shove, and the little boy, his chin still quivering rebelliously, reluctantly obeyed. Then Jeffrey turned his full attention on his stony-faced wife. "This, my dear, is for you," he said, dropping a nondescript-looking gray cardboard box in her lap. "Merry Christmas."

He stood outside in the hallway until he heard her first shocked gasp of surprise. Then, smiling smugly to himself, he went back to his own room to wait.

It was nearly over, this ghastly farce they still called a marriage. She had finally given him the last bit of ammunition he needed. She herself had handed him the loaded pistol, all he had to do now was pull the trigger. By her own actions she had condemned herself, vindicated him, and relieved him of the responsibility of continuing this ridiculous charade any longer. She had played him for a fool from the first, and for that she would pay, and pay dearly.

He had tried to make her into an Oliver, but she had insisted on staying Kirsten Harald. He had wanted her exclusively for himself, yet she had remained the common property of the entire world. He had never been able to purge her of Michael Eastbourne—the proof of which lay in black and white in that ordinary gray box. She still wore him around her like a halo, the way had had once worn his bracelet around her wrist. She had stolen the love of his children, hoarding it for herself while depriving him. As a result, his daughter was dead and his son barely spoke to him anymore.

The ache in his groin reminded him of Kirsten's greatest failure. To spite her, he angrily ground the heels of both hands into the subtly pulsing place between his legs. He pressed in, relaxed, pressed in, relaxed, repeating this pattern until the reassuring throbbing had blossomed into a full-blown erection. Then he unzipped his fly and closed his eyes. It took less than a dozen strokes to bring him to orgasm. With the image of a naked Dierdre fixed firmly in his mind, he came, catching the rich hot flow of his semen in his carefully cupped hand.

We won't have to wait much longer, he promised her tantalizing image as he cleaned himself up with a freshly laundered, white linen handkerchief, not too much longer at all. He readjusted his trousers, slipped a clean handkerchief into the breast pocket of his blazer, and went back in to see Kirsten; he had already given her more than enough time.

"Congratulations, my dear Kirsten," he said with a smirk, indicating the open cardboard box in front of her, "you nearly managed to get away with it."

"There was nothing to get away with," she replied, her mouth scarcely moving as she spoke, she was still that rigid with shock.

"I wouldn't call a fifteen-year affair with Michael Eastbourne nothing."

"I haven't had a fifteen-year affair with Michael Eastbourne."

"No?"

"No," she repeated emphatically. "I've never been unfaithful to you, Jeffrey, never, I swear it."

"I don't happen to believe you, Kirsten." He put the lid back on the box and picked it up again. "Neither, I may add, will the courts. You look surprised. Well, you certainly didn't think I was going to turn a blind eye to this, did you? Not when your old friend Claudia went to so much trouble. I really ought to find some way of thanking her properly for what she did." He watched with malicious delight as Kirsten's ravaged face registered a dozen different emotions while she sat there listening to him. "Maybe I'll even name the new wing we're building onto the institute after her, what do you think?"

"I think you're vicious and despicable," was her answer. She was so disgusted by the sight of him, she felt sick to her stomach. Who was this man, she wondered, this man she thought she knew but obviously had never really known at all. "You and Claudia make the perfect pair," she added quietly, "you're both evil."

"Evil?" Jeffrey laughed. "My wife, the lying, conniving adulteress, has the nerve to call me evil?"

When every instinct was screaming for her to scratch his eyes out, Kirsten forced herself to remain calm and not make matters worse.

"Well, evil or not, I intend to divorce you, Kirsten. I want you out of my house and out of my life as quickly as possible." She took his news without flinching. "Oh, by the way, in case you're even thinking about trying to get custody of Jeff, you can forget about it right now. If you're not fit to remain my wife, you're certainly not fit to bring up my son." At that she blanched. Her skin became so pale, it was practically transparent; even her eyes seemed more crystal now than amethyst. "I'd advise you not even to contemplate fighting me, Kirsten, because if you do, I'll destroy you."

The moment he left, she reached for the telephone beside her bed. Her hysterical sobbing made her speech almost incoherent, but Nelson was still able to make out several key words: lawyer and private investigator.

* * *

"He can't do this to me, he can't, he just can't," Kirsten kept muttering as she paced Scott Hamlyn's large cork-paneled office on the fortieth floor of the Empire State Building.

Her lawyer, a lanky redhead with a narrow, sensitive face and a reassuring sense of solidity about him, rested his elbows on the oak and brass campaign desk his parents had given him when he graduated Harvard Law in 1950, and watched his client pace away some of her anger. After two months he had gotten used to her pacing. Not that he blamed her. If he had been in her position, he would have been pacing too. In his twenty years of practice as one of the city's top divorce lawyers, he had never seen a more vindictive divorce action than the one filed against Kirsten Harald.

Jeffrey Powell Oliver II was out for blood. He was angry, vengeful, and single-minded. But it was his enormous wealth that made him truly lethal. By virtue of his wealth, he was a longstanding member of an exclusive club that automatically and loyally closes ranks against the invasion of outsiders in staunch defense of one of its own—no matter what. The weight of his family name alone had already granted him virtual immunity from the laws governing the more average man, while his own broad sphere of influence and well-placed contacts had so far rendered him impervious to even the most skillfully planned attack.

Scott had tried everything: he had bargained and harangued; he had argued precedents and threatened to file a countersuit. Nothing had made the slightest difference. Jeffrey Powell Oliver had left nothing to chance. He had stacked the cards tight and high, and they were all in his favor. He had what every opposing attorney dreads most—a water-tight case.

Kirsten threw herself into one of the two chocolate-brown-suede tub chairs facing Scott's desk and continued to seethe sitting down. It seemed she lived every waking moment in a state of contained anger these days. Sixty-seven days to be more precise. Sixty-seven days since that snowy morning in early January when a red-nosed bailiff had slapped a bulky blue-backed document into her hands and informed her that by accepting it, she had been "duly notified and served."

Not only had she been served with Jeffrey's petition for divorce, she had also been ordered—as they had so delicately phrased it—to "vacate the premises within twenty-four hours of receipt of said notice." Like some hapless tenant being evicted by her landlord for nonpayment of rent, she was being evicted by her own husband from the home they had shared together for nearly eleven years. To humiliate her still further, two court-appointed peace officers stood guard over her while she packed her bags.

She hadn't even been allowed to say good-bye to Jeff. With cruel and calculated forethought, Jeffrey had arranged for Dierdre to take him for the day—where, he refused to say. He himself put in an appearance at the house for exactly ten minutes—whether to gloat or merely to see that she was complying with the court order she couldn't decide—then left again without so much as a parting word to her. What had begun in silence had ended in silence. In twenty-four hours, Jeffrey, with all the knife-wielding precision of the surgeon he had wanted to be, had ruthlessly and cold-bloodedly severed her from eleven years of her life.

Kirsten put her head in her hand. She felt dizzy; but then, she found she felt dizzy most of the time now. One by one the supports that had kept her firmly rooted and standing upright all her life had been cut out from under her, leaving her to teeter unsteadily on ground that shifted hazardously beneath her feet. She had suffered too many shocks, endured too many losses, all of them coming too close together. Before she had even been able to recover from one, she had been hit with another. She had met each new, devastating blow with the courage and resiliency that had always been her hallmark, but her abundant reserves of energy had finally been depleted, her boundless strength sapped; now all that remained to fuel her was her anger.

"Scott?" She peered up at her attorney through the splayed fingers of her right hand. "Tell me he can't do this, please, tell me he can't."

Scott Hamlyn picked up a paper clip and toyed with it a moment before he answered her. "I'm afraid he can, Kirsten." He saw a convulsive shudder shake her small body as though it had no more weight or substance than a leaf, and he wanted to put his arms around her and promise her everything would be all right. But he didn't, for the simple reason that he couldn't make her such a promise.

"Do you mean to tell me he stands a good chance of being granted sole custody of Jeff?" Scott nodded. "And that the courts can really deny me all visiting rights?" He nodded again. Further words failed her; she was too incredulous, too dazed to speak. She knew she should have chanced it that day—taken Jeff and run—because now it was too late.

"Jeffrey's contention is that you're an unfit mother, Kirsten," Scott continued, "that you're a harmful influence on your son, and as such you pose a genuine threat to his safety and well-being."

"That's nonsense and you know it." She was out of her chair and pacing again.

"I know it and I intend to prove it."

"Then why are his chances of being granted custody of Jeff better than mine?" No sooner had the words left her mouth than she took them back with a weary wave of her hand. "Never mind, you don't have to tell me again. It has nothing to do with the facts; I was simply born on the wrong side of the bay." She thought about her son, her precious son whom Jeffrey was trying to keep from her, and her weariness evaporated; the full force of her anger returned, stronger even than before.

"Scott!" It was a command as she leaned across his desk and looked him straight in the eye. "You can't let them win, you can't let them take my son away from me. No one has the right to deprive me of my child, no one; not Jeffrey, not the courts. I love him, Scott, I love him desperately. He's all I have left in the world."

She pushed away from his desk and resumed her anxious pacing. Her fists were doubled as she walked back and forth in front of him, her agony so intense it was almost visible.

"Dear God"—she let out a moan—"I want to lead a normal life again. I want some peace, just a little peace." She stopped pacing and stared blankly out of the window. "Do you know how many times I've had to change hotels these past two months because of the news media? Every time I open the door of my room, flashbulbs go off in my face and reporters start firing questions at me. I can't walk through the lobby without someone shoving a microphone at me or following me with a TV camera. No one will rent me an apartment or lease me a co-op because they know where I go, the press goes. I feel like a freak, Scott; I feel hounded, hounded and trapped." She made a helpless gesture with her hands. "And I miss Jeff." Here her voice broke. "I miss him so much. I still drive out to Greenbriar every day hoping to catch a glimpse of him at recess or at lunchtime. But they keep him inside now, you know, they won't even let him out to play with the other children. He's every bit as trapped as I am."

For the past two months she had been forbidden by law to either see or attempt to contact Jeff in any way. That she had been served with a restraining order denying her the right to see her son until the case could be heard was a situation she found as degrading as it was intolerable. That the courts even had the power to issue and enforce such an order was to her inhuman and totally unacceptable. And it was an order which, much to Scott's consternation and against his repeated advice, she continued to ignore.

Because of her refusal to abide by the order, Jeffrey had had all the locks on the house changed, the high wrought iron fence surrounding the estate closed and electronically controlled, and the grounds patrolled twenty-four hours a day. He had even had the telephone number changed and unlisted. Every letter she mailed Jeff was returned still sealed to her rented postal box, every gift she had delivered to him was sent back unopened to the store it came from. In desperation, she had started calling Dierdre. It wasn't long before her number was changed and unlisted too. She had even called Lois Holden once, but Lois had hung up on her immediately. What Scott had warned her about had happened: the ranks of Long Island's social elite had closed around her husband, swallowed up her son, and locked her out.

"Kirsten?" Scott was touching her lightly on the sleeve. "Go back to the hotel and rest, all right? You must be exhausted. And try not to worry, we're not through fighting yet."

She took part of his well-intentioned advice: she did go back to her hotel, but she didn't rest. How could she, when her son was out there thinking she had abandoned him?

They weren't contesting Jeffrey's divorce action, but they were contesting his petition to be granted sole custody of Jeff and to deny Kirsten all visitation rights. They lost. On a drizzly afternoon in late September, Kirsten sat rigidly beside Scott in an impersonal, windowless courtroom crammed to capacity with morbid strangers and members of the ubiquitous news media to hear herself declared an unfit mother. To suffer the public humiliation of being told she presented a threat to the welfare and safety of her child, and was therefore denied all future access to him. To have what was a very private agony exposed for the rabidly curious of the world to feed on.

While pandemonium was breaking loose all around her, Kirsten didn't move; she didn't even appear to be breathing. Her entire world was gone. She had now been stripped of everything—her music, her marriage, her children. She was a woman who had lost it all; she had nothing left to lose.

On the afternoon Scott filed his first appeal, Kirsten drove up to Greenbriar in a leased limousine identical to Jeffrey's new slate-gray Chrysler Imperial. She had timed it well. Hers was the first car in line outside the main entrance to the school, hers was the familiar car Jeff would be looking for. At precisely two o'clock, a pair of carved oak doors swung open and children began spilling down the wide stone steps of the nineteenth-century Gothic-style mansion, the youngest ones first. Kirsten held her breath.

Jeff had the back door partially open, when Kirsten grabbed him firmly around the waist and pulled him into the car.

They were through the iron gates of the former Vanderbilt estate before anyone realized what had happened.

28

The sirens and flashing red lights came out of nowhere to surround them.

The rented limousine careened to a screeching stop on the soft shoulder of the road and the frightened driver practically leapt from the car in his haste to absolve himself of any wrongdoing. In the backseat Kirsten was clinging desperately to Jeff. His arms were wrapped tightly around her neck, his tear-streaked face crushed against hers. With her mouth buried deep in his straight black hair and her eyes closed, she told him again and again how much she loved him.

Hands began pulling at them from every direction, trying to roughly and swiftly separate them. Tightening her hold on her son, Kirsten kicked out with her legs, twisted and turned her body from side to side, and yelled for them to leave the two of them alone. Jeff could feel his grip on his mother weakening, and he began to scream.

"Please, Mommy, don't let them take me. Mommy, I miss you," he sobbed. "Please, don't let them take me. Mommy!"

Kirsten was a woman gone wild. She was savage, brutal, as she fought to hold on to her son, driven by the most basic of all primordial instincts—a mother's need to protect the flesh born of her flesh. But in the end she was outnumbered and overpowered. And Jeff was snatched away from her, still screaming.

"Jeff!" She jumped out after him, only to be shoved back inside the limo again. "Jeff, I love you, I love you Jeff!"

"Mommy!"

His voice grew fainter as he was carried to one of the patrol cars and placed on the backseat beside two uniformed police officers. Her last glimpse of him was his anguished face pressed up against the rear window of the car, his mouth opening and closing as he continued to call out to her; and the image promised to haunt her the rest of her life.

Scott and Jeffrey's attorney, Preston Howlett of the esteemed Madison Avenue law firm of Howlett, Massey, Steeves, and O'Brien, arrived at the police station within minutes of each other. When the desk sergeant asked Howlett if his client intended to prefer charges, the dapper seventy-one-year-old attorney shook his head.

"Not for the moment," came the curt reply as he fixed a pair of sharp blue eyes on Kirsten. "But we reserve the right to do so should Miss Harald make any further attempts to contact the boy." Turning to Scott, he said, "I'd advise you, counselor, to caution your client against trying anything this foolhardy again. She's been cited for contempt of the restraining order a half dozen times already; kidnapping charges aren't quite as easily dismissed."

"I want my son," Kirsten demanded, lunging at the man who was Jeffrey's lawyer and who had been his father's lawyer before him. Scott pulled her back. "I want my son, Mr. Howlett. You had no right to take him away from me."

"We didn't take him away from you, Miss Harald," the man replied smoothly. "We were awarded custody of the boy by the courts."

"It's the same thing."

"Kirsten, please." Scott was losing his grasp on her arm. One of the policemen who had been watching the exchange started toward them. "Kirsten, please, let's just go."

"No!" She wrenched her arm free. "Get Jeff back for me,

Scott, or I'll go after him again myself." Looking up at the white-haired Preston Howlett, who had all the power and prestige of the establishment on his side, she said, "I'm not the unfit parent in this case, Jeffrey is. Oh, yes, Mr. Howlett, your very respectable and very proper Jeffrey is."

"I think you'd better get your client out of here," the desk sergeant suggested to Scott in a tone slightly less than conciliatory. "She's just looking for trouble."

But Kirsten wouldn't be moved. "Why don't you ask Jeff who he wants to live with, Mr. Howlett?" Her voice was rising. Scott grabbed her firmly by the elbow and started tugging her toward the door. "Or maybe you already have, and that's why you're so afraid of me, why you're so afraid of letting me see him."

Scott practically wrestled her out the door of the station and into his car. But even then she refused to sit still. Her nerves were strung so tightly, her emotions so highly charged that her whole body appeared to be outlined by electrical sparks. She could still feel the imprint of Jeff's hands on her neck, of his cheek against hers, of his body cradled in her lap. She could still smell the familiar clean sweetness of his skin and hair. In the twenty brief minutes they had spent together, she had known her first real happiness in over a year. But it wasn't enough, not nearly enough; she wanted more. She wanted her son for more than just twenty minutes; she wanted him forever.

"Kirsten?" They were now only five blocks from her downtown hotel and this was the first time Scott had spoken. "Kirsten, how could you have done it?" His voice was so low, so obviously distraught, she barely heard what he was saying. "Did you honestly believe you'd get away with it? I know how you feel; I can understand your frustration and sense of helplessness, but to try kidnapping? You've played right into Jeffrey's hands. We'll never win our appeal, never. They might even deny us the *right* to appeal now."

Without even turning to look at him, Kirsten said quietly, very quietly, "You're wrong, Scott, you couldn't possibly know how I feel. You're not a mother."

It was three months before they had their answer. When Scott finally telephoned her with the news, Kirsten didn't know whether she was prepared to hear it or not. Her lawyer gave her no time to make up her mind.

"We were denied the right to appeal, Kirsten, just as I expected we would be." Kirsten sucked in her breath and grabbed hold of the receiver with both hands. "I'm afraid your abducting Jeff really finished it for us."

After swallowing hard several times, she managed to ask, "What recourse do we have?" When he didn't answer her immediately, she began to panic. "Scott?"

He cleared his throat. "None."

"None?" She was beside herself, her emotions dancing dangerously out of control. "None, you can't mean that, you can't! There must be something we can do."

"Kirsten, listen to me, and listen carefully. They've closed the door on us for now, and I'm emphasizing *for now*. I'm going to continue filing motions to appeal and I'm—"

"But, Scott, the motion didn't work this time, what makes—"

"Let me finish, please. I'm also going to file a petition before the Supreme Court. Unfortunately, that could take years."

"Years!"

"They receive thousands of petitions every year and they agree to hear only a few hundred of them. There's a chance we might be one of the lucky ones."

Kirsten doubled over and clutched at herself to keep her insides from spilling onto the carpet. "And if we're not?" she asked in a strangled voice.

"We'll have to wait until Jeff reaches the age of majority. Jeffrey won't have any legal control over him then."

"What's the age of majority?"

"Eighteen."

"Eighteen!" The shock of it straightened her instantly. Eighteen, dear God, Scott, he's only six-and-a-half now. We're talking about eleven-and-a-half years. He'll have forgotten me by then. Jeffrey will have had all those years to poison his mind against me." She shook her head in utter disbelief. "Nearly twelve years," she intoned, "twelve years. And just what am I supposed to be doing with myself in the meantime?"

"Picking up the pieces and living your life," Scott offered gently. "You still have your career, you know."

Kirsten nearly laughed out loud when she heard that. Her career. Her career! But then, she couldn't blame Scott. He didn't know; no one did.

Scott was worried. He didn't like the sudden silence at the

other end of the phone. "Kirsten, I'm coming over," he told her. "I don't think you should be alone right now."

She hung up while he was still speaking.

She didn't realize how cold it was until she reached Patelson's. Snowflakes were clinging to her eyelashes, dusting her hair and soaking through her fine wool sweater. She hadn't bothered putting on her coat, she hadn't even remembered to wear gloves. She purchased the piece of sheet music she wanted and left the store, fingering the bright new penny the salesgirl had included with the rest of her change. The wind had come up, the snow pelted at her mercilessly as she crossed the street half blinded by the driving flakes.

At the foot of the stairs leading up to the main entrance of Carnegie Hall, she stopped. The steps were almost entirely covered with snow now. Tucking the thin paper bag holding her sheet music under one arm, she dropped to her knees on the bottom step and clasped both hands under her chin. Scott was right. The key to her future lay in her music. Once she got her music back again, everything else would fall into place. All she had to do was rededicate herself to her dream and believe.

With her eyes closed and her head bowed, Kirsten repeated, word for word, the same pledge she had made on that very same stone step nearly thirty years before. She swore to forsake everything in the name of her music, to resist all temptation and remain faithful to her goal no matter what. Then she kissed the shiny new penny the salesgirl had given her and placed it on the topmost step to seal her pledge.

She went around to the studio entrance of the building and took the elevator up to the eighth floor. She found a deserted room and went inside. The number on the door stirred something deep in her memory. Of course. Room 851. It was the room where she was supposed to have auditioned for Eduard van Beinum. She sat down at the Baldwin, opened her sheet music, and hastily scanned the first page. Five flats. Four-eighths time. Andantino molto. The left hand beginning first—a single chord—then the right hand joining in. All these details she noted in a matter of seconds. She felt very much like a novice. And in some ways she was.

She exercised her fingers until they were warm and tingly and completely relaxed. Then she drew in a last, deep breath and began. The notes were at once strange and familiar to her, the melody both forgotten and remembered. Her hands moved lightly over the keys, gradually but steadily gaining confidence and strength, until she knew that what she was hearing was what she had always heard: the uniquely rich sound for which she was famous. It had set her at the very top of the golden mountain once; it would set her back up there again.

With the sound of her celebrated signature piece, Claude Debussy's "Reflets dans l'Eau" swirling so sweetly around her, she drifted upward and entered a state of perfect peace.

It was close to midnight when the elderly cleaner spotted the light under the door of Room 851. He waited a moment, but when he didn't hear anything, he opened the door and went inside.

"Hey, lady," he called out to the woman at the piano, "you shouldn't be in here so late."

Obviously she hadn't heard him. He moved a bit closer to her, then stopped dead in his tracks. She was sitting there so stiffly, she could have been a statue. Her eyes were glazed and staring, her hands poised like a pair of frozen claws two inches above the closed lid over the keyboard. He didn't think he had it in him, but he found himself running out of the room. He grabbed the first telephone he could find, dialed the operator, and told her to get him the police.

29

Kirsten was cushioned by a wonderful nothingness, living deep inside a large, clear bubble. But she wasn't alone in her bubble, she had her music with her for company. What had originally begun as only a faint ripple, so light it was hardly more than a whisper, had gradually been growing stronger. At times it was a shy patter of raindrops, at others a gently rolling stream. The gathering crescendo of a waterfall. A flash of lightning accompanied by a triumphant peal of thunder. Rising, continuously rising. Until it was howling all around her, with all the fury of a hurricane.

Out of the nothingness came a gradual redefinition of shapes as well. A window. A chair. A pillow. The bed. A glass of water. And faces. Faces she had never seen before. There were twinges, too, momentary pangs, tentative proddings. Reminding her that she was beginning to feel again. She fought this part the hardest. Feeling meant pain. She didn't want to feel pain again. Slipping back was easy. Better. Safer. A grateful return to nothingness and its absence of feeling.

Her recovery became a game of hide-and-seek after that. A fading in and a fading out. Elusive shadow tag. A cautious step ahead, two determined ones back. The pattern occasionally reversing itself. Whenever she resisted too strongly, the music would urge her forward, until it, not she, was the dominant of the two opposing forces. When at last the music seized complete control, her final defenses crumbled and then collapsed altogether.

She started up the long, steep staircase in front of her, stopping several times in her upward climb to catch her breath. But when she saw the top coming nearer and nearer, she took the remaining steps two at a time and arrived at the summit in a burst of glorious, golden sunshine.

"Welcome back, Miss Harald." A young woman was bending over her and smiling. "You've been away quite a while."

Two months had passed since the night the elderly cleaner had found her seated at the piano in a cataleptic trance. Two months during which her exhausted mind had—as the doctors she met with over the next few weeks explained to her—sought refuge from the battery of shocks that had been chipping away at her resistance over the last few years.

Her first steps back were hesitant, her direction unclear, her ultimate destination hazy. But she did precisely what they had told her to do—she began from the beginning again. Like a child learning to walk for the first time, she began by putting one foot in front of the other and relearned how to walk. And once she was as sure of herself as they were, they released her from the hospital and sent her back into the world again.

The woman who emerged from the protection of her three-month cocoon was far different from the woman who had spun that heavy chrysalis around herself in the first place. This one was muted, almost bland, as devoid of passion inside as she was devoid of expression outside. She was, in effect, a human slate from which all emotional extremes had been erased—at least for a time—leaving her to exist in a state of blessed indifference.

She checked into the Algonquin Hotel on West Forty-fourth Street and in a way it was like coming home again, home to the past. It was familiar and it made her feel safe. It reminded her of that most precious time in her life when she had been part of a family and deeply loved.

She pretended the doorman was her father, and each time he held the door open for her, she rewarded him with a dazzling smile. Coming into the dimly lit, dark wood-paneled lobby was like being ushered into the well-worn living room of a turn-of-the-century home. With its groupings of small tables, velvet upholstered sofas and chairs, lamps with finely pleated shades, and tasseled wall sconces, it represented coziness and comfort to her, and she spent her first few days at the hotel just sitting in a corner wing chair, unnoticed and undisturbed, sipping tea and watching the people come and go.

When she wasn't sitting in the lobby, she was sitting cross-legged on the floor in her roomy corner suite, walking herself slowly through her life, using her scrapbooks and photo albums as much for a guide as for companionship. Then, once her tour of the past was completed, she took the gold charm bracelet out of its worn brown leather pouch and went through it charm by charm, recalling not only the interiors of each of the various concert halls she and Michael had played in together, but also the concertos they had played and the gowns she had worn on each of those nights.

How strange it seemed—she hadn't allowed herself to think about Michael in a very long time. Michael, dearest Michael. Michael, who had been so much a part of her dream. But she couldn't think about him without also thinking about Roxanne and Clemence Treaves and Claudia, and what the three of them had done to that dream.

On her fifth day at the hotel she made two telephone calls and set up two appointments, one for eleven o'clock that same morning, one for three that afternoon. Then she ran the water for a bath. While she was waiting for the tub to fill, she took a long, hard look at her reflection in the full-length mirror on the bathroom door, to see for herself the woman she had become.

She wasn't particularly displeased by what she saw, but she *was* surprised. She was paler than she had ever been, she had lost weight, and there was a frailty to her smallness that her proud carriage had always belied. Her eyes had lost the radiance that used to turn the irises from mauve to purple according to her mood: they seemed slightly faded to her now. There were tiny lines around her eyes, her cheekbones were more pronounced, and the heart shape of her face was more sharply defined. But her hair came as a complete shock to her. It was heavily salted with silver, as though it had been frosted by an expert colorist at Kenneth's. And she was not yet thirty-nine. Her mother hadn't started going gray until she was fifty, while her father's blondness had made it next to impossible to see any gray at all.

When she got dressed, she chose a dress of lightweight lavender wool crepe by Albert Nipon with a bow at the neckline and a finely pleated bodice, dove-gray suede Charles Jourdan shoes with a matching clutch, dove-gray kid gloves, and a pair of gray pearl and diamond clips as her only pieces of jewelry. Her hands felt strangely naked without her diamond engagement ring and wedding band, but she noted rather wryly that their absence certainly made wearing gloves a lot easier.

Scott rose to greet her. She entered his office as though she were sweeping onto a stage, and once again he was reminded of what a magnificent performer she had been.

"If I didn't know better," he said, ushering her quickly to a chair, "I'd say you'd spent the last few months at La Costa."

Her laugh was warm but abbreviated, as though it were something to get out of the way quickly in order to make room for more important matters. Taking his cue from her, he didn't waste time mincing words.

"Jeff's been sent to some private boarding school. No," he hastily answered what he knew would be her next question, "I don't know which one. They've taken great pains to keep it secret." He didn't have to explain to her that the closing of ranks extended to privately endowed boarding schools as well as to courtrooms. "I've made dozens of phone calls, had several people working on it, but nothing." His curt nod indicated the thick brown folder tied with a broad brown ribbon and sealed with a large red wax seal that was sitting on top of his desk. "I have no idea what's in there," he added. Inside the folder was the report of the private investigator he had hired for her.

Kirsten glanced only briefly at the folder. "What about your latest motion?" she asked somewhat impatiently. Scott shook his head. "And the Supreme Court?"

"Nothing so far."

"Then if you can't find Jeff for me, I'll find him myself." She heard her attorney groan.

"Believe me, Kirsten, if I felt for one moment that you could get away with it, I'd even help you myself. But what you want is impossible. I also think you don't fully comprehend the precariousness of our situation. Provoke Jeffrey in any way, no matter how slight, and he can have you sent to prison. Not only can he have you charged with obstruction of justice, he can still have you charged with attempted kidnapping." She looked as though she were about to interrupt, and he held up his hand to stop her. "Let's just say for argument's sake that you do succeed in locating Jeff. Don't you think Jeffrey's going to be better prepared to stop you even faster this time? Or let's take it a step further. Let's say you actually get away with it; you have a day with Jeff, a week, a month. Now it's no longer *attempted* kidnapping, but *actual* kidnapping. You certainly won't see Jeff if you go to prison and you certainly won't stand a chance in hell of ever regaining custody of him. Don't break the law, Kirsten. People who break the law and get caught are punished for it."

"What if I don't get caught?" In spite of the tinge of humor in her voice and the momentary gleam in her eye, she half-meant it and Scott knew it.

"Kirsten." He said her name with exaggerated slowness. "We're going to have an even tougher time getting an appeal through now because of your recent breakdown. So please, please, please, don't even think about making what's already a less-than-hopeful situation even less hopeful."

Kirsten considered saying something, then quickly changed her mind. Getting up from her chair, she picked up the heavy brown folder and tucked it under her arm. "Your investigator must have found quite a lot of dirt mixed in with all that rich Long Island soil," she remarked with uncharacteristic sarcasm.

"And just what do you intend to do with the information, providing there *is* any *real* information in there?"

"As my attorney, Scott, you wouldn't want to know."

"Kir-sten?"

She laughed off his raised eyebrows and the warning she heard in his voice and headed for the door.

"Nelson, I want you to officially announce my retirement."

The aging former shoe salesman from Brooklyn did a double take. But before he could say anything, Kirsten held a finger to her lips and motioned for him to come with her. She owed it to him. Of all people, she owed Nelson Pendell the truth. She led him into the same soundproofed studio where she had first auditioned for him, seated herself at the piano, and showed him precisely why she wanted him to make that announcement. To her utter dismay, he broke down and wept.

"It's going to take time, Nelson," she told him, gently rubbing his back while he wiped his eyes and blew his nose. "I need time to heal myself first, then I'll heal my hands. On my own and in my own way. Maybe Jeffrey was right all along. Maybe I loved my music too much. Maybe I did put it before my family. I don't know. What I do know is that it's cost me everything I had. He may even have been right when he called me an unfit mother. I may have given Jeff my gift, but it may have been the only thing I was really capable of giving him. I don't even know about that anymore."

Nelson enveloped her in a giant bear hug and wouldn't let go. Kirsten batted her eyes in a frantic attempt to keep them from brimming over, and she would have succeeded, too, if Nelson hadn't started sobbing all over again.

"Oh, my dearest friend," she said softly, stroking his hair and gulping on her own tears, "don't cry for me, please don't cry. I swear to you it's not over. I *will* play again, I will. And I'll still expect you to represent me."

His laugh was choked and hoarse. "Then promise me it won't be long. I'm already seventy, Kirsten Harald; don't make me wait until I'm really old."

"I won't, I promise." Opening up his warm, beefy hand, she pressed something cool and flat into his palm, then closed his fingers around it again. "Hold this for me, Nelson," she said. "Keep it until Michael and I play together again."

It was only after she had gone that he opened his hand. He was holding a charm, a flat gold charm cut in the shape of a grand piano, both sides blank, as though it were waiting for something to be inscribed on it.

                    *   *   *

The news of Kirsten Harald's retirement shook the music world with the same intensity that her grand entrance had inspired seventeen years earlier. Reactions varied from shock to disbelief to regret, and in a very few instances, glee. There wasn't a TV show or radio program, newspaper or magazine, that didn't feature a number of stories on her. The most influential men and women in music—from composers and critics to conductors and fellow musicians—were interviewed for their reactions and comments. Every record and tape she had ever made was quickly gobbled up and hoarded by people as collector's items, while the record companies hastily produced and distributed more of them at nearly double their original price. A musical era had passed. And she was being eulogized as though she herself had actually died.

As soon as Eric Sheffield-Johns heard the news on the BBC, he called the number of the last hotel he knew she had stayed in, only to be told that Kirsten Harald had checked out over five months before. He spent the rest of the day closeted inside his study, working his way through a bottle of Napoleon brandy, while he stared morosely at a framed copy of the famous photograph Antony Armstrong-Jones had taken of her for her debut recital at Wigmore Hall.

In her bedroom, Claudia put her copy of *The Times* down and went to look for her scissors. Then she neatly cut the story out and pasted it into the latest of the two dozen scrapbooks she had been collecting on Kirsten over the years. She happened to glance at one of the many photos she had of Kirsten and Michael together—the two of them deep in a passionate embrace—and felt a stabbing pain in her heart. Even after all this time she still couldn't bear the sight of someone else touching the treasured girl she had loved and lost.

In his Vienna office, Clemence Treaves raised his crystal flute of Dom Pérignon at precisely the same moment that his niece, Roxanne Eastbourne, was raising hers in her bedroom in Boston, where she was recuperating from a second mastectomy. In lieu of clinking their glasses together, they settled for tapping them against the receivers they were each holding, then drained them dry.

Michael Eastbourne was scanning his copy of the *San Francisco Chronicle* as he unlocked the door to his suite at the Mark Hopkins Hotel. When he caught sight of the headline, he dropped the paper on the floor and had to lean up against the wall momentarily for support. Then he sank down onto a corner of the queensize bed, put his face in his hands, and cried as he hadn't cried in years.

In New York, Andrew Beaton was getting ready to leave his SoHo studio when NBC's Nightly News came on. As he watched them air a clip from one of her earliest concerts, he backed his way toward the row of low metal filing cabinets where he stored the sketchpads of every subject he had ever painted. Just as he was reaching into the drawer for hers, the *Time* cover he had done of her flashed onto the TV screen. Damn, he thought with a painful catch in his throat, she really had been what true art was all about.

On Long Island, Lois Eldershaw Holden dropped the results of a fruitful day of shopping at Bergdorf's and Saks onto the beige marble floor in the front hall, kicked off her black patent Delman pumps, and padded in stocking feet toward her music room. She had heard the news from the manicurist at Elizabeth Arden and had left the salon with only one coat of clear polish on one hand. Sitting down at the Steinway, she played an entire Grieg sonata through without feeling even slightly winded. She was so excited, she happily proceeded to play another one.

Jeffrey Powell Oliver III stood in the middle of the empty conservatory and stared at the exact spot where his mother's piano had been. He was home for the Easter holidays, and he kept hoping she would come through the door and announce it was time for their Easter egg hunt. But she didn't. And he knew she would never come through that door again. He shuddered as he thought about what he had heard his father telling his aunt Dierdre over the phone. *The great Kirsten Harald's dead and buried,* he had said. *The queen is dead, long live the queen.*

Jeff gulped down the tears that kept coming no matter how hard he tried to stop them and crept back upstairs to his bedroom. His mother was dead. She would never hug him or kiss him or play duets with him or tell him she loved him again, ever, ever again. Still snuffling softly, he got down on his knees in front of his giant red toy box and started to dig deep inside it. Past all the plastic soldiers; the metal horses, cars, and trucks; the stuffed pandas, dogs, and monkeys; the rubber balls, Bolo bats, and yo-yos. Until at the very bottom he found what he was looking for: a single record. His most prized possession. He had taken it one day while his father was busy packing up the rest of whatever she had left behind.

As long as he had this record of hers, he knew she would never really be dead. He planted a tender kiss on the album cover, pressed it tightly against his chest, and bowed his head. Then he made a solemn promise to himself. One day he would play this piece whose name he still couldn't pronounce properly; and when he did, the whole world would know that he was the son of Kirsten Harald.

Kirsten was leaving. To remain in New York would mean being reminded of everything she needed to forget for a while. And so she was about to become exactly what Jeffrey had always accused her of being: a vagabond. She was off to see the world; she, who had never seen any more of the world than its concert halls and its finer hotels. With the money from her divorce settlement, her continuing music royalties, and the proceeds from the sale of some of her more important pieces of jewelry, she would be able to live abroad comfortably for years.

What she needed most now was time and anonymity. Time to find herself again and the opportunity to do her searching in private and in peace. Then, once she was whole again, and when she had found a way to repay them all, she would come back and reclaim what was rightfully hers.

Her airline ticket said Dublin, because to her it seemed the most logical place to begin a world tour. As she strode through the TWA terminal—a small, slim figure in a tailored black silk suit, her beautiful face shielded by a pair of dark glasses—she half-expected to be accosted by the usual battery of reporters and photographers. But for the first time in all the years that she had been embarking and disembarking from planes, Kirsten Harald went unnoticed. The spotlight had been switched off; she was finally being granted the privacy she had been craving for so long.

But as her jet lifted off smoothly into the cloudless night, she took a long last look at the receding skyline of New York, and vowed to switch that same spotlight back on one day.

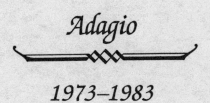

Adagio

1973–1983

30

Athens was Kirsten's rainbow and her pot of gold too. A golden city swaddled in a celestial cloak of constantly changing colors. Warmed by a canary sun and cooled by an aqua sea. The course of its days still charted by the sun god Apollo. Beginning at dawn in a pastel sweep of pink and blue, the blues brightening through siesta time, turning violet at dusk, deepening to amethyst with the first evening star, ending on a note of indigo with the rising moon, and then fading slowly to black.

But life in Athens didn't end with the night. On the contrary. The setting sun released it. It thrived in the dark. From the light-bathed Acropolis to the inky waters of the Aegean, Athens seethed and bubbled with life. It was a fevered pulse, clogging the streets, the squares, and the tavernas with people. It moistened the air with retsina and ouzo, and spiced it with dolmadas and moussaka and spinakoppita. It was rich with baklava, redolent with jasmine and gardenias, running over with bouzouki music, dancing, and laughter.

Even from her third-floor apartment at the foot of the Lykabettos, the sharp, pine-capped hill northeast of the Acropolis, Kirsten was still able to hear the sound of the city's laughter. It was what lured her out onto her small balcony most evenings—just as it had tonight—and made her sit in her wicker chair with a glass of ouzo, sometimes for hours, until she grew sleepy enough for bed. She slept well in Athens. It was here that she had had her first good night's sleep since leaving New York. Perhaps that was the main reason she had decided to stay on.

She had spent an entire year roaming Europe. A virtual vagabond—homeless, rootless, directionless. An orphan and an outcast. Cut adrift from everything familiar and dear to her. She had fought hard to play the ordinary tourist the way she had so naturally played the extraordinary star. And she was still struggling, to rise above the pain and the emptiness and the devastating sense of loss that made her days and nights almost unbearable.

Her travels had taken her to ten countries—Ireland, Scotland, Holland, Belgium, France, Spain, Portugal, Switzerland, Italy, and, of course, Greece. But her memories of most of those ten countries were vague. She had floated from city to city viewing everything around her through a heavy filter of grief.

She went to bed each night praying for some surcease from the pain. Yet, even in sleep she couldn't escape. She had lost everything—her career, her family, her world—and everything she had lost was cruelly recreated and exaggerated as she slept and woke, slept and woke, slept and woke. Each morning found her exhausted, her pillow soaked with tears, the sheets tangled from her nightly battles with the demons that haunted her.

But after she had spent eight months abroad, her psychic wounds were no longer as raw, the pain was no longer as acute. She learned to suppress the faces that had blurred her vision and to submerge the feelings that had ravaged her system. She did so by superimposing upon her memories all the various sights and sounds around her. It didn't make the pain vanish completely, but it did make living more tolerable an experience. And after a while it even made the living pleasant.

She looked for some way to keep herself occupied. She found it by becoming a collector. A gatherer of handicrafts, a hoarder of native mementoes, a curator for the bits and pieces of every place she visited. Collecting became her obsession. It became her reason for getting up and getting going each day. It was a harmless and amusing distraction, but one which, more important, kept her thoughts focused outward instead of inward.

With each subsequent city and town she visited, she became increasingly more adept at sublimating, at living her life almost entirely on the surface, in a state of suspended emotion. She knew that as long as she didn't allow anyone or anything to penetrate her newly formed and delicate surface, she would survive. There was a wonderful comfort in not feeling anymore, even if *not* feeling was as alien to her as not being able to play the piano.

By the time she arrived in Athens three months before, she had already thought about stopping someplace for a while.

Her first good night's sleep in a year settled the matter of just where that place would be. She cabled Scott immediately—he was still the only person she kept apprised of her whereabouts—then went about the business of making a temporary home for herself.

She may have found herself a haven in Athens, but she still hadn't found a way of living in it thought-free. The past was still her ever-constant companion, although in her present numbness, it did less damage than before. She was even teaching herself to compartmentalize—which made her feel strangely cold-blooded at times—dividing everyone she thought about into three separate and distinct categories. There were those for whom she was in perpetual mourning: Meredith, her parents, and Natalya; those she missed: Michael, Eric, and Nelson; and those she had sworn to repay: Jeffrey, Claudia, Roxanne Eastbourne, Clemence Treaves, Dierdre, and Lois.

Then there was Jeff—and here the stifled feelings stirred and strained against their confinement—her beloved Jeff. Cherished heart of her heart. Scarcely an hour passed when she wasn't rededicating herself to the pledge she had made: that one day she would return to reclaim both her son *and* her music. She could think of no sweeter revenge than her retaking of the golden mountain with her precious son beside her.

She finished her ouzo, took a last deep breath of the jasmine-scented July air, and stepped back inside the apartment. Her new home was a large one-bedroom corner apartment in a modern five-story brick and stucco building, with a gentle cross-breeze that kept it comfortably cool even on the hottest days. Although minimally furnished, with everything she had collected during her travels, the overall impression one got was of cheerful clutter.

The wooden floors were covered with gaily patterned rugs, some woven, some hooked. The walls were hung with straw baskets of varying shapes and sizes; carved masks; cuckoo clocks; hand-painted wooden shoes, and even a pair of forest-green suede lederhosen. Every available surface was covered with lace or tartan plaids and topped with hand-carved statuettes and ceramic figurines, tiny clay animals and birds, and dozens of framed photographs.

On impulse she had purchased a secondhand upright and set it against the narrowest wall in the living room. There was no sheet music inside the scarred wooden piano bench, and the lid covering the keyboard had never been raised; it simply stood there like a silent sentinel, a reminder of what she had once been and would one day be again.

"Kirsten?"

The small voice calling out to her in the semidarkness made her jump.

"Aren't you asleep yet, Markos?" she whispered, tiptoeing over to the couch where a six-year-old boy was curled up underneath a lightly woven striped cotton blanket that she had bought in Portugal.

"I'm thirsty," he complained as he threw off the blanket and sat up.

"How about a nice cold glass of orange juice?" She could see him shaking his head. "It's freshly squeezed."

"What I'd really like is a glass of retsina."

"Yes, I'm sure you would."

"So, can I have some?" His small face looked so hopeful, she hated to disappoint him.

"No, you can't."

"Just a little, please?"

"Uh-uh." Kirsten put on her sternest face, then promptly ruined the effect by bending down and ruffling his hair with her fingers. "One glass of freshly squeezed orange juice coming up."

"Bah!" To protest the unfairness of it all, Markos lay down again and drew the cotton blanket up over his head.

Smiling, Kirsten headed for her small kitchen. Of all her discoveries in Athens, Markos had been the most unexpected, as well as the most sweetly rewarding. He was the son of Larissa and Alexandros Pallis, a young Greek couple living three doors away from her. The day she moved into the building, the Pallises had appeared at her door—Larissa carrying a plate of freshly baked baklava, Alexandros a bottle of ouzo, and Markos four glasses. The bonding between them had been instantaneous.

In spite of her initial protests, Larissa and Alexandros had insisted on introducing her to their wide and eclectic circle of friends, who in turn had inducted her into the bustling nightlife of the city. Her way of reciprocating was to look after Markos on those nights when the Pallises weren't home—which was quite often, because they weren't only high-spirited socializers, they were also devoutly idealistic intellectuals-turned-agitators who were violently opposed to Greece's six-year military regime.

Thirty-one-year-old Alexandros was a professor of economics at the National Polytechnical Institute of Greece known as the Polytechnic; thirty-year-old Larissa taught ancient history there. She came from the north, he came from Crete—his looks were as darkly handsome as hers were delicate and fair.

They had both been politically active as students; now as teachers they had aligned themselves with all the other professionals and intellectuals who were protesting the country's military regime headed by ex-artillery colonel Georgios Papadopoulos, the man responsible for overthrowing King Constantine in 1967. Not only did they meet in secret to discuss the tyranny of the regime, but the group the Pallises headed also published a weekly four-page tabloid designed to inform the public of the government's corrupt practices and repressive policies, and to call for its ouster. In the past year alone, the military police had searched the Pallises' apartment three times; the Pallises themselves had been arrested twice, detained overnight, then released the following day; and yet they stubbornly persisted, undaunted and unafraid.

Now as Kirsten watched Markos drinking his orange juice, she wondered where Larissa and Alexandros were tonight, and couldn't help shuddering. She was desperately afraid for them and for the young boy stretched out so comfortably on her sofa. Her heart skipped a beat—as it so often did when she looked at him—for Markos was one of the most beautiful children she had ever seen.

He was tall for his age, his body well formed, with Larissa's golden good looks and a pair of golden-brown eyes that could be as limpid as liquid honey one moment and as hard as rock crystal the next. They weren't the eyes of an adult, nor were they strictly the eyes of a child. But then, Markos Andreas Pallis wasn't either one or the other himself; he was an eerie combination of the two. More like a little man. And that was what Kirsten called him: her little man. He was exceptionally bright and precocious, as fluent in English as he was in Greek, high-spirited like his parents, and equally fearless.

"I'm still a bit thirsty," he said as he handed Kirsten his empty glass.

"Then how would you like some water?" She knew he would make a face, and he did. But he also yawned; that at least was a favorable sign. "No more excuses now," she said, plumping up his pillow and giving it one final, authoritative whack. "It's late. Your parents will think I'm a terrible baby-sitter if they see dark circles under your eyes tomorrow."

"I'm not a baby," he protested. "I'll be seven next week."

"Really?" She pretended to be surprised.

"Yes, really. And you promised to take me someplace very special, remember?"

"I did?"

Genuine panic flared in his golden eyes, and Kirsten knew the game—one her own children had always insisted they play—had gone too far. She gave him a quick hug to reassure him, then kissed him tenderly on the forehead.

"Of course I remember," she whispered. "I was only teasing you." His tense body began to relax. Taking his face in her hands, she smiled at him. "How could I possibly forget two things that are so important—your birthday and our first concert together?"

The Athens Symphony performed every Monday night between June and October in the Odeion of Herodes Atticus just below the Acropolis, and Kirsten had promised to take Markos to one of the concerts for his birthday. Now she regretted ever having made him that promise. She hadn't been near a concert hall since her own last recital the day before Meredith's disappearance. The sudden shooting pain in her abdomen caught her off guard. She winced, nearly dropping the empty juice glass.

"Kirsten, what's wrong?" Markos instinctively reached out for her arm. "Does something hurt?"

She got her breath back and shook her head. "No, nothing hurts," she said, "I'm fine." His eyes told her he didn't believe her. "Really, I am. Now, give me a great big hug and try to go to sleep." He hesitated, but only for a moment. Then he wrapped his slender arms around her neck and kissed her continental-style on both cheeks. She squeezed her eyes shut against the stinging threat of tears and hugged him back.

She was halfway to the kitchen when he called out, "When are you going to teach me to play the piano?"

As always, that question made her freeze; and as always, she gave him her usual answer. "One of these days."

"When the piano isn't being used for other things, right?"

Kirsten turned and held a finger to her lips.

"I know, I'm sorry." He lowered his voice to a whisper and burrowed under the blanket again. "Good night, Kirsten."

"Good night, my little man."

On the way to her bedroom a few minutes later, she glanced over at the upright standing so innocently against the living room wall. At least it was finally being put to some use. For the past month it had been the hiding place for the heavy metal plates used to print the Pallises' outlawed weekly tabloid, *The Democratic Voice*.

Kirsten spent most of the Monday night concert monitoring the changing expressions on Markos's young face. He was mesmerized; his eyes never left the stage. His rapt attention reminded her so much of Jeff, she sat through the performance misty-eyed and aching, with a lump in her throat that refused to dissolve. From time to time he would sweep his hands back and forth in front of him in an imitation of pianist Nikos Capralos, the evening's featured soloist; otherwise he sat perfectly still, his chin in one hand, simply staring. At the end of the concert he jumped up, shouting and clapping, his face flushed, his eyes pure liquid gold.

"Did you really play up there like that, Kirsten?" he asked excitedly as he took her hand to leave.

"Yes, I did," she told him.

"Were you ever afraid?"

"All the time."

"You were?" He was astounded. "I wouldn't be. If I'm not afraid of Papadopoulos, I wouldn't be afraid of something like that."

Several people had turned to stare at him, and Kirsten anxiously sought to divert his attention. "How would you like to go to Zonar's for ice cream?" she asked. His response was an immediate nod. In that respect, he was no different from other children—he adored ice cream, especially one particular dish called the "Chicago Special" that was a regular feature of Zonar's, the popular sidewalk café on Venizelou Avenue.

By the time they returned home, it was close to midnight. The elevator doors opened at the third floor and Markos quickly dug into the pocket of his khaki shorts for his house key.

"I wonder if my parents are home yet," he said to Kirsten in a low voice as the two of them started down the silent corridor.

"Well, if they're not," she whispered back to him, "you can come and spend the night at my place." She watched him fit his key into the lock, then stop without turning it. "What's wrong?"

The door wasn't locked. Markos gave it a slight push with his fingertips and it swung open.

"My God!"

It was Kirsten's involuntary gasp of surprise that gave him a start, not the sight of his home having been turned upside down. He was used to that.

"You wait here," he said.

For one startled moment Kirsten actually obeyed him. Then she remembered he was only a seven-year-old boy and hurried after him. She was trembling as she picked her way through the ransacked apartment, terrified of what they might find among the overturned tables and chairs, the upended lamps, rolled-up rugs and emptied drawers, the stripped beds, scattered books, and slashed paintings. Her blood was running cold in her veins, yet Markos seemed virtually unperturbed. She found his reaction—or, rather, his lack of reaction—to the chaos around them the most frightening thing of all. There was something unnatural about a seven-year-old boy viewing the ruins of his home as calmly as if he were some seasoned general surveying yet another littered battlefield. But then she quickly reminded herself that this was Athens, not Long Island. Markos wasn't some wealthy socialite's sheltered son; he was the son of political activists, and he had lived in a state of siege all his young life.

"Do you think they've been arrested again?" she asked almost hesitantly.

Markos shook his head. "They were meeting at the Economideses tonight, they'll be safe there. No, the police were looking for the plates again."

Kirsten's mouth went dry. "Stay here," she ordered. He was about to protest, but she silenced him instantly. "Do as I say, Markos. I want you to stay here. Now, promise me." He didn't respond. "Promise me, Markos!"

"Oh, all right," he grumbled. "I promise."

"Good boy." She gave him a kiss and left.

She was convinced she could hear every step she took as she walked down the long corridor, but she knew it was impossible. It was her heart she was hearing, not the rubber soles of her canvas espadrilles on the thick carpet. Just outside her own apartment she stopped. The door was slightly ajar. From inside came the sounds of men's voices, muffled and indistinct, and the opening and slamming of drawers. Throwing back her shoulders, she took a deep breath, pushed the door open, and marched determinedly into the small front hall.

The uniformed military officer leafing through a stack of magazines on the low cherrywood coffee table in front of the sofa in her living room straightened up immediately. He barked something in Greek and a moment later two other officers came hurrying into the room.

"Who are you?" Kirsten demanded before any of them could speak. "And what are you doing in my apartment?"

The youngest of the three men, tall, with a wiry build and wearing glasses, stepped forward. His eyes were black and penetrating and his thin black mustache framed a pair of exceptionally full lips. He snapped Kirsten a brisk military salute and introduced himself.

"Colonel Dimitrios Pattakas, madame." His voice was thin, almost reedy, and he spoke with only a faint accent.

Kirsten faced him without blinking. "Just what are you doing here, Colonel?"

"We understand you are a close friend of Alexandros and Larissa Pallis, madame."

"That's not an answer."

"Neither is that, madame." He said it without the slightest trace of humor in his voice. "Do you wish me to repeat the question?"

Kirsten eyed him coldly and shrugged. "I know the Pallises."

"You more than know them, madame. You have been observed in their company a great deal these past three months."

She shrugged again. "We're neighbors."

"And are you a sympathizer as well as a neighbor, madame?"

"A what?"

"A sympathizer."

"I'm an American."

The man snickered. "That is not what I asked you, madame. Are you—"

"I'm a citizen of the United States," she interrupted angrily, "and if you and your men don't leave immediately, I intend to contact the American embassy and lodge a formal complaint against you."

To her chagrin he greeted her bluff with a snort of laughter. "This city is under martial law, madame. Complaining to your embassy would serve little purpose." He took hold of her chin with his gloved hand and forced her to look up at him. Kirsten could see her face reflected in his glasses and concentrated on that. "Why are you in Athens, madame? Why Athens when you could have chosen a hundred other cities?" When she didn't answer him, he continued doggedly. "In less than two weeks we will be holding a referendum, and there are a great many people, your neighbors among them, who would prefer if such a referendum never took place. So I ask you again, why are you in Athens, and are you or are you not in sympathy with your neighbors?"

Kirsten peeled his hand away from her face and answered him in cool, measured tones. "I'm in Athens, Colonel Pattakas, for the simple reason that I choose to be here. I've been touring Europe for the last fifteen months, and Athens is just another city on that tour. As for my being in sympathy with the Pallises, all I can say is I'm completely apolitical. But if I were politically inclined, I would never presume to interfere with the workings of someone else's country." She made a brief, impatient gesture with her hand. "It's late and I'm very tired, so if you're quite through here, I'd—"

"Oh, but we are not through at all." Pattakas cut her off in mid-sentence and ordered his men to resume their search of the apartment.

"What precisely are you looking for?" Kirsten asked, as if she didn't know. But he was no longer paying any attention to her; he was peering over at the piano. Suddenly her heart became a triphammer loud enough for him to hear. He started across the room and she went after him, her back clammy, her chest tight, her legs like rubber bands. He looked as though he were about to raise the lid over the keyboard. If he so much as pressed down on any single key, all he would get would be a muffled thunk.

"Please." She put out her hand and touched the sleeve of his uniform. "I'd prefer if you didn't."

He looked surprised. "You no longer play at all, even for yourself?" Now it was her turn to look surprised. He cracked a slightly self-conscious smile. "I heard you perform once," he said, "here in Athens, nearly ten years ago. It was a most memorable experience for me. I was truly saddened, madame, to learn of your retirement."

His abrupt about-face rendered Kirsten momentarily speechless. But as soon as she recovered her voice, she uttered a soft "thank you" and lowered her gaze in an effort to appear appropriately moved by his admission. "I'm afraid I use it only for decorative purposes now." With a mournful sigh she indicated the flowered Spanish shawl draped over the piano and the various artifacts clustered in small groups on top of it.

"A pity, madame, a very great pity indeed."

Playing on his startling change in attitude toward her, Kirsten led him away from the piano with a coquettish shrug of her shoulder. He responded to the overture by immediately beginning to stroke his mustache, using slow and precise outward flicks of his thumb and forefinger, while he fixed his eyes meaningfully on her face. She could feel a slow flush starting at the base of her neck. It had been a long time since a man had looked at her the way Colonel Dimitrios Pattakas was looking at her now.

A moment later—to Kirsten's profound relief and Pattakas's more than obvious disappointment—his two men came back into the room shaking their heads. He nodded curtly and told them to wait for him outside. An icy prickle of apprehension began climbing up Kirsten's spine as soon as she was alone with him again. But her fears were unwarranted. Pattakas was once again the efficient soldier, all traces of his manly posing gone. He snapped her another crisp salute, then headed, back straight, shoulders squared, for the door himself. On the threshold he paused.

"I apologize for having disturbed you, madame. It is a shame we could not have met under more pleasant circumstances." A slight nod and he was gone.

Kirsten realized how badly she was shaking only when she tried to pour herself some ouzo; the bottle kept knocking against the side of her glass like a pair of teeth chattering.

"May I have some too?"

Kirsten gasped, nearly dropping both the glass and the bottle. But it was only Markos.

"I'm sorry, I didn't mean to frighten you."

Without even thinking, she handed him her glass and filled herself another one. Markos glanced over toward the piano. She shook her head and he heaved a sigh of relief. Taking their glasses with them, they went to sit on the sofa in the living room. Markos insisted she tell him everything that had happened and not leave out a single detail. She was only halfway through the story when he gave a loud yawn, curled up against her with his head in her lap, and promptly fell asleep. It wasn't long before Kirsten fell asleep herself—still sitting up, still with one arm around Markos's shoulder.

She woke once, briefly, after having dreamed that it was her own son she was holding, and not someone else's.

From the end of July until the end of October, Kirsten didn't miss a single Monday performance of the Athens Symphony. That first concert with Markos had made it impossible for her to stay away. Her emotional armor had been pierced, imperceptibly but irrefutably, and it was through that one tiny hole that the music had reentered her system. It had swelled up her body and invaded her brain, its effect more powerful than the most powerful narcotic.

She felt like an addict; she craved more. She had been deprived long enough. To deny herself music was to deny herself life. And more than anything, she wanted to live. She had to live. There was still so much for her to do.

When a number of the world's most highly acclaimed orchestras came to the city during the annual Festival of Athens, she attended those concerts too. But they were sheer torture for her. She would sit in her seat, tense and expectant, twisting a handkerchief in her hands, and watch as one familiar face after another paraded past her. While a part of her kept hoping one of those familiar faces would turn out to be *his* face—Michael's face, handsome and tender, with that gentle smile she knew so well—she was relieved when it never was.

Here were some of the orchestras with whom she herself had once played. And here she was, no longer the world-renowned soloist, but just one more faceless paying member of the audience. When her battered ego screamed for her to stand up and be recognized, her pride held her back.

And yet, after every performance she would go to one of the tavernas frequented by the touring musicians, find herself a discreet table, and wait for them to arrive. Then she would sip on a glass of some local white wine and just watch them. But deep inside her there was a battle raging. She alternated between loving them and hating them. Envying them and admiring them. Revering them and reviling them. She was afraid of being recognized, but even more afraid of *not* being recognized. She wanted to jump up and join them, yet she made no move to do so.

When they left, she left. But when she went home, it wasn't to sleep; it was to try to play.

She used the musicians the way a religious fanatic uses a scourge. And while she used them, she prayed that through the miracle of osmosis she might absorb them inside herself, make their music her music, their hands her hands, their instruments hers.

But to her increasing despair, the music continued to live on solely inside her mind; her hands remained crippled; her piano mute.

The newly appointed concertmaster of the Philadelphia Orchestra would talk of nothing else. *"You'll never guess who I saw"* became his standard form of greeting everywhere he went. There wasn't a person he met who was spared his greeting; everyone was subjected to it equally. When his hapless victims invariably guessed incorrectly, he patiently provided them with a clue. *"Athens,"* he would say, *"at some dinky sidewalk café."*

Some would be good sports about it and guess again; most simply shrugged and gave up. *"Kirsten Harald!"* he would shout jubilantly, *"Kirsten Harald!"* Occasionally he drew a blank, but usually he was rewarded with either a smile, a *"No kidding"* or a *"Well, well, well."* Once in a while he even got a genuine *"Wow!"*

But whatever their reactions were, he really didn't care. He, Paul Bell, had seen Kirsten Harald at a sidewalk café called Lakoniki in Athens, and he was ecstatic.

31

On November 25, the country awoke to find a new government in power in Athens.

Although the ruling military junta had won the July referendum that had seen Greece declared a republic with Georgios Papadopoulos as its president, the summer had been marred by an ongoing series of nationwide protests and strikes. Then, on November 13, a mob of angry students had seized the Polytechnic, set up a radio on the campus grounds, and called on all of Athens to join them in overthrowing the government. The people listened. Twelve days later, their rebellion paid off. At five A.M. on the morning of November 25 an army coup placed Georgios Papadopoulos under house arrest.

Lieutenant General Phaidon Gizikis was sworn in as president. In an immediate purge, thirteen generals were "compulsorily retired" and ten army colonels arrested—including a certain Colonel Dimitrios Pattakas. The curfew was lifted from the city, and the climate was one of unrestrained euphoria. In a swell of renewed optimism, the people of Athens celebrated their victory, and Kirsten celebrated with them.

She spent the entire day with the Pallises and their friends as they took their celebration first to the streets, then into the tavernas, then back to the streets again. They ended up at her apartment at three in the morning, all of them gathering around the piano while Alexandros removed the metal plates from inside it for what everyone hoped would be the last time. Raising them high above his head like some youthful Moses holding up the clay tablets containing the Ten Commandments, he said, "For six years *The Democratic Voice* was a voice of protest; now its message will finally be one of victory and of peace." There were cheers, a smattering of applause, and several of the men even crossed themselves. Leaning the heavy plates up against the wall, Alexandros picked up his glass of retsina and saluted Kirsten with it. "To you, my dear friend," he said in a voice choked with emotion, "or rather *our* friend, for risking so much for a cause that was never yours."

"To Kirsten!" It was one loud declarative roar, her name rolling off their tongues as easily as it had once rolled off the tongues of her adoring audiences. If her smile seemed overly bright and her violet eyes glassy, no one thought anything of it; it was a highly charged moment for all of them.

By five they had all gone, except for Markos. He hung back, looking anxious and uncertain, as though he were actually afraid to leave. Something had changed for all of them tonight; nothing would ever be quite the same again; and suddenly he wanted it back the way it was. Sensing his ambivalence, Kirsten went to him and pulled him into her arms.

"Nothing's really changed," she assured him as she held him close to her chest, "you're still my little man." Burying her face in his thick blond hair, she squeezed him as tightly as she could. "Nothing's changed, my Markos, I promise."

The young boy sighed and batted his tears away. The knot in his stomach eased and he could smile again. "Now you'll finally be able to teach me the piano," he said hopefully, in all innocence. "Do you think we could start tomorrow?"

Now it was Kirsten's turn to sigh. "Not tomorrow I'm afraid."

"Then when?"

"One of these days."

"But that's what you always say."

"Markos!" Larissa came to the doorway, her arms folded, the toe of one sandal tapping impatiently on the floor. "Say good night to Kirsten now and come to bed."

Standing on tiptoe, he obediently pecked Kirsten on both cheeks, then whispered hurriedly in her ear, "You will teach me *one* day though, promise?"

Kirsten was laughing as she watched him go. "I promise," she called after him.

She was still smiling when she locked the door and turned out the light in the hall. It was easy to smile; "one day" was the safest promise she had ever made.

Christmas was a week away and suddenly all Kirsten could do was cry. Everything made her cry. The streets crowded with last-minute shoppers. The colored lights, the glittering ornaments, the decorative wreaths. The laughter. The parties. The expectation in the air. The promise of togetherness, of families sharing in the spirit of the holiday. Joy to the world, she would think bitterly each time she reached for her handkerchief. But where was the joy in her world, she asked herself.

She wanted what everyone around her had: closeness and warmth; a sense of belonging; a family. She wanted Jeff. She wanted Meredith. She wanted her parents. She wanted it back the way it was at the beginning, when she and Jeffrey had their whole marriage ahead of them. She wanted what she knew she could never have: the past. And she wanted *not* to want it.

She tried to tell herself she wasn't alone, that she did have a family just like everyone else. The Pallises were her family now, and would be for as long as she wanted. It helped, yes, it helped; but in some ways it also made everything worse.

She was right in the middle of another of her crying jags, when there was a knock at the door. Hastily drying her eyes and blowing her nose, she hurried to answer it.

Before her stood her past.

She blinked, waited for the apparition to fade and disappear, then blinked again. It was still there. Was wishful thinking responsible for this, she wondered. Was this simply a product of her overactive imagination?

"Hello, Kirsten," the apparition said.

It *was* the season for miracles, wasn't it, she asked herself. Could this one be hers?

"You were all a certain concertmaster could talk about last week. Apparently you're all he's talked about for the past three months."

His smile was tender, his eyes warm, and Kirsten could feel herself melting.

"Michael."

All of her was bound up in his name: her despair and her longing; her regret; her bitterness and her pain; her dashed hopes and her faltered dream.

"I tried, Kirsten," he whispered hoarsely, tears bright in his gentle hazel eyes. "I swear to you, I tried."

"Michael, oh, Michael." She began to waver. He was who he had always been, but she wasn't. He still had it all, she had nothing.

Looking at her, he knew what she was thinking.

"If my prayers could change what happened," he said, "I'd be on my knees right now. If my arms could heal you, I'd never stop holding you. And if resenting me will make it easier for you to live with your pain, then it's something I'll have to accept. But don't, Kirsten, don't ever envy me. Don't think for a moment that I've been spared, that I've got everything."

She sucked in her breath. He was crying; she had never seen him cry before. She moved toward him as if in a dream. She put out her hand to touch him and the shock of touching him was registered in every part of her body. It wasn't an apparition; it really *was* Michael.

He crushed her to him. She heard him take a deep, quivering breath, felt him shudder as he buried his face in the hollow of her throat and weep until he had wept himself dry. Then he cupped her face in his hands and kissed her the way he had always kissed her: beginning with her forehead, her eyelids, the tip of her nose, her chin, and finally her mouth. She felt the soft pressure of his lips on hers and for a moment she was paralyzed, uncertain even of what to do. But instinct took over from the vacuum she had been living in for so long and reminded her. Her lips parted; she returned the pressure, and when he slipped his tongue between her parted lips, she opened her mouth wider and extended her own tongue in welcome.

"Oh, Michael." She whispered his name between kisses. "Michael, it's been so long, so long since anyone's held me." His kisses grew harder, more insistent, more demanding. "Keep holding me," she urged him. "Please, just keep holding me." She was on a carousel, spinning round and round, growing light-headed and dizzy, but she never wanted to get off. They were still kissing, still holding on to each other as she led him down the hall and into her bedroom.

Shedding their clothes, they sank to their knees on the bed and faced each other. Instead of their mouths this time, they used their hands, reaching out to touch what the years had kept apart. And when their bodies craved far more than touching, he gathered her into his arms and drew her down on top of him.

Where he was tender, she was demanding; when he met her demands, she coyly withdrew. He sought her out and took her higher. She soared above him, then stopped and pulled him after her. For one brief, pulsating moment, they were evenly matched, but then the game began again.

They ached for release and fought against it, neither of them wanting the delicious agony of anticipation to end too soon. They longed to rediscover everything they had once known about each other, and in their quest they left no part of themselves untouched or unexplored. They shaped and reshaped each other a thousand times, using their fingers, their mouths, their teeth, their tongues. Kissing and biting, fondling and stroking. And through it all he remained hard and hungry inside her.

It was only when their passion bordered on exhaustion that they finally gave in to it. One last, deep thrust was all it took to hurl them over the edge and into the ecstasy of mutual orgasm. Her body's floodgates were open; she was spilling, falling, out of control and calling his name. And he was there to catch her, to hold her and to keep her intact until the pieces of her scattered self could fuse again.

She lay in his arms afterward with her head on his chest, listening to the steady thumping of his heart. She knew she was smiling; in fact, her entire body seemed to be smiling.

Her lips were puffy, her skin tingled, there was a wonderful soreness between her legs, and her bloodstream was sizzling with life. She wanted to jump up and shout, because every sensation meant only one thing: she could feel, she could still feel.

And absurdly enough, she also felt hungry. She was ravenous, hungrier than she had been in a very long time. But when she admitted as much to Michael, he didn't seem the least bit surprised. They took a quick shower together, then while she prepared a Greek salad and heated up some of Larissa's homemade moussaka, Michael set the table and uncorked a chilled bottle of Santa Elena.

"I still can't believe it," she told him when they were sitting down.

"Can't believe what?"

"That you're really here." He smiled and squeezed her hand. Her bottom lip quivered. "Oh, Michael, there's so much I have to tell you."

He brought her hand up to his mouth. "And I you."

He told her first about Paul Bell, and that made her smile. She thought of the fountain pen he had once given her, a pen she still had, although the lavender ink inside it had dried up long ago. Then he told her he was presently with the Cleveland Symphony.

"Why Cleveland?" she wanted to know.

"Daniel, our oldest, has been teaching math at Western Reserve University for the past two years. He and his wife, Kelly, made us grandparents last year, and Roxanne wanted to be close to them. Also, George Szell had just died and they were looking for a new conductor." Kirsten winced. Michael, a grandfather? It wasn't possible. Not this handsome virile man across from her. A grandfather was old, with white hair. "Unfortunately," Michael continued, "Kelly suffered a miscarriage three days ago. That's why Roxanne didn't come to Europe with me." He speared a black olive and popped it into his mouth.

Kirsten chewed thoughtfully on a chunk of feta cheese for a while, swallowed it with some difficulty, and poked around for a slice of tomato. "How long will you be in Athens?" she finally forced herself to ask.

"I really shouldn't be here at all," he admitted. "Right now I'm supposed to be in Rome. I've got a concert there tomorrow night."

"All right then, when do you leave?"

"At ten in the morning."

Nothing ever changes, she wanted to say, but didn't. Instead, she asked him what hotel he was staying at.

"I'm not." The meaningful look he gave her actually made her blush. "That is, if you don't mind."

"Mind?" She raised her glass to him and smiled. "How could I possibly mind?" She wondered if he remembered the night they had never gotten to spend together in Berlin exactly fifteen years ago; the night he had given her the gold charm bracelet.

They talked late into the night and then they made love again. It was all the sweeter an experience because after so many years they finally had what they had never once had before: time. Precious time, theirs to share and to cherish at last, at long, long last. Tucked inside the tender circle of Michael's arms, her body stretched out along the length of his, every part of her touching a part of him, Kirsten thought her heart would break out of sheer joy. But when she heard him yawn and saw him close his eyes, panic clamped an icy hand around her full and happy heart, and began to squeeze the happiness out of it.

"Oh, Michael, don't," she whispered fearfully. His eyes fluttered open. "Don't fall asleep."

"I'm exhausted, Kirsten." He tightened his grip on her and pressed his lips against her forehead. "I'm not as young as I used to be." He chuckled as he said it, but her panic wouldn't go away.

"I'll keep you young," she told him, and she was only half joking.

"Too late."

She sighed and bit down hard on her bottom lip, but that didn't stop it from trembling. "I'll be all alone if you fall asleep." She mouthed the words silently as her eyes began to fill. A single tear slipped out from between her lashes and fell with a tiny plop onto the pillow. Another trickled down her cheek into her mouth, leaving a salty taste on her tongue. She had forgotten how lonely real loneliness could feel.

She tried to relax enough to fall asleep herself, but it was impossible. Her thoughts wouldn't let her. After a while she stopped trying. She cast her mind as far back as she could—all the way back to the beginning—and then, while Michael slept peacefully beside her, she relived every single moment the two of them had ever spent together.

She drifted off shortly before dawn but awoke with a start almost immediately. For a moment she was disoriented. She couldn't remember where she was; she thought she was back in bed with Jeffrey again. And then she saw his face, the lock of chestnut brown hair falling across his forehead, the faint brush of stubble on his chin, and she smiled.

She coaxed him out of bed with a kiss and a tickle; he responded by lunging for her and pulling her down onto the floor with him.

"For someone who's not as young as he used to be, you're pretty frisky," she teased as his mouth ran wild across her body.

"You said you'd keep me young, remember?" He stopped in his hungry exploration just long enough to answer her. "I thought I'd see if you're as good as your word."

She was. And he was even better.

Afterward, they took a long, leisurely bath together, then had their breakfast out on the balcony.

"I didn't notice any sheet music on the piano," Michael said, his offhanded remark shattering the idyllic peacefulness of the morning and instantly putting Kirsten on her guard. "You're still playing, aren't you?" He had seen the way her body had tensed and he suddenly felt terribly apprehensive. "Kirsten, you *are* playing."

"No, Michael." She shook her head slowly. "I'm not."

"But why, don't you want to?"

"It's not a question of wanting to or not wanting to."

"Then what is it?"

"I can't."

"What do you mean, you can't?"

When she told him, he refused to believe her, so she took him back inside, sat down at the piano, and showed him. She watched him struggle hard to mask his feelings, and she felt sorrier for him at that moment than she did for herself.

"You'll play for *me*. Don't shake your head, Kirsten, you can and you will." He grabbed hold of her frozen hands and began to rub them briskly between both of his.

"Are you magic?" she asked him with one of her impish grins, but he was all seriousness now.

"We'll let you be the judge of that." He continued to massage her hands until they were tingly and throbbing with heat. "Relax this time," he told her. "Don't think about anything, just keep your mind blank. Now close your eyes and take a deep breath. Hold it, hold it. Okay, now let it out slowly, very slowly. Good. Now again. Keep breathing that way, deeply, in and out, in and out. Good. Now place both hands on the keys and concentrate on the rhythm of your breathing."

With her eyes still closed, Kirsten followed his instructions exactly, hearing nothing but his soothing voice and her own deep breathing. Her fingers touched the keys and her breathing automatically quickened. He urged her to slow it down, to remain calm, and not to hurry. Once again she did what she was told. Breathing slowly and evenly, she struck a single note. Then another and another one after that. Next she tried an arpeggio, followed by a scale. At first she used only her right hand, then she used only her left, then both. She played the first Chopin prelude she had ever learned, then she began her beloved Debussy.

"Try, Kirsten, please try."

She could hear him speaking, but his voice sounded very far away.

"Harder, Kirsten, harder."

She opened her eyes and looked at him. He was staring down at her hands, his face pale and horror-stricken. She hadn't been playing at all; her hands hadn't moved. They were still fixed rigidly in place, poised and petrified, two inches above the keyboard. The only music she had heard was the music inside her own mind, born of her desperate need to believe that Michael really *was* magic and that he possessed the power to set her free.

"You see?" She took her crippled hands and tucked them away in her lap. "I told you, didn't I?"

Michael shook his head, combed his fingers agitatedly through his hair a number of times, then shook his head again. "Yes," he admitted, his voice sounding hoarse and strained, "you told me. But it doesn't have to be that way." Gripping her by the shoulders, he gave her a slight shake. "I'll help you," he said, "whenever I can I'll work on it with you. Don't look at me like that, I do want to work on it with you. Please, Kirsten, please let me help you."

She shrugged herself free and stood up. "And when will you find the time to help me, Michael?" she asked, digging her hands into the pockets of her cotton skirt and tightening them into hard fists. "No, this is something I'm going to have to do on my own." Her eyes followed him as he went to stand in front of the window. "I did it to myself, therefore I'm the only one who can *un*do it. But thank you." She ran to him and flung her arms around his neck. "Thank you for offering, Michael, thank you for wanting to help." He groaned, and she silenced his protest with a kiss. "Let's not talk about it anymore," she pleaded. "Let's not waste what little time we've got left. All I want now is for you to hold me and to keep on holding me until you have to leave."

Twenty minutes later he was gone. She didn't ask when she would see him again, and he didn't volunteer it. That hadn't changed either. No promises made, no promises to break. But if nothing else had changed, she had; she had no expectations now. And because she had none, it made his leaving much easier. It made the closing of her apartment door less devastating and the sudden cold rush of emptiness into the room less fearsome. Their night together had been a glorious gift—long overdue, but finally delivered—and for sixteen hours she had been happy again.

She saw him only twice more over the next year, but both times were sweet and satisfying. Although he begged her to let him try to help her with her playing, she refused; she much preferred to spend whatever precious time they had making love. Or talking. Or watching the sun set over the city. Or lying, comfortably and companionably, and saying nothing, in each other's arms.

In between visits she had her daily routine; and she had the Pallises and their friends. But above all she had Markos. He was still her greatest pleasure, her secret, treasured delight. A fitting replacement for the child she had lost and the one who had been stolen from her. The busier Larissa and Alexandros became at the university, the more time she and Markos spent together. And the more dependent she became on him.

In March 1975, Michael surprised her by calling her from his rented home in Shaker Heights. He wanted her to be the first to know: He had just been appointed permanent conductor of the New York Philharmonic.

"I've been waiting all my life for this appointment, and now it's mine." He was thousands of miles away from her, but not even distance could diminish the jubilation in his voice. "It's New York, Kirsten, can you believe it, New York at last! The student finally gets the chance to follow in his teacher's footsteps. God, if only Toscanini were still alive; if only he'd lived long enough to see it happen."

Kirsten swallowed hard and rubbed her eyes with the heel of her hand. She was strangling on her emotions; she could barely force out the words she needed in order to congratulate him properly. How she managed she didn't know, but she did. Yet when she put the phone down, she was shaking. Feelings she couldn't explain had taken control of her and were throttling her body from the inside. There was a bitter taste in her mouth—the taste of gall—and no matter how hard she tried, she couldn't get rid of it.

It was only then that she understood what the feelings were, and exactly what was happening to her. She resented him, she actually resented him. His family, his career, his success, his dream coming true. Everything she had suppressed, everything she had tried so hard not to feel, she was feeling now. She was horrified by her feelings, but she just couldn't help herself. She resented Michael and she envied him. Because in spite of what he had told her a year ago, he *did* have everything.

The piano! Kirsten gasped, and forced herself to stand up straight. Someone was playing the piano. She staggered out of the bedroom, holding on to the wall for support. Markos, it was Markos, sitting at the upright, picking out one of the Greek folk songs he knew. Seeing him seated there was like seeing Jeff again, and suddenly she was gripped by the truth she had refused to see.

She loved Markos. She loved him as though he were her very own.

But he wasn't hers; he belonged to someone else. He was only hers to borrow for brief periods of time.

Like Michael, just like Michael.

Once again she was seized by the same terrible fear that had haunted her most of her life: that she was condemned to getting only bits and pieces of people. That she would never have all of anyone, and no one would ever have all of her.

32

"Well, pet, I hope you'll be happy now." Eric Sheffield-Johns continued to stroke his wife's long, faded blond hair while he stared absently out of her bedroom window. "You ought to be; I've finally managed to get Wynford for you."

Although Nigel, the fifth Earl of Wynford, had been dead for years, his widow, Constance, had gone on living in the house until her own death eighteen months before. By the time the estate had been put on the auction block by the National Trust, Eric was ready. Enough of his holdings had been successfully liquidated to enable him to put in a bid that no one else had topped. For the past two weeks he had been sole legal proprietor of the Wiltshire property Claudia had coveted all her life. And this afternoon he would be driving her north for her first glimpse of the house she hadn't seen in forty-eight years.

He had already toured the estate once on his own, feeling very much the country squire and rather liking the idea. But then, Wynford itself was easy to like. It was a spectacular piece of old England, as noble as the countryside surrounding it. Nestled in the shadow of the gray stone walls and crenelated towers of Longford Castle, whose extensive grounds had been landscaped originally by the renowned Capability Brown, Wynford Hall was a rare treasure of Georgian architecture that merited being preserved no matter what the cost. And preserve it was precisely what Eric intended to do.

He bent to kiss the top of Claudia's head, then went to order the car brought around.

Claudia waited until he was gone, then lifted herself out of the faded chintz-covered wing chair she had been sitting in. She plucked several dead flowers from one of the deep purple African violets on the window ledge and crumbled the paper thin blooms in her hand. She was occupying the third-floor flat herself now, and had been for the past three years. Kirsten had disappeared—some even said she was dead—and she wouldn't be needing it anymore. And it had been years since anyone else had lived in it. Peering out the window, she watched Eric having the car packed and wondered where he was off to. It took her another few minutes to remember. How tiresome it was, being so forgetful all the time. How could she possibly have forgotten?

Eric, sweet, devoted Eric, was taking her home. After all these years, she was finally going home again.

Kirsten's face was expressionless as she watched the driver load her suitcases into the trunk of the taxi. Everything else had already been shipped; all she was bringing with her were her clothes. She thought of the plane ride ahead of her—two really, since she had to change planes in Lisbon for Faro— and immediately tensed. Unlike the other trips she had taken in the two years since Michael's surprise telephone call, this one would not be a return trip. This time the ticket she had purchased from the Alfa Tourist Agency on Hermou Street was one way: to a tiny town in the south of Portugal called Tavira. The next place she would be calling home.

"Wait for me, please," she instructed the driver in Greek, and went up to say good-bye to the Pallises again. The tears in her eyes and the heaviness in her chest reminded her that despite her attempts to try to remain calm and detached, it was impossible to leave Larissa and Alexandros, and especially her beloved Markos, without feeling a devastating sense of loss.

And yet it was time she left. She had grown too attached to the three of them, too dependent on them for companionship and for the familial warmth she still missed so dreadfully. She had started traveling again and that had helped put some distance between them. But the only real answer to her growing dependency was to move.

"You couldn't have chosen a worse day to leave," said Alexandros as he gave Kirsten one last warm hug. "Didn't you hear they're rioting everywhere to protest the new law that restricts the right to strike?"

"I heard," Kirsten told him. So much had changed, yet nothing had changed.

"Dozens of people have already been hurt," added Larissa, "and one person's been reported killed. Do you think you should risk trying to get to the airport in the midst of so much confusion?"

"At the moment I don't have much choice. My flight leaves in two hours; all I can do is try."

"And if you don't get through, you can always come back here and stay with us," Markos piped up, his amber eyes dancing.

"You'd like that, wouldn't you?" Kirsten teased him. She reached out to ruffle his hair, but he ducked. She wasn't offended; she knew he was only protecting himself. He had already used every excuse he could think of to try to convince her to stay: his upcoming eleventh birthday (she wouldn't be there to take him to his annual birthday concert); the piano (she still hadn't taught him to play it, even though he had recently taken up the bouzouki); and especially her choice of Tavira (it was practically a medieval town whose people were still living in the Middle Ages).

"Do you realize you're almost as tall as I am now?" she said, trying again to coax the unhappy boy out of his shell. "I'm sure the next time I see you, you'll be as tall as your father."

"Does that mean I won't be seeing you for a long time then?"

"No, it doesn't mean that at all." It was a losing battle, and the look in both his parents' eyes told her so. Their son adored her, and he still hadn't reconciled himself to her leaving. But Kirsten decided to give it one last try. "Come here, my little man," she called softly, and held out her hand to him. "Come on, Markos. Please?" He wavered another moment, then finally gave in with a shrug and a sigh. They walked down the long, carpeted corridor toward the elevator hand in hand.

"You do understand why I'm leaving, don't you, Markos?" she asked him.

He hung his head and stared down at the carpet. "Not really," he answered in a muffled voice.

"I'm leaving because I stayed here much longer than I ever intended to, and because I need to be alone again for a while. Athens isn't my home, Markos; Tavira won't be either. None of the places I've visited these last five years has been my home. New York is still my real home, Markos, and I plan to go back there someday."

"But will I ever get to see you after you go back?"

"Of course you will."

"How?"

"You'll come and visit me."

"New York's too far away."

"No, it's not. *I* got here from New York, didn't I?"

"I suppose."

"Besides, that day is still a long way off; you'll be visiting me in Tavira first."

"And you'll be coming back here to visit us, won't you?"

"We promised, didn't we?" He nodded grudgingly. "We even shook hands on it, remember?"

"I remember."

"And what's the other promise we made?"

"That I'm not to tell anyone where you are."

"Good boy."

She hadn't told Michael about the move; he was another reason she was leaving.

She had used her traveling as a defensive shield against him too. As a result, she had seen him only once more. And then, just briefly, when the New York Philharmonic arrived in town the previous August to take part in the Festival of Athens. Although Roxanne had accompanied him on the trip, he had left his wife to shop and had come to her apartment to spend one single stolen hour with her.

It was an awkward meeting, not at all like their other three meetings. They didn't even attempt to make love; they talked instead, speaking in stilted sentences while sitting on her balcony sipping ouzo, and stopping only occasionally for a hasty kiss or a quick embrace. Roxanne was like an uninvited guest at their all-too-brief encounter, her ghostly presence acting as a physical wedge between them. But more than anything, it was Kirsten's own distance that helped to keep that wedge in place. In the end it had made Michael distant too. There was little time for questions, even less for explanations—not that she would have offered him any.

The truth was she didn't want to have to explain herself—or *not* explain herself—to anyone anymore. She was tired of having to protect her feelings and everyone else's. She was tired of dissembling, tired of settling for only bits and pieces. What she wanted now was what she had wanted five years ago and lost: anonymity and the blessed numbness that went with it. Only her leaving would get that back for her.

She glanced at her watch and saw she was running late. "Quick, Markos," she said, "one last hug before I go." To her dismay, he didn't move. "Markos?" Without waiting any longer

for him to respond, she wrapped him in her arms and covered his face with kisses. Just as she was about to release
him, he let out a moan and threw his arms around her neck.
"Oh, Markos, Markos," she said, hugging him tightly. Then,
before the pain could get worse, she took his face in her
hands and kissed him gently on both cheeks. Smiling bravely,
he did the same to her.

"I love you, Kirsten," he whispered, his luminous amber
eyes flooding as he began backing away from her. "I love
you." He repeated it twice more, then turned and ran back
down the hall.

Tavira, with its population of thirteen thousand, is the most
picturesque little town in the Algarve. It lies at the mouth of
the Ribeira de Abbeca and was once a bustling port. But its
harbor has long been sanded up, and although many of the
townspeople still fish for a living, most of them are farmers,
working the land the way their fathers did and their fathers
before them. Set on a series of slopes high above the Mediterranean, the land looks like one enormous fertile garden.
Its orchards abound with lemons, oranges, tangerines, peaches,
pears, plums, and apricots. Its fields are rich with maize,
sweet potatoes, beans, tomatoes, cabbages, cucumbers, peas,
peanuts, squash, and watermelons. It is truly a town in
perpetual harvest, and anyone with a patch of soil has a
garden of his own.

Kirsten's small house, with its two bedrooms, living room,
dining room and kitchen, was identical to the other small
houses on the winding, sun-baked street just three blocks
south of the most important building in the town, the Church
of the Misericordia. The front of the house had an unobstructed view of the harbor below, the back had a tiny garden, and like her neighbors, Kirsten grew many of her own
vegetables. As much as she loved the town, with its slightly
drowsy air and sense of peacefulness, she had befriended
none of her neighbors in the seven months she had been
living there, and remained cautiously aloof whenever she
went out. To further safeguard her privacy, she had no telephone, and whatever mail she received was delivered to the
local post office.

She didn't sleep as well in Tavira as she had in Athens, but in
spite of that and her intense longing to see Markos, she was
fairly content. Tavira was her Garden of Eden, her piece of

elusive paradise, her sliver of heaven high above the earth. It was easy to find contentment among these simple people who celebrated their nights on the terrace of some taverna, feasting on a dinner of freshly caught fish or chicken with clams, drinking wine and listening to the tortured laments of a fado singer, and who highlighted their days by shopping at one of a hundred outdoor markets and journeying to any number of local county fairs.

Tavira is a town that loves fairs. Its two largest take place in August and October, its smaller ones the third Monday of every month. But the most popular by far is held the week before Christmas. And Kirsten, like all the other inhabitants of the town, had been eagerly anticipating this particular fair all fall.

The first day of the fair was disappointingly overcast, however, the air saturated with the threat of rain. But Kirsten refused to let the ominous weather deter her. She dressed the same way she always did when she went out—in a scoop-neck cotton blouse, full skirt, and flat-heeled sandals—but as an added precaution against the elements she tucked a heavy, fringed wool shawl inside her large straw marketing basket.

By noon her basket was crammed with oversize hand-painted wooden forks and spoons, small hand-carved wooden dolls, clay animals, and two bottles of locally made strawberry brandy. She stopped at one last stall, bought a hand-loomed woolen blanket for her bed, then set off in search of someplace to have lunch. She chose a small sidewalk café deep in the heart of the town's tiny artists' quarter, and ordered a tuna steak with rice and a glass of white wine.

She ate quickly, keeping a cautious eye on the leaden sky, then picked up her basket again and began a hurried tour of some of the artists' open-air stalls. None of the paintings or sculptures she passed appealed to her, but when she happened upon a display of small, unframed watercolors, she suddenly found herself intrigued and completely captivated.

Some of them were taped to a rough wooden table, others to a large plywood board that was leaning up against the trunk of a strawberry plant. They were all either landscapes or seascapes, painted in exquisite and minute detail, with a breathtaking delicacy that was reminiscent of the early works of Monet and Pissarro. The scenes were more dreamlike than real, as though the artist had viewed them all through a netting of finest gauze. And she knew she had to have at least one of them.

Kirsten was surprised that whoever had painted the watercolors wasn't around to sell them. None of the works had even been signed. And when she inquired about the artist at a number of nearby stalls, all she got was a series of shrugs. She went back to the stall to wait, and would have waited awhile longer had the sky not begun to edge from gray to black. Unless she started for home immediately, she risked being caught in the middle of a typical Tavira downpour. She would simply have to come back for the watercolors another time.

She didn't return to the artists' quarter until two days after Christmas. She headed straight for the watercolor exhibit, then stopped short in exasperation. There was no one around this time either. But several new watercolors had been added since her previous visit—all of them detailed studies of local wildflowers. There was such a poignancy to them, such a bittersweet quality to their rendering, it seemed to her that only a woman who had suffered the way she herself had suffered could have painted anything so wrenching and so touching.

She strode over to a group of local men gathered around a stall directly across the street and tapped one of them on the shoulder.

"Could you tell me where I might find the woman who painted those pictures?" She spoke slowly and enunciated each word very carefully as she pointed out the pictures she meant.

There was a hasty exchange among the men before one of them finally shook his head and indicated a spot somewhere behind her.

"No woman," he told her. "Is man."

Kirsten glanced over her shoulder, trying to locate the person he meant, and nodded. She saw him now. She thanked them and hurried back across the street. Squinting into the sun, she peered up at the tall, suntanned man in the wide straw hat who had appeared out of nowhere and was now ambling over to the plywood board leaning up against the strawberry plant.

"Excuse me," she called out, wondering as she did if the man even spoke English, "but I'd like to buy one of your paintings."

He turned around and Kirsten gaped.

His eyes were much the way she remembered them, only now they seemed more smoky than green, as though a film had formed over them and dulled their brilliance. But their effect on her hadn't changed at all. They pierced the outer layer of her skin, blazed an unswerving path straight to her very core, and turned her knees to jelly.

33

Andrew Beaton took a closer look at the woman standing directly in front of him in the blazing sunlight and thought: it couldn't be.

"Kirsten . . . Kirsten Harald?" He swept the hat from his head and reached for her hand, recalling at the last moment that she had never cared much for shaking hands. "Don't tell me you're hiding out here too?"

Hiding, she asked herself, but that was as far as her thinking got. She was still too stunned to conjure more than a single word at a time. A grin began to spread across his face, framed now by the golden sweep of a trim mustache and narrow beard, and her pulse quickened.

"I can't believe it's you."

"That makes two of us." He continued to study her with an intensity that made her blush.

But she was studying him no less intensely. His hair was still thick, still combed straight back from his high forehead, only now it was streaked a dozen different shades of blond by the sun. His tall, muscular body had been more precisely defined by time, and in his open-necked white shirt and faded jeans he could still pass for a college fullback. Once again the blatant maleness of him aroused a familiar turbulence deep inside her.

Giving herself a swift mental shake, she nodded toward the watercolors. "Are those really yours?" she asked.

"You sound surprised."

"I thought they'd been done by a woman."

"Now, that's a pretty sexist thing to say." At the hurt expression on his face, Kirsten burst out laughing. "I think I'm insulted. Should I be?"

She was still laughing—she couldn't remember the last time she had laughed this way—but she did manage to shake her head. "No," she assured him, "you shouldn't be."

He didn't seem too convinced. "Is that a formal apology?" "It is."

He took off his hat again and swept her a low bow. "In that case, madame," he said, "your apology is accepted."

A flash of gold caught her eye. It was only as he straightened up again that she realized what it was. It was a ring. A broad gold band hanging on a heavy gold chain around his neck. Following her gaze, Andrew instinctively closed his hand around the ring as though he didn't want her looking at it.

So he was married. The name Marianne immediately sprang to mind. Kirsten's stomach started on a swift and painful downward spiral. Her acute reaction baffled her, causing her to be more than a little annoyed with herself, and she quickly seized on his work to get her out of trouble again.

"All of your paintings are exquisite, Andrew," she told him. Suddenly it hurt to say his name. "I can't decide which of them to buy." Had he even heard her, she wondered. He now seemed a million miles away. "Andrew?" She was not only testing herself by saying his name again, she was also testing him.

Looking at her without really seeing her, he merely shrugged. "You don't have to decide right this minute."

Part of her wanted to shake him, part of her wanted to simply walk away. But she had never been one to walk away from a challenge before. And that was precisely how she now viewed Andrew Beaton: as a challenge. Wetting her lips with the tip of her tongue and giving her head a toss, she met the challenge of him head-on.

"Are you living here in Tavira?" she asked, her eyes blazing defiantly as she dared him to pick up the gauntlet.

If he was at all aware of having picked it up, he gave no outward sign. "Not really." He motioned toward the harbor. "I live on board my boat, and have for the past three years."

"How long have you been in Tavira, then?"

"About two weeks, I guess."

"Where are you the rest of the time?"

"Here, there, everywhere." He was anxiously fingering the ring again. "I'm a veritable Flying Dutchman, Miss Harald, a man without a country, with nothing more strenuous to do than sail and paint, paint and sail. And on occasion sell what I paint." The bantering tone disappeared from his voice and he grew serious again. "I came to Europe, you see, a year after I"—he stopped abruptly as he stumbled over the words—"ah, after I . . . my wife and two daughters were killed in a plane crash." Kirsten gasped. "I was piloting the plane, a Cessna. The landing gear jammed and I had to crash-land. Marianne and my two girls died before anyone could get to them. The *Time* reporter traveling with us broke two ribs and a leg. I was lucky." Here he laughed, a short, bitter and cynical laugh. "I walked away with a broken finger and a few bruises."

Kirsten was in shock, caught totally off guard by Andrew's grim revelation. When her mind finally stopped reeling, it began to fixate on the name of his dead wife: Marianne. The lovely face in the painting. Marianne. The luminous face of love. So she had been right after all.

"After they died," Andrew continued, "it was almost impossible to look at my face in the mirror. I couldn't see myself without seeing them and remembering that I was the one responsible for their deaths. So I eventually stopped looking." He gave his beard a self-conscious pat. "I even stopped doing simple things like shaving. Then I stopped painting portraits. I just couldn't bear to look at any more faces. I find all my subjects in nature now; I can deal with that. There's no pain in a landscape or a seascape, there's only beauty."

"I'm sorry, Andrew," she said, keeping her words soft. "I'm so very, very sorry." But his pain was so palpable, so fiercely accusing, she finally did what perhaps she should have done in the first place—she turned and started walking away.

"Kirsten?" Andrew came after her immediately and caught hold of her wrist. "I hope I didn't scare you off. I usually don't go around blurting out my life story to people that way. I guess I've been alone so long, it just felt good to have someone to talk to. Especially someone who understands English." His smile was infectious; she found herself smiling back at him. "Have dinner with me tonight?" She hesitated, suddenly unsure. "Please?"

In the end she agreed. But all the way home she wondered if she had made the right choice. She had come to Tavira expressly to be alone, to live a life free of emotional encumbrances. And what had she done? She had accepted a dinner invitation from one of the most attractive men she had ever met, a man who still needed his own aloneness every bit as much as she needed hers.

She recognized the signs all too well: it was taking her far too long to get dressed. She cautioned herself against feeling anything, especially excitement. Andrew Beaton had extended nothing more to her than a polite dinner invitation—a token gesture from one expatriate to another. And she would have to take care. He was no longer that same brilliant young artist who had painted the world-acclaimed pianist all those years and all those hurts ago. Now he was a man in exile, in hiding from himself and the rest of the world.

Like her. Too much like her.

"You look positively enchanting," was Andrew's appreciative comment as he seated himself across from her on the terrace at Gilao's, a small taverna huddled in the shadow of the eighteenth-century Church of Santa Maria do Castelo. Kirsten blushed and tucked her hands underneath the table to keep him from seeing just how tense she was. "Sangria?" he suggested.

"That'll be fine." She needed a few more minutes to compose herself. But as soon as their waiter poured them their drinks and placed the large, frosty glass pitcher of sangria in the center of the table for them, Andrew raised his glass in a toast, forcing her to do likewise.

"To old acquaintances," he proposed.

"To old acquaintances." They clinked glasses, and Kirsten was relieved that she was actually able to bring hers up to her mouth without spilling any of the dark, fruity red wine down the front of the new dress she was wearing.

Studying her carefully while he sipped his drink, Andrew came to the conclusion that Kirsten Harald was even more beautiful now than when she was younger. Her hair was more silver than black, and it framed her heart-shaped face like a pair of sterling-silver hands. The amethysts in the wide silver hoops she wore intensified the violet of her eyes, and against the soft whiteness of her dress, held up by the thinnest of straps, her skin glowed like burnished honey-tinted marble. If he were sketching her, he would have— He stopped himself instantly and tossed the notion aside.

"Andrew?" He started at the sound of his name. "Do you realize I know very little about you?"

"I'd have thought just the opposite was true after this morning."

"I mean your background, things like that."

He toyed with the stem of his wineglass and smiled. "It's the clever artist who gets to know his subjects without his subjects ever getting to know him."

"Well, I'm not your subject anymore," Kirsten retorted, "so I'm afraid that excuse just won't work."

Andrew gazed at her through narrowed eyes and leaned back in his chair. Stretching his long legs out in front of him, he hooked his thumbs through the belt loops of his jeans and gave her a look that said *Brace yourself, because here it comes.* Kirsten hunched forward, her elbows on the table, and waited expectantly. But instead of launching into his story, he aimed a lopsided grin her way and said, "You're sure now?" She nodded. "You really want to hear this: names, dates, everything?" She nodded again and he shrugged. "Okay."

He wondered where to begin and exactly how much he wanted her to know. "I suspect our backgrounds were pretty similar," he started by saying. "Deprived. Deprived in almost every way except for love." Kirsten's eyelids began to prickle, and she took a long, deep, steadying breath. "My parents were both born in Belfast, but they emigrated to Chicago the year after they were married. My dad worked as a foreman at a meat-packing plant; my mom worked at the notions counter at Woolworth's. By the time I was born they were far too old and still too poor to have another child. They'd already raised two boys. Jimmy was nineteen when I was born, Hank—Henry really—was seventeen. Home was a third-floor walk-up in a roach-infested tenement on the north side. The only way out of there was to muscle your way out." He made a fist to show her precisely what he meant. "Both Jimmy and Hank were experts at that. Hank was a boxer, Jimmy was a hood."

"A hood?" Kirsten winced at his use of the word, but Andrew didn't blink.

"It's true, he was. He was a car thief, he ran numbers, he broke bones. You name it, he did it. But as tough as they both were on the street, that's how gentle they were with me. I was like a pet to them, something small and defenseless, something to protect. They swore I'd never have to be like them. It was Jimmy who put a stick of charcoal in my hand and told me to make something decent of myself. I guess he'd gotten tired of my stealing his pens all the time. But it was my mother who taught me about beauty; she was the one who showed me how to see beyond the surface ugliness of things."

"I know the feeling," she said. "Music was *my* way of getting past the ugliness."

He finished his drink and refilled both their glasses. "The day I graduated high school, Jimmy was released from prison for the second time. He thought we should celebrate and took me to some bar on Oak Street. We had a few beers and left around midnight. Never take a shortcut through the alleys of Chicago at midnight." His hands were cupped so tensely around his wineglass, Kirsten was afraid he might crush it. "To this day, all I can remember seeing were two pairs of yellow headlights and three shapes coming toward us. They weren't interested in me; they were after Jimmy. I had this small knife"—here his voice faltered—"a lousy, fifty-cent penknife I used for sharpening pencils. I took it out, and the next thing I knew, there was a knee in my gut and I'd dropped it. I must have passed out, because when I opened my eyes, the lights and the shapes were gone, and Jimmy was lying on his back with my knife in his chest." Kirsten clapped her hands over her mouth. "No one was ever arrested for Jimmy's murder. Not that the police tried very hard. I couldn't identify anyone, and to them it was just another case of the underworld taking care of its own and saving them the trouble. After a while it no longer mattered. As far as I was concerned, I'd as good as killed Jimmy myself."

Kirsten thought of her own lingering guilt about Meredith. "Did you ever stop feeling guilty?" she asked him.

"For the most part, yes, but completely?" He shook his head. "No, not completely. I'm still convinced he wouldn't have died if I hadn't pulled out my knife."

"What happened to your painting after that?"

"For a while everything I did was ugly. Ugly, because that was all I could see, and because it was the only way I could work out my anger. Picasso had his blue period, I had my ugly period. Thankfully, it didn't last too long. I landed my first official commission my second year at Northwestern. It was for the portrait of a debutante named Paige Rheinholt Dirksen, the grandniece of Senator Everett Dirksen. Brother, was I impressed: the boy from the north side painting the girl from the north shore." He laughed at the pleasant irony of the memory. "That portrait changed everything for me though. It helped me get my first cover at *Time*. And the rest, as they say, is history."

Whether it was or not, he had said more than enough for one evening.

They ordered a second pitcher of sangria, then they ordered dinner. Kirsten recommended he try the baked stuffed clams, which was a specialty of Gilao's, while she decided on cod poached in a white wine sauce with fresh basil. All through the meal they kept the conversation light, chatting together easily and companionably about any topic that came to mind; then after a glass of port and a complimentary dessert plate of fresh figs and almonds, he walked her home.

They stood outside her front door as awkwardly as two teenagers at the end of their first date. Kirsten, clutching her key in her hand, wondered if she should invite him in for a cup of coffee or a nightcap; Andrew stared down at the tips of his loafers and tried to decide whether to kiss her good night or to settle for a simple handshake instead.

"Well." Kirsten cleared her throat, gave her head a toss, and held her hand out to him.

That seemed to settle the matter, but not quite. As he took her hand, Andrew bent down, planted a hasty kiss on her cheek, then bolted. He felt like the world's biggest fool. A forty-four-year-old man behaving with all the grace and subtlety of a fourteen-year-old boy. But Kirsten Harald represented something he didn't want to have to think about dealing with—at least not yet. Not until he had dealt with all the ghosts first.

Michael Eastbourne stared at the handsome boy with the liquid honey eyes and asked him to repeat what he had said. So he did. It was just as unbelievable the second time.

"And she left no forwarding address, no phone number where she could be reached?"

The boy just shook his head.

"How long has she been gone?"

He calculated quickly. "Seven months."

"Seven months!" Michael's shoulders slumped. "Thank you," he said, his voice finally revealing the strain he was under. "I'm sorry if I disturbed you."

No sooner had Markos closed the door than he went running back to his bedroom to add a postscript to his weekly letter to Kirsten. She would be so proud of him when she

read about how well he had kept their secret. But just seeing
that same man again had stirred up something inside him. It
reminded him that Kirsten was all alone in the world and that
she still needed someone like him to protect her. Not for the
first time in his life he found himself wishing he were a man
instead of a boy.

The flight from Athens to Amsterdam gave Michael too
much time to think. He had his answer now. It explained the
disconnected telephone number and her not being there the
last time he had flown to Athens especially to see her. If her
intention had been to punish him, she had certainly succeeded. Her message to him was clear. It said: leave me
alone; I can't bear to have you remind me. And that hurt.
God, it hurt.

He downed his bourbon and ordered a second. Had she
resented him that much? Had she blamed him, even hated
him? He rubbed his eyes with one hand and toyed with the
empty miniature of Jack Daniel's on the lowered tray table in
front of him with the other. He thought of her hands and
unconsciously flinched. Her hands, her exquisite, gifted hands.
Hands so blessed they had changed the sound of music
forever. Hands that were stilled now.

He drained his second drink gratefully. The pain was beginning to subside, the ragged edges were softening. He had
failed her; it was no wonder she had run away from him. He
hadn't helped her play again. His faith in her hadn't been
enough. Or was it that her faith in him had been less than it
should have been?

He nearly laughed out loud. He had seen himself as om-
nipotent. The magician who, with a single wave of his baton,
would break the spell she had cast over herself and set her
free. He had even pictured himself sweeping her onto the
stage of Carnegie Hall and reintroducing her personally to
the world that his own wife had helped steal from her. He
sighed as he leaned his head back and closed his eyes. He
was a fool, he told himself, a weary, aging fool. He was no
knight errant off on some sanctioned holy quest; he was only
a conductor of orchestras. And a man. A mere man, who
would have given anything to have been her god—just this
once.

34

Andrew lay across his bunk on his back, his hands tucked behind his head, staring out the porthole at the clear Mediterranean night, and fought the urge to weigh anchor and sail out of Tavira while it was still dark. All the way back to the boat he had been jumping out of his skin, dancing inside with a restless energy that had yet to subside completely. And all because of a face from the past. A past he had buried along with his wife and two daughters.

But it was a face he had never totally forgotten. A face that combined the beauty of the surface with the beauty of the soul. The sensuous artist and the sensual woman. Ingenuousness and genius. A combination so unique and so rare, he had uncovered it only that one time.

He turned onto his side, and in the flickering darkness the three faces on the mahogany wall of the cabin were as clear as day. He had painted their portraits six months before the crash—three separate oils which he had then set into the large ornate wooden frame he himself had carved and gilded in twenty-four-carat gold leaf. The results had been astonishing; breathtakingly dramatic. A glorious triptych, dedicated not to God, but to the three loves of his life: Marianne, Michelle, and Andrea. Little did he know at the time that guilt would ultimately turn his monument to love into a personal testament to grief. An altarpiece before which he still continued to pray, humbled and heartsick, for forgiveness and healing.

Marianne. He sighed as he mouthed her name. The last time he saw Kirsten Harald he still hadn't proposed to Marianne Mathison. But he did the very next night, as soon as he was certain his first New York exhibition was going to be a success. Marianne. He had broken his most important rule—never to mix his painting with his personal life—when he fell in love with her. She had just graduated from Columbia with a masters in social work; her parents had commissioned him

to paint her graduation portrait, and she had adamantly refused to pose for it in a cap and gown.

Ah, Marianne, Marianne. Turning his head, he looked out
at the night again. She was twenty-three when he found her,
thirty-five when he lost her. But what they had compressed
into those twelve short years had been heaven.

After six days of fierce internal struggling, Kirsten finally
worked up enough courage to go back to the artists' quarter.
Why she was even bothering, she didn't know. Andrew Beaton
certainly hadn't come looking for her. In fact, he had done
just the opposite; he had acted as though he couldn't get
away from her fast enough. For all she knew, he might not
even be in Tavira anymore. She felt her determined stride
break, become slightly less determined. Stopping for a moment to think, she told herself it wasn't too late, that she
could still turn around and go home.

"Why should I?" This asked aloud through tightly clenched
teeth, causing two elderly women to turn their heads and
peer at her strangely. She returned their stares with a stare of
her own, then marched, shoulders back, chin thrust out
stubbornly, around the corner and into a brilliant stab of
sunshine.

Even from a distance of one hundred yards it was impossible to miss him, towering over everyone else, his blondness
surrounding him like a beacon.

"I was beginning to think I'd lost a customer," Andrew said
by way of greeting. Suddenly Kirsten wished she were six
inches taller. "That *is* why you're here, isn't it?"

"Can you think of a better reason?" Her smile was part
impertinence, part indifference. Touché, his own smile told
her in return.

"You actually made up your mind then, did you?"

But she was no longer looking at him, she was looking at his
work. "They're gone," she exclaimed in genuine dismay.
"Don't tell me you sold them all."

"Would that surprise you?" He folded his arms and watched
her with one eyebrow arched speculatively.

"No, it wouldn't surprise me, why should it? You're good."

"Thank you, I'm flattered."

"And I'm disappointed," she scowled.

"Don't be."

"Oh?"

"They're all back on the boat."

"You beast!" She bared a pair of imaginary claws at him. "How could you do that to me?"

"Do what?" He feigned innocence.

"Tease me."

"Who else do I have to tease; no one around here understands a word I say."

"You are wretched." But she was laughing as she took a playful poke at him.

"Ouch!" He yelped in mock pain. "Does that mean you don't want any of them now?"

She gave him a shrug of total indifference. "Who knows?" she declared breezily. "I might want one of these instead."

"Ah, capricious woman," he sighed, rolling his eyes. "Mind if I watch you look?"

"Not at all." Although her reply sounded nonchalant enough, it was hardly the way she was feeling. With Andrew standing so close to her, it was practically impossible for her to concentrate. "You're blocking my light," she complained. "I can't see." The truth was she could hardly breathe.

"Sorry." He backed off a bit.

It helped, but not that much. His bigness continued to loom over her like a shadow, taking up all her space. After five minutes she was still staring blindly at the same landscape.

"Say, do you think you could hold off making this all-important decision awhile longer?" Andrew was squinting up at the sun and calculating the time. "At least until after lunch? Because I'm famished, and I've just discovered this terrific little restaurant that serves the best mussels you've ever tasted." He interpreted her hesitation as a yes and promptly steered her off down the street.

The restaurant turned out to be only slightly bigger than a shack, but behind it was a surprisingly large flagstoned terrace with a spectacular view of the Ribeira de Abbeca. Andrew ordered for both of them, and the mussels *were* wonderful. But what she found even more wonderful was the way he was opening up to her again.

"Do you know what I love about my life now?" It was a rhetorical question, but she shook her head anyway. "The sea. To me it's one long, unending challenge, a continual battle of wills. Poseidon's on one side, I'm on the other, and the two of us disagree about absolutely everything." Kirsten smiled at the image she had of two bearded titans locked in perpetual combat. "He keeps me guessing and I keep him stimulated. Whenever I'm feeling especially mellow, he'll send up a squall just to irritate me. When I'm lazy, he'll brew up a storm just to make me work. But if I'm ever in a foul mood and would give anything for a good, strong gale, there's not a hint of a breeze anywhere, and the ocean's as calm as a pond." He gave his head a shake, popped one last mussel into his mouth, then signaled their waiter and ordered some more.

With her eyes focused on her own growing mound of empty shells, Kirsten asked cautiously, "Do you ever think about going back?"

"Back?" he repeated. "Back where?"

"To the States."

"God, no, what for? Everything I want and need I've got with me. No, Kirsten, I'm afraid that's where you and I are different. I'm here to live; you're just here to wait."

She could feel her appetite fading as a host of unwelcome memories sought to overtake her. Quickly she steered the conversation back to him again. "So you plan to spend the rest of your life as the Flying Dutchman, then?"

"Why not?"

"And where will you go when you leave Tavira?"

"That, my dear lady, is in the laps of the gods. I'll simply do what I always do—pull out my trusty map, close my eyes, and point. I don't care where it is as long as it's warm. Even thinking about the cold makes me shiver now. I hated our Chicago winters, and New York's weren't much better. No, I intend to live in perpetual summer from now on and leave the topcoats and boots to everyone else. And if they call me a coward or a dropout, it'll be only because they're jealous." His green eyes were sparkling as he said this. "I haven't met a man yet who wouldn't trade his gold-chip stocks and three-piece suits for the chance to pull a Gauguin, and live happily ever after in some nice, warm paradise."

As she sat there listening to him, Kirsten had the feeling that she was already about to lose her newest friend. But it wasn't until she was halfway through her second glass of Madeira that she felt brave enough to do something about staving off the inevitable awhile longer. Fortified by the wine, she brazenly invited him to her house for dinner that evening.

"I'm a pretty good cook," she added almost defiantly when she noticed a slight hesitation on his part.

"I don't doubt it."

"But?"

"No buts, just a condition."

"A condition?"

"Yup, that we make dinner together." Her jaw dropped. "Chauvinist!" He pointed an accusing finger at her. "I'm a pretty good cook myself, I'll have you know."

At first Kirsten found it strange to have such a giant of a man working beside her in her tiny kitchen, but after a while it seemed like the most natural thing in the world. He insisted on preparing his famous "shrimps Beaton" for her, and she agreed to make the vegetable rice to go with it. They worked on a salad together, using tomatoes and cucumbers from her own back garden; then, while he sliced a melon for dessert, she set the table in the dining room and lit a pair of dusty-rose candles.

She was pleased and surprised at how easy it was to be with him. The conversation was easy, so was the laughter. And as the evening progressed, with the wine flowing as freely as the conversation, she realized she had never shared this kind of camaraderie with anyone else before. Deep in her unconscious, a warning light began to flash, but she was much too relaxed to notice.

"You *are* a good cook," she told him, cleaning up the last of the spicy tomato sauce he had made for the shrimp.

"Any time you want to trade recipes, let me know."

"I certainly intend to."

Pouring them each some more wine, he nodded toward the piano in the living room. "Are you still playing?"

At that, some of the pleasure went out of the evening.

"No," she said, so softly he almost didn't hear her.

"You're kidding."

"I stopped after Meredith died."

"And you haven't played since?"

She shook her head. He seemed to be waiting for some kind of explanation, so she gave it to him—quickly, in brief, broken sentences.

"You'll play again," he said.

It could have been Michael speaking. "Sometimes I wonder."

"You will, but only when you really want to."

"The same way you'll paint portraits again when *you* really want to." She had meant it as a gentle rebuke, but it didn't come out that way. His face immediately began to close over.

"We're not talking about me right now, Kirsten, we're talking about you." Suddenly the entire tone of the evening seemed to be changing. "The only reason you can't play is because you're still punishing yourself for what happened to Meredith." She started to say something, then changed her mind. "Don't bother, I'll say it for you. I should know, right, because I'm an expert on guilt."

Kirsten stared down at the floor. She should never have told him the truth about her hands, never. Not only had it ruined their evening, but it was bringing back everything she had managed to forget for a few hours. Meredith saying she loved her more than anyone else in the world. Jeff's tear-streaked face pressed against the back window of the police car. Michael telling her he would help her play again; the look in his eyes when he realized he couldn't.

"Kirsten?"

She didn't hear him. She was being swallowed up by her memories again. She was lost, trapped inside a whirling vortex, surrounded by hundreds of colliding images. All of them swirling around her, pressing in on her, making her feel dizzy and claustrophobic.

"Kirsten, are you all right?"

She put her head in her hand, felt how clammy her forehead was, and waited for the dizziness to pass. "I think you'd better go," she finally said, her voice trembling and thick.

"At least let me help you clean up first."

"No, don't bother, I'll do it all in the morning."

"Are you sure?"

"I'm sure."

"Kirsten, I'm sorry if what I said upset you."

She fended off his apology with a weak wave. "It doesn't matter."

"But it does."

"Please." There was a sob in her voice now. "It's late and I'm tired, so if you don't mind . . ."

"Sure." He came around to her side of the table and gave her shoulders a gentle squeeze. "In spite of what you might be thinking, this was one of the sweetest evenings I've spent with anyone in a very long time. Thank you." He kissed the side of her face and left before she could move.

She waited a few more minutes, then got up from her chair and walked on wobbly legs over to the piano.

"Please, Michael," she whispered into the sudden stillness of the room, "please help me prove him wrong." She pictured Michael sitting on the bench beside her, his hazel eyes warming her face, his voice low as he hypnotized her with his words, telling her that all she had to do was believe in him and in herself and she would be able to play again.

After flexing her fingers to relax them, she placed both hands on the keys and pressed all ten down at once. She counted to five, then tried again. And again. And again. She should have known better! Snatching her hands away, she slammed the lid down with a frustrated bang. It seemed the closest she would ever get to a keyboard was the two-inch space directly above it.

She barely slept that night or the next. Dreams of Michael, of Meredith, and of Jeff kept waking her up; thoughts of them kept her up. Once again her past was invading her present. Leaping out from behind the flimsy barricade that usually contained it, it wrapped its strong, bony hands around her throat and began to squeeze. Instead of fighting it off this time, she succumbed to it. She allowed herself to feel everything it wanted her to feel: each ache of longing, each stab of pain, each pang of regret, each unshed tear. Then, once her catharsis was complete, she gathered up all her runaway feelings and locked them up again.

But with them all safely tucked away, there were others that were only too eager to take their place. And they all involved Andrew.

To her, Andrew Beaton was something of a conundrum. Contradictory and compelling. Someone who left her breathless, bemused, and slightly bedazzled. He was a ride on a roller coaster, a carousel, a magic carpet, and a Ferris wheel. He was evanescent. As impermanent as smoke. As intoxicating as champagne. Appealing, and therefore dangerous. Her only hope was to stay away from him.

But chance decreed otherwise.

The very next afternoon she came face-to-face with him over a barrel of sweet potatoes at the outdoor market just four blocks from her house. She immediately changed her mind about the potatoes and moved on to a stall selling freshly picked medlars. Andrew moved right along with her. She pretended she didn't see him.

"You couldn't be avoiding me, now, could you?" He picked up one of the small apples, checked it for bruises, then put it back again.

"I just decided I didn't want any sweet potatoes, that's all." Without looking up, she sidled over to a stall piled high with pomegranates.

"Changed your mind about the medlars too, huh?"

Kirsten bit down hard on the inside of her cheek to keep from smiling. If nothing else, at least Andrew Beaton was persistent.

"No pomegranates today either?" With a shrug of his shoulders he followed her over to a bin of unshelled almonds. "Pass these almonds up and all you'll have left will be those sorry-looking grapes over there."

She gave the grapes a cursory glance and then made the fatal mistake of looking up. His gaze locked with hers. She tried to look away and couldn't. His grin only made it worse. Cursing him roundly, she gave in, not only to his irresistible smile, but to her own ridiculous urge to smile back at him.

"Do you realize you still haven't bought one of my watercolors," he threw out casually, "or"—and he paused to emphasize the word *or*—"come by for my shrimp recipe yet?"

"Have I insulted you again?"

"Immeasurably." He put both hands over his heart and grimaced appropriately.

"Poor Andrew," she said, sliding easily, too easily, back into his games again. "How can I make it up to you?" Before he could suggest something, she came up with a suggestion of her own. "What about one watercolor *and* one recipe? No? Two watercolors and one recipe, then? I couldn't possibly say two recipes, because I've tried only your shrimps. Okay, you win, three watercolors and one—"

"How about one watercolor, one recipe, and one swim over at Ilha de Tavira?"

Ilha de Tavira was a spit of land between Tavira and the sea.

Kirsten shook her head. "Uh-uh, too cold."

"You call this cold!" Andrew gave her a disgusted look. "Chicken."

"Not chicken, merely sensible. Besides, I'm not wearing a bathing suit."

"We'll stop off at your place and get you one."

"I still say it's too cold."

"And I still say you're chicken. Let's go." He caught hold of her upper arm and began hurrying her across the street.

"What about your own bathing suit?"

"I'm wearing it." He gave her a wink that reminded her of Eric. "Since I never know when the swimming urge may strike, I'm always prepared."

Kirsten felt a tremor of excitement at his words, and she wondered if she were allowing herself to be drawn into the kind of game she wasn't prepared to play yet.

It's not too late, she told herself all the way down to the beach. It's still not too late, she insisted as she changed into her black one-piece maillot inside a damp and deserted cabaña. And then it *was* too late. She hovered uncertainly at the water's edge, shivering and clutching herself, and watched as Andrew came loping toward her. As cold as she was, she could feel herself growing hot with embarrassment at the intimidating sight of him. There was so much of him—all of it muscled, glazed golden, and brushed with fine gold hair.

"You lied," she shouted above the pounding of the surf when she noticed what he was wearing.

"No, I didn't, I just stretched the truth a bit." He gave the elastic waistband of his navy blue cotton briefs a snap that made Kirsten wince and look away. "It's almost as good as a bathing suit," he insisted, laughing at her appealing shyness. "Come on, give me your hand."

The moment the first breaker slammed into them, Kirsten forgot all about being shy. Suddenly she was very grateful for his size. Breaker by breaker, bit by bit, the danger of the game began to dissipate—swallowed up by the sea and absorbed by the sky. Soon all that remained of the game was the joy and the fun of it.

She and Andrew chased waves like children. Each time they found one, they would plunge headfirst into its blue-green heart, turn, and race with it toward the shore. By the time they finally surfaced again, they were coated with sand, both of them laughing and gasping for air, and eager for the next one. When they eventually grew tired of chasing waves, they chased each other. In and out of the water they ran, improvising games as they went. Playing tag and hide-and-seek, shrieking with laughter, spitting out mouthfuls of sea-water, swiping at stinging eyes with wet hands, and barely stopping to catch their breath. He bobbed her up and down like a top; she climbed onto his back and rode him like a dolphin. Then, when they were both exhausted and chilled, they joined hands and ran up the beach to get their towels.

Kirsten dried herself off as best she could, but she still felt cold and wet. Seeing her shiver, Andrew wrapped his own towel around her and started to rub her vigorously up and down. She was so startled by the unexpected gesture, all she could do was stand there in frozen shock. But she didn't remain frozen for long; the surface of her skin seemed bent on betraying her by beginning to tingle excitedly.

"Better?" he asked.

"B-better," she admitted through blue lips as her entire body caught fire and burst into flame.

"Then why are you still shivering?" He was behind her now and his mouth had grazed her ear when he spoke. "Hmm?" The answer to his question was another uncontrolled shudder.

How could she tell him her shivering now had nothing whatsoever to do with the cold, when she didn't want to admit it even to herself?

"I think you'd better go inside and get changed pronto." He whisked his towel away, and she felt naked and exposed. "I don't want to be responsible for your catching pneumonia." He gave her bottom a light whack. "Now, go."

By the time he dropped her off at her front door, she was aching with frustration.

"What about the recipe and the watercolor?" she asked flippantly to keep him from seeing how genuinely disappointed she was at being returned home so soon. "Weren't they part of the same deal?"

"They still are," he assured her.

Her eyes framed the question she herself was too proud to ask; his told her that the next move was up to her. Then with a jaunty wave, he headed up the path whistling. Kirsten gritted her teeth in vexation and slammed the door behind her.

That night she lay in bed with her arms wrapped tightly around her pillow and her hips grinding in a steady, undulating rhythm against the mattress.

What Andrew had started, Andrew would have to finish. She would wait. And the anticipation would make the waiting all the more exciting.

She fell asleep with that subtle pulse still throbbing between her legs and an eager half smile hovering about her lips.

*   *   *

She waited until noon, then she simply couldn't wait any longer. She was out of breath by the time she reached the artists' quarter and started across the street toward his stall. A moment later she stopped dead in her tracks

She couldn't believe what she was seeing.

Where the watercolors had always been, there was now a display of crude wood carvings.

Andrew had taken his works and left.

35

Twelve-year-old Jeff Oliver couldn't have been happier.

It was snowing, the school was deserted, and he still had another few days of Christmas vacation all to himself. His decision to remain at Choate over the holidays had infuriated his father and raised the usual number of eyebrows among his classmates. What else can you expect from such an oddball, they seemed to say; but then, they had been calling him an oddball for years. Not that it mattered what they called him. There was only one thing in the whole world that mattered to Jeffrey Powell Oliver III, and that was his music.

As much as he had originally dreaded being sent to the Wallingford, Connecticut prep school, he had come to dread going home even more. Going home meant having to endure his father's endless critical scrutiny; staying behind meant peace and quiet, but more important it meant the auditorium, where the piano was kept. If his father knew that most of his monthly allowance went on sheet music and weekly piano lessons with Harriet Badgerow, the wife of his geography tutor, he would have had a stroke. But he didn't know. And hopefully he wouldn't know until it was far too late for him to do anything about it.

Jeff was whistling as he cut across the crunchy snow-encrusted front lawn of the auditorium, the sheet music he had wrapped inside a plastic bag tucked firmly under one arm. For whistling, he always chose Bach or Mozart, but when it came to playing, he much preferred the dreamy and romantic melodies of Brahms or Chopin, Liszt and Rachmaninoff. Just like your mother, Harriet Badgerow had commented once; then she had promptly clammed up, as though she expected to be struck down for saying what she said. But those four words had been enough for Jeff. They had served to confirm what he already knew.

Shaking the snow out of his hair, he shrugged off his duffel coat and gloves, dropped them onto the faded maroon velvet seat of an antiquated wing chair, and trotted over to the piano. It was an old and poorly tuned upright, but at least it was a piano. He blew into his cupped hands to warm them, then limbered up his fingers with a couple of exercises his teacher had taught him. Flipping through his sheet music, trying to decide on which piece to begin with, he selected Mendelssohn's "Albumblatt" and opened it up in front of him.

From the very first note he played he could feel it happening, just the way it always happened. The lightheadedness. The sensation of floating, of being lifted up and out of himself. Of becoming one with the music, and feeling for certain that he was still alive.

For Jeff, the only tangible proof of his existence lay in his music. It was who he was; it gave him shape and definition. It filled his lungs with air, forced the blood through his body, and regulated his heartbeat. But his music was also his closest friend: his sole companion and only confidante. It made the loneliness easier to bear; it chased the nightmares away; it held him whenever he needed to believe he was still loved.

But most important of all, it lessened the terrible pain of missing her.

If his memory of her had grown vague over the years, her hold on him had grown only stronger. While all the boys he knew were being groomed to follow in their father's footsteps, he was the lone exception. He had no intention of following in his father's footsteps; he had no desire to grow up into a proper Long Island gentleman, Oliver or otherwise.

As far as he was concerned, he was a Harald. His *mother's* son. And like his mother, he was going to become a pianist.

Kirsten was miserable.

There were lead weights attached to her ankles, a thousand crazed butterflies on the rampage in her stomach, and ice water in her veins. She tried telling herself Andrew owed her nothing, he was free to come and go as he chose, but it didn't do any good. She was still miserable. She couldn't believe he would simply vanish like that.

But whether she believed it or not, Andrew Beaton *had* vanished.

She spent the rest of the day wandering listlessly around the house. She dusted, washed the kitchen floor, rearranged a few paintings in the living room, and lined up the books in her bookcase first according to height, then according to color. At one point she even tried to eat something, but ended up throwing it into the garbage instead.

Twilight found her puttering around in the back garden. By the time it was too dark to see, there wasn't a dead leaf, dead flower, or single weed left anywhere. Never had her little garden been more thoroughly or meticulously groomed.

She tried eating again at ten, and actually managed to swallow a small piece of cheese before her throat closed up. With a sigh of frustration she threw out her second meal of the day and settled instead for a glass of strawberry brandy. The potent liqueur went straight to her head. She downed a second glass without thinking twice about it, then stumbled into her bedroom, lay down on her bed still fully clothed, and tried to will herself into a woozy sleep.

Two hours later she was still wide awake. The effects of the brandy had worn off and she could feel the start of that terrible emptiness inside her again. Damn you, Andrew Beaton, she cursed as she slammed her fist into her pillow. Damn you, damn you, damn you. She turned on the lamp next to her bed and tried to read. But after going over the same sentence fifteen times, she slammed the book shut and went over to her small writing desk to finish her latest letter to Markos.

The pen was barely in her hand before she put it down again. Remembering what Markos had written to her in his last letter made her heart give a small, exultant leap. So Michael had been there looking for her. Twice in fact. That made her smile. But even as she smiled, she could feel the emptiness inside her spreading—she was really no different from Andrew. Michael, she whispered, oh, Michael, I'm sorry. The smile faded, then disappeared completely. A moment later it was replaced by something else: inspiration.

She flew to the night table beside her bed, opened the top drawer, and pulled out the worn brown leather pouch containing the gold charm bracelet. Why hadn't she ever thought of this before? It took her five tries before she was finally able to fasten the bracelet around her wrist. Then, with her heart hammering wildly in her chest, she sat down at the piano and raised the lid on the keyboard.

Let it work, she prayed, repeating the words over and over again as she began to limber up her fingers. Please, God, please let it work this time. The bracelet felt cool against her skin; the charms danced and tinkled like wind chimes in a breeze. Michael was there in the bracelet, there in each of the gold charms, waiting to work his magic on her. Please, God, please. She was ready now. Closing her eyes, she took a long, deep breath and placed both hands on the keys.

It was six in the morning, the translucent pink of another Tavira sunrise was just beginning to stain the room, when she finally gave up. Staggering over to the sofa, she collapsed onto it, utterly exhausted and depleted, and fell into the sleep that had been eluding her all night.

It seemed only moments had passed when she heard him call her name. Opening her eyes slowly, she found to her astonishment that it was nearly dusk, and that the shadows stealing across the floor were tinged with scarlet. She raised her hand to rub the sleep away, and the charms on her bracelet began to jangle. Beckoning for him to come closer, she started to tell him about the dream she had had.

Andrew moved closer to the sofa, only to stop short at the sound of some other man's name. Michael, who was Michael, he wondered.

"Kirsten?"

Her startled gasp made him jump.

"Andrew!" Her eyes were wide, the pupils so dilated they all but consumed the violet irises. Where was Michael? Hadn't she just been trying to play the piano, and hadn't he been sitting right there beside her?

"Kirsten, what is it, what's wrong?" Andrew crouched down beside the sofa and watched with some concern as she struggled to pull herself together. He caught a flash of gold as she rubbed her eyes again, and found his curiosity piqued more than ever.

Kirsten pushed herself into a sitting position and focused on the man kneeling in front of her. Suddenly she was seeing him clearly for the first time.

"Andrew! I thought you'd gone," she blurted out.

"Gone, no."

"But you weren't at your stall yesterday."

"I went back to Ilha de Tavira."

She didn't know whether to laugh or cry. Whether to throw her arms around him and tell him how happy she was to see him or pound him with her fists and shout at him for having left without telling her he was coming back.

"I wanted to surprise you," he said.

"Surprise me!" Her hands went self-consciously to her hair; her stomach's rumbling reminded her that she hadn't eaten in almost two days. Oh, he had surprised her all right.

But Andrew seemed not to notice; he was grinning as he got to his feet again. "Since you've been having so much trouble deciding on which of my watercolors you wanted, I thought I'd make the decision for you. Now, wait right here."

He disappeared into the kitchen and Kirsten hastily began combing her fingers through her hair and moistening her dry lips with the tip of her tongue. She was anxiously smoothing out some of the creases in her crushed cotton skirt when he came striding back into the room with both hands hidden behind his back.

"Could you switch on a lamp for me?" he asked, indicating with a sharp sideways nod that his hands were otherwise occupied. She scrambled to do as he asked, then sat down on the sofa again, her hands clasped between her knees, her eyes as bright as a child's with anticipation.

With a flourish he brought his hands out from behind his back and held up two nine-by-twelve-inch watercolors for her to examine. "Well, what do you think?"

She sucked in her breath. "Andrew, they're exquisite!" Both scenes depicted the sea and the beach at Ilha de Tavira: one at sunrise, the other at sunset. The morning scene was a study in opalescent pink, salmon, and aqua; the evening scene a jeweled wash of coral, garnet, and sapphire. "They're truly exquisite," she repeated, "both of them."

"Then that settles it." He set them down gently on top of the coffee table. "They're both yours, with my compliments."

The smile she gave him was dazzling. "Thank you," she whispered hoarsely, barely managing to get the words out; the lump in her throat wouldn't let her say anything else. She longed to hug him for his wonderful thoughtfulness, but the painful memory of all the hours she had spent thinking he had gone held her impetuousness in check.

"You're more than welcome." Andrew eased his hands into the back pockets of his jeans, rocked back on his heels, and studied her for a moment through critical eyes. Something was troubling her. There was an ineffable sadness behind the warm smile she had just given him. He watched her toy with the charms on the bracelet she was wearing and felt his stomach muscles automatically tighten. "Kirsten," he asked softly, "is there something wrong?"

She continued playing with her bracelet to keep from having to meet his gaze. Yes, there was something wrong. And it all revolved around her absurdly violent response to his disappearance. In the short time she had known him, he had succeeded in stirring up too many feelings in her. Feelings that made her vulnerable when she had hoped never to be that vulnerable again. She didn't want to feel anything for him, not when she knew she would only have to say good-bye to him one day. Not after she had already said good-bye to almost everyone else in her life.

"Kirsten?" He tipped her face up for a better look at her, but she shook him off.

"There's nothing wrong," she told him. "You just startled me by coming here, that's all."

"You mean by showing up here uninvited?" He rubbed the back of his neck and shot her a sheepish grin. "You're right, I wasn't thinking. I might have embarrassed both of us."

Kirsten's cheeks began to burn. "That wasn't exactly what I meant."

"What did you mean then?"

"Nothing."

"You're disappointed in the paintings."

"No, I'm not, I think they're wonderful. And I'm touched." She stared down at her hands. "It was a very sweet and thoughtful thing for you to have done."

"But?"

"But you just disappeared!" The words were out before she could stop them.

"I didn't just disappear. I was at Ilha de Tavira, painting." He went to stand over by the piano. "You know, we never said anything about being accountable to each other for our time, Kirsten."

"I never asked you to account to me for a thing," she snapped. "But I *was* disappointed; I didn't think you were the kind of man to simply disappear."

"I'm not that kind of man. I'd never just disappear, believe me."

"Thank you."

"You're welcome."

She crossed her arms and sat there, fuming inwardly.

"I think I'd better leave," he said.

"Yes, I think you'd better."

But he didn't move. He just stood there looking at her, trying to find some graceful way out of what they had gotten themselves into, and for no reason. As always, whenever he was agitated about something, he started to play with his wedding band. Kirsten watched what he was doing, and her heart turned over.

"I thought you were leaving." Her tone was so cold, so penetrating, it snapped Andrew to immediate attention.

"I am."

A moment later the front door closed with a bang.

36

"Andrew, wait!"

He stopped halfway up the path.

She stepped down from the porch, then waited, her heart in her mouth, to see if he would turn around. His hesitation was only momentary, but to her it seemed like an eternity. In the light of the rising moon his face and one side of his body glowed pearlescent silver. She was barely breathing as he started toward her. Part of her urged her to run back up the stairs and lock the door; but the part that had sent her dashing outside after him made her stay right where she was.

He stopped just inches from her. Suddenly her heart was a stone being skipped across the surface of a lake. His hands reached out to clasp her shoulders and she stiffened, expecting him to crush her. But his touch was gentle, as gentle as a sigh.

Andrew could hear the blood drumming in his ears. His hands felt huge and clumsy; she was so small, her shoulders so narrow. He was afraid he might hurt her, bruise her, out of nothing more sinister than simple eagerness. Casting about for an image to hold on to, he pictured her as a piece of finely spun Venetian glass. And he used that image to keep his eagerness in check and his touch whisper-soft.

"Kirsten." Four years of devastating aloneness were summed up in the serious way he said her name. Taking her face in his hands, he rubbed his thumb back and forth across her smooth, flushed cheeks and said her name again. Then he smiled at her.

The warmth of his smile melted the outermost layer of resistance enclosing her heart and allowed her to smile back at him. But despite the smile, she was in agony. She ached all over—her mouth, her back, her breasts, her groin. All of her was tense and expectant, taut with repressed desire.

Bending down, Andrew touched the sensitive hollow of her throat with his lips. She shuddered; the ache grew stronger.

"Andrew." She gasped out his name like a plea. She needed him to put an end to her agony; she needed to be kissed.

But he refused to be hurried. He was intent on discovering each of her other features first. This he did with tender and protracted thoroughness before he finally reached her mouth. And even then he took his time. Beginning with its farthest corner, he traced the outline of her mouth with the tip of his tongue. Then he slipped it slowly between her parting lips and ran it across them like a letter opener slitting open an envelope.

Kirsten was on fire. A tiny flame marked every place his mouth had touched. Yet, she was still waiting.

A moment later, her waiting was over.

His kiss was deep, full, and searching, made all the more sensual by the bristly softness of his mustache and beard. It was unlike any kiss she could remember. Its taste, its texture, its intensity—all of it was different. It was like being kissed for the very first time.

He broke their kiss just long enough to catch his breath. Then he began to track a moist, teasing path up and down the slender column of her throat with his tongue. She immediately arched her back to intensify the tingling sensations his tongue was creating. Their thighs connected. She heard him groan. Locking her hands behind his neck, she rubbed back and forth against him, feeling him harden as she herself began to soften.

He kissed her again, open-mouthed and savage, and they continued to kiss until they were both too weak to stand. Then, with his mouth still clamped around hers, Andrew picked Kirsten up and carried her into the house, kicking the door shut behind them.

As they began to undress each other, she couldn't believe a man so big could be so gentle. He was like some great, golden treasure that was hers to explore. And explore him she did, uncovering every golden bit of him with her curious fingers and hungry mouth—his broad shoulders, the curly mass of blond hair on his chest, his taut belly and narrow hips, the muscled legs that seemed to go on forever.

Mindful as always of just how small Kirsten was, Andrew took special care to be tender with her. When all he wanted was to enter her, he held himself back with a control that was herculean, and continued to caress the sweet, inviting flesh she was offering him. The small breasts, so round and firm, their nipples pointed and cherry-red; the tiny waist, the smoothness of her hips and legs, the lush triangle of black hair nestled between her thighs.

They tasted of themselves and of each other; they were slick with their bodies' juices; both of them wet and warm and growing warmer. Finally, when he couldn't hold back any longer, he gathered her close, tucked her firmly against him and guided himself inside her. Her hot wetness seethed forward to welcome him, and he closed his eyes.

As their bodies were joined together now, so were their mouths. Each breath they drew they drew together, from the same energy source, keeping the circle unbroken. Something hard was digging into her chest. It was his ring. She shifted, moved her hand. The charms on her bracelet jangled in her ear.

She thought of Michael.

He thought of Marianne.

Together they made themselves forget.

Nothing had prepared Kirsten for the feeling of having Andrew inside her. She, who had doubted her capacity to ever fully feel anything again, was feeling more acutely and more profoundly than she had ever felt before. She was at the edge before she knew it, each insistent thrust of his body pushing her closer and closer. She pulled back; she didn't want to let go just yet. But that delicious tingling was starting, the thrumming that signaled the beginning of the end. She turned her head to the side and moaned as the first pulsating wave of her orgasm overtook her. The wave subsided, another rose in its place, stronger and more violent. Her rhythmic moans kept pace with his rhythmic pumping as she came, again and again and again.

Andrew felt the force of her contractions along the entire
length of his penis. It was time. Time to loosen his grip on
the past and on himself. He quickened his pace. He was
already so close, it was only a matter of seconds before he felt
it. A great, surging rush; a purging release, exploding from
him in a series of ecstatic bursts. And when it was all over, he
felt a calm unlike any calm he had ever felt before.

They lay entwined in each other's arms, neither of them
saying a word. Their hearts were full, their bodies sated.
Both of them were feeling a little shy now, and more than a
little afraid. Tonight they had taken a step away from the
past, but it was only a step. The proof of their continuing
bondage to that past was still suspended from the chain
around Andrew's neck and hanging from the bracelet around
Kirsten's wrist.

Jeffrey and Dierdre were the perfect couple; everyone said
so. They were seen everywhere together: at dinner parties,
dances, and the most exclusive restaurants; at the theater,
the opera, and the ballet; at gallery openings, debutante
balls, gala charity benefits, and political fund-raisers. They
played tennis together, went sailing together, and took trips
together. They even spent the occasional evening alone
together.

But Jeffrey wanted more. Dierdre didn't.

He wanted to combine their two households, she wanted
to keep them separate. He wanted to marry her, she didn't
want another husband. He wanted her to be a mother to Jeff,
she much preferred being his godmother.

"If I'm perfectly content with the arrangement just as it is,"
she kept saying, "Why can't you be?"

Why indeed? How could he explain without admitting his
failures to her? Beginning with his own treacherous hands.
Continuing with Kirsten. And now with Jeff. When he had
gotten rid of the mother in the hopes of reclaiming the son,
he had failed there too.

He couldn't bear to have her know about the failures,
because then she would know the truth about him. She
would know that in his ambitious reach for the stars, he had
been forced to settle for a handful of failed dreams.

Perhaps it was time he resigned himself to the fact that
nothing was ever going to change. And if Dierdre was to be
his life's last dream, then perhaps maintaining the status quo

wasn't that steep a price to pay for the privilege of holding on to that dream.

"Do you know I still look for Jeff in every dark-haired six-year-old I see?" Kirsten confided to Andrew. The two of them were sitting together on the blanket she had spread out on the grass in her back garden, just holding hands and gazing up at the stars. "I keep forgetting he'd be thirteen now. His birthday's the day after tomorrow."

Andrew heard the tears in her voice and gave her hand a hard squeeze. "I stopped looking for Michelle and Andrea when I stopped looking at myself in the mirror," he admitted.

"What about Marianne?"

"It's funny, but I never really looked for her anywhere." He tapped the center of his chest. "I didn't have to, she was always right in here."

Kirsten looked away. Even after six months, she still felt a twinge when they talked about his dead wife. She even felt it when she caught him staring at her as though he didn't know who she was. And when his eyes suddenly filled with tears for no apparent reason.

For the past six months they had been treading separate paths through the exhilarating obstacle course that was their relationship. It was tempestuous, lusty, and tender too. Volatile, comforting, irritating, consoling. Demanding and frustrating. Fulfilling, maddening, satisfying. Predictable only in its unpredictability.

Andrew and Kirsten were alternately frank and secretive in turns. They inched forward and they withdrew, trading each other parts of themselves as though they were trading stamps. But as open as they were, they were both relieved to know they still had their separate coats of protective armor to retreat behind whenever they wanted.

"Kirsten, who's Michael?"

Andrew's question took her by such complete surprise that for a moment Kirsten couldn't speak.

"Michael?" It came out sounding slightly strangled.

"Michael."

She asked how he knew the name and he told her. Tugging up a blade of long grass, she began to shred it with her fingers.

"He gave you the bracelet, didn't he?"

Kirsten responded with a very reluctant, very brief nod.

"Can't you talk about him?"

She took a deep breath, brushed the shredded grass from her lap, and drew her knees up to her chin.

"Now, that's the most blatant piece of body language I've ever seen." Andrew chuckled and reached out to ruffle her hair. She smiled in spite of herself. "Okay, no more questions about the mysterious Michael."

She rewarded him by leaning her head against his shoulder. Then after a few minutes she whispered, "Michael is . . ." She paused, wondering if she really wanted to do this. "Michael Eastbourne." She pushed his name out as quickly as she could, then clamped her mouth shut.

"The conductor?" Andrew nodded in instant recognition. "He was one of the few men I wanted to paint and never did."

"Really?" For some unfathomable reason her heart was beginning to pound.

"Really." He turned, kissed her lightly on the brow, then turned away again.

"Maybe you will one day."

"And you'll arrange it."

She pretended she hadn't heard that. "I'm serious, Andrew, why shouldn't you paint him one day?"

"For the simple reason that I don't intend to paint anyone one day."

"Chicken."

"Hah! Talking about chicken, how's the playing coming along?"

This was one of their favorite ways of protecting themselves. Whenever a particular subject became too painful, they immediately picked a fight. But tonight Kirsten refused to rise to the bait. Instead, she switched the subject to something else.

"Do you realize I've still never seen your boat?" Andrew sighed as if to say, Here we go again. "I don't think that's particularly fair, do you? I mean, you've been here dozens of times, you've seen *my* home. Why won't you let me see yours?"

"It isn't a matter of letting you or not letting you."

"What is it then?"

"I guess I'm just not ready, that's all."

Kirsten's tone instantly softened. "It's only a boat, Andrew," she said. "It may have her name on it, but it was never her home." She saw him wince, but continued anyway. "It's been *your* home, Andrew, only yours. Why are you still so protective of it, why won't you share it with people?"

"People?"

"All right, me."

"Did it ever occur to you that I might not want to share it with anyone, even with you?"

"I'd be an intruder, right?"

He didn't have to answer her, she already knew what the answer was. Even now, he still considered her an intruder. As close as they were, that was how far apart they were. She thought about all the times he disappeared—sometimes for days, sometimes for weeks—sailing off someplace alone, but always with the promise that he would be back. And he always had come back. So far.

Out of the corner of his eye Andrew could see her making a fist. He recognized the warning sign and wondered if he should do something to mollify her or simply wait. He decided to wait. As soon as he noticed her hand beginning to relax again, he was seized by the impulse to reach out and stroke it. But he didn't. If he so much as touched her now, it wouldn't end there. It seldom did.

A simple touch never stayed simple, it ultimately evolved into an embrace. A single kiss never stopped at one, it always led to a second, then a third. And they always ended up making love. Making love so passionately and so gloriously it took his breath away just thinking about it. Their lovemaking was the glue that bonded them together, healed the rifts between them and evened up all the scores. He couldn't get enough of her—of her beauty, her body, her sensuality. She was a stimulant and an intoxicant. She made him needy, too needy. And he had vowed never to be that needy again.

"It's late, I'd better go," he said, getting to his feet, then holding out a hand to help her up.

Kirsten angled her wrist to try to read the time on her watch. "It's not late, it's only ten."

"I want to be up at four."

"Four, why four?"

"Didn't I tell you?" His voice became muffled as he bent down and picked up the blanket. "I'm sailing for Gibraltar in the morning."

Her hands were shaking as she reached out to take the blanket from him. "How nice." Her voice was tight, her lips pursed.

"I've been pretty good." He laughed in the hopes of taking the edge off his announcement, but his laugh sounded strained even to him. "I've been landbound for nearly a month now; that's a record for me." He followed her into the house, then tried to put his arms around her to kiss her good-bye. She swatted him away as though he were a fly.

As she stood there glaring up at him, it suddenly came to her. She knew exactly what she was going to do. She would go to Athens. She hadn't seen Markos in over a year. She needed to see him now more than ever. And she needed what only the Pallises could give her: the warmth and comfort of a family. Surely it couldn't hurt, not if she stayed only a short while.

She felt infinitely better now, so much better, in fact, that she threw her arms around Andrew's neck, gave him a swift, deep kiss on the mouth, and stepped away from him, grinning.

"Have a wonderful time," she told him, ushering him to the front door and even opening it for him. "I know I will."

Andrew stumbled down the steps looking slightly dazed. Had he missed something, he asked himself. And if he had, what the hell was it?

37

Kirsten returned from Athens revitalized and brimming with the kind of contentment only a loving family circle can create. Although her original intention had been to remain with the Pallises a week, it had taken very little convincing on their part to get her to extend it to two. But staying that extra week had made it that much harder for her to leave. It was only after Markos had promised to visit her in Tavira the following July that she was even able to leave at all.

She slept late the morning after her return, then roused herself in time to go to the market for groceries. After putting everything away, she found she was far too lazy to think about cooking, and decided to have lunch at one of the local tavernas instead. She wandered aimlessly through the streets while she tried to make up her mind about what she wanted to eat, but nothing seemed even remotely tempting. She had just stopped to gaze out over the crowded harbor, when it came to her in a rush. A rush that had very little to do with food and a great deal to do with how much she suddenly missed Andrew.

What distance had successfully blunted, proximity had not only sharpened again, but exaggerated. Here he was everywhere—an integral part of every sight and sound and smell of the town they were both temporarily calling home. Had he returned from Gibraltar yet, she wondered, or would this be the one time he broke his promise to her and didn't come back at all. No sooner had she asked herself that than she could feel the old familiar panic start.

Resisting every impulse to race down to the docks and look for his boat, she forced herself to start walking again. Before she was even aware of having decided on where to go, she was standing in front of Gilao's, the first restaurant she and Andrew had ever eaten at together.

As she breathed in the mingled smells of salt sea air and cooking spices, she waited impatiently for someone to seat her. She was now so hungry, she could almost taste the baked stuffed clams and feel the icy splash of sangria as it hit the back of her throat. When her stomach began to growl, she gave up on the maître d' and started scanning the terrace in the hopes of locating an empty table on her own. Suddenly she froze. Her eyes widened incredulously as they focused on an achingly familiar face. And across from that face, with her back turned to Kirsten, sat a woman whose ash-blond hair was twisted into a single long, heavy braid.

Her heart raced, then stopped. She reached out to steady herself and found to her embarrassment that she was clutching the arm of the maître d', who had finally materialized and was ready to show her to a table. Blurting out something indistinguishable to him, she turned and ran back into the street.

She sagged against the wall of a nearby building, trying to catch her breath. She felt betrayed, utterly betrayed. And yet she knew betrayal was the one emotion she had no right to feel. They had agreed, right from the start, never to be accountable to each other for the way they spent their time. They owed each other nothing—neither explanations nor apologies. But then, if she truly believed all that, she had to ask herself, why had seeing Andrew Beaton with someone else left her feeling so terrible?

*   *   *

That night she went to bed early, not because she was especially tired, but because she didn't want to have to think anymore. After three unhappy hours of tossing and turning, she finally gave up in disgust and went into the kitchen. There was only one cure for her insomnia, and that was a cup of hot chocolate.

The fact that it was July made no difference to her. There was something soothing about the sweet, foamy drink, something especially comforting and reassuring. It not only reminded her of her own childhood, but of her own children. Hot chocolate had been as much a favorite in the Oliver household as it had been at the Haralds. Meredith had always added a marshmallow to hers, while Jeff had always insisted on two maraschino cherries in his. Why cherries? Because the marshmallow melted, the cherries didn't. They were always waiting there at the bottom of the mug for him when he was finished—as happy a surprise as the plastic toy at the bottom of a box of Cracker Jacks.

But tonight the hot chocolate wasn't working. Tonight the memories were too close, too strong. She shut her eyes and saw the face of her nine-year-old daughter in front of her. Even after all these years it was inconceivable to her that she would never see her eldest child again. Meredith's death had opened up a hole inside her that had never closed over; and it never would. It remained a cold and barren place, empty and black, a void nothing would ever be able to fill.

She opened her eyes and there was Jeff. Her son, her beloved son.

"Oh, Jeff, my darling," she cried aloud to him, "do you think about me at all? Do you even remember anything about me?"

She could feel the tears beginning and angrily blinked them away. Slamming her half-full cup of hot chocolate down on the counter next to the sink, she stomped into the living room.

"Don't think," she commanded herself as she sat down at the piano in the dark. "Don't think, don't think, don't think." She repeated the words while she worked on some relaxation exercises, and she was still repeating them as she shook her hands up and down rapidly several times to increase the flow of blood to her fingers.

She needed a fresh image to focus on and immediately seized on Jeff. She imagined him at the Steinway in the conservatory before Jeffrey had ordered the piano removed from the house. She saw herself sitting next to him, showing him—no. She stopped, rethreaded the thought as though it were a piece of film, and began again.

They were onstage together at Carnegie Hall, seated at matching Steinways. Her heartbeat quickened, beads of perspiration broke out across her upper lip. The piece they were scheduled to play was a concerto written especially for dual pianos. She searched her memory for just such a composition and came up with Mendelssohn's Concerto in A Flat Major. Tonight they were playing with the New York Philharmonic; Michael Eastbourne was conducting. A trickle of perspiration slithered down the center of her spine. She was wearing lavender and diamonds; Jeff was in black tails, but instead of the traditional white bow tie, his was lavender—to show the world they were a team. Smiling happily at the thought, she brought her hands up to play.

She looked over at Jeff and their eyes met for just an instant. She grinned at him, he winked at her, then bowed his head low over the keyboard. Her eyelids were starting to sting. She glanced up at the podium, waiting anxiously for Michael to cue her. The muscles in her hands began to tighten; she could feel the strain in her fingers all the way up to her shoulders. She tried to get herself to relax again, and couldn't.

After two hours she gave up and went back to bed. But all she did was lie there, with her eyes open and her arms aching, for the rest of the night.

By eight in the morning she couldn't bear it any longer. She showered, slipped into a thin cotton sundress, and left the house without even stopping to have her morning coffee. As she threaded her way down the dusty rock-strewn path that led to the harbor, her palms grew moist and a dull throbbing started up behind her temples. By the time she was within sighting distance of the *Marianne*, she could hardly breathe. The last of her courage deserted her then, and she stopped dead in her tracks, unable to move.

What if that girl had spent the night with him? What if they were together at this very moment? And if they were together, did she really want to know about it? Without thinking, she took an uneasy step backward. Then she got angry. How dare he invite some stranger to his boat when he still refused to let her on board.

Torn between confronting him and simply leaving him alone, Kirsten momentarily chose to do nothing. And then she saw him. Sitting out on deck with what appeared to be a sketchpad open on his lap. Her heart gave a small, happy leap. There was no sign of the girl anywhere. But what did that prove, she asked herself. She could still be inside the cabin sleeping or making breakfast or . . . Andrew had spotted her and was waving, actually waving. She automatically waved back.

She was nearly alongside the boat when he stepped down onto the creaking wooden dock to greet her. Disappointment surged inside her at the way he still wouldn't let her get too close to where he lived. But all other thoughts fled the moment he pulled her into his arms and started to kiss her. She gave herself over completely to the welcome warmth of his embrace. Safe in his arms, she yearned to dissolve, to lose herself inside him so that she would never have to live as a separate entity again.

Andrew's head was spinning. That first glimpse of Kirsten had left him weak-kneed with desire and a dozen other pent-up emotions. Kissing her now, feeling how the curves of her body fit so snugly and insistently into his, he cursed himself for the way he had left her again. He cupped one of her breasts and began to circle its stiffening nipple with his thumb, knowing as he did that no matter how he fought it, she was and always would be an unchecked fire with the power to consume him. A fire that neither distance nor denial would ever be able to quench.

In the two weeks they had been apart, he hadn't once stopped missing her or wanting her, and he couldn't afford such feelings. He couldn't afford to get so close to her, not when their time together was limited. The parallel paths they were on were only going to diverge someday and send them off in opposite directions. She would be leaving, he would be staying; it was as simple and as painful as that. One of these days it was all going to end.

"Did you have the wonderful time you said you were going to have?" he asked as soon as he could breathe again.

Kirsten laughed. Trust Andrew to remember everything she said word for word. "I did," she answered. "Did you?"

"Naturally."

After that they both began speaking at once. As soon as Kirsten admitted she had gone to Athens to visit the Pallises,

Andrew seemed only too eager to tell her about his own trip. What he neglected to say, however, was that because of her he had cut his trip short and returned to Tavira earlier than scheduled, only to discover that she was still away.

All the time he was talking, Kirsten found herself listening to him with only half an ear. She wasn't as interested in his trip as she was in the mysterious blond—a subject he seemed determined to evade if not avoid completely. But she was just as determined not to let him off the hook.

"And what about *her*?" she finally interrupted him to ask.

"What about who?"

"Your sailing companion."

"What sailing companion?"

"All right, then, your lunch companion." Quickly she admitted to having seen him at Gilao's.

"Oh, *her*."

Kirsten crossed her arms and waited, but all she got was one of his maddening, broad-shouldered shrugs. "An-drew," she sang, tapping her foot impatiently on the dock.

"I met her only yesterday, so there's really not much to tell." In spite of his denial, he still looked a bit sheepish. "She stopped by the stall and bought three of my best watercolors. She told me she was Dutch and that she was crewing for some charter clipper based in Marseille. The minute she left, I closed up and went over to Gilao's to have lunch. I'd just started eating when I noticed her waiting in line for a table. She saw me, came over, asked if she could join me, and I said yes. You wouldn't have wanted me to be rude to a patron of mine, now, would you?" The look Kirsten gave him was blandly noncommittal. "By now she's on her way to Algiers. End of story."

She accepted his explanation and the soft kiss he planted on her mouth for emphasis with an inner sigh of relief, but when he tried to put his arms around her again, she wriggled away and began inching toward his boat. He watched for a moment, then started after her.

"Just where do you think you're going?" he demanded.

"Nowhere."

"Nowhere? It sure looks like somewhere to me."

She pointed to the sketchbook he had left lying on his deck chair. "I thought I might sneak a look at your latest work."

"You don't have to sneak a look, I'll be happy to show it to you."

She had one foot on the deck, one leg poised to swing over the side of the *Marianne*, when Andrew caught her around the waist and lifted her down. "Oh, no, you don't. No one comes aboard without a formal invitation from the captain."

The smile she trained on him was bright and full of mischief. "All right then, Captain, formally invite me."

Although he was smiling back at her, his green eyes were beginning to cloud over. "I will, Kirsten, you know I will—"

"But not yet." He shook his head. "Oh, Andrew." She sighed as she locked her hands behind his neck. On tiptoe, she brushed her lips back and forth across his until she heard him groan. "Andrew, Andrew," she whispered, using her mouth and her body and all her powers of persuasion to seduce him into changing his mind. As she felt him growing hard, her genuine passion for him swept through her like a wild hot wind and turned her legs to jelly. She began tugging at the buttons on his shirt. "Andrew!" Her voice was hoarse and urgent now. "Make love to me, Andrew, please make love to me."

His own hunger was like a frenzied drumbeat echoing throughout his entire body and demanding to be released, but he held back. Part of him longed to carry her on board the *Marianne* and make love to her on the bed he had never shared with anyone. But another part of him wouldn't allow it. His boat was his last place of refuge, the one remaining buffer between him and the rest of the world. Once that barrier was removed, he would be completely at her mercy, and at the mercy of all those reborn feelings that stubbornly refused to die.

"Kirsten, not here." His lips were warm and moist against her throat.

"Yes, Andrew, here."

He closed his mouth over hers. "No." With his tongue he stifled her next protest while his hands caressed away the remainder of her resistance.

In the end, he took her home and made love to her on the hooked rug in the living room, again in the shower under a pulsating cascade of lukewarm water, and once more in the tumbled shelter of her double bed.

In spite of all the precautions they took to guard against it, the bond between them grew thicker and tighter with each passing month. Although Andrew continued to take the occasional trip on his own, Kirsten had finally learned to believe him when he said he was coming back. She even welcomed his absences because it enabled her to devote herself entirely to finding some way of unlocking her willful hands. In her constant search for fresh incentives and newer images, she discovered she was starting to rely more and more on thoughts of Andrew, and less and less on her memories of Michael. There were even times now when, to her sad surprise, she had difficulty remembering exactly what Michael looked like.

She and Andrew now saw themselves as a couple, and so did the rest of Tavira. But with a slight difference. They saw them as two people totally apart, two people intent on saving themselves only for each other. Although they were never less than cordial, it was clear to anyone who met them that they neither welcomed nor needed the company of others. And so, in deference to their unspoken wishes, the villagers were careful to leave them alone.

It was the end of May, and it seemed to Kirsten that for days Andrew had been holding something back from her. Just as he had come to know her moods, she had come to know his, and whenever she noticed him beginning to withdraw inside himself, she respected his need for privacy and never intruded. But this time was different; it was lasting too long. Perhaps what he needed was some gentle coaxing. And so she broke her long-standing promise never to interfere, and went in after him.

She cooked him one of his favorite dishes—pasta primavera the way her mother used to make it—plied him with two pitchers of sangria, then proceeded to make slow, tender love to him. When he was lying spent and satisfied beside her on the living room couch, she leaned over him in such a way that only her lips were grazing the sensitive rim of his ear, and whispered, "Out with it, Andrew Beaton, I want to know what you've been hiding from me."

He shuddered as her whisper shot through him like quicksilver.

"Tell me, Andrew." With one hand she began slowly stroking his chest. He shuddered again. Her hand traced lazy circles across his stomach, then slid behind him to caress his buttocks. "Tell me, or else."

His voice was husky. "Or else what?"

"Or else I'll stop."

He grabbed hold of her hand to make certain it remained

precisely where it was. "Don't," he said. "I'll tell you whatever you want to know."

"Out with it then."

Andrew wet his lips. "Last week an agent of the Castilho Gallery in Lisbon approached me and asked if I would mount a show of my watercolors at the gallery in July."

"And?" she prompted him.

"And that's it."

"That's it?" Her ministrations ceased abruptly. "You mean you didn't say yes?"

"I told him I would think about it."

"Andrew, what's there to think about? It's a wonderful offer and a wonderful opportunity for you. How could you just tell him you'd think about it?"

"It seemed easy enough, all I did was say—"

"You'd think about it, terrific." Arousing him again was now the farthest thing from Kirsten's mind. "I don't understand you. You've been asked to mount a show at the most prestigious art gallery in Lisbon and you act as if you couldn't care less."

Andrew shifted his weight on the couch. "I do care, believe me, but I don't think I'm ready to handle a show just yet. You know what a show means. It means a lot of hard work, a lot of publicity, a lot of standing around trying to make small talk with a bunch of strangers who probably don't even speak English." Kirsten rolled her eyes. "It reminds me of everything I very happily left behind when I decided to leave New York. I'm sorry, Kirsten, but it just smacks too much of civilization for me right now."

"You'd think you were some Tarzan who's been hiding out in the jungle so long he doesn't remember how to behave around civilized humans. Well, you're not. Oh, Andrew, Andrew." She grabbed him by the shoulders and shook him. "Don't you dare turn down this chance because it reminds you of everything you left behind in New York a long time ago. This is now, this is Lisbon, and you are still a remarkably gifted artist. Be glad of it, damn you, be proud. Someone like Luis Castilho doesn't mount shows for pity, he mounts them for profit. And he wouldn't have asked you to exhibit in his gallery if he didn't think you could make him money."

"I'd feel like a freak," he grumbled, "a curiosity. Step right up, folks, the man doesn't paint portraits anymore, he doesn't even trust himself to use oils, but he sure can paint a mean little watercolor."

His bitter self-deprecation ripped at Kirsten's heart and made her feel like weeping, but for his sake she kept a tight rein on her emotions. "If you really feel that way," she said, "maybe it's time you tried oils again."

She could feel him tense. "I'm not ready, and you know it."

"I don't know it." Her voice was gently chiding. "I'm taking only your word for it."

They sat together in thoughtful silence for a while, until Andrew finally said, "I might consider it if you'd come to Lisbon with me."

Kirsten perked up immediately. "Of course I'll come with you," she cried. Suddenly she couldn't stop hugging him or trying to cover every part of his body with kisses. But as soon as he told her the dates of the show, her heart sank. He saw the anguished expression on her face and braced himself for the worst.

"What's wrong?" he asked.

"I can't go. Markos will be here that week."

Andrew let out a groan. "Couldn't you ask him to come some other time?"

"It's too late. He already has his ticket, and as soon as he leaves here, he'll be going to Crete with his parents for a month."

"Well, that settles it then, I'm not doing the show."

"Oh, yes, you are. With me or without me, you're doing that show."

"Trying to get rid of me, wench?" He grabbed hold of her and started nuzzling the most ticklish part of her neck.

Kirsten began to squirm. "Me, trying to get rid of you?" she gasped between giggles. "Now, why would I do a thing like that?"

"I don't know," muttered Andrew from deep in her collarbone. "You tell me." But Kirsten was laughing too hard to tell him anything.

It took her another week of home-cooked meals and spectacular lovemaking, but she finally convinced Andrew to call Luis Castilho in Lisbon and tell him that he would mount the show.

38

When Markos arrived to spend the week with her, Kirsten was astounded at the difference the past year had made in him.

"How much did you grow?" she demanded, turning him around to examine him closely from every angle. "What happened to the boy I knew last summer?"

"He's gone," laughed Markos as he basked in her attention. He was extremely proud of the three inches he had grown since they last saw each other; it made him feel much more like the man he desperately wanted to be. "Now we'll see who's boss," he told her with a wide, self-satisfied grin.

"Oh, we will, will we?" she shot back at him. "In spite of your height, my dear young friend, I think age still wins out in that department."

"But I can take better care of you now that I'm taller than you are."

He looked so serious, so earnest, Kirsten had to laugh. "Do I really look that helpless?" She pinched his cheek affectionately. "I might be small, but you know what they say about small packages, don't you?"

"No, I don't." So she told him. "You Americans," he scowled. "You make jokes about everything."

"Only about things that matter, like the truth."

"There, you see, you did it again."

"You did it again," she mimicked, playfully mussing his hair with her fingertips. He promptly slicked his hair back into place. "Uh-oh." Kirsten shook her head in mock dismay. "All the signs are there," she said.

"What signs?"

"Adolescence." Markos's scowl deepened. "You know, the age when boys, excuse me, young men, don't like having their hair touched."

"Really, is that true?"

"So they tell me."

He watched a shadow pass over her face and knew exactly

what she was thinking. All the protective urges in him came rushing to the surface. He hurriedly changed the subject.

"The New Democracy Party's in trouble, did you know that?" Kirsten cleared her throat and said no. "My father says if an election were held tomorrow, Papandreou's socialists would probably win it." He chattered on for another few minutes about the current state of affairs in Greece, then motioned toward the shawl-draped piano in the living room. "I see you're still using it as a decoration," he remarked with just enough sarcasm to make Kirsten laugh appreciatively.

"Where else would I put my shawl?" He would never know how hard she had been working to try to disprove his statement. Catching sight of the bouzouki that he had left propped up against the side of his suitcase, she noted dryly, "And I see you're still carrying your own music around with you everywhere." It was true; the last time they were together, he and his bouzouki had been virtually inseparable.

To her amazement, Markos actually started to blush. "I've learned quite a few new songs in the past year. I thought you might like to hear them."

She had a mental image of this handsome young man down on one knee serenading her, and knew she wasn't far wrong. "I'd love to hear them," she said. "Now, how about a tour of the place?"

But he seemed distracted the whole time; she finally understood why when he asked, "Where are the paintings *he* did?"

"By *he*, you mean Andrew." Markos nodded. She pointed to the two watercolors that she had hung on a diagonal by themselves over a small curio cabinet, and Markos made a beeline for them.

He stood with his arms folded, his head tilted thoughtfully to the side, studying first one, then the other. He had come prepared to hate them, but he didn't; he couldn't. They were far too beautiful to hate. He couldn't even muster up any hatred for the sensitive man who had painted them. He let his breath out slowly. Perhaps his fears had been unfounded after all.

"So when do I get to meet this Andrew?" he asked.

"I really don't know."

"Oh?" His suspicions began to surface all over again.

"He's in Lisbon," she explained, "mounting a show at one of the art galleries there." The pride in her voice was unmistakable, but still he was wary. "So for now it's just you and me; that shouldn't be too much of a hardship, should it?" Markos shook his head. "Good, now that we're both agreed, why don't we get you unpacked? Then in an hour or so we'll go into town and have dinner. What do you say to some baked stuffed clams?"

Markos brightened. "At Gilao's?" She had told him all about the clams at Gilao's.

"If you like."

He nodded eagerly. Gone, temporarily at least, was the concern of the man; back again was the natural exuberance of the boy.

With Markos for company, Kirsten found the only time she truly missed Andrew was when she got into her empty bed at night. Their days were filled with laughter and happy chatter and a wonderful warmness. When they weren't out exploring the town and the surrounding countryside or swimming at the beach at Ilha de Tavira, they were sipping lemonade in her back garden and Markos was playing his bouzouki for her. They tried a different restaurant each evening for dinner; she taught him the Portuguese words for mussels (mexilhões), small clams (ameijoas), octopus (polvo), and a fish stew much like bouillabaisse (caldeirada), then watched with pride as he ordered for the two of them.

"Do they have any special wines in Tavira?" he asked one evening. "You know, like our retsina?"

"Lagoa," she told him. "It's the major regional wine of the Algarve."

"Could we order some?" When she hesitated, he gave her an imploring look. "Please? Retsina or Lagoa, what difference does it make, I always have retsina at home."

In the end she gave in.

The week flew by all too quickly. Before either of them realized it, they were on their last full day together. They spent the morning shopping at a street fair for gifts for Larissa and Alexandros, then, while Markos continued on his own, Kirsten returned home and began bottling the peach, pear, and ginger preserves she had made for him to take back to his parents. Her tiny kitchen smelled like a fruit orchard at harvest time, ripe and pungent and sweet. She hummed happily to herself while she worked, filling a number of small glass jars with preserves, then tying a different color ribbon around the neck of each one and looping it into a wide decorative bow.

She didn't realize there was someone else in the kitchen with her until a pair of man's arms grabbed her around the waist from behind. She let out a startled shriek and narrowly missed dropping the glass jar she was holding.

"Gotcha!" Andrew tightened his hold on her and leaned forward to kiss her on the neck. "Something smells good in here, and I don't mean the preserves," he whispered in her ear. Turning her slowly in his arms, he kissed his way around to her mouth.

All the questions she wanted to ask him dissolved in the heat of his embrace. Each time she tried to speak, he silenced her with another deep, searching kiss.

"Andrew, I—"

"Later," he urged her.

"But I want to know how—"

"Shh, not now."

There was plenty of time to tell her what an exhilarating experience it had been, plenty of time to tell her he had sold every one of his watercolors and had gotten orders for more, plenty of time to tell her the only thing missing through it all had been her. But right now all he wanted to do was make love to her.

Scooping her up in his arms, he carried her into the bedroom and laid her across her bed. Eager fingers worked at unbuttoning her blouse while his lips followed, burning a path from the base of her throat to the warm, sweet valley between her breasts. Kirsten moaned and arched her back to get as close to him as she could. He was just about to ease her out of her skirt when she let out a gasp and sat up, clutching her opened blouse.

"Markos!"

"My God, I forgot all about him." Andrew watched as she hastily did up her blouse and straightened her skirt. "Where is he?"

"I left him at one of the street fairs, but he should be back any minute now."

Reluctantly Andrew got up and went to check himself out in the mirror. As much as he wanted to meet Kirsten's little Markos, he still wished they could have timed things better.

Having expected a boy, he was totally unprepared for the self-assured young man with the physical beauty of a young

Greek god to whom he was introduced only moments later. And as the two of them shook hands, he found himself again regretting that he had given up painting portraits.

Kirsten stood back and just watched them size each other up. If the moment hadn't been such a sensitive one, she would have burst out laughing. There they were: Andrew, the great golden bear of a man; and Markos, the slim golden youth, facing each other like adversaries ready to go to war over the honor of the fair maiden. But before they could, she placed a hand on either of their shoulders and suggested they go outside into the garden.

"Just let me finish off in here," she said, indicating the preserves she still had to bottle, "then I'll make some lemonade and come join you."

"Let me help," both Andrew and Markos offered simultaneously.

Kirsten fought hard to keep a straight face. "I think I can manage by myself, thanks. And since you two don't have very much time to become acquainted, I suggest you get started." Andrew and Markos exchanged wary glances. "Go on."

She covered her mouth with her hand to stifle a laugh as she watched them both trying to fit through the narrow doorway at the same time. Andrew stepped aside graciously, deferring to Markos. But Markos, with a defiant gleam in his amber eyes, insisted Andrew go first. Age before beauty, Kirsten couldn't help noting with a loud crow of pent-up laughter the moment they were safely out of earshot.

She knew she was dawdling, but she wanted to give them as much time alone together as possible. She didn't quite know why; it was just something she felt she had to do. Suddenly it seemed very important to her that the two golden men in her life get to know and like each other. She kept peering at them through the kitchen window, watching with interest as their body language gradually began to change. Before long they were both leaning toward each other in their chairs instead of away, and she felt her eyes growing misty.

The three of them had dinner together that evening at Gilao's, where they all had the baked stuffed clams and shared a bottle of Lagoa among them. The conversation flowed back and forth with the kind of happy ease that usually comes only with time, and Kirsten could tell from the looks they kept getting from the other diners that everyone considered them to be the perfect family. She, of course, knew better. What they really were was a family out on loan, and only for this one night.

Markos left for Athens on board a noon flight the next day, and Andrew looked every bit as stricken by his departure as Kirsten was. When he embraced the boy and said good-bye to him, it could have been a father embracing his son, and Kirsten witnessed what was happening between them with a rising lump in her throat. Finally it was her turn. She hugged Markos until her arms ached, then she took his face in her hands and kissed him fiercely on both cheeks.

"I'll be back next year," he assured her as his eyes began to fill. "Maybe I'll even stay for two weeks instead of one."

"I'd like that."

"Do you think Andrew would?"

"You'll have to ask him."

"I already did." Through his tears Markos was grinning broadly. "He's promised to take me sailing on his boat."

Although Kirsten was careful not to say anything, her stomach muscles contracted with a sharpness that was undeniable.

After one last kiss Markos was gone, and her entire body began to ache with loneliness. Andrew came over and put his arm around her shoulders. She tensed when she first felt his touch, then slowly relaxed again. Next year was still a long way off; a lot could happen in a year.

Andrew kissed the top of her head and gave her shoulders a squeeze. "Markos adores you, as if you didn't know," he said with a tinge of wistfulness in his voice. "And he left me with some pretty specific instructions as to your proper care and handling. Don't laugh. That boy means business. If he were ten years older, I'd be looking at him as the competition."

Kirsten's heart lifted. She was beginning to feel all giggly and flirtatious. "I wouldn't worry if I were you." She slipped her hand into the back pocket of his jeans and gave his right buttock a pinch. "You don't have any competition."

Don't I, he thought unhappily to himself. But his rising desire quickly pushed the thought away. "What do you say we get out of here," he whispered with a kiss on the mouth for emphasis, "and pick up where we left off yesterday?"

39

Lois Holden could breathe again.

She tucked the small metal inhalator back into the pocket of her black velvet hostess gown and rearranged herself on the beige and white striped moiré love seat in her sitting room. If there was anything she detested, it was fighting, especially with her closest friend, and over a matter that was none of her concern. Or shouldn't have been. But then, she supposed the ties of family were stronger then the bonds of friendship, and that it did give Dierdre some rights.

"If Jeffrey ever found out about what you've been doing all year, he'd . . ." Dierdre paused and allowed the thought to dangle between them unfinished.

"He'd what?" Lois prodded. But Dierdre didn't answer; she just took another sip of her coffee. "I'll tell you what he'd do, nothing, because there's nothing he can do. If Jeff doesn't take lessons from me, he'll take them from somebody else. What do you think he did before he started coming to me; he only went through every half-decent piano teacher in Wallingford." She laughed with secret delight at her victory over all those other teachers. She had him now. He was hers, hers to shape and to mold. And he was the way she would finally pay Kirsten Harald back for all the years she had spent dying in her shadow. She, Lois Eldershaw Holden, would see to it that the son supplanted and then surpassed the mother. What rapture! What sweet revenge!

Dierdre set her cup and saucer down on the small marquetry table next to her, patted both corners of her mouth with her napkin, and said, "I still can't believe he'd go to the trouble of having someone drive him all the way here every Saturday just to take a two-hour piano lesson from you."

"When you want the best, you make every effort to get the best," was Lois's huffy reply. Dierdre rolled her eyes. "You don't know the first thing about genius, do you, Dee? Oh, don't look at me like that. He *is* a genius. If you thought Kirsten Harald was great, you should hear him. Jeffrey made a big mistake when he tried to keep Jeff from playing the piano. All he did was alienate the boy. It was a big mistake," she repeated, "possibly even a fatal one."

Hackles rose on the back of Dierdre's neck; it could have been Kirsten speaking. "Don't you think you're becoming a bit too involved in all this?" she asked, phrasing the question as tactfully as she could.

"What do you mean by 'too involved'?"

"I mean"—Dierdre gave her napkin a flick—"he's not your son or anything, yet you talk about him as if he were."

Lois bit her lip and looked down at her hands. "He could have been my son."

"Oh, Lois, I'm sorry." Dierdre was instantly contrite. "I didn't say it to be hurtful, it's just that I'm so concerned about you."

Lois sighed. Dierdre was the only one she had ever told about Alec. He had had mumps as a teenager and it had left him sterile—a fact he had carefully concealed from her until they had already been married for years and his position in her life was secure. "I appreciate your concern, Dee, I really do," she said. "But you needn't worry, I'm not afraid of Jeffrey." To her dismay, her eyes were beginning to fill. "Every minute I spend with Jeff is more than worth it. He's awesome, truly awesome; and what he does with that piano is nothing short of miraculous. I'd risk the wrath of God himself just to be able to say that I had a hand in shaping him."

Stunned by her friend's vehemence, all Dierdre could manage was a muted, "I understand."

But Lois shook her head. "No, you don't," she said, "you don't understand at all. You couldn't, because you've never had a dream."

"Who ever heard of playing blind man's bluff at Christmas?" Kirsten complained as Andrew led her by the hand along what felt like a bumpy wooden bridge. "I thought it was reserved strictly for birthdays."

"I decided not to wait that long."

"For what?"

"You'll see."

"That's the problem, I wish I could see."

Andrew laughed. "You've been such a good sport up to now, just hold on a bit longer, we're almost there."

"Where?" The scarf he had tied over her eyes had grown damp and was making her skin itch.

"If I told you, I'd be defeating the whole purpose of the game, now, wouldn't I?"

"Hmmph," was her only answer to that.

"Watch your step here," he warned her. "Better still, I'll carry you."

She felt herself being lifted into the air and set down gently on a wooden floor that seemed to be moving beneath her feet.

With a flourish Andrew whisked off the scarf and swept her a low bow. "Welcome to my floating home, m'lady. As your captain, I'm here to do your bidding." He straightened up smartly, snapped her a mock salute, then promptly added, "But only for today, mind you, because it's Christmas."

Kirsten was stunned. She rubbed her eyes as much to clear them as to convince herself she wasn't dreaming, then took her first curious peek at the one place that had always been off limits to her. She had been starving for details of his boat for so long now that whatever she saw, she instantly devoured. The dark oak-paneled walls and highly polished wood plank floors. The gleaming brass fittings and globe-shaped hurricane lamps. The framed maps and antique compasses he had used for decoration. The bunks, chairs, and portholes covered in matching green and blue plaid. The narrow, compact galley.

She walked gingerly, hands at her sides, wanting to touch everything yet holding back for fear of breaking something that didn't belong to her. With each careful step she took, her curiosity diminished and her discomfort increased. It was difficult to shake the feeling that she was less a guest than a trespasser in a world that had heretofore belonged only to Andrew and his memories. Turning to him with a painful catch in her throat, she asked him why he had decided to show her his boat now. And he answered simply, "Because it was time."

Taking hold of her hand, he guided her slowly through the rest of the boat. But even with him walking so close by her side, she still felt uncomfortably like an interloper. Marianne herself may never have set foot on the boat her husband had named in her memory, yet she was everywhere. In the dozens of framed photographs he kept of her. In the wool tapestries she had woven, the ceramic pots she had thrown, the hand-dipped candles she had made. But nowhere was she more in evidence than in the breathtaking family portrait that hung like an icon on the wall in the main cabin. The moment Kirsten saw it, she thought of Daphne du Maurier's haunting novel *Rebecca*. Then she thought of making love to Andrew under the watchful gaze of his dead wife and immediately began to shake.

She couldn't get off the boat fast enough.

Although Andrew never knew the reason for Kirsten's abrupt departure, he realized it was going to take more than just coaxing to get her back to the boat again—it was going to take time. And he was right. It took nearly a month before he was finally able to convince her to go sailing with him one afternoon. But no sooner had they left the shelter of the harbor for the open sea than he began to question his choice of afternoons. Clouds were banking in the northwest, the wind was picking up, and as plumes of seawater began arcing through the air, he realized he had never stopped to ask Kirsten what sort of sailor she was.

He needn't have worried. She was witnessing nature about to throw a tantrum and she was fascinated. Every sensation was a heightened experience for her: the force of the wind lashing at her hair and tearing at her clothes, the sting of saltwater on her face and tongue, the smell of sulphur from the gathering thunderheads. Throwing back her head, she took a long, deep breath of the moist, tangy air and flung her arms out to welcome whatever surprise the elements had in store for them.

"You'd better get below," Andrew shouted above the crackling of the sails and the howl of the wind. But Kirsten shook her head. "Don't be so stubborn, I don't want you washing overboard."

"You'd save me," she shouted back as she got a tighter grip on the metal railing that skirted the stern.

"How can you be so sure?"

"I know you."

Whatever he said next was lost in a ripple of low, growling thunder. As she watched him at the wheel, steering the boat he loved through jagged pyramids of foam-topped waves, she recalled what he had once said about his ongoing war with Poseidon, and felt a surge of desire inside her. With his blond hair and beard slicked down with seawater, the muscles in his arms straining, his big body taut and his long legs spread for better balance, he was a man more than nobly equipped to battle the gods and win.

As if reading her mind, Andrew glanced back over his shoulder at her and grinned. "I told you Poseidon was an ornery one, didn't I?"

"Do you think there's a message in this somewhere?"

"What kind of message?"

"You know, the kind of message that says I should stay away from your boat from now on."

Andrew laughed. "Don't worry, we'll find some way to appease him."

"And what would you suggest?"

"A sacrifice might help."

With that he tugged the wheel sharply to the right to meet a menacing wave head-on. They sliced through it cleanly, but a sheet of blue-gray water separated itself from the body of the wave and washed onto the deck with a belligerent roar. There was no more talking after that.

Wave upon wave hurled itself at the small boat, assaulting it, battering it and threatening to overturn it, but Andrew's grip was steady, his sense of direction sure. With Kirsten as his resolute and admiring witness, he continued to guide the *Marianne* through the tumultuous sea in as straight a course as he could manage. They plunged from one dark trough to another, emerging only to scale some new ragged peak before catapulting downward all over again. It was an exhilarating seesaw of a ride, with spears of rain slashing away at them the whole time and chilling them to the bone.

But as they neared the harbor, some of the bluster went out of the sea god's fight and the waters began to grow calmer again. Teeth chattering, her body cold and trembling, Kirsten nestled close to Andrew while he steered the boat back to its mooring. After all the excitement of their unexpected adventure, she was beginning to feel strangely let down, and she could tell by his expression that he was feeling the same way.

"What do you say to a nice hot shower?" he asked her.

"I say yes."

She started for the steps, only to have him catch her by the wrist and haul her back again.

"How about a kiss first?"

"I think it can be arranged." With a gentle tug she brought his face down closer to hers.

Their mouths met and they could taste the salt on each other's lips and tongue. They deepened their kiss and suddenly they couldn't seem to break it. Finally Andrew scooped Kirsten up into his arms and carried her down the steep, narrow wooden steps to his cabin.

They forgot about their shower; and as Andrew began to make love to her, Kirsten even forgot about the portrait.

After that, she accompanied him on most of his voyages, and it wasn't long before she came to look upon the *Marianne* as her second home. In September they took their longest trip ever—to Casablanca, Tangier, and Tunis—returning to Tavira one evening just as the sun was beginning to set.

"Do you ever think of keeping this up forever?" Andrew asked, his tone part serious, part playful, as he wound a strand of Kirsten's silvery hair around his finger.

"Keeping what up," she replied, her own tone lightly teasing, "sailing the globe as the Flying Dutchman's lady?"

"Why not?"

"You know why not." Yet, listening to the gentle sound of the waves slapping against the hull of the boat, she wished there was no "why not." How simple it would be to say yes to him. But saying yes to Andrew would mean saying no to her music and to Jeff and to the dream that still burned at the very core of her being. "You could always come back to New York," she suggested. She heard him groan. "There are plenty of places you could sail all along the eastern seaboard—Long Island Sound, Nantucket, the Cape—"

"Too cold."

"The Carolinas—"

"Still too cold."

"The Keys." When he didn't comment, she continued. "The Caribbean. See, the list is endless."

"Hah!"

"Just give me one good reason why not."

He pushed himself to his feet, turned, and leaned over the back railing of the boat. "You know why not."

Kirsten gazed up at the star-filled sky. "What would you call this?" she spoke softly, focusing on the Pleiades, but directing her question at Andrew. "A stalemate or check-mate?" Whether or not he had heard her, her question went unanswered.

She shivered. The night air was cold and getting colder. She allowed her eyes to sweep the hills overlooking the harbor and pretended she could see her own little house huddled among all the others in the darkness. After having been gone a month, she was surprised at how much she missed it.

"Come," said Andrew, intruding upon Kirsten's thoughts, "I'll take you home." She seemed a bit taken aback.

"The moment we arrive, all safe and sound, you can't wait to get rid of me, I see." She was trying to make a joke of it, but it wasn't working. Andrew's expression was unusually grim. She immediately became alarmed. "Is something wrong?" she asked.

"No, nothing. I'm just tired, that's all."

Standing up, she locked her arms around his waist. "Wouldn't you like me to stay and put you to bed?"

He returned her hug but said, "Not tonight."

She pulled away from him, stung, and went below to pack.

"Did you know they have a nickname for you in town now?" Andrew sounded more like himself as he helped Kirsten off the boat and onto the dock. "They call you La Branca."

"The white one?"

"Catchy, don't you think?"

"La Branca." Kirsten tried it out herself, rolling the "r" dramatically as she spun the two words off her tongue. "I like it," she said, "but I think I'd like La Prada even more."

"The silver one, sure, why not?"

"And at today's prices, I'd be worth a small fortune."

"Aha! I knew it." Andrew was laughing as he flagged down the only visible taxicab on the entire waterfront. "You've been sneaking looks at the newspapers again."

"Sometimes the urge to know what's going on in the outside world is completely overwhelming." She pretended to swoon and fell backward into his lap in the taxi. He held her in his arms all the way up the hill to her house, but as soon as he saw her to the door, he turned to leave.

"I suppose I couldn't lure you inside with the promise of a glass of strawberry brandy or a cup of hot chocolate?" Kirsten asked, trying hard to keep the tremor out of her voice.

"If I came in, I'd only stay."

"And we can't have that, now, can we?"

"Kirsten, please. I'm bushed, all I want to do right now is sleep." He kissed her long and hard on the mouth, then bounded down the steps and up the path.

Kirsten stared after him with tears in her eyes and panic

churning up waves inside her. Was it her imagination, or had there been something very final about that kiss?

Despite what he said, Andrew didn't get to sleep at all. He spent most of the night alternating between pacing his cabin and pacing the deck. The restlessness was back again; the same twitchy feelings that had had him jumping out of his skin the night he and Kirsten had gone out for their first dinner together. He thought of the question he had asked her tonight and winced. What had possessed him? Had he been testing her or testing himself? Asking her if she had ever considered keeping this up forever. And if she had said yes, then what?

True, there had been times during the trip when he had fantasized about the two of them sailing off into an endless series of sunsets together, yet there had been other times when he had felt stifled by all the closeness. He had never shared his boat with anyone for so long before. Only with memories. And they didn't take up very much space. But having Kirsten on board for a month had changed everything.

It had left no room for *him*.

The memory of Marianne and the reality of Kirsten had combined to crowd him out and cram him into a small, airless corner. For the first time in his life he had known how it felt to be claustrophobic.

All he wanted now was to get his space back again.

The next morning Kirsten woke up to find that a letter had been slipped under her front door. With her heart in her mouth, she tore it open and read:

My beautiful La Branca,

When I said I was tired, I meant it; I still am. When I said I needed sleep, I meant that too; I still do. But what I need even more right now is time. Time to myself, time to be on my own awhile, time to have time, if that makes any sense.

We've been as close as a single heartbeat for so long now, I sometimes wonder if my heart even remembers how to beat on its own. I think it's something I have to find out. And when I do, I'll be back. No matter what, I *will* be back. I promise.

Andrew

She didn't believe it; she refused to believe it. She had to see for herself.

The harbor looked exactly the same. It sounded the same, smelled the same, even felt the same. Boats were bobbing about at anchor. Sea gulls were circling. Fishermen were emptying their bulging nets onto the docks. Mackerel and cod and sardines were being piled into high slippery silver pyramids. She heard the screeching of the gulls and the laughter of the men. She smelled the salt of the sea and the stench of the dying fish. She felt the heat of the sun on her face and the coolness of the breeze in her hair.

Yet she saw, heard, smelled, and felt nothing.

It was true. The *Marianne* really was gone.

Andrew was gone. Again.

She had been right about the kiss; he *had* been kissing her good-bye.

He had promised to come back. Again.

She went back to the harbor twice a day for the next four days. Then she stopped going. Instead, she took out a large detailed map of the world and scanned it for places she had never been before. It had to be someplace exotic—like Fiji or Burma or Thailand or Samoa. Or perhaps even the Galápagos. What was it Andrew had once said about pulling a Gauguin? She traced a line from Tahiti to the Marquesas Islands, then back to Tahiti again. And thought to herself, why not?

She felt better than she had in five days. Exhilarated even. There was nothing like the anticipation of a trip, the promise of some far-off adventure, to start the adrenaline flowing again. And to put the pain in its proper place—at least temporarily.

Changing her clothes, she set out for town, but more specifically for the post office to use the telephone. One call and she would as good as be on her way. She was humming a lively mazurka out loud, when she heard someone call her name. It was Antonio Zenha, one of the clerks at the post office, and he was waving an ominous-looking yellow envelope in his hand. The melody caught in her throat and died.

"Senhora Harald!" The man was practically panting by the time he caught up with her. His swarthy face was running with sweat and the top of his bald head glowed red in the sun. "I am on my way to your house when I see you. Here, Senhora, is telegram for you."

She stared blindly at the envelope in her hand for what felt like forever. Then she forced her resistant fingers to pull out the folded cable and open it. She tried telling herself that a telegram didn't necessarily mean bad news; it could just as easily be something good. Maybe it was from Andrew, letting her know he had changed his mind about leaving and was on his way back. Maybe it was from Scott, telling her they had won their latest appeal, or that Meredith's killer had finally been caught. Maybe it was from Larissa and Alexandros, saying Markos was coming to Tavira for a surprise visit.

Maybe, maybe, maybe. Too many maybes. But at least the maybes were safe, safer than knowing for certain.

She glanced at the cable quickly, and just managed to make out Scott's name printed on a single strip of white tape before she glanced away again. She didn't know whether she was disappointed or relieved. But whatever she was, she knew she had to put an end to her ordeal.

Drawing a full breath, she forced herself to look closely and carefully at the piece of yellow paper that was rapidly turning soggy in her damp hand. At first nothing she read penetrated. Not one of the bold black printed words went any farther than her eyes. She read the entire message through to the end, then read it over again. By the third reading the words finally succeeded in reaching her brain.

She wasn't aware of having walked home. It was only when she heard the front door close with a click behind her that she even realized where she was. She looked for her arms and found them wrapped around her waist. She discovered, at the same time, that she was doubled over.

"*No!*" She screamed her denial into the room. "No, no, no, no, no!"

When the tears began, they swallowed up the screams.

Another of her life's supports was gone. Like her parents and Natalya. Once again she felt she was off balance, confused, lacking all sense of direction.

The boy of the streets had died in the street. In the middle of Fleet Street to be precise, with the empire he had built all around him.

Eric Sheffield-Johns was dead.

40

It was like taking a giant step back in time as Kirsten slowly mounted the steps of the Church of St. Martin-in-the-Fields in Trafalgar Square. Behind her dark glasses her eyes were red and swollen, and in spite of her tan, she looked pale and drawn. She was wearing a simply cut black wool coat; a heavy black lace mantilla covered her hair. With her head carefully bowed, she slipped into the last row of wooden pews and clasped both hands under her chin in silent prayer.

Oh, Eric, she whispered to the man who had been a second father to her and whom she had adored with all her heart. *Eric, my dearest Eric, I can't believe I've lost you too.* Then, as she had a thousand times in the last eight years, she begged him to forgive her for having kept silent, for having kept her whereabouts a secret, even from him.

Peering cautiously at the hundreds of people streaming into the church to pay their last respects to Eric today, she couldn't help but think how he would have loved it, the spectacle of it all, and all of it for him. The mourners were representative of the many different worlds Eric had touched and influenced during his lifetime; politics, publishing, the arts, business, fashion, photography. She recognized almost all of them; she herself had known most of them.

Would Michael be here, she wondered. And if he were, would Roxanne be with him? She wanted to know, yet she didn't want to know. Bringing her clasped hands up to her mouth, she leaned into them and closed her eyes.

She remained seated that way all through the service and through the numerous lengthy eulogies that followed, hearing the words being spoken, but not really listening to them. She was lost somewhere in another time, when Eric Sheffield-Johns had loomed so large and so important in her young life. There was a wistful smile on her face as she relived each precious moment they had shared together, some of them so vivid, they might have happened only yesterday.

She waited until the church was nearly empty, then got up

and walked slowly down the aisle toward the main altar. It didn't seem possible that the man with the mischievous wink and wry wit could be lying silent and still inside this flower-draped bier. She touched a small, exposed corner of the ebony casket and imagined she was touching a bit of Eric instead. Recalling what Horatio said to the dead Hamlet in the first play of Shakespeare's that Eric had ever given her to read, she thought of how appropriate it was, and repeated the words out loud to him now: "Good night, sweet prince, and flights of angels sing thee to thy rest."

Bending down, she kissed the cool wood of the casket, then stepped back again and removed her dark glasses to wipe her eyes. A muted squeaking sound caught her attention. She turned to see a tall woman in a navy blue wool cape pushing a wheelchair across the floor. Kirsten's eyes widened in horror.

"My God, Claudia!"

The wheelchair squeaked to a stop.

"I beg your pardon, mum."

Kirsten barely heard the woman, all she could hear was a loud drumming inside her head as she stared at the wreckage of Claudia Sheffield-Johns.

Her fine white hair was drawn back into a bun at the nape of her neck. Her face was so pale as to be almost transparent; her skin was tracked with a hundred delicate lines, and her eyes were faded and vacant. Dressed all in black, her thin frame now skeletal, she would have looked like the harbinger of death itself had the slight fixed smile on her otherwise impassive face not lent her features the innocence of a fallen angel.

"Claudia?" The name was a puff of wind hanging in the still air of the deserted church.

"She can't hear you, mum," said the woman in the cape.

Without taking her eyes off Claudia's face, Kirsten asked, "How long has she been like this?"

"Since before I came to Wynford, I'm told."

"Wynford?"

"Yes, mum, Wynford." The woman's smile was tolerant. "I've been there myself nearly two years now. But they say she was like this some years before that."

"Wynford." Kirsten kept repeating the name disbelievingly. "I'm sorry," she said, "I don't understand."

"Wynford, mum, you know, the home up in Wiltshire."

When she realized that Kirsten didn't know, she explained. "It's a rest home, mum, bought by Mr. Sheffield-Johns himself several years back. They say it was one of the grandest estates in Wiltshire in its day. Now it's far and away the finest rest home thereabouts. For them's can afford it, mind you," she confided with a sly nod.

Kirsten stood there stunned. So Eric had finally kept his word; he had finally managed to buy Wynford for Claudia. Fresh tears welled in her eyes at the tragic irony of it all. Claudia had come home to Wynford at last, and would probably never know it.

The woman seemed impatient to be off. Claudia hadn't moved, hadn't so much as blinked the entire time the two of them had been standing there talking. Before she could stop herself, Kirsten leaned down and planted a gentle kiss on the withered forehead of the woman who had been both friend and betrayer to her, then watched as she was wheeled away out of sight and out of her life forever.

She was just slipping her dark glasses back on when she sensed someone behind her. Michael! She whirled around expectantly, her lips parting in a smile.

"You are Kirsten Harald, are you not?" Her smile froze. The man was a stranger to her. Short and stocky, with snapping blue eyes and thinning brown hair, he was conservatively dressed in a three-piece charcoal gray business suit and carried a black homburg.

"Yes," she answered somewhat guardedly, "I'm Kirsten Harald."

"Now, that's a bloody relief." She expected him to take out a handkerchief and mop his sweaty brow next, but he wasn't sweating, and she saw no evidence of a handkerchief anywhere. "I am Godfrey Montague of the firm of Montague and Smythe, solicitors. My card." He deftly snapped a business card of heavy ivory vellum at her and continued. "I am the executor of the estate of the late Eric Sheffield-Johns." He allowed a moment for his card and his announcement to penetrate. "If you hadn't appeared here today, we would have been rather hard-pressed to know what to do next. As it was, I bloody nearly missed you." He indicated the lace mantilla covering her hair. "I have something for you, Miss Harald, a letter." From the inside breast pocket of his jacket he withdrew a long, slim white envelope. Kirsten's heart twisted as she recognized Eric's handwriting. "If you'll be so good as to come round to our offices at nine tomorrow morning, I'll have all the necessary papers ready for your signature." Setting his hat on his head, he tapped the brim lightly with his forefinger. "Good day to you, Miss Harald. And," he added as an afterthought, "my most sincere condolences."

Kirsten sank weakly into a pew to read what Eric had written her only a month before his death.

Kirsten dearest,

My greatest sorrow is knowing I shall never see you again. My greatest joy has been loving you like the daughter I never had.

If life is a series of wrongs committed and wrongs redressed, then let me, in Claudia's name, redress a terrible wrong. If it is also a series of beginnings and endings, then let me, in my own name, provide you with the opportunity to begin.

Suffice it to say, lamb, that I know. I finally discovered (thanks to Claudia's occasional moments of lucidity these last years and her own meticulous records) how grievously you were wounded. That we could have given so freely with one hand while snatching it all back with the other is a shame I shall carry with me to my grave.

I am, therefore, begging your forgiveness, and asking that you accept as proof of our eternal devotion to you, the town house in Belgravia.

A separate trust has been established for its care and maintenance for as long as you choose to keep it.

Use the house, Kirsten, use it to begin at the beginning again. Then take that glorious gift God gave you back to the world. It has gone without far too long.

I kiss you, Kirsten dearest, and embrace you with all my heart.

Adieu—
Eric

The letter fluttered to the floor. Kirsten put her head in her hands and began to weep. So in the end Eric had known, and he had left her the town house as recompense. While she had been begging his forgiveness, he had been begging hers.

Begin at the beginning again? Could she? Would being in London, where it had all begun for her once before, make

the difference? She could count the remaining years of her
exile on the fingers of one hand now. Was it possible? Could
she who never believed in miracles believe in them now?

She walked from the church in a daze. It was only as she
started across Trafalgar Square that she realized she hadn't
seen Michael at the service after all.

"Roxanne?"

Her eyelids fluttered open and she smiled. "Sorry, darling,
I must have dozed off."

Michael brushed a strand of auburn hair back from his
wife's forehead and kissed her just above her left eyebrow.
Would she lose that beautiful thick hair of hers once the
chemotherapy started, he wondered. The thought of it made
him queasy, and he hastily bent down and kissed her again.

"My poor, brave love," he whispered, his voice breaking as
he continued to stroke her hair and kiss her.

Not so brave, thought Roxanne, not so brave at all. It was
happening just as she once predicted it would. Bit by bit
they had stripped her of her womanhood. First her breasts,
now her uterus and ovaries. What else was left?

"They buried Eric yesterday," he told her.

"You should have been there," she said, gazing up at him
with her clear green eyes. He shook his head.

"I had far more important things to do." He cracked a
smile and she smiled back. But a moment later his composure slipped; his eyes filled with tears. "Oh, Roxanne." He
buried his face in the warm, smooth crook of her neck and
wept while she held him.

When he finally pulled away, he felt slightly embarrassed.
Of all the times for him to break down in front of her. He
wiped his eyes and blew his nose, then went to stand at the
window with his back to her. The day was appropriately
bleak, a typical October day, overcast and lit by a dull silver
light. The wind flattened a dried russet-colored leaf against
the window, then flicked it away again. It all seemed so
effortless. Like dying. One good, strong gust and . . . death.
Everything reminded him of death these days.

"I should have canceled tomorrow's concert in Dallas," he
said, his back still turned to her.

"Nonsense, I'm fine," said Roxanne from the bed. "Besides, you'll be gone only those two days."

Michael sighed and pressed his forehead against the win-

dowpane. It felt cool and soothing compared with the over-
heated hospital room. He thought of the trip ahead of him
and sighed again. Another airport, another plane, another
hotel room. God, he was getting tired of it all.

They had been warned to expect her.

The butler's name was Tobin now, the chauffeur's Hughes.
Nella was the housekeeper, Yvonne the cook, Patricia the
only downstairs maid and Jean the upstairs maid. But other
than the staff, nothing about the house itself had changed.
Kirsten handed Tobin her coat, purse, and gloves, then started
on a slow tour of the house she had called home for one of the
most important and exciting years of her life. As she went
from room to room, she was once again that gauche and naive
girl from Ninth Avenue seeing its splendor for the first time.
All wide-eyed and innocent, eager to absorb everything around
her, and grow.

She was Alice coming home again to Wonderland.

Her mouth was dry as she climbed the stairs to the
third-floor flat. She expected a faded and dusty mausoleum,
cobwebs heavy in the corners of each room, drapes closed
against the light, white sheets covering the furniture, the
smell of mold and disuse in the air. But that wasn't what she
found.

At first she thought she was hallucinating. She blinked her
eyes once, twice, then a third time.

"It can't be," she said aloud.

But it was.

It was the same flat she had left twenty-six years before.
Somehow Eric had managed to find the same floral chintz
fabric Claudia had originally used, and used it again. The
rooms even smelled faintly of fresh paint—just as they had
then. Not a single detail was different. There were even pots
of fully blooming African violets on all the windowsills.

She floated through the rooms on gossamer wings, tears
spilling down her cheeks.

"Oh, Eric," she cried, her head thrown back and her arms
wide, "I accept your challenge. I *will* begin again here, I will,
I know I will."

She had saved the conservatory for last. It spread before
her, hushed and still, parquetry floors gleaming, everything
just the way she remembered it. The miniature trees. The
ebony concert grand. The glass case holding Michael's baton.

But something new had been added, something she had never seen: her signed copy of Claude Debussy's "Reflets dans l'Eau" in a simple sterling silver frame, hanging on the wall directly above the glass case.

Yes, here the magic would finally work, she was sure of it.

Andrew settled back in his chair on deck and poured himself another glass of wine. Gazing up at the stars overhead, he searched for a constellation to toast and decided on Hydra. As companions, the stars might have been less than ideal, but they did help to keep some of the loneliness at bay. He took a sip of his wine and watched as the stars in Hydra's formation shifted and rearranged themselves in a configuration resembling a woman's face. He put out his hand. Her features instantly dissolved and trickled through his fingers in a single shimmering stream.

He was anchored off Cadiz, and in the ten days since he had left Tavira, he had done nothing but sail and think. He hadn't even done any painting; he was too afraid any subject he tackled would find some way of turning into a woman's face, just as Hydra had. And if he happened to paint her face, so what, he asked himself for the hundredth time. What precisely would it mean, that by committing her face to paper, he was therefore committing himself to her?

He had told her he wanted time, but the time he had wanted so badly was now weighing heavily on his hands. All he could think about was her. As much as he had loved Marianne and his two daughters, what he had come to feel for Kirsten Harald transcended simple love. And that terrified him. There was too much need involved in his feelings. It left him open, at risk, and in danger of being mortally wounded. He had loved Marianne and lost her; he had loved his daughters and lost them too. He simply didn't want to love and lose again.

He spent the night tossing restlessly on his bunk, then got up shortly before dawn and brewed himself some coffee. He took his mug, his sketchpad, and several sticks of charcoal up on deck with him, and settled himself cross-legged on the hard plank floor. Squinting out at the rising sun, he commanded himself to capture exactly what he saw. His first strokes were tentative, shaky, and unsure, but as he regained his confidence, so did they. Stroke by stroke, page by page, he could feel a return of the freedom he felt had been so threatened. Each successive sketch he did was further proof of the one vital truth he had forgotten: that as long as he had his art, he would never lose his freedom.

An hour later he looked at what he had done. He was amazed, but hardly surprised. There wasn't a single sunrise in the lot. Every sketch was a sketch of her face.

The judge held up a pair of large brass scales. In one round pan was a stack of sheet music, in the other a hooded man.

"Choose," said the judge.

"I can't," she answered. Choosing one meant forfeiting the other. "I want them both."

The judge laughed. "You can't have them both. You must choose one of them."

"I don't want to choose, I want them both."

"That's what you said before, and look what happened. Now, choose!"

"No! I want them both!"

She woke up still saying, "I want them both."

For a moment she couldn't remember where she was. The African violets reminded her. Even after two weeks she still couldn't get used to waking up in her old bedroom in the house that officially belonged to her now. She still expected to find Claudia bustling about and chattering while she sat up in bed and had her first cup of tea of the day. She still expected to find Eric seated at the breakfast table, the usual stack of newspapers at his feet. She still expected it all to be exactly the way it used to be—even though she knew that was impossible.

Claudia was gone, Eric was dead. Of the three of them, she alone was left.

She smiled as she got up and got dressed. She was hardly alone here. The entire household revolved around her; the staff coddled her, worried and fussed over her. And she quite enjoyed it. She knew they all thought her strange, never leaving the house except for a brisk walk once a day to St. James's Palace and back, then spending the rest of her time closeted inside the conservatory trying to force the magic to work.

It hadn't worked yet, and she refused to leave London until it did.

This morning she went directly to the piano instead of stopping to have breakfast first. She was still feeling the aftereffects of her latest recurring dream. She knew all there was to know about the interpretation of dreams, yet she wondered if she might have purposely been overlooking some very basic truths in this newest one.

Sitting at the piano now, she cast her mind back over the dream and started sifting for clues. Then she began to free-associate. Her thoughts became increasingly more jumbled and confused. Her body started to tremble; her head began to pound. The truth was a gleaming object she had merely to bend down and pick up.

And the truth had to do with love.

Her mind balked. This wasn't the truth she had been looking for. But it was too late; she couldn't put it back now.

She heard Natalya warning her, drumming it into her over and over and over again. Stay away from love. Love detracts from music; it drains and depletes. It dilutes the dream. Stay away from love. And she had listened.

In pursuing her dream, she had ultimately forfeited love.

Jeffrey, during their entire marriage, had never once told her he loved her. Even Michael, in all the years she had known him, had never told her he loved her. And Andrew, whose love for his dead wife still held him in thrall, didn't want to love her.

But then, she herself had never been free to love either.

She, who always thought she had had it all, had never *really* had it all. She had been missing love and hadn't even known it. All these years she had been punishing herself for having had it all and failing, the same way she had been punishing herself for Meredith's death. She had used her music to keep her safe from love just as she had used her daughter's death to keep her from her music.

She was sobbing uncontrollably. For the first time in her life, she finally understood the true meaning of the word *all*.

And *all* was precisely what she intended to have one day.

Above her sobbing she could now hear another sound. Obviously one of the servants had turned on a radio. She looked down at her hands. Her shriek brought the entire staff running. Her hands—those two granite talons that had held her prisoner all these years—were moving. They were flesh and blood and they were moving across the keys.

"Americans," sniffed the butler.

"Artists," sighed the cook.

What the devil was there to cry about, pianos *were* for playing, were they not?

41

Kirsten was a woman reborn.

For the next six weeks she remained sequestered in the London town house rediscovering her music. With the sheet music Eric had bought, supplemented by what she went out and bought herself, she relearned every piece she had ever known and forgotten: every prelude, sonata, mazurka, scherzo, waltz, étude, fantasie, gavotte, and polonaise. Once she had those perfected, she tackled the concertos, beginning with Rachmaninoff's Second.

She stopped practicing only long enough to eat and sleep. She thought of nothing but her music during the day and dreamed of nothing else at night. After practicing on her own for the first two weeks, she invited the staff to become the first audience to hear her in over ten years. They were pleased and honored to oblige. At first she was as nervous as they were, but the nervousness passed quickly enough for all of them. Her seven o'clock recitals immediately became an established part of the household's daily routine; the servants even went so far as to give up their nights off so as not to miss a single performance.

She had Hughes scour the city's record shops—both new and used—for any old recordings of hers he could find. But he couldn't find any; they had long since become collector's items. She had nothing with which to compare herself, no yardstick by which to measure how she was playing against how she had played then. And so, in the end, she abandoned her search and relied solely on the one thing she had always relied on before: her instincts.

The days grew colder, and so did she. It was time she left; in a week it would be Christmas. That made her think of Andrew. They had met again three Christmases ago. What about this Christmas, she asked herself, then angrily brushed the question aside. For all she knew, Andrew Beaton had left Tavira for good.

She had Hughes buy a small canvas tote bag for her sheet

music, and packed reluctantly. The morning of her departure she took a quick tour of the house and bid a temporary farewell to each of the rooms individually. In the front hall, the entire staff had lined up to say good-bye to her, and there were tears in the eyes of each and every one of them. Blinking back her own tears, Kirsten went down the line slowly, shaking hands and kissing cheeks.

"Now, you'll remember to water the violets, won't you, Jean?" she asked. The upstairs maid bobbed her head. "But only from the bottom, and fertilize them every three weeks."

"I will, mum."

"And, Tobin, you'll remember to have the piano tuned once a month?"

"That I will, madam."

"Nella, you'll keep the rooms aired and you won't let anything get musty."

"No, mum, I won't."

"The humidity in the conservatory's very important, Patricia; you'll see it stays constant?"

"Yes, mum, I will."

"And, Yvonne, you won't forget to prepare those casseroles I asked for and store them in the freezer for me?"

"I've already begun, madame."

"Good, good." She nodded absently, her mind already on other things.

She felt that familiar catch in her throat as she watched Hughes carry her bags out to the car. Suddenly she didn't want to leave. She was afraid to leave. London had been her Lourdes; the magic had worked here. This was where the miracle had occurred.

What if the magic wouldn't work in Tavira? What if, by the time she got back, she couldn't play anymore?

"We'd best be leaving now, madam." Hughes was standing at her elbow, her airline ticket in his gloved hand.

"In a minute," she said.

She knew what she had to do. Hurrying back down the hallway, she burst into the conservatory and headed straight for the glass case that contained Michael's baton. She placed the palm of her right hand on top of the case like someone about to take an oath on the Bible.

"It won't be long now, Michael," she said in a soft and solemn voice, "I swear it."

* * *

In spite of her fears, the magic did work in Tavira; she was still able to play. Just as she had in London, she spent every hour of every day at the piano, stopping only to eat and sleep, then getting up to play again. Christmas came and went—and no Andrew. The smooth edges of her elation were beginning to fray. She missed him terribly. She began to dream about him at night, and at infrequent intervals during the day she would find herself gazing up at the two watercolors he had painted for her, and wonder where he was.

On New Year's Eve she decided to usher in the year nineteen eighty-one with a grand flourish. She even dressed for the occasion, putting on a white and silver embroidered peasant dress with a low, gathered neckline and flounced hem, and a pair of low-heeled silver sandals. She clipped a pair of silver and turquoise hoops to her ears and slid a half-dozen narrow silver and turquoise bangles onto each wrist. Then she frosted her eyelids silver, used a purple mascara on her eyelashes and a frosted mauve lipstick on her mouth.

"What a waste of feminine pulchritude," she told her reflection in the mirror. "Ah, well." She shrugged stoically, blew her mirror image a kiss, and went off to the kitchen to open the bottle of Mumm's she had brought with her from the duty free shop at Heathrow.

She took her glass of champagne out to the back garden and sat down on a wooden chair in the moonlight. The air was mild, slightly humid, and the stars in the clear night sky were as silver as the jewelry she was wearing. Sipping her champagne slowly, she stared up at the stars and thought only happy thoughts. Nineteen eighty-one would be a good year, she could feel it. She had gotten her music back. It wouldn't be long before she got her son back. The doors that had closed on her were beginning to open again. It was only a matter of time before she pushed them open all the way and reclaimed what was still rightfully hers.

She finished the glass of champagne, returned to the kitchen to refill it, and came back outside again. She was feeling slightly giddy now—light and bright and twinkly. She felt like the goddess of the moon . . . whatever her name was. She frowned and tried to think. Who *was* the Greek goddess of the moon?

"Selene."

Kirsten started. The glass slipped from her hand. She hadn't even realized she had asked the question aloud.

"Andrew!"

He had been standing there watching her for some time, too mesmerized to move. Her silvered beauty had been so much a part of the night, he hadn't dared move and break the spell. Until now, when she had spoken. He headed toward her, only to stop short when he saw her features clearly for the first time. The pain he felt was brief but devastating. The expression on her face was the same one he had captured when he had painted her portrait all those years ago. And he knew, in that one frozen moment, that he had already lost her.

Kirsten was standing there rigid, her arms at her sides. When her first impulse had been to rush to him and embrace him, her second was to stay right where she was and make him come to her.

"I shouldn't even be talking to you," she said, her voice a dusky whisper, when he was only inches away.

Andrew's smile was guarded. "Then don't talk, just let me look at you." He put out a hand to touch the side of her face. She moved her head. He let his hand drop.

"You ran away, you bastard," she told him through gritted teeth.

Andrew looked down at the ground. "Not a bastard so much as a coward," he admitted.

"And now?"

His answer to that was a shrug. "I came back, didn't I?" But that didn't satisfy her. "Kirsten, I came back because I decided I wanted to try living my life strictly for today instead of living it as a reaction to what happened yesterday. I've stopped looking for that guarantee of a lifetime of tomorrows. I want whatever's happening now to be what really matters. And I guess I was hoping you might feel that way too. Obviously, I was wrong." He turned to leave.

"Wait, please." She had never asked him for tomorrow. Their tomorrows had always been different. They had known it from the start, but they had started anyway. As far as she was concerned, nothing, absolutely nothing had changed. That made her sad. Yet it didn't stop her wanting him—for however long she could have him. She took a step forward, reached out, and touched his arm. It was like touching fire.

"Oh, God, Kirsten." He took her in his arms and kissed her with an intensity that consumed them both.

Then he carried her into the house and made love to her.

"Again," she sobbed, her body still thrusting in the dying moments of orgasm. "Oh, Andrew. Andrew, please, make love to me again."

And he did.

It was only afterward, as they lay sated and spent in each other's arms, that Kirsten noticed he was no longer wearing the gold chain with his wedding band on it around his neck.

"I have a surprise for you," he said, propping himself up on one elbow and looking down at her tenderly.

She could barely find her voice. "I have one for you too."

"You first," they said in unison, then burst out laughing. The tension that had begun building between them popped like a soap bubble. Andrew tugged on his jeans; Kirsten slipped into his shirt.

"I'll be right back." He bent down and kissed her lightly on the mouth.

"I'll be in the living room."

He found her seated at the piano, the only light in the room coming from two broad blue candles. He felt a clenching deep in his gut. So that was it; that was the reason for the expression on her face. As he walked toward her, holding up the large watercolor he had done of her and framed himself in a hand-carved silver-painted frame, she lowered her hands to the keys and filled the emotional silence with the joyous sound of sunlight dancing across the surface of a pond.

When she finished, neither of them spoke for a long time, then they both started speaking at once. Finally they talked in turns, and when they had talked themselves out, Kirsten poured the remains of the champagne into two crystal glasses and carried them into the living room.

"To art," proposed Andrew.

"To today," suggested Kirsten. She was leery of toasting art just yet, in case time turned out to be an Indian giver and snatched it all back.

The next time Kirsten went on board Andrew's boat, she found all traces of Marianne Beaton gone, except for the triptych, which was now hanging in the guest cabin. In its place in the main cabin hung a framed portrait of Kirsten,

one of the many Andrew had painted of her in the ten weeks
he had been gone. Although she was adamant about practicing eight hours a day, seven days a week, Andrew did manage to coax her away from the piano for the occasional trip. In
March they sailed to Majorca, in May to Sardinia, and in
June he actually got her away from the piano long enough for
them to sail to Sicily.

"Do you know I haven't heard from the Pallises in a while,"
Kirsten remarked to Andrew one evening as they were making dinner together in the narrow galley of the boat.

He nibbled thoughtfully on a carrot for a moment, then
said, "Instead of Markos coming to Tavira in July, why don't
we sail to Athens from here and surprise him? School should
be out by now, and we can take him back on the boat with
us. What do you think?"

"I think it's a terrific idea."

As excited as they were, they were anything but prepared
for what was awaiting them in Athens. As they walked from
the harbor, they were both shocked to realize how truly
isolated they had become from the rest of the world. It didn't
take them long to learn what had happened.

Throughout the spring, the country had suffered a series of
debilitating earthquakes. Tremors had even been felt in places
as remote as Epirus, Crete, and the Ionian islands. But the
worst of the quakes had had its epicenter in the Gulf of
Corinth. As a result, Athens had been the hardest hit. Scores
of people had been killed, hundreds injured, with damage
estimated in the millions.

"No wonder I haven't heard from them," Kirsten said,
clinging tightly to Andrew's hand as he helped her into a taxi.
"Something's happened to them, I know it, I just know it."
Her teeth were starting to chatter. "Markos." She whispered
his name and it caught in her throat. "Dear God, please let
him be safe, please, please, please."

Andrew thought of the golden-haired boy he had grown to
love and said nothing; he was too sick inside to say a word.

The city was still a pockmarked testament to the many
devastating blows it had sustained over the last four months.
The destruction was random—buildings lay in ruins beside
those still perfectly intact—as though some areas had been
specifically singled out for demolition, leaving others to survive virtually unscathed. As they skirted the base of the
Acropolis and continued northeast toward the pine-capped

Lykabettos, Kirsten's heart began to lift. Most of the streets were clear and only a few of the familiar landmarks they were passing had been damaged. Maybe there was reason for hope after all.

They rounded the corner and her heart plummeted. One glimpse of the vast mountain of bricks and wood and stucco that had been the five-story apartment building she had once lived in, and Kirsten would have collapsed if Andrew hadn't been holding on to her. With her sobbing convulsively in his arms, he directed the driver to take them to the main office of the International Red Cross.

All the time the records were being checked, Kirsten leaned up against Andrew for support and refused to let go of his hand. Even before the solemn-faced young woman in front of them could complete her search, Kirsten knew. A few minutes later the woman confirmed it.

"They're dead." Kirsten's frozen lips could barely form the words as she peered at the ledger and saw their two names for herself, written in the cramped scrawl of some faceless bureaucrat. Her knees buckled, and it was left to Andrew to ask the next question for her.

"What about Markos Pallis?"

The woman searched through her records again but could find no one by that name. As far as the Red Cross was concerned, fourteen-year-old Markos Andreas Pallis was neither officially dead, injured, or missing.

"Who would have reported him missing anyway?" Kirsten muttered on their way out of the office. "His parents are dead. He had no other family here in Athens."

"But what about relatives in some other part of the country?"

"As far as I know there *is* no family, Andrew, no family at all." She shook her head to force back the tears. "Years ago, Larissa made me promise that if anything ever happened to them, I would look after Markos. I promised her I would. Oh, Andrew, we've got to find him, we've simply got to."

A pattern was set after that.

They despaired in each other's arms aboard the *Marianne* at night and scoured the city hand in hand with renewed hope during the day. They visited hospitals and churches, youth shelters, schools, and hostels, questioning everyone they met and following up every possible lead. Then one of the priests they spoke with suggested they try the harbor.

"It's not unusual for many homeless children with no families to claim them to congregate there," the man insisted. "While it's true they must scavenge for food and shelter, they manage to survive surprisingly well. Some even band together to form small family groups of their own."

As shocking as the prospect was, Kirsten and Andrew took the priest's suggestion to heart; from then on they confined their search solely to the city's vast, sprawling waterfront. To Kirsten, every fair-haired person she saw was Markos, yet it never was. Each new day was as heartbreakingly frustrating as the one before. At the end of their second week of looking, they stopped to eat at a restaurant close to the harbor, but by then Kirsten's appetite was as diminished as her hope.

"Won't you even try some of the calamari?" Andrew held a forkful of the squid up to her mouth, but she shook her head. "One bite, that's all. Come on, Kirsten, you've got to eat something."

"Why?" She rested her chin in her hand and sighed. "I'm not hungry."

"Yes, you are; you're just too tired to notice."

She finally relented, opening her mouth like an obedient child, and began to chew on the squid without even tasting it. Andrew was just about to cajole her into eating some rice, when she suddenly pushed his hand away and sat up straight.

He was ambling down the street, headed their way, wearing sandals, a pair of torn gray trousers that were too short for him, and a soiled white shirt. His slow, shuffling walk was the walk of someone with no particular place to go. He had both hands in his pockets and his head was bowed, but from time to time he raised it to give the trash cans he passed a cursory glance.

Kirsten jumped to her feet, shouting. Andrew dropped his fork and started after her.

At the sound of his name the boy stopped, stared for a moment, then headed straight for Kirsten at a run.

She wrapped her arms around him and wouldn't let him go. Through her tears she kept hearing him whisper, "I knew you'd come, I knew you'd come," and she thought her heart would break. Her precious little man was no longer lost, no longer missing and unwanted. He was found now. He was here with her and Andrew, safe, and wanted, very, very much wanted.

"We didn't know," she told him as she went on hugging him. "We didn't know about the earthquake or your parents.

We're so sorry, my darling Markos, so very sorry. If we'd known, we would have been here sooner, believe me."

"I was at school when it happened." His voice was so muffled she could barely make out what he was saying. "They were working at home that day; they were supposed to give a seminar together at the university later in the week. If they'd been working at the library instead . . . if . . ." He broke off and couldn't go on.

Kirsten held him until his tears subsided, then gave him over to Andrew. As she watched the two of them embrace, she remembered how it felt to be part of a real family again.

42

"Do you think I'll ever be as tall as Andrew?" Markos asked Kirsten as he helped her set the table for dinner.

"At the rate you're growing, I wouldn't be at all surprised."

"I'm already taller than my father was." Markos put a wineglass in front of Andrew's place, then cocked his head thoughtfully to one side. "Do you know I sometimes have trouble remembering my father? It's as if Andrew's my father now and always has been. Is that bad?"

Kirsten assured him it wasn't. "It's simply time's way of healing the hurt you've suffered," she explained. "It's much easier to recover from the loss of someone you love by finding someone else to love. You haven't really forgotten your father, Markos, you're learning to live with the fact that he's gone. A part of you will always grieve for him, but at least your grief hasn't kept you from loving others. That's not bad, that's healthy."

Markos thought about it a moment, then gave her a warm smile. "I always feel so much better after I've talked to you," he said. "I only wish I could do something to help *you* grieve less."

"But you *have*," she insisted, "just by being here."

It was still something of a shock to think that eighteen months had passed since she and Andrew had discovered the homeless youth wandering the waterfront of Athens. Since then they had borne happy witness to his remarkable trans-

formation, seeing him change from a silent, brooding shadow
back into a laughing, robust young man again. Nurtured by
the deep and genuine love they both had for him, Markos
had grown and flourished; and together all three of them had
flourished as well. They had grown into the family they had
only appeared to be that first night at Gilao's—bound to one
another as naturally as any other family bound by blood.

Kirsten's little house was a happy home these days. The
second bedroom was Markos's now, and he alternated between it and the guest cabin on board the *Marianne*. Andrew
had bought him a new bouzouki, and it was a nightly ritual of
theirs for Markos and Kirsten to play duets together after
supper. Andrew had also been teaching him to sail and paint,
and they were both astounded at the natural aptitude he
showed for painting. There wasn't a wall in the house or
aboard the boat that didn't boast its own Markos original
now.

The situation was idyllic in many ways, but hardly perfect.
There were arguments as in any other household, the inevitable clash of wills, the jockeying for position, the balking
against authority. When he wanted to, Markos could be a
superb manipulator, playing Kirsten and Andrew against each
other with devilish delight. Those were the times they invariably rolled their eyes and uttered the universal lament,
"Teenagers!"

They had enrolled Markos in one of the local high schools
in Tavira, and much to his chagrin, and Kirsten's relief,
Andrew had proven to be a strict disciplinarian. Most of the
arguments they had revolved around his schooling—which
was understandable, yet unavoidable. Markos was too knowl-
edgeable and too mature for such a parochial kind of educa-
tion. But for the moment it was all that was available to them.
As a reward for his bearing up so bravely all year, Kirsten had
taken him to London in August for a month. He had been in
his element in London—the most eager and absorbent of
young sponges—so achingly reminiscent of Kirsten herself
her first time there.

Even now the tender memory of that trip made her smile.

"Kirsten?" Markos was studying her with a puzzled frown.
She seemed so preoccupied these days; she always seemed to
be drifting off somewhere.

She shook herself free from her thoughts with great effort.
"Hmm?" She was looking at him as though she were seeing

him clearly for the first time. His resemblance to Andrew was uncanny. They looked so much alike—both so tall, so well built, and so blond. "I was just thinking," she said.

"And only about good things, I hope." It was Andrew. He came loping toward them, a sketchpad tucked under his arm, a broad grin on his face.

"Well, you certainly look pleased with yourself today," Kirsten remarked, raising her face for a kiss.

"I am." He planted a kiss on her mouth, gave Markos a one-armed hug, then thrust his sketchpad at him. "Here, have a look."

Markos's eyes were wide as he thumbed through the sketches. "They're all of the flower vendors at the market," he exclaimed. "Andrew, they're wonderful."

"I thought I'd give the two of you a break and pick on someone else for a change." He took the sketchpad back and was about to hand it to Kirsten, when she just seemed to float past him and out of the room. He glanced over at Markos and scowled. "She's still doing it," he said, tossing the sketchpad onto the dining room table and combing his hands through his hair the way he always did when he was upset about something. "Has she said anything to you?"

Markos shook his head. "Nothing."

"Damn!" He felt so helpless.

This time Kirsten took the precaution of locking her bedroom door after she closed it. She had procrastinated long enough. Taking the folded newspaper clipping out of her skirt pocket, she reread it for the tenth time that day. And for the tenth time that day her reaction to it was exactly the same: that same sharp intake of breath, that knife slash in her belly, that prickly wave of heat coursing through her veins.

The clipping was an announcement of a piano recital at Boston's Symphony Hall. An all-Brahms program. The pianist: Jeffrey Powell Oliver III.

She had been carrying the clipping around for two weeks now. The recital had taken place only last night, yet she still couldn't believe that her son, her beloved Jeff, was really a pianist. A pianist! It was a miracle, nothing short of a miracle. Somehow her son had found a way to take what she had given him and used it. Used it brilliantly. He was seventeen, only seventeen, and he was already performing in public. If Scott hadn't mailed her this clipping, she might never have known.

Had there been other recitals, she wondered, recitals Scott hadn't read about, recitals he might have missed?

All the feelings she had suppressed through the years in order to stay sane had surfaced during the last two weeks, and she had no desire to force them back down again. Everything she had been waiting for was within reach at last; the time had finally come for her to act. She walked over to her clothes closet and opened the door.

The bulky brown folder was where it always was, on the topmost shelf next to some shoeboxes. She felt surprisingly calm as she took the folder down, blew the dust off it, and sat down with it on her knees at the foot of her bed. But as calm as she might have been on the inside, that didn't keep her hands from shaking when she untied the wide brown ribbon and broke open the red wax seal. She was about to put an end to nearly eleven years of wondering.

"Who's F. S. Dukes?" Andrew asked Kirsten, waving a large brown envelope at her.

She nearly dropped the glass she was washing in her haste to put it down.

"H-he's a man." She was so flustered, she could hardly speak.

"I gathered as much."

"He did some work for me in New York."

"New York?" Andrew glanced at the postmark. "You're right, New York." He handed her the envelope. "Is this a secret between you and F. S. Dukes, or is it something you can share?"

But Kirsten didn't hear him; she had already left the room.

Andrew thought of going after her, then decided against it. Obviously this F. S. Dukes, whoever he was, had something to do with the strange way she had been behaving lately. He tried to shake off a deep sense of foreboding and couldn't; the feeling only got worse as the day progressed.

When Kirsten sat down at the dinner table that evening, she looked drawn and anxious, and her eyes were puffy from crying. Andrew and Markos exchanged hasty glances, but said nothing. It was unusual for any of their meals to be either silent or strained, yet this one was both. When she realized no one was eating, Kirsten decided it was time she put an end to their waiting. Looking first at Markos, then at

Andrew, she clasped her hands in front of her and leaned forward in her chair.

"I'm sorry if I've seemed so preoccupied these past few weeks," she began nervously, "but I've been doing a lot of very serious thinking." She paused, wet her lips, then said, "I'm flying to New York the day after tomorrow."

"What!" Andrew exploded; Markos sucked in his breath and held it.

"I can't discuss everything with you right now, but I want you to understand just how vital this is to me. I'm going back to see my son, to see Jeff. He turns eighteen in June, you know. That means he won't be a minor anymore, he'll be legally free then to decide whether or not he wants to see me again."

"But why go back now?" Andrew interrupted. "Why not wait until June?"

"Because I want a fighting chance." Her expression was grim, her jaw set determinedly. "For all I know, he's either forgotten me or been so poisoned against me he may not even *want* to see me again. And if that's the case, I'm going to need time to change his mind. I haven't waited all these years to risk losing him permanently now. He's still my son, and I intend to get him back."

Andrew was gazing at her quizzically. "How?"

"By letting him get to know me all over again." Her answer was purposely vague, and Andrew knew it was the only answer she meant him to have.

"But why the day after tomorrow?" he persisted. "Why so soon?"

The smile she gave him was sad and wishful. "Maybe because it's New Year's Day. Maybe because I need to believe it'll magically make a difference. A new year, a new beginning. It's supposed to be symbolic of fresh starts, isn't it?" She leaned over and grasped his hand. "But I also think I'm leaving then because I don't want to give either of you enough time to try to change my mind." Her voice broke, her bottom lip began to quiver.

"And F. S. Dukes?"

"He's the private investigator my attorney once hired for me. I contacted him in New York a few weeks ago and had him do some follow-up work for me."

"How long will you be gone?" Markos wanted to know.

When she didn't answer immediately, he became alarmed. "You're not going to stay in New York, are you?"

Kirsten took his hand and squeezed it. "Do you remember when you were little I told you that New York was my real home and that I'd be going back there one day?" Markos nodded. "Well, that day has finally come."

"But you still haven't answered me."

Kirsten and Andrew locked glances. They had kept their promise these last two years, living every today they had shared to the fullest. Although in her more vulnerable moments she had longed to ask him for an eternity of tomorrows, she never had; there was still so much she had to do alone, while Andrew himself seemed perfectly content to leave the future open. She recalled her recurring dream in London, when she had so boldly declared, "I want them both," and smiled. She had her music back, it was true; the time had come for her to take her son back, but it seemed love would have to wait awhile longer.

Turning to Markos again, she told him truthfully, "I might be gone a few weeks, perhaps even a few months. I really don't know."

"But suppose he wants you to stay, will you?"

"Markos." Andrew shook his head, but the youth persisted anyway. "Will you stay, Kirsten, will you?"

"This is only a visit, Markos," she assured him. "I'm not even thinking about the future right now."

"Then if it's only a visit, why can't we come with you?"

"You have school."

"They have schools in New York too."

"Andrew hates the cold. He'd never think of coming to New York in January."

"You're damned right I wouldn't," Andrew said, more for Markos's sake than anything else.

There were no duets after dinner that evening, and when Kirsten and Andrew made love later that night, there was an urgency to their lovemaking that reminded her of her stolen times with Michael, when neither of them knew when they would be seeing each other again.

"I'm going to miss you, Kirsten." Andrew's voice, for all its tenderness, was tense and unhappy.

"Then why don't you come with me?"

"You said it yourself, I'd never think of coming to New York in January."

"No, my darling," she said, stroking his cheek, "*you* so much as said it when you told me you had nothing to ever go back there for."

"I still don't."

"And I still do."

"But you also have something to stay *here* for now."

"I know I do, and I'll be back, I promise. You can't get rid of me that easily." How strange it was to have the positions reversed. Couldn't he see how desperately torn she was, couldn't he tell? She began to trace his perfect profile with her index finger. "Sometimes I feel I've been waiting eleven lifetimes, not eleven years for this moment," she said in a husky voice. "I not only swore to get my son back, you know, I also swore I'd return to the concert stage one day. And that's precisely what I intend to do. They stole my life from me, Andrew; I've waited a very long time to see them pay for what they did. I've even kept a nice neat list of all their names inside my head. Well, now they've finally started to pay. Claudia, poor soul, was the first." She made a check in the air with her finger. "But she's only the beginning, Andrew, only the beginning."

He turned to look at her in alarm, wondering if what was in her voice would also be in her face. It was. It was there in an expression he had never seen before. It went beyond hardness to a kind of ruthlessness that made him shudder. Her features were so stonily set that for a moment he didn't recognize her.

"We both knew this was inevitable, didn't we, Andrew?" Her face had softened, so had her voice.

"Yes, I guess we did," he conceded. "But then why am I so damned surprised?" He laughed at his own rhetorical question. "Kirsten." He pulled her close and whispered into her hair. "Kirsten, I don't want to lose you."

But she had drifted off again and didn't even hear him.

Kirsten took another step back in time as she traveled by taxi from JFK Airport through the congested streets of New York City. It was a cold, crisp afternoon, when the breath of every pedestrian and the exhaust from every car and bus hung in the frigid air like so many clouds of white smoke. In spite of her suit and coat, she couldn't stop shivering, and she had to ask the driver twice to turn up the heat in the cab.

Being back in Manhattan for the first time in nearly eleven

years made her feel the way she had felt when she had arrived in London for Eric's funeral—only worse. London had never been her home; New York *had* been, once.

But it didn't feel like home anymore.

Regardless of what she might have told Markos, she was virtually an outsider here. An interloper. An uninvited stranger returning to a world that had continued to spin without her. Many of the city's familiar landmarks were gone. New skyscrapers competed with the old for their share of the smog-stained sky. Old hotels bore new names. There was more noise, more dirt, and more traffic than she remembered. More of everything except space and clean air and sunlight. She thought of Tavira, and her shivering got worse.

If New York had been undergoing changes, so had the music world. In nineteen eighty-two alone, pianist Glenn Gould had died, the New York Philharmonic had given its ten thousandth performance at Avery Fisher Hall, and Michael Eastbourne had resigned as conductor of the orchestra. He had reportedly returned to Boston with the intention of resuming his career as a guest conductor.

It seemed she was returning as a virtual stranger to that world as well.

She checked into the New York Hilton under the assumed name of Madame La Branca and unpacked the few things she had brought with her; the rest she would have to go out and buy. Her head was spinning as she called room service and ordered a shrimp salad and a glass of white wine for her dinner. Although she was sorely tempted to phone Scott, she didn't. She couldn't afford to let anyone know she was back in town. She thought longingly of Nelson, whom she knew to be alive and well and, at the age of eighty, still a driving force as a manager, and felt a tug at her heart. *Hold on, my friend,* she whispered, *hold on. It won't be much longer now.*

For the fourth time in as many days, she walked from the hotel to the nondescript white brick apartment building on West Fifty-third Street, and pressed the buzzer next to the name E. Shaw in the lobby. But when she again got no answer, she took up her usual position directly across the street to wait. She tucked her gloved hands into her coat pockets, stamped her feet to keep them warm, and tried to distract herself from the cold by counting backward from one thousand by threes. Her black velvet cloche with its gathered half veil was managing to protect her head fairly well, but not her ears. After only an hour they were beginning to feel frostbitten. She decided to give up for the moment, find someplace nearby to have a cup of coffee, and come back later.

Just then she noticed a woman turn into the walk of the building she was watching, and her heart leapt expectantly. At last. Kirsten rushed across the street, caught hold of the lobby door as it was closing, then followed the woman onto the elevator. The woman pressed six, Kirsten pressed seven. Her pulse was racing as she stared up at the lighted numbers and counted them off to herself, one by one. When the other woman got off at the sixth floor, Kirsten waited an extra second, then darted after her. Just outside the door to Apartment 606, the woman paused and glanced suspiciously over her shoulder in Kirsten's direction.

"Are you looking for someone?" she inquired.

"I was," replied Kirsten, "but I think I've found her, thank you." From the puzzled look on the woman's face, Kirsten could see she hadn't been recognized, and that was reassuring. Advancing a bit farther, she said, "Don't you remember me?"

"Should I?" The woman hastily unlocked her door, but as she opened it, Kirsten's arm shot out and held it open. "If this is some sort of game, I'm not amused," she snapped.

"It's not a game. I'm Kirsten Harald, Lois."

Lois Holden gasped. "I don't believe you."

Kirsten raised her veil and took off her dark glasses.

"My God, it *is* you." Lois took a step back, her eyes wide, her mouth falling open. "But how did you find me? No one knows—" She caught herself in time.

"I obviously do." Lois's features seemed in imminent danger of collapsing. "As a matter of fact, if I hadn't waited so long to read the report of the private investigator I hired, I would have known about it eleven years ago."

Lois reached into her purse for her inhalator. "What is it you want?" she demanded.

"I want to see my son."

"That's impossible. Jeffrey would never permit it."

"I have no intention of asking for Jeffrey's permission. *You're* going to help me."

"The hell I will!"

"Tell me, Lois"—Kirsten was having increasing difficulty

keeping her voice controlled—"does your husband Alec know about this little hideaway of yours?"

"Of course he does."

"You're lying."

Perspiration was beginning to form above Lois's top lip and her breathing was becoming labored. "Just what do you want from me?"

"You're Jeff's piano teacher. I want you to arrange for me to meet with him."

"No!" Lois ducked inside the apartment, but Kirsten was right behind her. Closing the door herself, she leaned her weight against it and refused to move.

"I think I might be able to get you to change your mind," she said, a low note of warning in her icy voice.

Lois took a quick puff from her inhalator and studied Kirsten warily. "Would you please get to the point?"

But Kirsten wasn't in any particular hurry. "I lived on Long Island long enough to know how important appearances are," she said, "and just how eager everyone is to maintain them, no matter what the cost. Yet you know as well as I that appearances can be deceiving." She watched as Lois began to fidget uneasily. "How do you think Alec would take it if he knew his wife was being unfaithful to him?"

"What kind of a twisted joke is this!"

Kirsten continued as though Lois hadn't spoken. "What do you think Jeffrey would say if he knew his perfect Dierdre was also being unfaithful?"

"Unfaithful?" Lois snorted. "They aren't even married."

"I find that rather curious, don't you? After all, the two of them have been inseparable for years."

"How would you know?"

"As I said before, Lois, I know a lot more now than I did then."

"You know absolutely nothing."

"That's where you're wrong. I know everything." Kirsten's insides were beginning to churn. "And one of the things I know is that you and Dierdre are lovers, and have been for years."

Lois blanched. For a moment it even looked as though she might faint. "That's a lie," she almost screamed.

"It's no lie, Lois; I have the report and the photographs to prove it. How else would I have known about the apartment and the name E. Shaw on the board downstairs? How else would I have known that Dierdre Oliver is the only person who's ever visited you here? Does the name the Pink Lady mean anything to you?" The Pink Lady was a notorious lesbian bar on Eighth Avenue.

Lois put her hands over her ears and moaned. Kirsten felt physically ill. She knew she would go to her grave regretting what her desire to see them all punished was driving her to do.

"Should I continue?" she asked.

Lois shook her head. "Just tell me what you want me to do," she whispered.

"When are your lessons with Jeff?"

"Tuesdays at four and Saturdays at two."

"Where?"

"At my house."

Today was Wednesday. "Call and tell him that his next lesson will be held at Carnegie Hall in Room 851. Tell him to ask for Madame La Branca."

"Madame La Bra—" Lois stopped, incredulous. Then she snickered. "Don't tell me you actually plan on giving him a piano lesson?"

"What's so unreasonable about that? I *am* a pianist."

"And after you've given him this one memorable lesson, then what?"

"Who said anything about giving him only one lesson?"

Lois gaped. "You're not seriously thinking of becoming his permanent teacher, are you?"

"And what if I were?" Kirsten challenged her.

"You can't. I won't allow it."

"*You* won't allow it?"

"He's *my* student, Kirsten, mine, do you hear me?"

"But he's *my* son!"

Lois opened and closed her mouth, but no sound came out. She could see everything she had been working toward crumbling in front of her eyes. She took another puff of epinephrine. It didn't help; she took another. Her heart was racing so feverishly now she could hear it rattling inside her chest and echoing in her ears. She had never counted on this happening, never. Jeffrey, when he found out about what she was doing, had been difficult enough to handle. But this! How dare the urchin come back, how dare she!

"You have no right . . ." Her voice was a wheezy gasp. "No right, damn you, no right . . ."

"I'm sorry, Lois, but I'd say you're the one who has no right, no right at all, to try to use my son to compensate for your own failure." Lois sucked in her breath. "All these years you've blamed me for what happened to your career. Did it never occur to you that it might have been your fault and not mine? Did it never occur to you that you just weren't good enough?"

Lois drew herself up proudly. This nobody from nowhere would never see her cowed or humbled. Steering the painful conversation away from herself, she was snide as she said, "You'll never be able to pull off this little charade of yours, you know. How long do you think Jeff will be able to keep it from his father?"

Kirsten was losing patience. "I can't worry about that right now. Besides, I doubt he'll recognize me. You didn't. And he was only a little boy when I left, remember."

"Jeffrey's still bound to find out."

"Who's going to tell him, Lois? You? Are you really that eager for Alec and Jeffrey, not to mention the rest of Long Island, to learn the truth about you and Dierdre?"

"You are despicable," spat Lois. Kirsten let the remark pass. "And just how am I supposed to explain why I'm suddenly dropping Jeff as a pupil?"

"I'm sure you'll think of something." Kirsten opened the door to leave. "You must be quite an expert at deception by now."

The two women stared hard at each other for a moment, the same bitter adversaries they had always been. Kirsten put a mental check mark beside the next two names on her list and left the apartment, leaving the door for Lois to close. When she did, she did it quietly. Kirsten smiled. In spite of everything, Lois Eldershaw Holden was still very much the proper lady.

She prowled the cramped studio like a caged animal with no room to move and no air to breathe. She could barely feel her fingers or toes anymore. Her legs were two numbed stalks scarcely able to support her weight, and her stomach had looped itself into a wriggling python of terror and doubt. She took out her gold compact, anxiously checked her face one more time in the tiny mirror, then put the compact back into her purse again. She was wearing a royal blue and white wool tweed Chanel suit, a royal blue silk blouse tied in a full bow at the neck, and a pair of large, metal-framed aviator glasses tinted blue to conceal the true color of her eyes. On the surface she looked more like a fashionable forty-nine-year-old Long Island matron on her way to a Junior League luncheon than a highly agitated, near-hysterical mother about to see her son for the first time in eleven years.

She had prayed for the strength she needed to survive the next few minutes, but she was rapidly losing her courage. She was so panicky, all she could think of was grabbing her coat and getting out of there.

The knock at the door made her jump.

She froze. Her heart wedged itself firmly in the middle of her throat and cut off all the air to her lungs. There was a second knock, slightly louder this time, and then the door opened.

Finale

1983

43

The universe shrank until its sole focus was the seventeen-year-old boy walking toward her. He was tall, with a slender build and a shock of straight black hair falling across his high forehead. He had Jeffrey's long, straight nose, her mouth and cheekbones, and a firm, square chin that offset the dreaminess in his soft blue eyes. Wearing a Harris tweed jacket over a pale blue crewneck and white Oxford cloth shirt, gray flannel trousers, and black loafers, he looked more like an ordinary prep school student than an extraordinarily gifted musician. After absorbing and memorizing every detail of his appearance, Kirsten turned her attention to his hands. They were a man's hands, long and fine-boned and strong, yet they were her hands too. And it was all she could do to keep from flinging her arms around him and telling him that the moment she had been waiting for all these years had finally arrived.

She was with her son again, she was finally with her son! The waiting was over. She wanted to dance and shout for joy.

Every fiber of her being was screaming out to reestablish some kind of physical contact with him. She ached to touch him, stroke him, hold him, kiss him, brush back the hair from his forehead just as she always had when he was a child. The mother in her strained to reclaim what still belonged to her—the flesh born of her flesh—even now, even after all this time. She was bursting, choking on her feelings, strangling with a dozen different needs that for the moment would have to go unmet. She didn't dare act on a single one of her many desperate impulses; she didn't dare risk recognition, and with it the possibility of rejection.

His smile tore at her heart as he extended his right hand to her, saying, "You must be Madame La Branca. I'm Jeff Oliver."

She longed to scream, I'm not Madame La Branca, I'm your mother! but she didn't. She simply slipped her small hand into his larger one and replied in a carefully muted voice, "A pleasure."

The formalities over, Jeff went to hang his jacket on a peg, keeping up a steady stream of conversation the entire time.

"I always knew Lois would take off for Arizona one day, but I never expected it to happen quite this soon. She's asthmatic, you know, and New York winters are very hard on her. I sure hope I didn't have anything to do with her leaving so suddenly; I seem to have this knack for burning out my teachers." Kirsten hung on his every word, fascinated. Had the Jeff she left behind ever been this talkative? She couldn't remember. "Anyway, I'm glad she was able to find me someone else on such short notice. You've come highly recommended, madame."

I'm sure, Kirsten thought cynically. She did applaud Lois's ingenuity, though; she recalled that Lois had inherited her parents' house in Phoenix.

"I understand you've been teaching in Europe," said Jeff as he concentrated on removing some sheet music from the well-worn black leather attaché case he had brought with him.

"Yes." Kirsten cleared her throat. "For quite a few years now."

He was so forthright, so open and earnest. She just stood there, staring at him, while her insides turned cartwheels and she went from hot to cold, then back to hot again. But whatever she was experiencing, he seemed blissfully unaware of it as he began to describe the most recent pieces he and Lois had been working on together.

While he talked, Kirsten drifted. She saw them as they used to be, and the mother in her wept because her son didn't remember her. *Oh, Jeff, my darling, my angel,* she implored him in her mind, *look at me. Look at me and remember. I'm your mother, Jeff, your mother.*

"What did you say?" She came bouncing back to earth with a jolt.

"I said I'm giving a recital at Carnegie Hall on March twenty-fifth."

Kirsten grabbed on to the piano for support. Carnegie Hall, it wasn't possible. Only seventeen, and already playing Carnegie Hall.

"Is something wrong?" he asked.

She shook her head. Her dream. He would be living her dream for the two of them without her.

"There's no conflict, is there? I mean, none of your other students are performing that night, are they?"

She wanted to laugh at the utter absurdity of it all. "No, there isn't any conflict, I assure you." Anxious to change the subject, she clapped her hands once in a brisk and business-like manner, then motioned him over to the piano. "Now, young man," she said, "let's hear what you've been working on for today."

He began with Beethoven's "Pathétique."

As Kirsten listened to him play, she could barely suppress her mounting excitement. He was inspired. There was great-ness in every note he played, genius in the totality of the sound he created. To say that Jeff was gifted would have been an insulting understatement. He wasn't merely an extension of his music, nor was his music a simple extension of him: he *was* his music.

Her son, her precious son had fulfilled his promise and her prophecy. He had it in him to be the best, and she told him so.

"Now I wish you'd tell my father that," he said, pivoting around on the stool to face her. "God knows Lois has tried often enough and so has my manager, but it doesn't make the slightest difference. If he had his way, he'd rather see me be a second-rate doctor than a first-rate musician. He still hasn't forgiven me for accepting a scholarship to Juilliard next fall."

Juilliard! Kirsten thought her heart would burst with pride. No, she doubted Jeffrey would ever forgive their son for going to Juilliard. A check mark began to take shape next to Jeffrey's name on her list.

When Jeff began Chopin's Polonaise in F Sharp Major, she found herself drifting off again. There was so much she wanted to know about him. Where did he go to school? Did he have a lot of friends? Did he have a girlfriend? How many hours a day did he practice, and where did he do his practicing? What did he do in his spare time? Did he have any hobbies? Was he interested in sports? In art? Did he ever go to the theater, the opera, or the ballet? What kind of popular music did he like? Did he drive a car?

There was so much to learn, so many lost years to make up for. And so little time to do it in.

When their two hours were up, Kirsten felt cheated. It had come to an end too quickly; she wasn't ready to let go of him yet. What if he left now and never came back? What if Lois

changed her mind about going to Phoenix? What if she went
to Jeffrey and told him the truth?

What if this was to be the first and only time she ever got
to see her son?

"Should we stick to the same schedule as I had with Lois?"
Jeff was asking her, but she didn't hear him.

"I'm sorry?"

He repeated the question. "Are those days convenient for
you, because if they're not, we can always make some other
arrangement."

"No, no, they're fine, really." She glanced pointedly at her
watch. "Are you in a hurry, I mean, is there somewhere in
particular you have to be right now?"

He shrugged. "I was just going to drive back to school."
School, she wanted to pounce and didn't. "Why?"

"Would you like to continue awhile longer?"

"Would I, I'd love it! Lois was always exhausted at the end
of our two hours." Jeff hastily pulled off his jacket and hung it
up again. "Madame," he said, giving her a wide grin, "I think
you and I are going to get along fantastically."

Dierdre wanted to scream.

She was so lonely, so wretchedly, miserably lonely. Every
part of her cried out to be soothed and stroked and comforted, and there was no one around to do it. What a rotten,
selfish thing for Lois to have done. She had given her no
warning, none whatsoever. Just a brief telephone call then
poof, two days later she was off to Phoenix. And she wouldn't
be back now until April.

She stared bleakly into the mirror of her vanity and patted
a few of the curls on her short blond wig into place. Even
with her make-up and false eyelashes, she still looked washed-
out and pasty. Thank goodness the lighting in the club was
pink; she would need all the help she could get tonight. The
thought of having to start off the evening sitting at a table by
herself made her stomach churn. But she had no choice; she
couldn't bear to spend another night alone.

When she was dressed, she used the back stairs and let
herself into the garage. She pressed one of a series of black
buttons on the wall and watched as the wide garage door
opened upward with a smooth, well-oiled whirr. Then she
got behind the wheel of the white 1979 Chevy Camaro and

started the engine. As always, she was careful not to turn the headlights on until she was safely out of the long driveway.

Glancing nervously in the rearview mirror, she first checked herself, then checked the road behind her. All was clear. She immediately snapped on the lights and drove off with a burst of delighted laughter that astonished her.

Wouldn't poor Jeffrey just die if he knew?

Jeffrey shifted his position slightly to take some of the pressure off his knees. The closet door was open just enough for him to see every detail of her luscious body. She was the best one yet. She really knew how to take her time, washing herself as though she had hours, alternating between using a washcloth and a large oval bar of soap. She was sitting in the tub facing him; her eyes were closed and her full, pink-tipped breasts seemed to be floating on the surface of the water and pointing directly at him.

He continued to stroke himself, slowly and evenly. Thank God, he was finally getting hard. It was taking longer and longer these days. And this was the only way he could get hard now. He hadn't made love to Dierdre in years, something which didn't seem to bother her in the least. She had never particularly enjoyed their lovemaking anyway, and had agreed to all his various games with the greatest reluctance. Well, he didn't have to resort to games anymore. He thanked God for that too. Poor Dierdre. The woman was frigid, just as he had always suspected she was.

The girl in the tub had gotten to her knees. Jeffrey whimpered. He was big now, big and hard and heavy with desire. He watched her rub the soap over her pubic patch in sweet lazy circles and tried to hold back. But the tingling had already started. The feeling was building; he was beginning to pant. He worked himself up and down, up and down, faster and faster. He was almost there, almost there. Yes. Yes, yes, yes, he was coming. Oh, God, yes, he was coming!

"Ah, ah, ah, ah, ah . . ." He couldn't suppress his short, rhythmic moans any more than he could contain the thick flow of semen spurting out of him.

The girl in the tub heard his moans, yawned once, a long, leisurely yawn of pure boredom, and put down the soap.

Kirsten was humming softly as she stepped off the elevator into the lobby. In another twenty minutes she would be seeing Jeff again. She was still humming when she swung through the double glass doors and walked out into the madly swirling snow that had been falling all day. Nothing, not even this surprise March storm, could dampen the wonderful warmth she felt inside. The furnished apartment she had sublet was only three blocks from Carnegie Hall, yet it could just as easily have been three steps or three miles. She had absolutely no perception of distances when she was on her way to see her son.

Although two months had already come and gone, and the bogeymen she had imagined lurking around every corner had never materialized, she was still reluctant to let her guard down; she was still too afraid of being taken by surprise.

After that first joyous meeting with Jeff, she had been tempted to savor her victory and run. Run before it turned sour and exploded in her face. But she hadn't run. She had stayed, more determined than ever to see her plan through. The easier it got, the harder it got. She kept expecting every time to be the last time, and she was both surprised and grateful when it wasn't. She kept waiting for something to trigger Jeff's dormant memory, and fearing that once he knew who she was, he would send her away. So far that hadn't happened. She kept imagining the door of the studio being flung open and Jeffrey striding into the room to drag their son off the piano stool and out of her life again. But that hadn't happened either.

Her only regret was that they had so little time together. Their lessons were intense, emotionally demanding, and physically draining; there was no room at the end of them for idle conversation. She still knew practically nothing about her son's life. Despite his initial frankness, he had quickly turned reticent; he seemed reluctant to volunteer any further information about himself, and she hesitated to question him for fear of having it sound like prying. But there was one thing she had learned about him: he was just the way she had been at his age—totally committed to and obsessed with his music.

The studio was cold and Kirsten was shivering in spite of the long-sleeved wool dress and matching shawl she was wearing. She gave up trying to keep warm by pacing and decided to sit down at the piano and play for a while. But she couldn't concentrate. Jeff was late. Glancing out the window at the falling snow, she began to wonder if he was even coming at all. Her spirits tumbled. She couldn't bear having to miss even a single second with him. There were so few of them as it was.

What she needed was a distraction. She found it the moment she began one of the Greek folk songs she and Markos had played together in Tavira. Markos. How she missed him. And Andrew. She felt a pang of hungry longing at the thought of Andrew. He was smart to have stayed behind; the cold really was intolerable. She pictured him on board the *Marianne*—outlined by the golden sun, framed by the blue sky and the aqua sea—and started to smile. God, she missed him.

She wrote him a long letter every evening and mailed it every morning; and whenever she received one from him, she read and reread it until she knew every word by heart. Recently he had begun to enclose tiny pen and ink sketches of Markos and himself in each of his letters. He and Markos always wore exaggerated frowns on their faces, and there was usually either a clock or a calendar dotted with question marks somewhere in the background.

He wanted to know, without asking directly, when she was coming back; she wished she had an answer for him.

The calendar reminded her. Jeff's recital at Carnegie Hall was only four days away. He expected her to be there, of course, but did she dare? What if she were recognized? She had been wrestling with the question for weeks now.

How could there be any question? This was Carnegie Hall. How could she not see her own son perform at Carnegie Hall?

She was desperate to be a part of that very special evening. She deserved to be a part of it: not only was she his mother, she was his teacher as well. She had every right to be there. She wanted to stand in the wings with him the way Natalya had always stood with her. She wanted to pace for him, offer him words of advice and kisses of encouragement. She wanted to watch over him while he played and wipe the sweat from his brow each time he came off. But more than anything, she wanted to sweep onto the stage to the sound of thunderous applause and share the final bow of the night with him.

Yet did she dare chance it?

Jeff stopped with his hand still on the doorknob. He stood there motionless, his heart beating wildly. There it was again.

The melody that had haunted him all his life. The recording he had played until the grooves were worn out. The piece he had sworn to learn one day. But for some reason he never had. It was as though he had been saving it for something. He didn't know quite what. Maybe a miracle.

"Please, don't stop, I love that piece."

The sound of Jeff's gentle voice so close to her made Kirsten jump. She tried to recall what she had just been playing and couldn't.

"You know, the Debussy," he prompted her. " 'Reflets dans l'Eau.' "

Kirsten paled. For a moment she thought she was going to pass out. Only Jeff's hand on her elbow kept her from keeling over.

"Are you ill?" he asked, his voice quivering with fright. "Do you want to lie down? Should I go and get you some water?"

She made a vague, fluttering gesture with her hand. "No, I'm fine. It's just a bit stuffy in here." Jeff was looking at her strangely; the room was anything but stuffy. "No, really, I'm fine," she insisted. And to prove it, she stood up. "Now, let's get these wet clothes off you before you catch a chill."

All through the lesson, Jeff was preoccupied, his mind everywhere but on the intricate passages of Liszt's exquisite third "Paganini" étude. With each mistake he made, Kirsten cursed herself for having slipped so stupidly. After all her worrying about someone else giving her away, she had practically done it herself. She had him stop the Liszt and begin Rachmaninoff's Sonata in B Flat Minor. It went no better than the Liszt. She suggested Chopin's Ballade No. 1, but he mangled it so thoroughly, she finally put her hands over her ears and wagged her head back and forth in a gesture that was pure Natalya.

"That bad, huh?" Jeff looked embarrassed as he closed his sheet music and stretched. "I'm sorry, I feel I really wasted your time this afternoon."

"No, you didn't. You can't be at peak form every day."

"But I should be."

He was so much like her. Impulsively, she reached out and touched his hair.

"Do you think it's too long?"

"What?"

He gave his head a shake. "My hair. My father says I look

like one of the Beatles." He grimaced. "That shows you how up-to-date he is on music." Kirsten looked away. "Well, what do you think?"

"I don't find it too long at all. Seiji Ozawa has always worn his hair long, so has Leonard Bernstein."

"Thanks." He shot her one of the grins that made her knees go weak. "It's nice to know I have someone on my side for a change."

She watched with increasing alarm as he put on his duffel coat and got ready to leave. "Do you really think you should be driving in this?" She indicated the snow that was still falling outside the window.

Jeff wrapped a burgundy wool scarf around his neck and picked up his fleece-lined gloves. "I'll be okay, I'm used to it."

"Do you have far to go?" She could feel herself holding her breath.

"Wallingford." At her blank look, he said, "Connecticut. I'm at Choate."

Choate. So that's where he had been all these years.

"Well, I'll see you Tuesday."

Kirsten followed him to the door. "Please, Jeff"—she put her hand on his sleeve—"drive carefully."

"I will." He flashed her a grin, gave her the thumbs-up sign, and headed off down the hall.

44

Jeff was in turmoil.

Between Saturday and Tuesday, when the sole focus of his concentration should have been the works he was preparing for his upcoming recital at Carnegie Hall, all he had thought about was the Debussy. By the end of his next lesson he was so agitated, he could hardly leave the practice studio fast enough. He felt as though he had a high fever; he had chills, he was palpitating, and he was nauseated. It would have been easy to blame everything on stage fright, but he knew better. He wasn't feeling this way because of his recital; he was feeling this way because of her.

With only that one piece Madame La Branca had stirred up his entire past, causing all the memories and all the unanswered questions to come tumbling out again. Nothing he did made them stop or go away. He was completely powerless against them; *they* were in control now, not he. And *they* were demanding to finally know the truth. It was either give in to them or lose his mind.

And so, instead of driving directly back to Choate, he went to the main branch of the New York Public Library on Fifth Avenue.

He was like a cat on hot bricks. Every part of his body was shaking and twitching by the time he sat down at an empty reading table armed with a stack of magazines, six reels of microfilm, and all three unauthorized biographies on her. He squeezed his eyes shut for a moment, took several long, deep breaths, then opened his eyes again. Reaching for the most recent of the three biographies, he turned to the narrow section of black and white photographs in the middle of the book, and braced himself.

The photos were every bit as blurry as his memories were. He rubbed his eyes. His hands came away wet, whether with sweat or with tears, he didn't know.

After that he was possessed.

He was starving and couldn't fill himself up enough on the details of his mother's life. He gulped it all down eagerly and greedily: the words, the black and white stills, the four-color spreads. It left him breathless and dizzy and soaked through with clammy sweat. After almost three hours, he was exhausted. Dropping his aching head onto his folded arms to rest, he closed his eyes. All he could see was a woman with a face so beautiful, he wondered how he had ever managed to forget her.

He was thirteen before he realized she wasn't dead, that what he had overheard as a distraught six-year-old had been an exaggeration of the truth and not the truth itself. But knowing she hadn't really died didn't make him feel any better, it had made him feel worse. If she hadn't died, then it could mean only one thing: she had left him on purpose. Even after promising she would never leave him, she had anyway. He had wanted answers, and there was no one who would give them to him, because no one, including his father, his aunt Dierdre, Lois, all their friends, even the servants, ever once mentioned her name in front of him. As far as they were concerned, Kirsten Harald Oliver had never existed.

But they were wrong. She *had* existed; she *still* existed. In him. He was her legacy. She may have left him, but in her place she had left her music.

He gasped.

Several people turned to stare at him. He was shaking again. His pulse was erratic, his breathing rapid and shallow. Thousands of tiny black dots began dancing in front of his eyes. Pushing back his chair, he bent down, put his head between his knees, and waited for the blinding dizziness to pass. Once it had, he straightened up slowly and began to gather up his things.

Suddenly it all made sense. He had hated her for abandoning him. That was why he had never learned the Debussy. It was his way of punishing her. If he hadn't been in a library, he would have leapt up onto his chair and let out a shout so loud it would have carried all the way across to Long Island.

He had his miracle now.

"Nervous?" Andrew asked Markos.

"A bit."

"So am I." Nervous was an understatement.

He still couldn't believe what he had done. On impulse he had purchased two plane tickets and wired Carnegie Hall the money for two tickets to Jeff's recital. Now he was not only on a plane—when he had sworn never to set foot on one again—but he was on his way back to the very city he had vowed he would never go back to: New York.

"Andrew, you're talking to yourself again."

"Am I?" He sighed. "I must be getting old."

"You, old? You'll never be old."

"Thanks, but I don't think I like the sound of that, especially thirty-five thousand feet over the Atlantic."

Markos had to stifle a laugh. "Won't Kirsten be surprised," he said, "when she opens the door and finds the two of us standing there?"

It was then that Andrew experienced his first pangs of doubt. What if she *wasn't* surprised? What if it made her angry instead? What if she thought they were intruding, interfering with a part of her life that had nothing to do with them? He hadn't stopped to think. He had been too caught up in his need to be with her and to help her share the joy of this momentous night. Oh, God. He groaned and put his head in his hand. What if he had made a mistake?

What if she didn't want them there?

Kirsten had been practicing most of the day in the hopes of forgetting about Jeff's recital at eight. But all she kept forgetting was her music. She glanced at her watch. Two o'clock. It was useless; she just couldn't concentrate. She got up from the piano and started pacing the floor. In precisely six more hours she would be watching from the wings as her son strode onto the stage of Carnegie Hall for the first time.

She had made up her mind to be there tonight. She had also made up her mind to tell him the truth. Her decision to be at the recital had left her no other choice—someone was bound to recognize her tonight and tell him first. She couldn't risk having that happen. Not when she had begun to sense his own growing suspiciousness. The Debussy had been her undoing.

And once he knew the truth about her, then what?

She didn't dare think about that now. If she did, she would go mad.

She remembered the sheet music she had bought him at Patelson's as a gift—duplicates of every major work she had ever played—and went to find a shopping bag large enough to hold it all. Her choice couldn't have been more fitting: The bag came from Bergdorf's, and of course it was lavender. It had to be a sign. She suddenly felt more optimistic about everything. Like mother, like son. Jeff, too, was specializing in the Romantics. What a magnificent team they would make someday.

The doorbell rang and she started. No one knew where to find her. Unless . . . Jeff? No, it couldn't be. It had to be a mistake. Someone had simply pressed the wrong buzzer. The bell rang again, three long, shrill, insistent rings. Smoothing her hair anxiously with the palms of her hands and moistening her lips, she made certain the safety chain was fastened, then cautiously opened the door a crack.

"As you can see, I'm a fairly persistent man; I've managed to track you down again."

She could barely get the metal chain to move, her hands

were trembling so badly. But once she had, she threw open the door and flung herself into Michael Eastbourne's outstretched arms.

For a moment, time stopped.

The last six years dissolved in a single heartbeat. The present faded and became the past. His lips found hers and once again they were kissing for the first time in the backseat of his rented limousine as it pulled away from the curb outside the stage entrance to Carnegie Hall. And when he released her, she felt that same sense of abandonment she always felt.

"Let me look at you," he said, his hazel eyes warm as he drank her in. "You're more beautiful than ever, you know." She could feel herself blushing.

"I'm completely white now." She patted her hair self-consciously.

"It suits you."

She touched the white at his temples. "You look so dignified."

He laughed and kissed the tender inside of her palm. She closed her eyes and swayed against him. "Oh, Michael," she murmured, "forgive me for never telling you where I went when I left Athens. But I needed so much to be alone."

He pulled her into his arms and began stroking her hair, soothing her the way he had always soothed her. "I know that, Kirsten, and I never blamed you for it. Oh, I might have hated you at times," he said with a slight chuckle, "but I never blamed you. Not after what you'd been through. If I blamed anyone, I blamed myself, because I couldn't be there for you, at least not the way I would have wanted to be had you asked."

She peered up at him with a sly smile. "Do you mean to say I should have been more demanding?"

"Who knows, if you'd been more demanding and I'd been a little less honorable, things might have been different for us."

What he was saying was making her tremble. He had taken her completely by surprise. She had been caught totally unprepared. For him, this conversation, everything. Before he could say anything more, she drew him into the living room, removed his topcoat, sat him down on the sofa, and curled up beside him with her legs thrown across his lap, her head resting against his chest and her arms wrapped around his neck.

"How did you find me?" she asked him after a while.

"I noticed you at Patelson's yesterday."

"Oh?"

"You seemed intent on buying out the entire sheet music department." Kirsten giggled. "You were completely oblivious to everything and everyone. I really didn't mind, though, because I got the chance to follow you back here. A discreet bribe to your friendly doorman took care of the rest."

"And just what brings you to town, Mr. Holmes?"

"A certain young man who's already causing quite a stir in the music world." His voice turned serious. "God, you must be proud of him."

That was all the encouragement she needed. Everything began spilling out of her then, a great, rushing torrent of words and emotions that she had kept stored up for nearly three months. It seemed the most natural thing in the world for her to be telling it all to the man who had known her longer than anyone else. And when she finally ran out of words, she poured them each a much-needed sherry, then curled up beside him again.

When Michael's glass was empty, he turned to her and said, "There's something I've got to tell you." Kirsten automatically tensed. "Roxanne died six months ago. She'd been dying in stages for years."

Suddenly she understood so much. Her feelings were mixed. But somewhere, entwined with all the rest, one of those feelings was envy. Roxanne was lucky to have had so loyal and loving a husband as Michael. She placed a check mark next to the name Roxanne Eastbourne on her list and sighed. There was only one name left.

"I'm sorry, Michael," she said as she hugged him tight. She was sorry, not for Roxanne, but for the man who had loved her.

It was his turn to talk now, and she listened without once loosening her grip on him or interrupting him.

"I wondered why you weren't at Eric's funeral," she said when he had finished. Now she knew. After a while she got up and poured them each a second drink. Then, "I'm playing the piano again, you know."

"Kirsten!"

"Yes." There were tears in her eyes as she told him how it had happened.

"I always said you would, didn't I?" His own eyes were unnaturally bright now. "Do you still have that last charm I gave you?" She nodded. "Wonderful." He grabbed her and squeezed her until she couldn't breathe. "I knew it, I just knew it. Oh, my darling Kirsten, it's going to be all right for us." Taking her face in both hands, he kissed her lingeringly on the mouth and said, "We have so much lost time to make up for, Kirsten, so many things to do we couldn't do before. I'm free now; we can be together. Everything out in the open. No more hiding, no more fear of reprisals. No more bits and pieces of each other, but all of each other, always. Oh, Kirsten, my darling Kirsten, will you marry me?"

She couldn't speak. She looked at the man on the couch beside her and saw a dozen different Michaels at a dozen different times in their lives. And never, at any of those times, had she expected to hear him say what he had just said. He wanted to marry her. He wanted them to have all of each other. Finally, and always.

She saw their two names linked together again—Michael Eastbourne and Kirsten Harald—not only in their professional lives this time, but in their private lives as well. Kirsten Harald and Michael Eastbourne. They would play together, record together, travel together, vacation together, live together openly as man and wife. Mr. and Mrs. Michael Eastbourne. Kirsten Eastbourne. She tried the name out in her mind to hear how it sounded.

Something was wrong. She couldn't quite decide what it was, yet something was definitely wrong. Michael had told her he was free . . . free . . . that was it, at least that was part of it. Michael was free now, but she wasn't. She thought of a tall, blond man with smoky green eyes and a blond beard and a boat called the *Marianne* and the way neither of them had dared to ask each other for tomorrow.

And suddenly a question that should have been so easy to answer wasn't easy at all anymore.

Michael had been watching her with a sinking heart. Now he took hold of both her hands and clasped them tightly in his. "You don't have to give me your answer now," he said. "Take your time and think about it." He could sense her uncertainty; he could feel her whole body wavering, and his tone became urgent. "Please, Kirsten, please promise me you'll think about it."

She nodded her head slowly, solemnly. "I will, Michael," she whispered. "I promise I will."

He kissed her tenderly one more time, then, as Kirsten watched him with a hint of irony in her violet eyes, he checked the time. She began to smile. Nothing had changed.

Touching her gently on the cheek, he said, "See you tonight." Then he left.

She stood there for some time, leaning up against the door, her mind racing feverishly. A single hot tear welled up and spilled down her cheek. A second tear followed. Then a third, and a fourth. For no apparent reason she was crying, in great heaving, gulping sobs, while her shoulders shook and her body shuddered convulsively. The man she had adored from afar all her life had just asked her to marry him; she should have been celebrating, not sobbing. Michael, her Michael, her dear, precious Michael had asked her to marry him. Why was she being such a fool; why was she crying?

Was it because her dear, precious Michael hadn't even told her he loved her?

She was positioned directly across the street from the main entrance to Carnegie Hall with her gaze focused on the poster of Jeff inside the wooden marquee box out front. Even from this distance she was still able to make out his features and see a hint of the wonderful dreaminess in his eyes. Her own eyes began to cloud over.

The shopping bag was getting heavy. She shifted it from her left hand to her right and slowly rotated her aching wrist. The gold charms on Michael's bracelet began to dance and jangle. It was a happy sound and it made her smile. She wondered if he would even remember the bracelet. Her smile dissolved, to be replaced by a frown of deep concern. Tonight after she told him the truth, she knew she might never see him again. She swallowed hard and looked back at the poster again.

With her eyes still focused on the face of her beloved son, she stepped off the curb, unaware of the approaching car.

The glancing blow of the car's left fender sent her sprawling onto the pavement.

Her world exploded in a burst of lavender and black.

45

Michael put his head in his hands and massaged his throbbing temples. The white curtain was still drawn around the cubicle; the doctors were still examining her. He would never forget what had happened. He could still hear the sound of squealing brakes as he went by the Russian Tea Room. He could still see the crowd gathering, the sheet music hurtling through the air, and the tall, suntanned man with the blond hair and beard bending over her after first dropping the gold charm bracelet that he himself had given her into the pocket of his green suede jacket. He could still feel his sense of outrage, then his desperate unhappiness as he had watched the man cradle Kirsten in his arms until the ambulance arrived.

Who was that man, he had asked himself, and what was he to Kirsten, if anything? The thought made him squirm, made his insides writhe. The man had to be someone, because at this very moment he was seated on one of the benches in the emergency room, one arm draped around the shoulders of a tall, blond boy who looked as if he were his son.

Andrew glanced up and narrowly missed making direct eye contact with Michael Eastbourne. He had recognized the conductor the moment he saw him coming out of Kirsten's apartment building that afternoon. How many other times had he visited Kirsten there in the past three months? He had felt so outraged, so betrayed, he had immediately checked his and Markos's bags at the Sheraton around the corner on Seventh Avenue, and then proceeded to drag the teenager through the city for the rest of the afternoon while he tried to decide what to do.

He had just picked up their tickets for the recital at the Carnegie Hall box office when the accident occurred. Nausea rose like a wave in his throat, and his whole body shuddered. He thought of the broken charm bracelet in his pocket and shuddered again. Had he come all this way only to lose her?

The sound of running footsteps made everyone look up.

Jeff was panting, his face flushed, his eyes wide and fearful, the black tails he was wearing looking strangely out of place in a hospital emergency room. The nurse behind the desk directed him to a bench and told him he would have to wait with the others. What others, he wondered. Without even bothering to look around, he leaned forward with his elbows on his knees and shook the hair out of his eyes. His blood was like a rushing cataract in his ears; the harder he tried to calm down, the more agitated he became.

He had just arrived at the concert hall when he saw the accident. The shock had momentarily paralyzed him and made him miss out on the chance to reach her first. But he had dashed into the street in time to see some man bend down, pick up the gold charm bracelet lying on the street next to her and put it in his pocket. If he had needed any further confirmation of what he already knew, he had it then. It was *her* bracelet. The one that had sounded like bells tinkling; the one she had always carried around with her in her pocket as though she were carrying around some deep, dark secret. Would he ever find out what that secret was, he wondered as his shoulders slumped and his blue eyes grew thick with anguished tears.

Ten minutes later the doctors emerged from the curtained cubicle. All three men were on their feet instantly. A young woman, a stethoscope protruding from the pocket of her long white lab coat, detached herself from the others and came toward them, a warm smile of encouragement on her pretty face.

"She's been badly bruised," she said, "but she's going to be fine. As far as we can determine, she hasn't any broken bones or any internal injuries, but we're going to send her up to X ray just to make sure."

"Can I see her?" all three men asked at once, and the doctor laughed.

"Of course, but only one at a time, if you don't mind. Are any of you family?"

Without hesitation, Jeff stepped forward. "I am," he declared. "I'm her son."

Michael and Andrew turned to stare at him, then at each other. Then they both watched as he disappeared behind the drawn white curtain.

Kirsten's whole body felt stiff and sore, and when she licked her dry lips with the tip of her tongue, even her mouth felt sore. Keeping her eyes tightly closed, she began flexing her fingers, one by one, just to reassure herself that as stiff as they were, they hadn't been injured. What a ridiculous thing to have happened to her. Tonight of all nights. Although the doctors assured her she hadn't been seriously hurt, she didn't believe them. If it was true, why wouldn't they let her leave? She had to attend her son's recital, they knew that. She started to sit up, only to have someone gently force her back down again.

"Jeff!" His face was so close to hers that she had only to raise her head a few inches and she could have kissed him. "Jeff, what are you doing here?"

"I saw what happened." His voice was quavering; his eyes were starting to fill again.

"It's serious, isn't it?"

"No, it isn't. You're only bruised."

"Then if I'm only bruised, why can't I get up?"

"Because they still want to X-ray you."

She scowled and gave her head an impatient toss. A spear of pain shot upward from the base of her spine to the top of her skull. But it was nothing compared with the pain she saw on Jeff's face as his features suddenly began to crumble.

With a tearing sob he flung himself across her body and wrapped his arms around her neck. She looked so tiny and so fragile that all he wanted was to hold her the way she had always held him. He had finally seen her without her tinted glasses, and although her skin was gold now, not ivory, and her hair was silver, not black, her eyes were still the color of amethysts, just as he knew they would be.

Kirsten closed her arms around her son's back and sighed. His heaving sobs were rattling her body and his tears were wetting her skin, but she couldn't have been happier. She was holding the man just as she had once held the boy, and she knew no moment would ever be as right as this one to finally tell him the truth.

"Jeff." She eased his head off her chest so she could look at him. "Jeff, I have something to tell you."

But he was smiling at her through his tears. "You don't have to, I already know. Mother."

Kirsten gasped. Suddenly the pieces of her shattered world were beginning to come together again. "But how?" she asked.

"You gave me a hint, remember?"

"The Debussy." He nodded.

Her eyes were brimming as she reached up and stroked his cheek. "Oh, Jeff, my precious Jeff, there's so much I want to say to you."

"And there's so much I need to know, but not now."

"Yes, now!" Frantic, she clutched at his sleeve. "You've got to know that I love you, Jeff, that I've never stopped loving you. I never wanted to leave you, never, but the choice wasn't mine to make."

"I think I know that now."

"Oh, God," she moaned, "there's so much I've got to make you understand, so much, so much."

"Later," he insisted. "We'll have plenty of time later. Right now I'm going to call and cancel the recital and—"

"Oh, no, you won't." Michael had slipped unnoticed inside the cubicle and was standing directly behind Jeff. "You're a professional, young man, and a professional always fulfills his obligations. Ask your mother. If you intend to make it to the top, that's the first rule you're going to have to learn."

"Michael." Kirsten watched Jeff's awed expression as she introduced the two of them. "He's right, you know," she told her son. "You can't cancel now, not if you want to be taken seriously, and I think you do."

Jeff was torn between wanting to stay with the mother he had only just found again and wanting to prove himself to her. "But I learned a new piece especially for tonight," he protested. "How can I play it if you're not there to hear it?"

"If you dedicate it to me," Kirsten assured him with the impish smile Michael knew so well, "I'll hear it." She didn't ask him what the piece was, she didn't have to. Like mother, like son. Yes, they were going to make a magnificent team.

Bending down to hug her again, Jeff whispered in her ear, "I'll be back as soon as the recital's over, even if I have to sneak in."

Kirsten kissed him on both cheeks, then lightly on the mouth. "Make me proud, my darling."

"You bet I will!"

A broad grin, that familiar thumbs-up sign, and he was gone.

Kirsten turned to Michael, glowing. "My son," she mouthed the words, her voice husky. "Oh, Michael, I've gotten my son back again."

He said nothing; he didn't trust himself to speak just yet. Settling himself on the edge of the bed, he opened her tightly clenched fist and studied her expression carefully as he placed a soft, warm kiss on the inside of her palm. Without having to ask, he sensed what was coming next.

"Michael, about your asking me to marry you," she began, only to have him cut her off.

"Shh, not now. You haven't had any real time to think about it."

"You're wrong." Her look was tender. "I *have* thought about it. You've been a part of my thoughts for so long, I sometimes find it hard to believe that in all the years we've known each other, we've spent less than a month's worth of days together. I cherish you, Michael." Her voice broke. "I do. But I can't marry you. I don't think we could ever build a future on something that barely was, do you?"

He looked down at the small, slender hand he was holding and shook his head. "I was hoping time would take care of all that for us."

"Oh, Michael."

They held on to each other for what felt as long as infinity and as short as an instant. Then he said, "You're sure your decision has nothing to do with him?" Kirsten looked confused. "You know, the blond one out there who looks a bit like a Greek god?"

"Andrew?" It wasn't possible. Andrew here? "Andrew!" She threw back the sheet and swung her legs over the side of the bed.

Andrew came running. He saw Michael Eastbourne back away from her, then all he could see was Kirsten herself. He gathered her up in his arms and covered her face with kisses. Neither of them noticed Michael leave. Neither of them noticed Markos tiptoe into the cubicle to stand, grinning happily, at the foot of her bed.

"Kirsten, we wanted to surprise you," Andrew said. "I even bought two tickets for tonight's recital, but then—" He stopped. For the moment, none of that really mattered. "Oh, Kirsten, Kirsten, you'll never know how much I've missed you." He kissed her long and hard on the mouth, then released her to look deep into her glorious violet eyes. "I love you, Kirsten Harald," he said. "God, how I love you."

She had been waiting a lifetime to hear those words, and it had taken her nearly that long to be able to acknowledge it.

But she was finally ready, ready to have it all. Smiling up at him, she said, "I love you too, Andrew. And I want those tomorrows now."

Jeff took one more bow, then stepped to the front of the stage.

"I would like to dedicate my final encore of the evening to my mother, Kirsten Harald. This piece belongs to her: Claude Debussy's 'Reflets dans l'Eau.'"

It was a full five minutes before the applause had died down enough for him to begin.

Encore

—❖—

1984

T he glare of the lights caught both of them full in the face and the audience rose to its feet. The entire New York Philharmonic rose too. Kirsten was radiant, her hair a silvered halo for her exquisite face, the heavy satin folds of her lavender Galanos encasing her slender body like the petals of a flower and giving her the illusion of great height. She turned to smile at her son, who smiled back as he squeezed her hand, causing the tiny round diamonds in her wedding band to dig into the sides of her fingers. With a final bow to the audience, they separated, each walking toward one of the two Steinways that stood facing each other in the center of Carnegie Hall's elegant stage.

It took a long time for the applause and the cheering to subside. From his seat in the front row, Andrew glanced over at Markos and winked; Markos winked back. Beside Markos, Nelson Pendell fumbled in the breast pocket of his tuxedo for a handkerchief. His wife, Bea, handed him hers. Directly behind Andrew and Markos, Lois Holden was wedged uncomfortably between her husband, Alec, and Dierdre, doing her best to keep her eyes focused straight ahead of her. The only one missing tonight from Kirsten Harald Beaton's much-heralded comeback concert was Jeffrey. Although his fear of losing Jeff completely had forced him to accept the boy's decision to live with his mother, he still refused to attend any of his performances.

After their marriage, Kirsten and Andrew had legally adopted Markos, and, together with Jeff, were living in the duplex co-op they had bought on East Eighty-third Street. They had kept the town house in London, while Andrew's boat—since renamed the *Kirsten*—remained anchored in the harbor at Tavira. They used both as their own private havens whenever they needed a vacation from the boys and from the rest of the world at large.

Andrew was again exhibiting at all the major New York galleries and only freelancing as a cover artist now. His

latest assignment: a sketch of Kirsten for the cover of *Ms.*
Magazine, as an example of the eighties woman who was
successfully combining marriage, motherhood, and career.

Kirsten closed her fingers around the gold charm suspended from a thin gold chain around her neck and smiled.
True to his word, Nelson had kept it safe for her. And true to
her promise, it had finally been engraved. It was happening
just as she had imagined it would. She and Jeff were performing Mendelssohn's A Flat Major Piano Concerto. He was
even wearing a lavender bow tie.

She checked off Clemence Treaves's name, the one remaining name on her list, then threw the list away. It was
over; she had won.

Michael Eastbourne raised his baton and the hall fell silent. He glanced first at Jeff, then at Kirsten. For a moment
their eyes met and held. The moment passed.

And then, there was only the music.

BANTAM BOOKS
GRAND SLAM SWEEPSTAKES
Win a new Chevrolet Sprint . . .
It's easy . . . It's fun . . . Here's how to enter:

OFFICIAL ENTRY FORM

Three Bantam book titles on sale this month are hidden in this word puzzle. Identify the books by circling each of these titles in the puzzle. Titles may appear within the puzzle horizontally, vertically, or diagonally . . .

P	R	O	M	I	S	E	S
Z	A	R		N	U		O
P	L	A	Y	I	N	G	
F	I	L		T	H	E	T
	L		'S		W		O
I	X			M	A	N	Y
F	L	A	S	H	B	A	C	K

Bantam's titles for September are:

IT'S ALL IN THE PLAYING

FLASHBACK

SO MANY PROMISES

In each of the books listed above there is another entry blank and puzzle . . . another chance to win!

Be on the lookout for Bantam paperback books coming in October: FAVORITE SON, WHITE PALACE INDOCHINE (U.S. only), CHILDREN OF THE SHROUD (Canada only). In each of them, you'll find a new puzzle, entry blank and GRAND SLAM Sweepstakes rules . . . and yet another chance to win another brand-new Chevrolet automobile!

MAIL TO: GRAND SLAM SWEEPSTAKES
Post Office Box 18
New York, New York 10046

Please Print

NAME _____

ADDRESS _____

CITY _____ STATE _____ ZIP _____

OFFICIAL RULES

NO PURCHASE NECESSARY.

To enter identify this month's Bantam Book titles by placing a circle around each word forming each title. There are three titles shown on previous page to be found in this month's puzzle. Mail your entry to: Grand Slam Sweepstakes, P.O. Box 18, New York, N.Y. 10046.

This is a monthly sweepstakes starting February 1, 1988 and ending January 31, 1989. During this sweepstakes period, one automobile winner will be selected each month from all entries that have correctly solved the puzzle. To participate in a particular month's drawing, your entry must be received by the last day of that month. The Grand Slam prize drawing will be held on February 14, 1989 from all entries received during all twelve months of the sweepstakes.

To obtain a free entry blank/puzzle/rules, send a self-addressed stamped envelope to: Winning Titles, P.O. Box 650, Sayreville, N.J. 08872. Residents of Vermont and Washington need not include return postage.

PRIZES: Each month for twelve months a Chevrolet automobile will be awarded with an approximate retail value of $12,000 each.

The Grand Slam Prize Winner will receive 2 Chevrolet automobiles plus $10,000 cash (ARV $34,000).

Winners will be selected under the supervision of Marden-Kane, Inc., an independent judging organization. By entering this sweepstakes each entrant accepts and agrees to be bound by these rules and the decisions of the judges which shall be final and binding. Winners may be required to sign an affidavit of eligibility and release which must be returned within 14 days of receipt. All prizes will be awarded. No substitution or transfer of prizes permitted. Winners will be notified by mail. Odds of winning depend on the total number of eligible entries received.

Sweepstakes open to residents of the U.S. and Canada except employees of Bantam Books, its affiliates, subsidiaries, advertising agencies and Marden-Kane, Inc. Void in the Province of Quebec and wherever else prohibited or restricted by law. Not responsible for lost or misdirected mail or printing errors. Taxes and licensing fees are the sole responsibility of the winners. All cars are standard equipped. Canadian winners will be required to answer a skill testing question.

For a list of winners, send a self-addressed, stamped envelope to: Bantam Winners, P.O. Box 711, Sayreville, N.J. 08872.

THE LATEST BOOKS
IN THE BANTAM
BESTSELLING TRADITION

Experience all the passion and adventure life has to offer in these bestselling novels by and about women.

Special Offer
Buy a Bantam Book
for only 50¢.

Now you can have Bantam's catalog filled with hundreds of titles plus take advantage of our unique and exciting bonus book offer. A special offer which gives you the opportunity to purchase a Bantam book for only 50¢. Here's how!

By ordering any five books at the regular price per order, you can also choose any other single book listed (up to a $5.95 value) for just 50¢. Some restrictions do apply, but for further details why not send for Bantam's catalog of titles today!

Just send us your name and address and we will send you a catalog!